I0590120

# DEVIOUS TEMPTATION

# D.L. DARBY

Copyright © 2025 by D.L. Darby

Identifiers: Print - 979-8-9927675-1-3

All rights reserved.

No part of this book may be reproduced in any form or by any electronic or mechanical means, including information storage and retrieval systems, without written permission from the author, except for the use of brief quotations in a book review.

The author acknowledges the trademark status and trademark owners of the products, brands, and/or restaurants mentioned in this work of fiction. The publication and use of these trademarks is not authorized, associated with, or sponsored by the trademark owners.

This is a work of fiction. Names, places, and events are either products of the author's imagination or used fictitiously. Any resemblance to persons living or dead, organizations, or events is purely coincidental.

Edited by Samantha Swart with Samantha Reads Spicy and Virginia Carey

Cover created by Charly Jade @ Designs By Charly

 Formatted with Vellum

# Also by D.L. Darby

# Content & Trigger Warnings

- Spanking
- Physical altercation (not between MCs)
- Revenge porn (not shared by the MCs)
- Explicit sexual scenes
- Food shaming
- Underage drinking
- Emotional distress
- Double penetration
- Unprotected sex
- Cheating (not between main characters)
- Snowballing
- Mention of an eating disorder by name

# Playlist

"older" - Isabel LaRosa
"Only Have Eyes For You" -
ButterflyTiger
"Now or Never" - K RHEN
"It's Giving..." - ili
"Used to This" - Maybe
"Scream" - WTRGRL, Zhone
"Make Me Feel" - Elvis Drew
"Cross That Line" - Joshua Radin
"Shakes" - Luke Hemmings
"OUT OF THE BLUE" - GRANT
KNOCHE
"Just Because I'm Okay" - Harvest
Son, Gabrielle Aplin
"Fall in Love" - 76th Street

*For Lauren, who demanded this book.*
*You're welcome.*
*But also, thank you. Lucy and Lawson wouldn't have a story*
*without you.*
*#laurensfault*

Someday we'll find it, the rainbow connection. The lovers, the dreamers, and me.

— *THE RAINBOW CONNECTION*, THE MUPPET MOVIE

# ONE

*Lawson*

LUCY BRADEE IS ALWAYS a rainbow of colors, but the one I associate her most with is red—from her gleaming, burnt copper locks to the cherry and strawberry patterns that usually adorn her 50s-style wardrobe.

And then there's the ever-present, giant 'No' symbol that hovers over her head whenever she's nearby.

The girl is off-limits in every way imaginable. Not only because she's newly eighteen and finishing her senior year of high school, but also because she's dating my son, Rhys.

"Stare any harder, Law, and you're going to creep the girl out. Although she's asking for attention in that outfit," Charlotte, my wife, chides as she sidles up next to me, grasping her glass of chardonnay like a lifeline.

Lucy's swimsuit *is* earning her the attention of most of the guys on the Montpier High football team. The white one-piece hugs her body like a mini dress, securing around her neck in a halter top that accentuates her naturally full breasts. The fabric is peppered with cherries, complementing her skin and highlighting her freckles against the tan the summer has kissed her flesh with.

It's a wonder Rhys isn't glued to her side, asserting his claim over her, instead of throwing a football back and forth in the pool.

"Is that how the pool boy in Boca caught your attention, Char? By wearing cherries on his Speedo?" I grimace at her *and* the unwanted image of them together that pops into my mind, before refocusing my attention out the windows over the farmhouse sink Charlotte *demanded* for the kitchen she never cooks in.

"God, are you still droning on about that? Get over it, Lawson. No one found out. Your reputation is safe." Her tone drips with condescending sarcasm as she leans into me, purposefully rubbing her fake double-D breasts against my arm.

I've never been a violent man, but sometimes I want to smack her just to see her lovely features show something other than haughty disdain for her life.

Her Caribbean blues are glazed over from her wine buzz, lids half-mast as she peers up at me suggestively, mauve-painted lips pulled wide in what she thinks is a seductive smile. "Why don't we go up to the bedroom, and I can take care of this little problem you seem to have?" She presses her hand against my hardening length.

My eyes find Lucy again. The image out the window is what's making my cock hard. Not my wife, who is entitled to half my net worth if I divorce her, even if she's a cheating slut. I'm not a pervert or into girls as young as my own kids, but Lucy is a goddamn rainbow in my otherwise dreary, gray life.

Charlotte continues to rub her palm against me, sliding into my joggers to wrap around my shaft and swiping her thumb over the bead of precum along the tip. As good as it feels, I swore I'd never go there with her again. Snatching her wrist, I pull her hand out and gently shove her away.

"No thanks, hon. I'm no longer interested in your contaminated body parts." My gaze drifts disdainfully down her body while I adjust myself.

Did I mention she got chlamydia from the pool boy?

I'll be forever grateful for the security cameras the neighbor suggested when we bought the place. *"You can never be too careful. If you know what I mean..."* He had nodded toward our wives, who were cackling while drinking margaritas in their backyard.

Charlotte lets out an unladylike snort as she pushes blonde curls away from her face, dropping her carefully constructed facade as the ultimate Stepford wife. The wine in her glass sloshes over the rim and splashes to the floor. "You'll have to give in at some point, Lawson. You're going to get real tired of your hand soon."

My lips pull up in a derisive smirk. "Who said anything about my hand, Char?"

Her nostrils flare, glassy eyes burning with contempt— which I find hilarious, considering *she's* the one who ruined our marriage. "You wouldn't dare!"

The object of my earlier attention walks through the French doors, raspberry lips lifted into a wide, knowing smile. Her deep hazel eyes light up with delight as she piles her long hair on top of her head, securing it with a white scrunchie. "Something smells delicious! Mr. Morgan, are you making your famous cookies?"

My wife snorts again into her glass. "Please stop inflating his ego, Lucy. Everyone knows Lawson's baking is terrible."

With a sneer thrown my way, she stalks out of the kitchen and upstairs to our bedroom.

Lucy watches my wife disappear before turning mirthful eyes to me. "Someone sounds like she's in for a wine-induced migraine later," she whispers, plucking a cookie off the cooling rack and sitting on a stool.

She smells like coconut tanning lotion and something sweet and floral. It makes my pants tighten again, so I turn toward the sink to finish the dishes and hide my evident arousal at her proximity.

I feel like a fucking predator.

"Mmmm," Lucy moans around a mouthful of cookie, firing up every single synapse in my body. "God, Mr. Morgan, these are so good. I don't care what anyone else thinks. My mom likes them too. She wants the recipe so she can recreate them on her vlog."

Chuckling, I shake my head and reach for the dish towel to dry off the last of the mixing bowls. "Family recipe. I'm afraid if I tell you, I'll have to kill you. And how many times do I have to remind you? Call me Lawson. Or Law. You don't have to call me 'mister.' It makes me feel old."

Her laughter fills the kitchen, and I throw her a smirk over my shoulder as Rhys walks in.

"Babe, what are you doing? I'm all wet, and I need you to dry me off," he says suggestively, his gaze ping-ponging between Lucy and me.

I try to ignore the urge to roll my eyes at his blatant attempt to be smooth. I love my son, but he, unfortunately, follows in his mother's footsteps and thinks the world is his oyster and that people were put on this earth to serve him.

He's hanging all over her when I turn around, dripping pool water onto the floor that he has no intention of cleaning up. A fierce jolt of protectiveness runs through my chest as he wraps a hand around her neck like a collar, tilting her chin up to capture her lips in an open-mouthed kiss.

Lucy's cheeks turn pink as she tries to push him away, peering at me apologetically at the gross display of impropriety.

"Okay, okay. I'm coming." She giggles, pecking him on the lips and allowing him to pull her off the stool.

"Yeah, you will be. As soon as all these fuckers leave," Rhys not so quietly murmurs into her ear. He winks at me over her head just before they disappear outside.

Releasing a long sigh, I slap the dish towel onto the quartz countertop with thinly veiled annoyance and scrub my hands over my face. Was I that bad when I was his age?

God, I hope not.

# Two

## Lucy

RHYS MORGAN IS, and always has been, my walking wet dream. The star quarterback of the football team, with tan skin, dark hair, and muscles for days—but not overly muscled like the linebackers.

And if his father, Lawson, is any indication of how my boyfriend will look when he's older, well, I'm going to be one lucky Mrs. Morgan someday.

But, over the last year, Rhys has developed an attitude that is really starting to get on my nerves.

"That was so uncalled for. Your dad didn't need to see that," I admonish as we join the other football players and cheerleaders enjoying the Morgan's gigantic pool.

Graduation is right around the corner. With prom next weekend and the National Cheerleading Competition coming up, the beginning of the last summer before the rest of our lives is starting to look promising.

"Oh, please. Like Mom and Dad didn't subject River and me to it all the time when we were younger." His hand slides from my shoulder to my butt beneath the bathing suit skirt, pulling me flush against his front. "Besides, we're adults now, babe. It's not like they still think we're virgins."

His words have my skin prickling with embarrassment, even though there's no one close enough to hear our conversation, and a sense of anger floods me at the mention of his mother.

Charlotte Morgan... is a bitch, to put it lightly.

No matter how many times I've tried to form a relationship with the coldhearted woman, she's always hit me with backhanded compliments and, sometimes, just straight-up rudeness.

Plus, she cheated on Mr. Morgan. So, she's obviously deranged.

I'll never forget *that* night when we were making out in the pool house, which doubled as a guest house for the nine months of the year the pool wasn't in use. His parents had stormed in—his dad screaming about how Charlotte had an affair with the pool boy when she was vacationing at their home in Boca Raton.

Mortified, I'd wanted to get out of there as fast as possible. But one look at Rhys' face had me staying by his side to comfort him long after his parents left.

That was the night we finally lost our virginities to each other.

Rhys rocks into me as his devastatingly gorgeous smile makes my knees weak and my vagina flutter.

Can vaginas flutter?

Mine pulses in confirmation as my boyfriend leans over me to run his tongue beneath my ear—the spot he knows makes me wet if he so much as breathes on it.

"Maybe we won't wait till everyone leaves." His voice is

thick and gravelly before he sucks on my neck softly. Everything from my belly button down turns to Jell-O, and he chuckles, nipping my lobe. "Does that turn you on, Luce? The thought of everyone watching as you sit on a pool chair, and I lick your pussy till your juices are covering my face?"

Biting my lower lip, I try to disguise the moan that escapes my mouth with a sigh. At only eighteen, Rhys has a way with dirty talk. I don't know if it stems from watching a lot of porn or if he's just naturally talented, but fucking hell, he knows how to send my pulse racing and heat all the liquids in my body to a roaring boil.

The thought of someone watching as he does things to me makes my lower body clench. It's like there's a cord wrapped around my heart, and with every beat, it tugs upward on that sensitive bundle of nerves between my thighs.

Rhys and I have never done anything so kinky before, even though we once talked about having a foursome with two of our teammates. But by the end of that conversation, we decided we weren't partial to sharing, just interested in being watched together.

And that's part of why I love him and our relationship so much. We have unwavering trust in each other to make those decisions together and to always be honest about our wants and needs.

"Get a room, you two!" someone shouts behind us.

Rhys laughs and steps back. Grasping my chin, he lifts my face to meet his bright cerulean eyes. "Seriously, I'm going to feast on that pretty pussy the second the last person leaves."

After that searing promise, I hide in the pool the rest of the afternoon to hide the ever-present wet spot between my thighs.

───────※───────

Rhys' hands wrap around my middle the second the front door closes behind the last of our teammates. "Come on. Let's go to the pool house."

His fingers drag across my stomach to dig into my sides. "Babe, you gotta lay off my dad's cookies. Those things are pure sugar."

The out-of-pocket statement jars me, and any hint of arousal I feel dissipates as I blink up at him. "Excuse me?"

The words hurt. I've never been as small as the flyers on the cheerleading team, so I'm the perfect main base. I have curves, and I'm proud of my body. I love the way I look. And Rhys has never uttered a single word about being unhappy with my appearance until now. Usually, such cruel behavior is learned from the man of the household, but Lawson has never been anything other than kind to me.

"He's right, Lucy. You want to fit into your prom dress, don't you? It's already a little tight as it is, dear." Charlotte's sardonic quip fills the space, echoing Rhys' sentiments and cluing me into the fact that *she's* the one his new attitude is coming from. She doesn't even look at us on her way to the dining room, nursing another glass of her usual chardonnay.

"CHARLOTTE!" Mr. Morgan's—Lawson's—incredulous voice rings out from the kitchen. Heavy footsteps sound from down the hall, and his angry face appears around the corner seconds later.

He's all fire and brimstone as he grabs her arm and yanks her down the hall, not even sparing us a glance. Rhys's hand grabs mine tightly, his breathing growing heavy as he stares at where his parents disappeared.

The nurturer side in me wants to comfort him, but the feminist side wants to demand why he'd say such a vile thing about my appearance.

I opt for silence.

The door opens and slams behind us, and I turn to see River, Rhys' younger brother, kicking off his shoes. "Hey, Lucy!"

Pasting on a warm smile, I wave and open my arms for a hug. "Hey, kiddo. Just get back from Rose's?"

"Yeah!" he exclaims cheerfully as he embraces me and ignores his older brother. "Her mom took us swimming in the pool in the garden on the roof!"

"That's great, Riv! I love it there." River is best friends with my little cousin, Rose. Well, she's not *really* my cousin —our mothers are best friends and have been for years, so we consider ourselves family.

Rhys is still staring down the hall, where we can hear Lawson's muffled—but clearly angry—voice as he yells at his wife, so I try to usher the younger Morgan toward his room. "Why don't you get changed and washed up for dinner? Your dad made steaks."

"And potatoes?" River cocks an eyebrow as he finally glances at his brother, who hasn't eaten a potato since we were sixteen.

"*Parmesan* potatoes." I wink, letting out a small laugh as the kid whoops and bounds toward his bedroom.

When I turn back to Rhys, he finally looks at me, his blue eyes shaded with guilt. "I'm sorry," he says, reaching for my hand again, having dropped it when River hugged me. "That was a dick thing to say."

"Damn right, it was." I pull him close, pushing up on my toes to kiss him chastely. "I forgive you. Don't do it again."

"Your mother isn't feeling well, Rhys. Looks like it will just be us for dinner. Did I hear River come home?" Lawson's voice startles me as he appears out of thin air. His stormy gray eyes are dark like a thundercloud—a hurricane force ready to unleash hell on his son when I go home for the evening.

Lawson has always reminded me a little of a storm, so intense when he's at the height of his anger—and I've seen him get angry plenty of times on the sidelines at our football games—but he's always devastatingly beautiful.

A force you find yourself drawn to and unable to look away from even though it has the power to kill you.

Rhys is attractive, but his father is painstakingly handsome.

That stormy gaze darts to me as I reply, "Yeah, I told him to get washed up and ready for dinner."

He smiles, his head tipping forward slightly. "Thank you, Lucy. Why don't you and Rhys set the table?"

A thrill runs through me at the command in his deep, husky timbre. Rhys clears his throat as Lawson returns to the kitchen, pulling my attention back to him, and his eyes hold a wariness I instantly know I don't like. "What?"

He watches me for a few silent moments, eyes sliding to where his dad disappeared before slowly moving back to me. He shakes his head, causing his dark hair to fall across his forehead. "Nothing. Come on. I'll get the plates and glasses. You can take care of the silverware."

# THREE

*Lawson*

STEAK JUICE SPLATTERS all over my 'World's Best Dad' apron that River gifted me for my birthday last year as I stab thick slabs of meat and move them from the grill to a serving platter.

*Fucking bitch.*

The two words replay in my mind like a broken record. Charlotte has everything she could ever want. Yet, instead of being happy, she chooses to live her life in self-induced misery. And she's poisoning Rhys' fucking brain with her bullshit.

My body thrums with anger. I've never touched Charlotte with anything other than a gentle hand, even when I found out she cheated. But hearing her say those words to Lucy? Hearing Rhys say what he said before his mother opened her over-injected lips?

I was already well on my way to scolding my son when my wife put in her two cents, and I couldn't stop myself from grabbing her and forcing her out of the room. I've never been more disgusted with anyone in my life.

It's a damn fucking shame that two members of my own family made me feel that way tonight.

River is chatting animatedly with Lucy when I enter the dining room. She's always been good with him, listening intently while he tells her about the day he had with his best friend. Rhys watches them forlornly as if he wants to join in on the conversation, but something is holding him back. His head swivels to me, blue eyes, which are so much like his mother's, staring blankly at me like he's lost and can't find his way back from the mess she's pulling him into.

They've grown closer over the last few months, and I can only imagine the bullshit she's feeding him behind my back—all the lies about her affair and why she did it. How I'm cold toward her and always busy working, so she sought comfort in the arms of a barely legal kid.

Ironically, I glance at Lucy, a radiant rainbow through the storm brewing in my house. She's changed into a pair of distressed, acid wash cut-off shorts—that barely cover her ass—and a plum-colored shirt that has a plunging neckline and fluttery sleeves.

"So, Lucy. Have you decided on a college yet?" I place half a steak on River's plate, ruffling his hair and kissing the top of his head.

She brightens up, nodding enthusiastically as she dishes out potatoes and green beans for River. "I settled on Berkeley! They have an excellent business administration program, plus a kickass cheer team."

I don't miss the way my oldest son flinches before a scowl settles over his face as he fixes her with a hard glare. He already signed a letter of intent with Ole Miss, and Lucy was still debating where she wanted to go. But if she's settled on cheerleading in college, she would have had to send in her tryout video months ago.

So that's the reason Rhys has become so sullen and unlike himself.

If Lucy knows Rhys is upset with her decision, she doesn't acknowledge it as she smiles at him. She cuts a steak into thirds, placing two parts back on the serving platter before cutting her portion into tiny pieces and pushing away the fat with her knife. There's a spoonful of green beans on her plate and a generous helping of salad in her bowl sans dressing.

And I can't help but notice the absence of the parmesan potatoes she and River love so much.

"California, huh? I never figured you for a West Coast girl." I flash her a smile, glancing between her and my oldest. "You can go surfing when you visit, Rhys."

He rolls his eyes. "Like I'm going to have time to go to California."

Lucy's smile falters, and she quickly interjects, "Well, I can always visit you if you don't have time to see me."

"I don't know why you couldn't just stick to Ole Miss. That was the plan." Rhys' tone is accusing, and Lucy's cheeks turn pink as she looks back down at her plate. A stray coppery lock falls into her face, and my palm twitches, itching to push it behind her ear—to cup her cheek in my palm and offer some sort of comfort.

"I'm not really hungry. Come on, Luce," Rhys demands. His chair screeches as he abruptly pushes back from the table and stands, waiting for her to join him.

River chews his steak quietly, looking down at his plate like he always does when there's strife at the dinner table. It twists my heart to see his sad face scrunched up as he tries hard to be invisible and not the subject of his brother's attitude.

But Rhys' ire is strictly for Lucy, who looks like she's walking death row.

And because it's none of my business, and I know my son would never lay a hand on her, I don't say anything as they retreat hand in hand to the pool house.

Diverting my attention to my younger son, I tap my hand on the table near his elbow. "How was your day, Riv?"

### <u>Lucy</u>

"What is up with you lately, Rhys? It's like you've been a completely different person these last few months," I state the moment he shuts the door to the pool house. It wasn't a necessary addition to the backyard, but the Morgan brothers convinced their father to build it, citing that it would be a perfect place for friends to hang out instead of Rhys' room in the basement, keeping Lawson and Charlotte up all night.

It's the perfect little home, with a loft that houses three sets of bunk beds. The downstairs has a fridge, multiple couches and loveseats, and a giant flat-screen TV where the boys play their video games.

"Nothing," he mumbles, grabbing my hips and pulling me against him. His lips are warm when they attach to my neck, sucking that spot below my ear I love so much. "I'm just going to miss you. That's all."

Heat floods my insides, both at his actions and his words. But we have things to talk about, and Rhys loves to distract me with sex when he doesn't want to have a conversation. "Babe. What's going on?"

Releasing a long sigh, he lets me go and runs a hand through his hair, pushing the long strands off his forehead. "Honestly, Lucy, I've been doing a lot of thinking. I mean, clearly, you're not interested in this..." He gestures between us. "...if you were even entertaining the thought of going somewhere other than Ole Miss. The plan was that you'd go wherever I went. So, what gives?"

He collapses onto a plush cream loveseat and widens his legs, patting the space between them like he always does when he wants to cuddle. But cuddling doesn't seem to fit the situation, and I know it's his way of trying to segue into sex.

Regardless, I go and straddle his lap, laying a soft kiss against his pillowy lips. "Of course, I'm interested in this... in *us*. But I'd be lying if I said Ole Miss is where I want to spend the next few years of my life. I'm ready for a change, for something different. You know how much I loved California when my family vacationed there last year."

Rhys hums in confirmation, leaning forward to nip my collarbone as he wraps one hand around my backside and the other at the base of my neck. "It's just so far away, baby. You're really going to deprive me of *this* for months at a time?" He bucks his hips, and his hard length presses against my already wet center as he drags his teeth along my skin.

Pulling my hair, he forces me to arch my back as he yanks down my shirt and bra. His lips find my nipple, sucking the stiffened peak hard before laving at it with his tongue. Twisting my fingers in his silky strands, I pull, relishing the husky moan that vibrates against my chest.

"Think about how good it will be when we finally do get to see each other." I try to push off his lap, but he pulls me back down forcefully. "Come on, Rhys. Let's go upstairs."

I try to get up again, and this time, he releases me. But only until I get to my feet. He loops his fingers into the waistband of my shorts and holds me in place, making quick work of the button and zipper before shoving them to the floor so swiftly that I have to grasp his shoulders to maintain my balance.

"Rhys—"

"Shut up." He leans forward to lick the arousal that's smeared along my thighs, his hands going to the waistband of his track pants to shove them down. With a groan, his tongue swipes along my center, languid and hot as the tip flicks against my clit. "Fuck. You're the best thing I've ever tasted."

A small smirk forms on my lips, and I peer down at him with a quirked brow, peeling my shirt and bra over my head. "I better be the *only* thing you've ever tasted."

Rhys stares up at me as he continues to lick, smiling against my core. When his teeth graze my sensitive flesh, I suck in a sharp breath as liquid heat floods between my legs. My gaze lifts to the window directly across from us, which reflects the one at my back. "Baby, seriously, come on. Let's go upstairs. Anyone could see us through the windows."

He seems completely unbothered, spinning me around

by my hips before pulling me onto his lap, his cock nestled between my butt cheeks. "We've always wanted to be watched."

Storm gray flashes behind my lids as my head rolls back on Rhys' shoulder. The thought of his parents—or, god forbid, River—seeing us has anxiety seeping along the edges of my pleasure. As if he can sense my hesitation, Rhys chases it away as he finds that spot beneath my ear, sucking on it while he palms my breasts. His fingers twist my nipples, and the breath stalls in my lungs as he squeezes his elbows into my sides and lifts me so his length slides between my legs.

"We don't have a condom." The words are hoarse as they leave my throat. I'm overstimulated as Rhys sucks at my neck, plucking my nipples and sliding the crown of his cock against my clit. I can see myself parted around his hard shaft, coating him in my juices with every pass.

"It's fine for one night," he assures me, grabbing my chin to turn my head. "I'll get you a pill in the morning."

There's no room for discussion as he captures my lips with a kiss, plunging his tongue into my mouth as he seats me on his cock. I cry out against his mouth as he stretches me, bare for the first time in the two years we've been intimate.

In the back of my mind, I know we shouldn't have sex without a condom. We're taking the risk of becoming another high school statistic of teenage pregnancy, upending our lives just before college.

I almost wonder if that's what Rhys is trying to accomplish.

"You're not getting out of our conversation," I whisper against his lips. My arm hooks around his neck, and my other hand grasps for anything to anchor myself as he fucks me, bottoming out with each satisfying thrust.

I'm too far gone to keep thinking about anything other than how Rhys plays every part of me like a violin— plucking at all the right cords to create a blissful symphony nearing its crescendo.

His lips trail down my neck as he picks up the pace, hitting that perfect spot inside me over and over again. "I never want to *get out* of you, Lucy."

"Fuck, Rhys, I'm so close." I let out a moan, pressing my head back into his shoulder as the beginnings of an orgasm pulses between my legs.

My lids flutter open, and I'm prepared to look over my shoulder and lock gazes with my boyfriend as we come together. But as my vision focuses, I catch sight of stormy gray irises through the window.

*Lawson.*

His pupils are blown wide as his gaze rakes down my body, taking in every exposed part of me, and his Adam's apple bobs as he swallows thickly. His hands are clenched into fists at his sides—the outline of his hardening length apparent behind his thin joggers.

When he meets my stare, a tidal wave of ecstasy flows through me as I come hard with a hoarse cry, legs spread wide, speared on Rhys' cock, completely bared to his dad through the glass. We're both frozen, watching each other as another wave crests, and I bite my lower lip to stop from crying out again.

From here, I can see his jaw tense, gaze darkening as

Rhys presses his forehead harder into my shoulder and roars his release against my back.

It's then that I finally close my eyes.

And when I open them again, Lawson is gone.

*Holy fucking shit.*

# FOUR

*Lawson*

HOLY. Fucking. Shit.

I did not just watch my son's *very naked* girlfriend come.

*Oh yes, you did, you piece of shit.*

Thoughts of Rhys storming into my home office at any second to shout at me have me pacing, whiskey tumbler in hand, as I try to process what just happened.

*She must think I'm disgusting.*

Two minutes pass. Then five. Ten. Twenty.

All the while, my heart beats erratically in my chest, thumping its way to a heart attack. Its message is loud and clear: *It's been a nice life. You can die now that you just willingly stayed and watched as your son's girlfriend got off while he was fucking her.*

Fucking hell.

I toss back another three fingers while I wait for the inevitable shitstorm that's about to fly through the house.

But it never comes.

*Did she not tell Rhys?*

After half an hour passes with no sign of life in the house except for River playing his video games in the basement, I settle at my desk and try to busy myself with work. I try to focus on anything other than how Lucy looked with a thin sheen of sweat coating her skin as she rocked her hips. Or her soft moans that crept through the thin walls of the pool house. Or the way she didn't break eye contact when she saw me watching.

The way she didn't fucking look away when she *realized*.

*Was it my imagination, or did she widen her legs when she came a second time?*

Fuck.

No.

I can't try to rationalize my way out of this. How will I ever be able to look her in the eye again?

Light knocking startles me from my thoughts, the soft tapping quiet enough that I assume it's River. "Yeah?" I call out, like I usually do to permit my kids' entrance into my private space.

Shuffling papers as the door opens, I glance up for a mere second to see what my son wants before jolting with shock at seeing Lucy in the doorway. She's dressed, her cheeks glowing with a post-coital flush.

Or perhaps she's just as embarrassed as I am.

"Hi," she greets quietly, gently closing the door behind her as though she's trying not to make a sound.

Words fail me as I watch Lucy walk further into my office, looking everywhere but at me. Her hair is a tangled mass of natural waves that dried haphazardly after her earlier dip in the pool, and she's making more of a mess of it as she idly twists the dark copper strands around her finger. "Listen... I—"

"I'm sorry."

"I'm so sorry."

We stare at each other for a beat, then speak simultaneously once more.

"What are *you* sorry for?"

"Rhys and I never should have done that in the pool house." Her cheeks must burn from how pink they are. The tip of her index finger is purple from how tightly she's winding her hair around it. Lucy continues to stare at the floor, directly in front of my desk, as she confesses, "I knew we should have gone upstairs. I'm sorry that we were in a place where River could have seen us. It was completely irresponsible, not to mention disrespectful."

I blink. "Lucy, I—"

"Please... don't, Lawson." Her face scrunches in a wince. "It's embarrassing enough as it is."

I nearly let out a groan at the sound of my first name on her lips. I was really hoping to hear her say it in some capacity, but definitely not under these circumstances.

With a nod, I lean back in my chair. "You two are adults. It's none of my business. As long as you're being safe..." I trail off as Lucy's face pales, expression glazing over as she gets lost somewhere in her mind.

Inwardly, I curse. If Rhys wasn't on my shit list for his little outburst earlier and the shit he said to Lucy about her weight, he sure as hell is on it now.

"It's fine. I'll take care of it," she whispers so softly that I barely hear her. "Your desk is a mess."

At the abrupt change of subject, I shake my head in

confusion. "What?" I glance down at where she's pointing. "Oh. Yeah, I don't have time to organize files. My assistant ended up on maternity leave earlier than expected. I'm afraid she will have quite the mess to sort out when she returns. You should see my *actual* office."

Lucy leans over the rich walnut and cleans up a stack of papers, looking completely at ease as though what happened forty minutes ago never occurred at all. The way she so effortlessly exists within my proximity after we locked eyes when she was in her most intimate state baffles me. "I could help out? I'm really good with organization."

*After what just happened, she wants to spend* more *time with me?*

I open my mouth to say the exact thing that flits through my mind but snap it shut so the words can't escape. After a few seconds, I ask, "Don't you have Nationals coming up?"

She peers at me from beneath dark, thick lashes. "Yes, but I don't have a job. We have two-a-day practices right now. I could come between them and do a few hours of work until you're caught up."

Unwillingly, and so goddamn against my wishes, my cock hardens again as I stare at her. "You'd *want* to do that?"

Lucy nods, the apples of her cheeks tinging pink again as she bites the left corner of her bottom lip. The same corner she bit to stop herself from crying out when she got off the second time. "I don't mind helping out."

The weight of her statement hangs heavily between us as her hazel irises slowly travel the length of my body. She's still leaning over my desk, and I know she's got a clear view of the effect she has on me.

Is she doing it intentionally? Or is she just curious?

*She's your son's girlfriend. Put an end to this now, Lawson!*

*There's nothing to put an end to. You're imagining it.*

While the proverbial angel and devil on my shoulders argue, Lucy stands upright, her freckles a stark contrast against the pretty flush on her face. "I should get home. Let me know if you want any help." She retreats immediately from my office without allowing me time to process what just happened.

"What the fuck was that?" I whisper to myself, completely mystified by the redheaded beauty.

───────── ∽ ─────────

I RAP MY KNUCKLES AGAINST RHYS' open door. He's lying on his bed, texting away on his phone with a surly scowl.

"Can I have a word?"

"What?" he asks flatly, not looking away from the screen.

On my way down to the basement, I debated mentioning that I saw him and Lucy in the pool house. Not that I *saw* them, but just that I know what goes on when they're alone in there. But my son isn't stupid. He knows I know, and he doesn't care.

Besides, I don't want him bringing it up with Lucy later

because I'm a coward and wouldn't know what to do if she confessed that I watched her come.

*Charlotte's right. I do need to get laid.*

"We need to talk about the bullshit you said to Lucy earlier." Crossing my arms, I lean against the doorframe. "I raised you better than that, Rhys. You don't talk to women that way."

"Relax, Dad. She had, like... five cookies. You know that shit isn't good for you." He continues to ignore me, and the need to cross the room and throw his phone against a wall flares brightly inside me.

"So the fuck what? Nationals are coming up. She said the squad is practicing twice a day. She needs the energy. If she wants the damn cookies, let her eat the fucking cookies. Jesus Christ, you sound like your mother."

My son rolls his eyes. "I apologized. Lucy is hot as fuck, and she knows it. My little comment isn't going to send her on a trip to bulimia town. Besides, it's none of your business what goes on between Lucy and me." He sends me a pointed glare. "She's not your concern."

"He's right. Calm down, Lawson. Rhys, your father is just upset because she's the only one who actually likes his cookies. And I think maybe he likes *her* a little too much." Charlotte's whiny voice cuts through our conversation as she appears behind me. I didn't even hear her approach, silent and slimy like the snake she is.

Rhys sits up as she nudges past me to wrap her arms around him. "I just wanted to come give my big guy a kiss and a hug goodnight."

My lip curls in disgust at her display. "What the fuck is

wrong with you?" I don't even try to hide my resentment for her from Rhys at this point.

Charlotte wasn't always this ugly. Before we had money, she was a kind, caring mother and the best wife a man could ask for. But everything changed as soon as I started making more deals at work and climbing the corporate ladder.

They say money is the root of all evil. But I honestly think the root of all evil stems from humans' raw need to prove themselves worthy. To whom? I have no clue. I suppose everyone is different in that aspect.

Even I fell prey to it.

We have three homes, multiple big toys, and enough wealth that my kids won't need to work if they don't want to—not that I'd ever admit that to them. But the need to prove myself a worthy provider for my family drove me to work the hours that I do, which in turn pushed my wife into the arms of another man.

"Nothing is wrong with her, you jackass," Rhys mutters, scowling at me before he pulls something up on his phone and tilts it her way. "And mom is right, you're a little *too* nice to Lucy. It's weird."

Disgust rolls through me as Charlotte settles on the bed next to him, laying her head on his shoulder as they watch the phone screen, dismissing me without another word. I'm not sure if it's because of their flagrant behavior or because my son has noticed my obvious proclivity for his girlfriend.

After checking on River, I retreat back to my office. It's the one place I know Charlotte won't bother me. My conversation with Lucy replays over and over as I pull up a work folder on my laptop and try to distract myself.

I remember the way she stiffened when I mentioned

them being safe, a clear sign they didn't use a condom. Is that normal for them? Does she let him inside her with no barrier often, even though they both know there's a risk of her getting pregnant?

Charlotte and I strived to make sure Rhys never felt like a mistake, but I know firsthand what an unplanned pregnancy does when you're straight out of high school. My oldest son's arrival put a wrench in every plan I ever made for myself.

Lucy said she'd take care of it, but I highly doubt Rhys will accompany her. And she shouldn't have to be subjected to the scrutiny of the pharmacy clerk due to her age.

Sighing, I scrub my face with my hands. "Fuck."

# FIVE

## Lucy

WHEN I WALK through the front door, my mom is sitting at the kitchen island with a glass of red wine next to her laptop. As soon as she sees me, she removes her thin wire computer glasses tiredly, pulls out the denim scrunchie holding up her waist-long strawberry locks, and rubs her scalp. "Hey, Luce. How was Rhys' party?"

My younger sister, Lorraine, and I get our hair from our mother—even though our shade of red is much darker. Our brother, Liam, somehow ended up with dark blond hair. Dad always jokes that if Liam didn't look exactly like him when he was younger, he'd wonder if our mother had an affair because no one in the family has hair that light.

"It was fine," I reply, passing through the kitchen and heading to my bedroom upstairs. "I'm tired. Got a lot of sun today. I'm gonna take a shower and head to bed."

On the way home, my brain went into overdrive, and it still hasn't quieted.

*Rhys and I had unprotected sex.*

*Lawson watched me come—twice. And it turned him on.*

*Rhys ignored my plea to talk afterward, leaving no room to discuss my decision to go to Berkeley instead of following him to Ole Miss.*

*Lawson got hard again when I went to apologize to him.*

*I liked the effect I had on him.*

*I* liked *it.*

"Hold up. Come here for a second. I want to get your opinion on this schedule for Terror Tot Summer Camp. You're way better at the activity time blocks than I am."

Fearing I may break down the second I look my mother in the eyes, I shake my head and continue to ascend the stairs. "I'll look at it tomorrow. I'm sorry. I have a headache, I'm exhausted, and I stink of the pool. I need a shower."

Liam appears on the landing, looking like he's ready to go out. "Where are you going? It's nearly nine." I eye his baggy sweatshirt that he's holding at the bottom as though he's hiding a bottle beneath the thick fabric.

"So? Curfew's at eleven." He rolls his eyes as we pass each other. My brother's only a year younger than I am but sometimes acts like he's still thirteen. The thing is, it's just that—an act. Liam is smart as hell, but for some reason, he makes really shitty decisions. He's one fuck up away from Mom and Dad hauling him off to a special school for troubled kids.

"Are you still hanging out with Thomas Becker? He's bad news, Liam."

"You're not my mom, Luce. Leave me alone." He flips the hood of his sweatshirt up and disappears downstairs.

Blowing out an exasperated breath, I storm to my

room, and it takes all my willpower not to slam the door. After a shower, I crawl beneath my butter yellow duvet and play with the frilly white lace at the edges as I will my brain to stop thinking about my boyfriend's dad. However, every time I close my eyes, the image of Lawson watching me is imprinted behind my lids.

His well-muscled figure, which is still toned to perfection from when he played football when he was younger. The way the veins in his arms popped as he clenched his fists. Dark, stormy-gray eyes, illuminated by the lingering fragments of the retreating sun's rays, peering at me with lust.

My body comes alive at the memory of when I unabashedly lowered my gaze to where he was hard, the outline of his cock straining against his pants. *That's* what made me come a second time.

Abandoning the lace of my blanket, I reach down between my legs, where I'm already wet, and begin to touch myself. And as I come for the third time tonight, it's not to thoughts of my boyfriend.

But of his dad.

---

"Rhys' dad stopped by this morning and dropped off a package for you," Liam side-eyes me as he unscrews the cap from the orange juice bottle. "Why isn't your *boyfriend* bringing you presents?"

Surprise rushes through me as I approach the small decorative cookie box on the island. Why would Lawson drop anything off? I pull my navy silk robe tighter as I sit on a stool, briefly wondering how his face would have looked if I'd answered the door wearing it with only my matching nightdress underneath.

My cheeks grow warm as I look up to catch my brother watching me warily, his right brow arched in suspicion. "What? And why do you say the word 'boyfriend' like that? I thought you liked Rhys?"

Liam shrugs his bare, sweaty shoulders. "He kind of turned into a dick this year, don't you think? He's not exactly nice to you, Luce."

I thought it was just me who noticed my boyfriend's change of attitude, but apparently not. I didn't think Rhys was mean to me, though. "I think he's just stressed about graduation."

The cookie box is white with little rainbows printed on it. A smile tugs at my lips, and I try my best to keep it from taking up my whole face since Liam is still watching me like a hawk eyeing a mouse on the ground. After using my nail to rip the sticker seal, I open the box to see a small white envelope sitting on top of a dozen of his cookies secured in one of the compostable cellophane bags I gave him for his thirty-sixth birthday this year.

Well, they were from me... *and* Rhys—who had completely forgotten what day it was.

My name is written across the envelope in Lawson's elegant scrawl, and there's a small, thick card inside that says,

"LIFE IS SHORT. EAT THE COOKIES."

I can't help my growing smile. But the elation in my chest quickly tightens and makes my heart thump harder as I realize there's a small slip of paper in the envelope as well. It simply says,

"INSIDE FLAP."

After checking that Liam is preoccupied with the fridge's contents instead of me, I shove the cookies over to check the part where the back of the box and the side connect. There's a little strip of silver sticking out—a familiar white pill encased in the original packaging that's been cut down so Lawson could hide it in the box.

*The morning-after pill.*

My cheeks start to burn as I realize that Lawson went out and got me an emergency contraception so that I wouldn't have to. My knees press together as my insides tighten. To have a man take care of it and save me the embarrassment of having to face the pharmacist's judgy eyes... Why is that simple act so hot?

Quickly, I shove the pill into the envelope with the card and slip of paper before tucking it into the pocket of my robe. Just in time, too, as Liam strides out of the kitchen and Lorraine walks in, followed by our parents.

"Good morning, darling. Are you feeling better?" Mom asks as she pulls two mugs down from the cabinet for coffee.

Running a hand through my mess of curls that I

stupidly let air dry as I slept, I nod even though her back is to me. "I am. Thanks. Will you make me a cup?"

Pulling a cookie from the box, I take a big bite as Dad slides onto the stool next to me. "Are you eating a cookie? Aren't you ladies headed to brunch club in a bit?"

"Quiet, Will. They're Lawson's cookies. It's fine." Mom gently shushes him as she places a mug in front of me. She plucks the cookie from my hand, breaks off a chunk, and shoves it in her mouth before giving the other half back to me. "God, these are so good. Have you asked him for the recipe yet?"

Lorraine holds a hand out silently for a piece, never pulling her eyes from her book, so I break the rest of the cookie up and hand her some. "Only every time he makes them, Mom. He says it's a family recipe."

"Well, you're practically family!" Mom throws her hands in the air with a laugh and a shake of her head. "Tell him to give up the goods!"

Her words make me think of Lawson's other *goods* that have nothing to do with his cookie recipe.

"Is that who was knocking on the door this morning? Why didn't he just send them home with you last night?" Dad's voice sounds far away as I daydream about what occurred yesterday.

Should I say thank you to Lawson for taking care of the pill for me? Should I even show up to help him organize his office? I feel like there's this line where he's on one side, Rhys is on the other, and I'm standing super close to the buzzing barrier between them, threatening to snap the divide.

Does this make me a bad girlfriend?

The attraction I feel for Lawson is all perfectly normal, isn't it? He's a young dad. Gorgeous and kind. And I can only hope that Rhys adopts more of his father's attributes as we get older, even if right now he's taking more after his mother.

"Luce?" Mom's sharp tone snaps me from my thoughts.

With a shake of my head, my glazed-over eyes refocus to find my parents both staring at me. Even Lorraine has pulled her mossy eyes from the pages of her newest fantasy novel and is watching me curiously.

"I'm sorry, what did you say?" I ask on an exhale.

"You should go get ready. We need to leave for brunch in twenty. Are you sure you're up for it? You look flushed, sweetheart." She reaches over the island to press the back of a hand to my forehead.

"I'm fine. I'll be ready soon." I get off the stool and put my hands in my pockets, fingering the envelope as I head to my room. Quickly, I change into a halter-style dusty blue dress with white polka dots and a pleated skirt before pulling my hair into a messy ponytail. A quick swipe of my favorite raspberry gloss and a few coats of mascara complete my look with five minutes left to spare.

I tap my nails against the blush-colored quartz vanity of my en suite, staring at the white envelope with my name on it before finally filling my water cup. I pop the tab on the back of the blister pack and swallow the pill, draining half my glass. After burying the trash beneath used tissues and clumps of hair from my shower, I grab the note about the cookies and bite my lip, deciding if I should throw it away as well.

As my fingers graze Lawson's handwriting, Mom's yell from downstairs startles me. "Lucy, let's go!"

Flinging the lid of my jewelry box open, I place the note under the top compartment before grabbing a pair of pink bow studs. Securing them, I grab my clutch and slip on a pair of white strappy sandals before heading downstairs.

BRUNCH CLUB IS a tradition my mom and her friends have had since they were young. Every Sunday, they get together for mimosas and family-style breakfast either at a restaurant or one of their houses.

Over the years, as their friend circle and families grew, it went from being a group of four to a party of ten. Originally, it was my mom and her three best friends, Daphne, Charleigh, and Kendall. Now, it's also my sister and me, Daphne's daughter, Rose, Daphne's ex-husband's wife, Evie, and their daughter, Nova, and Jess, my uncle Sean's long-time girlfriend.

None of my *aunts and uncles* are actually related to us, but my parents have been friends with them for so long that we might as well all be one big family.

"Are you guys excited to be starting fifth grade next year? I know River really wants Mrs. Southerd. What about you both?" I ask Rose and Nova.

The girls have been inseparable since Aunt Evie and

Uncle Eric adopted Nova when she was three. They are the complete opposite of each other: Rose with sun-kissed skin and bright blonde hair, and Nova with a snowy complexion and dark hair that she always wants to brighten up with colored clip-in extensions. They couldn't be more different, but I think that's what makes them best friends.

Rose scoops some fruit from a bowl while Nova plates herself some bacon before they smoothly switch dishes. "We want Mrs. Southerd, too. We obviously have to be in the same class as River," Rose states, as if I should have known that already.

I laugh and shake my head. *"Obviously."*

My little cousin has been stuck to River's side like glue since kindergarten. The aunts have made bets about when they'll start dating, but lately, I've noticed that Rose's eyes keep wandering to Liam whenever they're in the same room. The eight-year age difference is large enough that I'm not worried about warning my brother of her growing crush on him. I know he will shut that down himself if she ever tries to act on it.

She's too young to be worried about boys.

"Are you excited about prom next weekend, Luce?" Aunt Charleigh inquires.

"Ooh, yes. I hope you don't mind us all coming over before you leave. I want to see you and Rhys together in person. I'm dying to see his face when he sees your dress," Aunt Kendall adds as she takes a bite of stuffed French toast.

"I am excited," I respond indifferently with a small shrug. "But honestly, it's just a dance."

"Just a dance? It's a huge milestone, hon!" Aunt

Daphne cries incredulously. She tucks her blonde hair behind her ear, bright blue eyes shining as her expression turns playful. "But I guess you're already past the typical *what happens after prom* stage, aren't you?"

Mom slams her hands over her ears and starts singing loudly, "La la la la la la! I don't need to hear about my daughter having sex already!"

My aunts share an amused look as if they and Mom didn't just take me to get sexy sets of lingerie for my upcoming *milestones*.

"Really, Bree? You know what she's wearing under that prom dress. *You're* the one who picked it out!" Aunt Charleigh laughs.

"Not to mention graduation night. As a matter of fact, wasn't it *your* idea she wear that little number under Rhys' jersey?" Aunt Jess chimes in. She tosses back the rest of her mimosa and makes a face. "You know, the only reason I tolerate this shit is because I love them." She points at my mom and the other aunts. "But I need a Bloody Mary." Grabbing a bottle of champagne, she makes another mimosa, sliding it over to me discreetly before ordering a new drink.

My stomach flips as I pick up the glass and take a sip. I've had plenty of mimosas at brunch club before, but for some reason, today, the bubbles go straight to my head. Drinking isn't something I've done much of since Rhys and I stole a bottle of bourbon from his parents' liquor cabinet to take to our friend's house when we were sixteen. I thought I was going to die after a night of chugging it and whatever else everyone brought to our little get-together.

I'm not experienced enough to understand why some

alcohol—mainly the amber-colored ones—make me feel like shit while I'm perfectly fine with others.

Three mimosas later, my brain is giggly, and my mouth is foggy.

Or is it the other way around?

I take another bite of fruit. If I get more food in my stomach, it will help.

Aunt Evie slides over a small plate with half an Eggs Benedict on it. "You need to eat more than fruit, Luce."

Aunt Jess makes a hissing sound and grabs my champagne glass. "Yeah, no more for you, silly girl. Eat some carbs."

I stare at my favorite breakfast dish, wanting desperately to cut into it, and watch the egg cover the bacon and English muffin with its delicious golden yolk. Charlotte and Rhys' words from last night haunt me, though, and instead, I pull out my phone as my aunts' attention turns back to the adult conversation happening at the other end of the table.

Pulling up Lawson's contact, I debate sending him a message. The only reason I have his phone number is because once Rhys' cell died when we went to their Boca home for the weekend. Charlotte was supposed to be there when we arrived but was God knows where with God knows who, and Rhys didn't know the new lock code. Since he couldn't remember his dad's number off the top of his head, I reached out to Lawson on Iconic, a social media platform, and he gave me his number for emergencies.

This is an emergency, isn't it?

I need to say thank you. I don't want to be rude.

My body buzzes with excitement as I type out a message.

> Thank you for the cookies… and for the other thing.

He reads it immediately as if his phone were already in his hand and he was going to message me.

**Lawson Morgan**

> You're welcome.

His response is simple, sending a flood of disappointment rushing through me until I see the three dots that signal he's typing more.

**Lawson Morgan**

> I won't be home a lot this week. If you want to clean up the office between practices, I'll pay you what I'd normally pay my assistant. Just don't throw anything away, please.

My shoulders slump at his words. I was hoping that we would get a chance to spend more time together.

He clearly does not feel the same.

And now, I feel like an absolute idiot for getting excited at the idea of spending the week with him. Lawson is drawing a line in the sand, and I need to stop acting like a ho and respect that.

Lusting after my boyfriend's dad? What the hell am I thinking?

I love Rhys. What happened yesterday was inappropriate and absolutely can't happen again.

Pink takes over my cheeks in a mixture of embarrassment and too much champagne. Putting my phone away without replying, I grab my water glass and gulp it down before pulling the Eggs Benedict closer and asking Nova to pass me the platter of roasted potatoes.

I have practice later. I'll just work extra hard to work off the carbs.

# Six

*Lawson*

Do I have to work late all week?

Yes.

Is it because I picked up even more work than usual, so I didn't have to be at the house?

Also yes.

The memory of Lucy's brother answering the door Sunday morning replays in my head repeatedly. His calculating stare as I handed over the cookie box—how the cogs in his brain worked overtime as he tried to figure out why I was there at nine in the morning, with cookies, of all things, for his sister.

*"Wasn't she just there last night?"*

*Scratching the back of my neck, I nod and gesture to the box. "Yeah, but everyone ate them before she could set some aside to take home. I was making a batch for the office and thought I'd drop some off."*

All lies. And Liam stared at me like he *knew* I wasn't telling the truth.

The kid is way more intelligent than anyone gives him credit for.

Drumming my fingers on the desk, I take in my now spotless and completely organized office while waiting for Rhys to get ready to go to Lucy's. All week, I managed to avoid her. Tried to steel myself from thinking of her naked body and the way she looked down at my cock. She never responded to my last text message, yet she still showed up to clean my mess.

My days have been shit—downright dull without her bright colors and infectious laugh brightening up the room. I didn't realize just how much I enjoyed having Lucy around until the entire week went by and I hadn't seen her once.

Rhys appears in the open doorway, looking like the spitting image of me at his age, dressed in a black suit with an emerald tie and a red rose boutonnière. Something in my chest clenches as my reality slaps me upside the head. My son is getting ready to go to his senior prom with his girlfriend, who I've been lusting over.

I'm such a fucking shitty father.

"Ready? Mom is already grumbling about us having to go over there." Rhys smirks. It seems like tonight he's annoyed with Charlotte. Both of them have mood swings that shift faster than a dual-clutch transmission.

"Well, your mom doesn't *have* to go," I comment, like my son isn't already aware.

Rhys wanders further into my office, looking at all the colored binders with neat labels written on the spines. "Lucy did a good job. Funny that you never asked me to help you organize in here but had no problem allowing her to do it when you weren't home." There's a blatant accusation in his tone and hard stare.

"You never showed any interest in helping me. She offered. That's all."

His brows draw together, lips pinching into a thin line. "Yeah, you two seem to be awfully fond of each other all of a sudden."

"Would you rather me hate her like your mother does?"

His gaze drops, and he shakes his head, staring at the hardwood floor like he's got something on his mind. He doesn't move as I stand and approach him. "What is it, Son?"

"I don't know. I've been thinking a lot lately…"

"About?" I prod. Rhys is nearly as tall as I am now. We often get mistaken for brothers instead of father and son. It pisses him off, but I just keep telling him he should feel lucky he's got good genes.

"College," he sighs, turning to lean against the door-frame. "Football." Crossing his arms, he blows out a rough breath. "Lucy."

I keep quiet, letting him work through his thoughts.

"I love her, you know? I don't want her to go to California," he admits quietly. "But I know if I ask her not to go, then that will make me a selfish prick. But if she goes, I don't think we'll survive the long distance."

"If you love her, you won't ask her to give up her dreams and passions so that you can live yours, Rhys. If you love her, *truly* love her, what's a few years long distance?" My words summon a look of shame that flits across his face as he reaches up to scratch the back of his head, a quirk he gets from me. I rest my hand on his shoulder. "But you're also both very young. There's a whole world out there beyond Chicago."

I tell myself that I'm doing my job as a father and assuring my son that he doesn't have to hold onto his past while trying to navigate his future. But I'd be lying if I said there isn't a small part of me that wouldn't mind seeing Rhys and Lucy go their separate ways—not for me, but for them.

They both need to live their lives and find who they are away from each other.

"Would you have let Mom go to college on the other side of the country?"

I don't tell him that I was planning on breaking up with Charlotte until she told me she was pregnant with him. Instead, I try to dispel the seriousness of the conversation with humor. "Rhys, when has your mother ever done what I wanted her to do? Besides, we don't *let* our partners do anything, okay? We're not cavemen."

He laughs, the edges of his eyes crinkling with a smile. "Yeah, you're right. I guess I can't really tell Lucy she *can't* go. Can you imagine how that would go over?"

"About as well as me telling your mother I'm taking away her credit cards, and she's not allowed to go to Boca anymore."

∽

IN ANOTHER WORLD, I'd genuinely enjoy being a part of the Bradee's circle of friends.

Unfortunately for me, my wife can't seem to keep her damn mouth shut.

"These aren't terrible, but the gruyere ones you made last time were much better. Just my opinion." Charlotte holds her hands up after eating one of the homemade crackers Lucy's mother, Bree, made for a meat and cheese platter.

Bree's left eye twitches as she plasters a smile on her face. "So sorry they aren't to your liking, Charlotte. Here, have another glass of wine."

Rhys coughs a laugh into his hand while Bree's friends look at my wife like they want to skewer her and roast her over the fire in the pit in the Bradee's backyard. Lucy has a lot of her mother's features, from her red hair to the freckles over the bridge of her nose. They have a natural beauty, and I wonder if that's why Charlotte gives them so much grief.

My wife's beauty comes from a bottle, a scalpel, and many, many syringes.

Will, Bree's husband, tips his beer bottle back, gaze swinging to mine with a look that clearly says 'My wife is about to murder yours if you don't get her to shut her mouth.'

River's best friends, Rose and Nova, bound down the stairs in a fit of giggles. "Lucy looks like a mermaid!" Nova exclaims loudly as the girls throw their hands out and frame each side of the stairs dramatically.

Everyone collectively holds their breath as Lucy appears, and my heart skips a beat as her eyes instantly find Rhys. And I'm glad for it because if she'd looked at me first, I'm fairly certain I'd have to excuse myself to explain to my dick why it's inappropriate to get hard around the girl, especially in front of her parents.

As it is, my fists clench of their own accord at my sides as I try to tear my eyes away from the breathtaking image Lucy makes while her mom and aunts fuss over her. Her dress is emerald velvet and hugs her curves. There's a high slit on one side where the dress drapes in waves, while the other side is slightly shorter and straighter. It's strapless, and her breasts heave over the corseted top. Her makeup is simple, like always, but she's sporting a red lip that makes my insides sweat. Her hair falls in waves, pinned over her shoulder on one side, like a Hollywood starlet at a red carpet event.

"You are..." Rhys takes a deep breath. "Wow. I am one lucky guy."

He sure fucking is.

Lucy smiles widely, eyes darting to me briefly before she goes to stand in front of her boyfriend while he fishes a red rose corsage out of its box to place on her wrist.

"See, if you'd kept eating Lawson's cookies, you wouldn't have fit in that beautiful dress. It's just a tad too snug, dear," Charlotte sneers from behind her wine glass.

Will chokes on his beer as Bree whirls to face my wife. "Now, you listen here—"

Bree's friends try to intercept her, and everyone is talking at once to either try and calm her down or tell my wife off—who looks alarmed that everyone is so upset by her comment. Scrubbing a hand down my face, I glance over to see that my son is unaffected by his mother's words, but Lucy seems devastated.

"Don't listen to her. You look beautiful," Rhys whispers before kissing her forehead, completely unaware of her distress. "I'm gonna run to the bathroom real quick before we leave." If he notices that she's upset, he doesn't acknowledge it before he disappears into the guest bathroom down the hall.

"I... I forgot my clutch," Lucy murmurs amidst the chaos, escaping back upstairs. Her mom and aunts are still having words with Charlotte, who is holding her hands out as if she doesn't understand what the big deal is.

Anger courses through me, followed by utter embarrassment. I don't even bother trying to jump into the fray because I'm not on my wife's side. This has been a long time coming for her, and she needs to reap what she sows.

With everyone preoccupied, I mutter an excuse that I need to use the toilet as well, knowing the other guest bathroom is upstairs. After climbing the steps two at a time, I make my way down the hall, peering into the open doors to try and find Lucy. Eventually, I hear a sniffling sound and nearly run into her as she exits what must be her bedroom.

Startled, teary eyes blink up at me. "Lawson?"

"Hey," I offer lamely, leaning against the cream-colored doorframe. "I just wanted to check on you." Something my son should be doing. "Are you alright?"

I hate seeing her cry, even if the tears haven't fallen yet. Her eyes drop to my chest, and her lip quivers as she picks at her freshly manicured French tips. Without thinking, I straighten and reach for her hands, holding them in mine as I step in close.

"Please don't listen to anything Charlotte says. She's... she's..."

"Awful?" Lucy sniffs, squeezing her fingers around mine before shaking off my hold so she can dab under her eyes. She goes back into her room, and I follow her as she enters her en suite and grabs a tissue to fix her makeup.

Standing in the doorway, I nod in agreement. "Yes, she can be awful. I'm sorry she's so unkind to you."

"I just don't get what her deal is. I haven't done anything to warrant her hatred. I've been nothing but wonderful to Rhys for the past two years." Lucy grabs a golden tube and unscrews the cap, carefully applying more mascara to her bottom lashes.

Some of her hair escapes the clip and falls down her back, and my fingers itch to reach out and touch it. "She's just jealous."

Lucy's eyebrows screw together in confusion as she glances at me in the mirror before tending to her other eye. "What on earth does she have to be jealous of me for?"

Without skipping a beat, I reply, "Because you're taking away her son's attention. And because you're beautiful."

### Lucy

Lawson's words break the internal dam that's been holding back all my warm and fuzzy feelings for him. I've been building it all week, and with a simple phrase, he blows it up like dynamite.

"I'm sorry, I shouldn't be saying that." He scratches the back of his neck sheepishly.

As he turns to leave, I lunge toward him, wincing as my hair catches in the zipper of my dress. "Wait! Ahh!" My shoulders tighten to hold the garment in place as it tugs at a few stray strands.

Why does it always hurt worse when one or two hairs get pulled rather than a handful?

Don't ask how I know that the latter doesn't hurt as bad.

"What is it?" Lawson asks in alarm, getting so close I can smell his minty pine aftershave.

I try to turn my head, but the movement hurts. "My hair is caught in the zipper."

The corner of his mouth lifts into an amused half-smirk that I'm starting to think about entirely too often. "Hold still."

I can barely contain the rapid beating of my heart as it threatens to jump out of my chest at the touch of Lawson's fingers on my bare skin. He's so close I can feel his warm breath against my neck, causing my skin to break out in goosebumps. My breasts heave with every inhale that threatens to tear the fabric of my dress.

"I'm... uh... going to unzip your dress. Hold the front," Lawson softly commands.

"Yes, sir." The words escape before I can swallow them. They hang in the air around us.

His fingers still against my back. It's so quiet I hear a sharp intake of breath, followed by a soft groan that he tries so hard to conceal.

"Lucy..." My name falls from between his lips like a plea as his warm fingers finally move, gently untangling my hair. He's trying so hard not to touch me directly, but the barest hint of his fingers caressing against my spine has my entire body lit up like a sparkler.

When the strands are finally free, Lawson sweeps them back over my shoulder, tucking them securely inside my hairclip. As he slowly zips my dress back up, I turn to look at him over my shoulder, every part of me so aware of every part of him.

Our eyes lock, and he doesn't release me even when he's finished. A fiery trail follows his hands as they slide down my back to encircle my hips, fingers digging into my flesh possessively as his head slowly dips down.

"Lawson..." Our lips are a hair's breadth apart, and I slowly close my eyes and tilt my head up.

"What's going on here?" My brother's words cut through the thick cloud of lust that encases us, and we spring apart as though we've burned each other.

"Nothing!" My voice is high-pitched when I answer, whirling to grab my clutch from the vanity. "My hair got stuck in my zipper, and Lawson was just helping me untangle it."

"Yep," Lawson agrees, popping the p. "Good to see you, Liam." Without so much as a goodbye, he flees my room while my brother and I watch him go.

The dark brown rings around Liam's golden green irises are edged in red as he turns his gaze back to me, and I frown. "Are you on something?"

"Don't change the subject, Luce." He narrows his eyes at me. "I hope you know what you're doing." He turns away, leaving no opportunity for me to question him further about why his eyes are red or why he smells like a weed shop.

I am frozen, replaying what happened between Lawson

and me in my mind until Liam's door slams, spurring me to get a move on.

Downstairs, Rhys is waiting for me with a handsome smile, and his parents are nowhere to be found.

But as he helps me settle into his truck, I can't help but think about the near kiss I almost shared with his dad.

*No, Liam, I have absolutely no clue what I'm doing. I've lost my damn mind.*

# SEVEN

*Lawson*

IT'S JUST like Charlotte to tell parents we can host a graduation party, where both of us will be chaperoning, and then fuck off to Boca without so much as a heads-up. Just a short text stating she'll be gone for a week was all I got less than an hour before Rhys told his friends they could start arriving.

I don't know what it is about our house, or us, that makes the other parents feel like we're capable of keeping over thirty new graduates in line, but somehow, our place always gets offered up as the location for everyone to hang out whenever they celebrate something big.

It's an unspoken understanding that the kids will drink, so all of us parents feel like they might as well do it where they can crash when they're tired, and we know the liquor isn't coming from some random *"hey, mister"* at a gas station.

Charlotte wanted a big house where we didn't have neighbors right on top of us, and I guess I'm thankful for that because even though the lieutenant of the Neighborhood Oriented Policing Team's son will be in attendance, the last thing we need is nosy neighbors complaining about the noise and potentially sending an officer out who won't turn a blind eye to underage drinking.

As I clean the grill after making hot dogs and cheeseburgers, I frown across the backyard at my son, who is standing too close to a petite blonde I've never seen before. They're both wet from swimming, and he's grinning at her like they have a secret no one knows. Taking a pull from my beer, I try to tamp down the anger that rises beneath my skin as he tickles her before launching them both into the pool.

It's completely inappropriate.

Then again, I almost kissed Lucy on prom night, which is *way* more unacceptable.

It's been two weeks.

Two weeks of avoiding her at all costs.

I know the cheer team won Nationals—due to my unhealthy obsession of stalking Lucy's Iconic profile—and I was prepared to text her a congratulations before I nearly threw my phone across the room to stop myself. Rhys has been spending more time at her house, as well, so it's like she's been actively avoiding me, too.

But I didn't think Lucy would go so far as to not show up to the graduation party.

Regret runs rampant through my mind. I never meant to make things so awkward between us. I just... acted in the moment that night. She was right there. So beautiful. So warm. Surrounding me with her vanilla and lilac scent. Her whispered, "Yes, sir," plays in my fantasies as I stroke myself to completion. Then I try desperately not to throw up over how sick I am.

*She's eighteen-fucking-years-old, Lawson. You have to stop.*

Yet, here I am again, wondering about her and where she's at. Why is she not here? Why is my son flirting with another girl so openly?

Did they break up, and he just didn't tell me?

Is that why the girls from Lucy's cheerleading team are sneering at Rhys and whoever the blonde is?

It's none of my business. I keep repeating it over and over, even though my son's actions are reminiscent of his mother's, and his girlfriend deserves a hell of a lot better than that.

"Thanks for hosting the party tonight, Mr. Morgan!" Clarissa's—one of Lucy's teammates—bubbly voice cuts through my thoughts.

"No problem. Hey, where is Lucy tonight? And who's the girl with Rhys?" I try to ask as casually as I can.

Clarissa's eyes slide to the pool as her brows furrow. "Some chick from Fairmont. She's been showing up at all the parties. No idea who keeps inviting her." Her eyes slowly glide back to mine. "Lucy should be here later. She's celebrating with her family right now. Gonna be real interesting if she walks in on that." The raven-haired girl jerks her head toward my son before smiling mischievously as she picks up a skewer of fruit. "Where is Mrs. Morgan tonight?"

*Probably drunk off her ass by now and getting fucked by the guy who cuts our grass.*

"Went to check on the house in Florida. There was a...

landscaping emergency," I lie, glaring at the blonde who hangs onto Rhys' shoulders in the pool as she attempts to climb on for a game of chicken against another couple.

"Oh. Well, we women must take care of those *landscaping* emergencies. Maybe you could help me out sometime? Your lawn always looks trimmed," Clarissa suggests with a saccharine lilt. My head swings back her way at the obvious innuendo in her voice, alarm bells going off like big red flags. Her blue eyes sparkle with intent, causing my insides to churn uncomfortably.

Ignoring her, I turn away to go back into the house. "Rhys, I'll be inside! You guys make sure not to get into any trouble. I'll be checking in sporadically throughout the night."

"Got it, Dad." He doesn't even spare me a glance as the girl falls off his shoulders, and they begin to play fight. Everything about it sits wrong with me. I almost pull out my phone to ask Lucy when she'll be arriving so I can save her from having to 'walk in on that' as Clarissa put it.

*It's* none *of my fucking business.*

The music and rambunctious teenagers are giving me a headache that only something stronger than beer will fix. When they were younger, Rhys and Lucy broke into our liquor cabinet and stole a bottle, so I relocated all of the good shit to a place no one is allowed in if I'm not there. So, instead of relaxing in my room—where I can finally go because Charlotte is gone, and I can exist in my own space again—I head to my office. I can have the drink I so desperately need and work on some files for the coming week. Plus, the windows overlook the pool, making it easier for me to keep an eye on what's happening.

*You have to keep an eye on everyone, Lawson. It's not so you can see when Lucy shows up.*

## Lucy

"Hot damn, Lucy! Rhys is gonna come the second he sees you!"

"I'll give you a ride if he can't get the job done, Luce!"

With a snort and a roll of my eyes, I wave off the guys from the football team and make my way through the Morgans' house in search of my boyfriend. There are still a lot of people hanging around, even though the party is winding down, but these guys have literally seen me in a bathing suit. If I'd known showing up in Rhys' jersey would have caused such a commotion... well, I still would have done it.

The guys are completely harmless, so their comments don't offend me. If I were blackout drunk, I know that any one of them would put me in a room to pass out safely and lock the door so no one could get in.

"Baaaabe! You're hereee. *Finally!* Ugh, I tried waiting, buuut you took toooo long. I might be a liiiittle drunk," Clarissa slurs as Nathan Whaters slings her over his shoulder and heads for the backyard, no doubt taking her to the pool house.

"Don't put her on a top bunk, Nate! She rolls in her sleep!" I follow him to see if my boyfriend is in the pool. "Have you seen Rhys?"

"Not for a while!" he yells over his shoulder.

Clarissa picks her head up and grumbles, "You deserve better, Lucyyyyyy!"

*Deserve better? What's that supposed to mean?*

"Keg is gone!" someone yells from further in the house. A round of boos reverberates around the room, and people start calling their designated drivers to come get them.

"Hey, Lucy," Bethany, one of the football players' girl-friends, greets quietly as she sidles up to me while I grab a hard seltzer from the fridge.

"Hey, Beth. Looks like I missed the party."

She looks over her shoulder, scanning the room as she tucks her short blonde hair behind one ear. "Listen, I'm not trying to cause drama, but that girl from Fairmont who's been showing up at all our parties was here earlier. She was kinda all over Rhys in the pool."

My skin prickles with irritation. Allison Sweeny has been a thorn in my side all year since she transferred from out of state to our rival school. She's been fawning all over Rhys like he's the greatest thing ever to walk this earth since the second she saw him. And while I'm confident my boyfriend loves me, it hasn't escaped my attention that he doesn't seem to mind *her* attention.

"Was she now? Did she leave?" I ask before chugging my seltzer—one of the few alcoholic beverages I'm able to drink without it making me feel like the walking dead the next day.

Bethany follows me to the hall, where I throw my purse into a large coat closet. "I'm not sure. I haven't seen her for a while. But... Lucy... I haven't seen Rhys for a while either." Her big brown eyes are filled with pity.

A buzzing sound goes off in my ears as I stare at her. A heavy, crushing wave of anxiety swells beneath my lungs. "Where are Lawson and Charlotte?"

She looks confused momentarily, her taupe brows drawing together before shooting up toward her hairline. "Oh! Mr. and Mrs. Morgan? Rhys' mom hasn't been here all night, and his dad went upstairs a while ago. He looked kinda mad at Rhys if I'm being honest."

Something pricks my heart. "Did he see Allison hanging on Rhys?"

She nods.

I can't decide which news upsets me more: Rhys letting another girl hang on him or Lawson watching it happen.

"Jimmy was saying that Rhys is really upset about you deciding to go to Berkeley, especially since you're going earlier now for cheer."

"Bethany, baby! Let's go!" her boyfriend, Jimmy, shouts from the living room.

Her thick lashes flutter as she rolls her eyes. "I hope it's nothing. But if it does end up being... *something*, just know that you deserve better. Besides, we're all going off to college. There's plenty of other fish in the sea."

Bethany's words don't comfort me. As people begin to leave, with only a few who are too drunk to drive staying behind to pass out in the pool house, it becomes easier to see that neither my boyfriend nor Allison are amongst the crowd.

The stairwell leading to the basement is dark as I stand at the top of it, fingers twisting in the hem of Rhys' jersey. My nerves are fried, and the bottoms of my feet tingle with pins and needles as I take the first step down.

There's a night light at the bottom of the stairs for when River falls asleep playing video games so he doesn't wake up in complete darkness. It casts the den in a gentle glow, guiding me to Rhys' room.

At the first sign of the very thing I'm afraid of, my heart jumps into my throat, expanding to block my airway. The door is cracked, and the sounds of a bed squeaking grow louder with each step I take. It's clear what's happening. The familiar sounds of my boyfriend's groans join barely concealed squeaks that are obviously female, but I can't stop my feet from moving. Some insane part of me needs to see it to confirm my worst fear.

My lungs burn with their need for air as I gently push his door open. Blonde hair cascades down a naked back. A bare ass as Rhys pounds into her from below. His whispered words of encouragement as he brings her closer to release.

Air fills my lungs sharply, drawing their attention to where I stand, frozen in the doorway.

"Fuck! Lucy! This isn't what it looks like!" Rhys' clichéd excuse fills the room as he all but throws Allison off him.

I'm already halfway down the hall, furiously wiping at the hot tears that catch on my lower lashes, when I hear him shout, "Where the fuck are my pants?"

His heavy footsteps are loud behind me as I climb the stairs two at a time, trying to escape before he can catch up to me and try to feed me his bullshit excuses as to why he's cheating. The living room is empty when I reach it, and a curse falls from my lips when I remember I was dropped off and don't have a way to leave.

River's room is at the end of the hall, and knowing he's at a friend's house tonight, I make a run for it. No one will care if I lock myself inside until Rhys passes out, and then I can call someone to come get me.

"Lucy! Wait! Let me explain!" Rhys is nearly on my heels as I fly through the house.

"There's nothing to explain! It's pretty simple, your dick was in another girl. Got it. Message received!" I scream back.

Thick tears cause my vision to blur, and I know I'll never make it to River's room before he catches me.

"Lucy, please!"

We aren't supposed to go into Lawson's office without his permission, but he's permitted me to organize it, and I take that as a good enough excuse to try the door since it's closer than River's. Relief floods through me to find it open, and I rush into the room, slamming the door behind me and locking it just as Rhys' fists meet the heavy wood.

# Eight

*Lawson*

I'm three tumblers of whiskey in by the time the party clears from the house. I've never been more thankful for soundproofing. I'm barely able to hear anything when the thumping music cuts off in the living room.

So when my office door swings open while I'm standing at my minibar, pouring myself a fourth drink, it startles the shit out of me.

Lucy rushes in and slams the door behind her, stepping back to glare at it as she breathes heavily and wipes at her eyes. I'm too shocked to say anything, and she clearly doesn't notice I'm in the room.

Rhys pounds on the door. "Lucy! Talk to me!" His voice is muffled, but I can still make out his words.

"There's nothing to fucking talk about, you jackass!" With a rage-filled cry, Lucy turns away and pulls Rhys' jersey over her head, leaving her in nothing but a bra and underwear as she stomps toward my desk.

Objectively, I know I should have announced myself the

second she began to remove the jersey. But watching her expose a vast expanse of skin stuns me into silence.

Grabbing the scissors from a drawer, she begins to slice the blades through the fabric while muttering curses under her breath about my son being a lying, cheating bastard.

"Lucy, baby, let's talk about this, okay? I know I fucked up. I'm so sorry," Rhys' tone is strained and frantic on the other side of the door, but she ignores him and continues shredding the black and green material.

*I* knew *something was going on with the blonde.*

Afraid Lucy might hurt herself, I say her name softly, trying not to startle her.

She jumps anyway, spinning to stare at me with wide, teary eyes. Her raspberry-painted lips are formed in a surprised O. "Lawson? What are you doing in here?"

Trying my damnedest to keep my focus on her face and not let it wander down her exposed body, I swallow the lump in my throat before replying, "I could ask you the same thing." My voice comes out huskier than I meant it to, and I clear my throat in an attempt to make it go back to normal.

"Well..." She slams the scissors and what's left of the jersey onto the surface of my desk. "...I just caught my boyfriend fucking another girl." A fresh wave of tears spills from her eyes as her bottom lip begins to quiver. "I'm sorry. I was going to lock myself in River's room, but Rhys caught up before I could make it that far." She grabs her elbows, unwittingly pushing her breasts together, as she drops her eyes to the floor.

My son's pounding has ceased, and I see my cell light up on my desk. It's most likely him asking if I'm in here with her since we're talking too quietly to hear anything on his side.

"Fuck, Lucy. I'm sorry."

"Are you?" she bites out, gaze snapping up to mine as it fills with rage. "Because you apparently saw them together tonight but didn't say anything."

The ire in her eyes fills me with shame, but I shake my head and scratch my neck. "It's not my business."

"You should have said something!" she shouts before pointing at me. "You *know* what this feels like!"

My chest seizes, and I hold up my hands in surrender. "You're right." The admission cools the steam pouring from her, and she deflates. Instead of telling her I tried watching for her arrival all night, I murmur, "I'm sorry."

Silence extends between us for a few moments before she rubs her forehead with obvious frustration. "No. I'm sorry. It's not like you could have done anything."

"I didn't know... for certain if something was happening," I offer lamely. While Lucy's not paying attention to me, I allow my eyes to drift down her body, taking in every curve and dip that I've spent the last few weeks fantasizing about exploring and trying to commit it to memory like a creep because I'll never see her in this state again. "I should... uh... go get you some clothes."

Realization dawns over her pretty features as she looks down at herself and shrugs her shoulders. "It's not like you haven't seen me in a bathing suit." Then, in a quieter tone, she mutters, "Or completely naked, for that matter."

A cough escapes my throat, and I have to pound on my chest a few times to dislodge the bitter taste of the sarcasm in her words.

No, this is *nothing* like her lounging in her high-waisted bikinis by the pool. And it's somehow more intimate than her being bare. This is... this is lust-filled fantasies about centerfold models. This is pure art in the form of black and royal purple lingerie that hugs her curves and has my cock so rock hard I could balance my body weight on it. There's silk and lace and artistically placed appliques that hide her nipples, and I want to tear them from her body with my teeth.

I swallow another lump when she tenses her thighs, and my eyes snap back to her face to find her cheeks red as cherries. She's watching me take her in.

And she likes it.

"Here, put this on." I make quick work of the buttons on my shirt, handing it over without meeting her eyes. In a near panic, I cross the room to swipe my tumbler from the minibar and down the whiskey in one gulp.

Her voice is small, almost meek, when she speaks again. "I'm done."

When I turn back to her...

*Holy fuck.*

Somehow, all that lace and silk is a thousand times hotter beneath the open white button-down. It hits her thighs, the sleeves falling past her hands, and a tempting smile is plastered over her face as she rolls them up. "Can I have one of those?"

I follow her gaze to my empty glass and huff a laugh, even as I move around the bar to grab another one. "I thought you were never drinking hard liquor again?"

"It's the amber-colored ones that get me. Do you have

any tequila?" Lucy asks in a tone that implies she already knows I do.

As I contemplate asking if she's going to button up the shirt, she sits on the camel-colored leather couch, and it's clear that the answer is no. The damn lump I can't seem to get rid of grows larger. I swear I'm going to have to go to the doctor soon to see if it's a condition I can get rid of.

Rhys begins pounding on the door again as he releases a string of curses that are barely audible through the heavy wood, and I feel the weight of the situation on my shoulders. "I'm going to tell him to let you cool off for a bit."

Lucy snorts, shoving her fingers through her messy waves. "I don't care what you tell him. I don't want to talk to him."

With a sigh, I turn the lock and crack the door open, bracing myself on the frame to prevent Rhys from bulldozing his way inside. His eyes grow wide with shock, his cheeks burning cherry red as he looks over my shoulder and sees Lucy sitting on the couch in my dress shirt.

"What the fuck?!" he shouts, trying to muscle his way past me.

I push him back gently. "Calm down. I think you both need a breather."

"Are you fucking kidding me?! Lucy, get the fuck out here and talk to me."

"Hey!" I snap. "You don't get to fuck around on her and then talk to her that way." I dig a finger into his chest. "*You* fucked up, Rhys. She didn't do anything."

His eyes soften, chest deflating a little as he scrubs at his face. "Lucy, baby, I'm sorry. Please talk to me."

"I have *nothing* to say to you." I peer over my shoulder

to see her glaring at him, my shirt falling open to reveal her near nakedness.

Rhys' nostrils flare as he takes in her appearance. "Put some fucking clothes on when you're around him!"

He tries to muscle his way past me again, but I shove him back once more and hide her from his view with my body.

"Of course, you'd take her fucking side. Look at her, prancing around in front of you in her lingerie. Bet you're just loving this, aren't you, *Dad*?" he sneers.

Instead of anger, a wave of sadness crests against my chest. "No, Son. I'm honestly not. I expected better from you. In fact, I'm disappointed."

He shoves his tongue in his cheek before slamming his fist against the wall. "Fuck you!" he shouts as he leans into my personal space before stomping down the hall, swiping at a family photo. It falls and shatters, but he doesn't stop. I wait until he disappears from sight before I turn and close the door, locking it in case he tries to get in again.

Silence fills the room as I turn to the minibar. There's less Patrón in the clear bottle than I remember having, and I wonder if Lucy sipped on it while she organized what used to be my disaster of a desk. "I'm assuming you got dropped off?"

"Yeah," she states softly while playing with the hem of my shirt. Nestling into the corner of the couch, she tucks her legs beneath her and pulls them in tightly, leaving her thighs uncovered and flashing the barest hint of purple silk underwear. "My phone is in my purse in the hall, so I was going to wait a while before calling someone to come get me."

"I really am sorry, Lucy." I hand her the drink and move to sit on the other end of the couch. Before I can even get settled, she throws the tequila back in one swallow, even though there are at least three shots in the glass. "Whoa, there. Slow down, rainbow." I accidentally let the affectionate nickname I've never uttered out loud slip past my lips.

Her eyes meet mine over the rim of her glass. "Rainbow?" Her cheeks turn a shade of pink that highlights her hazel eyes.

I drain my glass, feeling the burn brewing in my own cheeks. Either from the whiskey or embarrassment—or both—I don't know. Getting to my feet quickly, I take our glasses and pour us both another drink, offering an explanation with my back turned away from her. "You're always wearing bright colors. Like a rainbow."

*You sound so fucking stupid, Lawson.*

When I turn back around, a small smile parts her plump raspberry lips, and I can't help but imagine how they taste. Or how they'd look wrapped around a part of me that is starting to become very partial to her.

*You're a bad man. You're a bad father.*

"I like it," Lucy whispers.

As I retake my seat, she reaches for her glass, and our fingers brush, creating a spark that nearly causes me to drop the tumbler.

Our eyes lock on the spot where our skin touches before slowly moving upward—hazel meeting gray as the air thickens between us.

A thump on the door breaks the spell, making Lucy startle.

"Dad, you need to stay the fuck out of it and open the damn door!"

I can only imagine how it looked when he saw his girl-friend in her lingerie and my button-down. Regardless of Rhys' transgressions, he's undoubtedly feeling pretty damn betrayed right now.

"God, your son sucks," she mumbles, scowling at the door.

I'm torn between letting them work it out and protecting her for a while longer. Either way, I'm fucked. One way or another, I'll be betraying one of them. It should be Rhys that I pick, no questions asked. But the fact that he willingly cheated on Lucy puts him right back at the top of my shit list.

I thought I raised my sons to be respectful, but the damage Charlotte has done to Rhys with her pandering bullshit is evident. Unfortunately for him, this isn't one of those times when I can take Rhys' side just because he's my son.

Lucy looks at me with tears lining her thick lashes again. "I'm sorry. I never meant to put you in the middle of this."

Of its own accord, my hand moves to her bare knee, my thumb swiping along her smooth skin. "You have nothing to apologize for. If anything, I feel like *I'm* the one who should be apologizing."

"It's not your fault."

"No, but he is my son."

"Well, this is *obviously* a trait he got from Charlotte." Lucy spits out my wife's name like it personally offends her before raising the glass to her lips, berry gloss coating the rim as she consumes half of the drink in one gulp. Her head lolls to the side to rest on a fluffy cushion, mussing her hair and making it look even more like she was just thoroughly fucked. My pants become extremely uncomfortable as my cock strains against the fabric. "Why did you stay with her?"

"Honestly? Because she's entitled to half my net worth, and I think it's more of a punishment for her to rely on an allowance." It's petty. But I don't give a shit. "Charlotte hasn't worked a day in her life. She'd request spousal support and claim that she never worked because she was raising the kids."

Lucy runs a finger around the rim of her glass. "What about if you ever meet someone else? Wouldn't you want a chance to be happy?" Her eyes are half-lidded as her tongue darts out to lick her lips. The bottom one disappears between her teeth as she stares at me, reminding me of the night I saw her in the pool house.

Simultaneously, we raise our glasses, pausing to share a laugh before finishing our drinks. My cock is so hard I know she'll see it if I get up to replenish them. As if she can read my mind, Lucy stands and holds a hand out for my tumbler.

"I guess it would depend on the woman." I stare at the curve of her ass that's covered in black lace as she walks by, and with her back turned, I take the opportunity to adjust myself, settling into a more comfortable position. It feels like the temperature in the room has risen about a hundred degrees, and I'd give anything to take a dip in the pool right now.

*Preferably with her.*
*Preferably with her naked.*

Our fingers don't touch this time when she passes me my drink. But as soon as she lets go, she raises a hand to brush it through my hair the way I've watched her do to Rhys a million times. "You should let the silver come through. Women love silver foxes."

My dick jumps so hard her eyes dart down to the movement, and the intimate gesture is short-lived as her hand falls away. A cloud of sweet lilac lingers in the air as Lucy takes her place on the other end of the couch. "Now that the initial shock is over, is it bad that I'm kind of relieved?"

Canting my head to the side, my eyes narrow. "What do you mean?"

She fists a handful of wavy curls and leans an elbow on the back of the couch, crossing her toned legs as she stretches them toward me on the cushion between us. "Rhys was so unhappy with my decision to go to California. Honestly, I'm not sure we would have survived the long distance," she explains dejectedly, staring off into space. "I guess it's better we broke up now. I can at least make peace with it before I leave. Who stays with their high school sweetheart anyway, right?"

It'd feel like pillow talk with her half-naked appearance and the alcohol, but the mention of my son's name on her lips sobers me a bit. "You know, Lucy, there *is* a great big world out there," I repeat the words I said to Rhys on prom night. "It's good for you both to explore what's beyond all this." I gesture out the window.

A frown twists her face. "You say that like we're going to get back together someday."

"Maybe someday you will." I lift my shoulders in a shrug. Still frowning, she shoots her liquor back. "You know, for a girl who swore once she would never drink again, you're doing work on that bottle."

A melodic laugh fills the room, and it's loud enough that Rhys will undoubtedly hear it if he is still outside the door. "I told you! It's the amber-colored ones I don't do well with."

Chuckling, I lean over to grab her glass. We both freeze as my large frame hovers over her. Slowly, she slides down the cushion until she's practically lying beneath me. "Lawson..."

Her sweet sigh spurs me to rise from the couch, turning so she can't see the extent of her effect on me. My balls are so blue they probably look like swollen blueberries.

As I debate pouring her another, she makes the decision for me. "About... that night... the one where you saw us in the pool house... and what happened in my bathroom—"

"We don't need to go there, Lucy." Abruptly, I turn toward my desk so she can't see the vulnerability in my eyes.

"What if I want to go there?" She's not slurring her words, but they're laced with the tequila she's been drinking like it's water.

"We can't. You're upset, and justifiably so, not to mention a little drunk. You wouldn't be bringing this up with an old man if you weren't."

Really, that's all this is—a silly crush that I shouldn't encourage.

"Don't you want me?" The words sound so fucking innocent, setting my insides on fire.

Fucking hell. I *want* to encourage it. "I'm not going to—"

Her voice is sleepy as she yawns, "Why not? There's no

one here, Lawson. It's just you and me. And honestly, we will probably never see each other again after tonight."

Her words make my breath catch—and not in a good way.

I haven't thought about the future or that we have no reason to see each other beyond tonight. Rhys has ruined any sort of relationship they might have had. And if I'm being honest, I'm thankful for it.

After everything that has transpired between us these last few weeks, I'm not sure I could stand idly by while they live their lives together. Watching her walk down the aisle toward him, seeing her for every major holiday, and announcing that they have a kid on the way.

Coveting her through it all.

But the thought of never seeing her again sets off a visceral reaction in my body because I also can't imagine my life without her in it in some capacity.

I've lost my fucking mind, but at least I can admit it—if only to myself.

And maybe, just this once, to her.

"Yes, Lucy." The truth slips past my lips in the barest of whispers, "I want you."

Silence greets me, weighing on my back like a wrecking ball. When I dare turn to gauge her reaction, steeling myself for what I might find, her eyes are closed, and her breathing is soft and steady.

With an amused huff, I raise my glass to drain what's left of my drink as I watch her sleep. My head swims from the alcohol, but I take my place behind the desk and continue working on the leasing offer I'd been drawing up earlier.

It's hard as fuck to concentrate when all I want to do is strip her down and have my filthy way with her.

*Jesus Christ, Lawson. Get a hold of yourself. You really do need to get laid by something other than your hand.*

Nearly twenty minutes go by before a whimper pulls my attention from the computer screen to the beautiful girl on the couch. Lucy moans again, her brows furrowing as she squirms against the cushions as though she's having a nightmare.

Abandoning my work, I cross the room in just a few strides to crouch beside her. "Lucy?"

Another moan escapes her parted lips, and my shirt falls open, baring all that silk and lace to me as she rubs her thighs together. Ignoring my hardening cock, I say her name again and try to shake her firmly.

With a gasp, she jackknifes up, staring blankly ahead. "Hey, you're okay," I soothe.

It happens in a blur.

One second, I'm comforting her, and the next, her lips are on mine. Plump and soft, and moving against me as though we've been kissing for years.

"Lucy—" I try to pull away, but she threads her fingers through my hair as she pushes me onto my ass. Our mouths part as she straddles my lap, and a fog of lust fills my brain as she starts to rock her hips.

A hoarse groan pours from my throat as she hungrily takes what she wants. I'm so fucking hard as she presses her chest against mine, grasping at my back to pull me closer. Her gloss tastes like actual berries as I give in to my desires and kiss her back with everything I have.

Kissing her makes me feel more alive than ever before.

*I'm going to hell for this.*

Lucy's lips part, allowing my tongue to tangle with hers. The taste of tequila and whiskey mixes in a smooth and sweet profile, combining with lip gloss and something else I can only describe purely as *her*. It explodes my senses as I become fully engulfed in everything about Lucy. Her taste, her sweet lilac scent, the smooth expanse of skin from her calf to her butt, and everywhere in between.

Her heels lock behind my back as she rubs against me harder, moaning into my mouth. My fingers slide beneath the lace that covers her ass, and I anchor her to me as I thrust upward. Without pulling back, she strokes down my arm until her hand reaches mine.

Then she places it over her pussy.

"Fuck, Lucy," I breathe as I look down to where my fingers slide back and forth over the purple silk. It's dark and damp.

A voice in the back of my head tells me to stop— warning me that this is an awful idea and that I shouldn't do this with her. But no matter how much I tell myself to pull away, I can't.

"Rhys," Lucy whispers my son's name like a fucking prayer, and it's about as effective as pouring a glass of ice water over my head.

*That* is enough to get me to stop. She isn't truly awake.

"Lucy."

*I'm such a fucking asshole.*

Her hips slow, but she continues to hold my hand to her even though I've stopped all movement. "Lucy!" I repeat, louder this time.

Her body jolts, chest heaving as clarity fills her gaze before morphing into confusion. "Lawson?"

A moment passes. Her hazel eyes dart side to side, studying my face, before dropping down to where she's still got my wrist in a vise grip, holding my fingers hostage against her dripping cunt.

My chest tightens as I wait for the inevitable disgust to fill her beautiful gaze. The revulsion that she will feel thinking I must have taken advantage of her.

Neither happens.

Instead, the devious little vixen's lips turn up in a smile.

Then she begins to ride my fingers again.

## Lucy

"Lucy, we can't," Lawson pleads hoarsely.

He's trying so hard to hold himself back. But all I want is for him to let go.

Tequila still addles my brain, making everything foggy, but I've never wanted anything as bad as I want Lawson to make me come right now. My entire body feels like it's being electrocuted from the inside out. I can feel the beat of his heart against mine, our pulses uniting as our bodies move together.

Am I surprised to find myself in his lap?

Yes.

I don't remember a damn thing after asking him if he wanted me, and even that's a little foggy.

Am I angry about it?

If I'm being honest, not at all.

Maybe it's the tequila or the fact that this tension has

been building between us since he willingly watched me fall apart on his son's cock, but the Lucy I am right now wants this.

*Badly.*

Tomorrow's Lucy can deal with the aftermath.

"Yes, we can." His eyes screw shut as I lift his hand to hold it up between us. It feels like molten lava is pouring through my veins and pooling between my legs.

Lawson's rigid cock is like steel beneath me, and I relish the almost pained "Fuck," that falls from his lips as I begin to ride him faster.

He tries to stop me. The hand that's splayed across my left butt cheek moves to my side to push me away, but as his eyes finally open again, they lock onto his glistening fingers.

"No one has to know." My words drag his darkened gray eyes to mine. "We can..." I nod affirmatively. "...just this once."

"Lucy—" I press his fingers to his lips, and his eyes turn nearly black as he holds his breath.

I cup his face with my free hand. "It's like the biggest fuck you to them both, don't you think?" I don't have to explain that I'm talking about Rhys and Charlotte.

It's petty and childish, but again, it's something tomorrow's Lucy can deal with.

Tequila Lucy wants to be a petty ho right now.

"It can be our little secret," I promise against the other side of his fingers. I don't think I can get any more turned on than I already am, but I can smell my arousal on him, and it heightens *everything*.

He swallows thickly, glossing his lips with my juices. His tongue darts out to lick them, causing my thighs to clench around his hips. "I don't want to take advantage of you. We've both had a lot to drink—"

"Don't worry. You aren't. I know what I'm doing, Lawson." I shift my hips again, rocking against his hard length. "I want you. Don't you want me?" I press his fingers down harder so they slip between his lips, and he can finally get a real taste.

A wave of heat pours from my center as he sucks them clean without breaking eye contact. When he finishes, he wraps my hair around his fist as his other hand cups my butt again. This time, his voice is rough and unrestrained. "Yes, Lucy. I fucking want you."

Effortlessly, he pushes off the floor with me still wrapped around him and turns to sit on the couch, settling me on his lap. The white button-down falls from my shoulders as he kisses up my collarbone to my neck, sucking on a spot that drives me absolutely wild.

Even though we're still wearing clothes, we might as well not be. The thin material of his dress pants does nothing to protect him from how soaked my underwear is. He pulls my head back to bare my neck to him as he thrusts upward, and I can feel him smiling against my skin as a string of curses falls from my lips.

Lawson comes alive beneath me, making me feel everything without ever removing our clothes. There's definitely going to be a mark on my neck where he alternates between roughly drawing my flesh between his lips and murmuring incoherent words against me. His fingers dig hard enough into my ass to bruise as he pulls me against his cock with every thrust. This memory will be burned into my brain to remember on cold and lonely nights.

We aren't even fucking, and this is one of the hottest experiences I've ever... well... *experienced*.

I know I don't have much to compare it to, but all I can think of is, how the hell will any guy be able to top this? It's like Lawson knows exactly what I need without me asking, and yet I can tell he's holding a part of himself back.

A delicious tingling pressure builds deep in my core. It spreads outward as he picks up the pace. He's close, too. Curses and peppered kisses caress my skin, joining the sounds I try to keep buried.

"Lawson," I whimper against his ear, trying to convey that I'm about to come but trying to hold on because I want us to do it together.

A quiet hiss leaves his lips as my nails dig into his back. "Let go, baby. I'm right there with you," he commands tenderly, raising his face to look at me.

My brows draw together, lips falling open as my release pulses through me. A cry begins to leave my throat, but Lawson swallows it, groaning into my mouth as he comes. That euphoric feeling of floating on a cloud overtakes me as our hips slow, and we settle into post-orgasm bliss.

We stare at each other, eyes wide, wondering if what just happened *actually* happened.

*Did I just dry fuck my boyfriend's—EX-boyfriend's dad?*

"Lucy—"

Preparing for him to tell me we just made a huge mistake, I quickly scramble off his lap. "Can you call me a Lyft?"

I can't handle hearing him say that this should never have happened. I'm mortified. And still turned on, even as I use the bottom of his shirt to wipe between my thighs. I kinda feel like I'm going to be sick. But only because I drank too much. At the same time, I don't feel drunk? Everything is just kind of hazy.

Regardless, I know for certain that I don't regret what just happened one single bit.

"Lucy, I'm so sorry." Lawson's tone is guarded as he picks up his phone.

Hopefully, there are drivers close by since it's graduation night.

"I'm not." I look like a mess, but I have nothing else to wear, so I start buttoning up his shirt. "I don't want you to be either."

His gray eyes shine bright with concern as he watches my face for any signs of distress until a ding sounds from his phone, and he looks at the screen. "Your uh... your ride will be here in a few minutes. Are you sure you don't want me to take you home?" He almost sounds hopeful that I'll say yes, but it could just be my imagination.

Patting my hair in an attempt to tame it, I shake my head. "I'll be okay."

Lawson takes a few slow steps forward as if he's trying not to spook me. "We should talk about this."

"There's nothing to talk about." I catch him off guard as I wrap him in a hug, resting my cheek on his chest. It takes a few moments, but his arms finally settle around me, and I feel the slightest pressure on the top of my head as his lips press to my crown. "One night, that's all this was, right? One night that we both needed." Tipping my head back, I breathe in his minty scent that mixes with the whiskey on his breath as our gazes lock.

"I just want to make sure you're okay," he expresses quietly.

Unspoken words charge the air around us. I can't imagine never seeing him again, but I know that after tonight—after this moment, right here, right now—there will be no reason for us to cross paths again.

"Lucy—"

A sharp ding sounds from his phone again, signaling that my ride has arrived. Lawson drops his hand and lets me go without another word, breathing out a sigh as he moves to crack open his office door. After looking both ways down the hall, he states, "Coast is clear."

"Thank you." I hurry past the threshold, not wanting Rhys to see me in my current state. But I'm only a few steps down the hall when I turn around.

Lawson watches me, regret written all over his face. Somehow, I know it isn't because of what we've done but for all we have left to say.

Unfortunately, his words from earlier ring in my ears. There's a great big world out there. And I need to go explore it.

"You're a good man, Lawson Morgan." Before I chicken out, I walk back to him and lay a chaste kiss against his lips. "I hope you realize that."

I don't give him a chance to reply, slipping out of his grasp before his hands can fully settle on my hips. But I hear his whispered words as I round the corner.

"Goodbye, Lucy."

# NINE

## *Lucy*

TWO DAYS PASS BEFORE I finally give in and talk to Rhys.

Forty-eight hours of non-stop calls and unannounced visits that I deny.

It took Liam threatening to break Rhys' arm for him to finally cool it and give me some space.

Two thousand eight hundred and eighty minutes to process what his dad and I did.

I haven't heard a word from Lawson.

"Luce?" Mom's voice questions from the other side of my bedroom door.

"Yeah? You can come in." I sit up, clutching my favorite decorative tangerine pillow. It has a beaded elephant on it that I like to run my fingers over when I'm thinking about things, watching a movie, or scrolling Iconic. I've had it for so long, it's lost half its beads. But it's still a welcome comfort, like a baby blanket or an old stuffed animal.

"Hey, honey. Rhys is here. He's waiting in the play-house," Mom says his name the same way she says raisins—

with a thick layer of revulsion. The sight of her hair thrown up haphazardly and a dusty smear of flour on her right cheek puts a smile on my face, even as instant anxiety sweeps through me at the reality that I need to talk to my ex face-to-face.

Not only because there's a part of me that needs to know *why* he cheated, even after we worked so hard to have healthy communication in our relationship, but because I don't know how to look at him without being instantly reminded of Lawson.

My feelings must show on my face because Mom sits on the edge of my bed to brush a hand through my hair. I wave her away, mindful to keep the mark on my neck hidden.

"I can tell him you decided that you don't want to talk after all if you'd like?"

Groaning, I flop back against my pillows, shaking all my limbs out in frustration—something Mom and I have done since I was little. "*Shaking away the ickies,*" as she always calls it.

When I'm done, I place my elephant pillow over my face and scream.

"Feel better?" Mom asks with an arched brow as I sit up again.

Expelling a long sigh, I nod. "Yeah. Ugh. This is gonna suck."

"You're handling it a lot better than I would have expected." From the reflection of my full-length mirror, I can see her appraising me as I get up to grab my cheer sweater.

"I don't know. I've thought about it a lot. I guess

breaking up just seems like the right thing to do anyway since we're going to different colleges."

Mom nods, biting her lip. "You know, I ran into Bethany yesterday at the store. She asked how you were."

"Yeah. Everyone already knows because I changed our relationship status on Iconic. I didn't realize it would blast the news to everyone on my feed." Going into my bathroom, I peel off my sleep shorts and pull on a pair of black leggings.

Mom hums. "She mentioned everyone went home around ten, which wasn't long after we dropped you off. But you didn't come home until after midnight."

I wondered when this line of questioning was going to start. Like Rhys, I've avoided everyone for the last two days, choosing to stay in my room unless absolutely necessary, like going to get a pint of cookie dough ice cream and an entire box of Girl Scout cookies—thin mints, obviously.

Freezing in my doorway, I don't turn around as I ask, "Is there a question in there somewhere?"

I've always had a great relationship with my parents. Liam is the problem child, not me. I know what Mom's getting at, and I don't want to lie to her.

"I locked myself in Lawson's office and waited until Rhys left me alone long enough to get my purse and call a Lyft."

There. It's not the whole truth, but it's definitely not a lie.

"Where was Lawson during all of this?" Her tone isn't accusatory, but it holds an edge I don't really understand. She's never been much of a fan of Charlotte's, but my parents have always gotten along with Lawson.

"I don't know, Mom. Maybe in his room?" I turn and slump against the doorframe, rubbing my forehead exasperatedly.

I am—not with her, but with the situation in general. A question about where Lawson was that night is the last thing I need to field right now.

Her eyes narrow slightly, lips pursing to the side as she studies me. It's the same look she gives Liam when she's trying to figure out if he's lying about something.

"I thought you liked Lawson? Why are you being all weird about him now?"

"I do like him, but I also know what you wore when you went to that house. It wasn't exactly appropriate attire to be wearing in the same room as a grown man."

*Oh, Mom. If you only knew.*

"Mom! Where are my headphones?" My gaze snaps to where Lorraine stands in the doorway of her room across the hall, just out of Mom's line of sight, pulling her headphones from around her neck and tossing them on her bed.

*Thank you,* I mouth.

She mouths back, *I got you.*

"Did you seriously lose those already, Lore? We just bought them." Mom forgets about her interrogation and goes to help my sister without another word.

I know she'll ask about it again later, but at least for now, I have a reprieve.

The playhouse is massive—nearly as big as the Morgans' pool house—and was built when my siblings and I were younger, but it's still used as a hangout spot. Now, it'll be the final resting place of Rhys' and my relationship.

Rhys is sitting on a picnic table, and to say he looks like

shit would be putting it nicely. His pallor is gray, and there are dark purple circles under his eyes. There's so much grease in his hair that it looks like he hasn't showered in days, and I briefly wonder if that means he's still got Allison's body fluids on him.

*Gross.*

But then he lifts his head when he hears my footsteps, and his beautiful blue eyes fill with tears, his face crumpling. It sends every negative feeling I've been harboring over these last two days flying out the window.

"I'm sorry, Lucy. So fucking sorry," he sobs, never breaking eye contact.

Part of me wants to embrace him, to comfort the boy I've been in love with for years. Yet, the other part of me screams that it shouldn't be *me* who comforts *him* in this scenario.

Rhys sniffs, attempting to get himself under control, when he sees that I'm not going to just jump into his arms and tell him everything will be alright. "I know there's no excuse for what I did."

A snort leaves my mouth as I cross my arms. "You got that right."

"I know I fucked up. I'm sorry," he repeats, sounding frustrated.

"What do you want me to say, Rhys? That I forgive you? Because I don't. We're better than *this*." I swing a hand between us. "At least we were. I mean... what the actual fuck?" I angrily pull at my hair in an attempt to keep my hands busy, so I don't punch him in the face.

"I know, Luce! I know! I've just been so fucking... *angry* at you!" He clutches the edge of the picnic table so hard the orange plastic gives under his strength, turning a creamsicle color as it warps. "We had plans, and you just went and ruined them and expected me to be okay with it!"

"Then you should have talked to me! How many times did I try to get you to tell me how you were feeling? This isn't on me, Rhys!"

"I know it's not. I... fuck!" He jumps off the table and begins to pace. "Allison was just there. And you... you weren't. It's almost like as soon as you made up your mind about Berkeley you've been intentionally pulling away."

My mouth falls open as I stare at him, completely dumbstruck. "We spend nearly every waking moment together. I eat dinner at your house more than I do my own. Spend more time with you and River than with Liam and Lorraine. What more do you want from me?"

"I want you to stick to our plan and come to Ole Miss with me," he says, dead serious. His jaw tenses as he fixes me with a dry-eyed stare.

"You're pathetic." Angrily, I spin around and head for the door. "I've *always* been there for you. And the moment I choose to do something for *myself*, you throw a fit."

"Oh, come on, Lucy! It's not like it wouldn't have happened anyway, right? One of us would have cracked. We never would have lasted long distance."

I spin on my heel, getting in his face. "Okay, *Charlotte*!" Even though my feelings about our college situation are the same, I would never have fucking cheated on him.

*You came awfully damn close, though, didn't you? And with his dad, no less.*

"I will *never* be your mother, Rhys! I will never sit on the sidelines and demand you buy me all the nice, expensive things I want but never use. I will never spend my days wine-drunk, waiting for you to pay attention to me and then complain that it isn't enough. I have dreams, okay? Things I want to do and see. You *know* this! So is it really *that* big of a surprise that I wanted to go to a different college?"

"No one is asking you to be my mom, Lucy. All I wanted was a little support!"

"And what about my support? What about what *I* want? Our future has always been about you. What about *me*?"

"You should have talked to me about it!"

"And you should have broken up with me before you fucked Allison, but here we are! You completely embarrassed me in front of all our friends. People said you two were all over each other."

His lip curls. "Is that what you're worried about, Lucy? Me *embarrassing* you?"

"No, it's just an unfortunate bonus to a shitty night I'll never be able to forget."

*Okay, so not all of it was shitty. Fuck, I'm just as bad as he is. At least I didn't do any physical shit when we were actually together, though.*

"Yeah, a night you spent with my dad in his office. Dressed in slutty lingerie and his fucking shirt! Wanna tell me how *that* happened?"

Blinking rapidly, I try to keep myself from stammering as I reply, "I-I was angry with you, so I cut up your jersey. I didn't even know he was in there until I'd already done it. He offered me his shirt when—"

"When he'd already watched you get undressed?" he questions, eyes scanning down my body for effect.

I rear back and glare at him. "What is that supposed to mean?"

"I've seen the way you look at him, Lucy. And the way he is with you... it's fucking weird. And I am telling you right now that I would *hate* you forever if something happened between you two." Rhys pins me with a cold, hard glare, searching for any hint that he might be right in his accusation.

My hands clench into fists, fingernails digging into my palms. I want so badly to yell, *"You got me! I fucked around with your dad!"* Just to get back at him. To see the look on his face when he realizes I'm not lying.

But I'd never cheapen my experience with Lawson.

And at the end of the day, Rhys is his son—I don't want to ruin their relationship.

"Fuck you, Rhys. Your dad was respectful. And I spent the night crying on the couch." I shove him away and turn around as angry tears fill my eyes. Partly from lying to him and partly because this is everything I never wanted to happen.

This sucks.

This isn't us.

As I dig the heels of my palms into my eyes, I don't flinch when Rhys' arms wrap around me from behind.

"I'm sorry, Lucy." He pulls me close, resting his chin on my shoulder as we both shake with grief. Some might say we're way too young to feel this much for our ruined relationship, but Rhys and I were friends long before we started dating.

We aren't just losing each other as lovers. I don't see how we can ever possibly be friends after this. And I'm just as much to blame for it as he is.

I turn, wrapping my arms around his waist as I rest my forehead against his chest. "This is for the best." I huff a watery laugh. "I wish it were under different circumstances, but it's better it happens now."

Through sniffles, he hums in agreement. "Maybe we can try again one day."

I say nothing, knowing that there is no way I'd ever be able to be with Rhys again in this lifetime. Not after what happened between Lawson and me.

"I think it's best if we don't see each other for the rest of the summer. I need... time... to process everything," I state when all our tears dry.

Rhys lets me go. "I love you. You know that, right?"

I nod, and a sense of calm relief rushes through me as I reach up to brush his hair out of his eyes one last time. "I love you, too."

We leave the playhouse together, sharing one last hug before he departs.

It feels like a huge part of my life is over. Instead of feeling sad about it, though, I'm filled with a strange sense of exhilaration for what's to come—like I'm getting a new slate.

I confidently let go of my past and enter the next phase of my life as a brand-new woman.

# TEN

## SIX YEARS LATER

*Lawson*

OF ALL THE companies that the Metropolis Investments Group has absorbed and taken under its umbrella, I have to admit that Benson Commercial Holdings isn't half bad. The team is composed of competent individuals with impressive portfolios, and the administrative team has a reputation for being highly organized and on the ball.

A guy with haphazardly-styled sandy blond hair nudges a man with slicked-back raven strands.

"So, how did your date with Lulu go last night?"

Either they're unaware that I'm their new boss—despite the company-wide memo that went out about the last-minute change in upper management—or they're so unconcerned about Chadwick Benson that they feel like it's ok to whisper about their personal lives even though he's speaking at the front of the boardroom about handing the reins over.

Like I said, not *half* bad.

The raven-haired guy smirks and rolls his eyes. "She

wants me. But the devious little minx is a pro at playing hard to get. She was all over me after a few glasses of wine."

I arch an eyebrow at his crassness while the young woman to my right, Anna, snorts. She's petite with honey-blonde hair and an unremarkable pair of dark brown eyes. "Is that why Lulu left before you even got your entrées?"

"How did you...?" The guy's face settles into a nettled look. "She fake-emergency'd me, didn't she?"

The blond man starts laughing quietly, and Anna smirks before glancing at me. A pink flush forms on her cheeks. "Sorry, Mr. Morgan."

Both males look at me questioningly, giving away that they clearly didn't read the memo.

My decision to return to the Windy City after nearly six years could have been better thought out. Cameron Crueller, a man I consider one of my best friends, even if he's quite a bit younger than I am, was supposed to take over the new Chicago office. However, I didn't want an upcoming promotion in the New York office, so they made the offer to him instead.

Chadwick continues speaking at the front of the room, utterly oblivious to his employees' side conversation. "Metropolis Investments has a stellar record for turning smaller operations such as this one into mega-successful firms. The fact that they can do so without laying anyone off is a testament to how prosperous they've become in the industry. M.I.G. is the future! And they are here to elevate this company and yourselves! So, it is with great pleasure that I introduce your new boss."

All eyes turn to me as he stretches his hand out in my direction. The raven-haired man's skin turns a ghastly pale as Chadwick announces, "Please join me in welcoming Lawson Morgan, the new Executive Director of the Chicago division for Metropolis Investments Group."

Applause erupts throughout the room. Multiple congratulations are tossed my way by faces that look eager and genuinely excited for something new. Benson Commercial Holdings has been around for a long time, and Chadwick is a relic. It's time for a fresh way of handling business, and M.I.G. has been itching to break into the Chicago commercial real estate game for a while now.

After shaking a few hands, I take my place at the head of the boardroom. "Thank you all. I'm happy to be back in Chicago, even if I have to return to the nonsense that is deep-dish pizza." I smirk and nod at the round of good-natured boos that sound from around the table. "In all seriousness, though, M.I.G.'s goal has never been to uproot a small company and completely change how they run their operations. We bought Benson Commercial Holdings *because* of the great work you're already doing. As Mr. Benson said, I'm here to elevate the newest division of M.I.G., not tear everything down. I look forward to getting to know all of you, and if you ever have any questions or concerns, I have an open-door policy. So, please, don't hesitate to drop in whenever you need."

Some of the females in the room look at each other with knowing grins as flirty smiles and hooded eyes flash my way. Each and every one of them is headed for disappointment when I make it clear that I strictly follow the company's zero-tolerance policy on interoffice relationships between management and employees.

Not to mention *my* zero-tolerance policy to bed women half my age.

As the room begins to clear out, I approach Anna, who is still scribbling on her notepad. "Anna, if you'd follow me, we can go over a few things I'm going to need over the next few months."

Her pen freezes, chocolate eyes moving around the room as she realizes I'm talking directly to her. She tilts her head to the side, blinking rapidly in surprise like she's just remembering her name is Anna. "I'm sorry, sir?"

"You are my assistant lead, aren't you?" I ask, gathering my briefcase and phone.

Understanding dawns over her features. "Oh! No, that's Lulu. She requested this morning off because Mr. Crueller was supposed to come tomorrow, but I will absolutely make a list for her. She's very thorough and did a lot of research on Mr. Crueller in preparation for his arrival. It'll take her a little bit to get your information from your previous assistant lead, but Lulu is gonna be upset she missed this meeting, so she'll probably have it down by the end of the day."

*Who the hell goes by Lulu? It sounds like the name of a show poodle.*

I have half a mind to ask if that's her real name when Chadwick interrupts, slapping a hand on my back and pulling my attention to him and another woman I haven't met yet.

"Lawson, this is Mary Peterson, head of our HR department. She'll show you to your new office because I..." He digs his thumbs into his tawny tweed suit jacket. "...am officially outta here."

Mary has mousy brown hair and blue eyes that appear too much like Charlotte's for me to want to look at her for longer than a few seconds. "Lead the way," I tell her before turning back to Anna. "When is... *Lulu* supposed to be in today?"

"Your assistant lead, Lucy, should be here soon. We're so sorry she wasn't here this morning, Mr. Morgan. She'd already gotten the time off approved," Mary answers for Anna.

*Lucy.*

Hearing her name makes my heart skip a beat. Just like it's done every other time I've heard it over the last six years.

*It isn't her, Lawson. She's probably still living it up in California.*

I squash all thoughts of the redhead I've never been able to forget and pack them away in a rainbow-colored compartment in my mind. My fingers itch to reach for my phone as I half-listen to whatever Mary is saying as we walk back to the elevator—something about themed parties once a quarter and how they are good for morale.

After spending an unhealthy amount of time stalking Lucy's Iconic profile after what happened between us, I blocked her so she could forever stay out of sight and out of mind. But what's that old saying? Absence makes the heart grow fonder?

Now that I'm back in Chicago, what could it hurt to see if maybe she's returned as well?

*Because she's eighteen fucking years younger than you, you pervert.*

Thoughts of whether Lucy ever came back after college dissipate as I enter my new office on the top floor.

It takes me by surprise how clean it is, given how Chadwick doesn't seem like the neat type. The mahogany desk matches the paneling on the wall, casting an old money atmosphere. The room's dark color is broken up by a cream and maroon oriental rug that takes up a good amount of space in front of the desk, and light blue vintage chairs with a golden jacquard print. Behind the desk, thick paneled blinds hang over large windows that take up two-thirds of the wall, with built-in cabinets below.

"Would you like me to email a copy of the revised rules to the entire office?" Mary inquires, switching gears as I browse the built-in bookcase behind the door. There are dozens of binders ranging from one to three inches, all color-coded and dated.

Mary laughs when I don't answer her. "Ah, yes. Lucy is nothing if not organized."

Meanwhile, I'm struggling to swallow the familiar, unwelcome lump that's formed in my esophagus. *It can't be.*

The system is the exact same, though.

"*I don't trust computers not to eat the data. Sure, you can back it up, but it takes time and costs money when you're dealing with this much information.*" Her words ghost the shell of my ear—a whisper of wind.

No, that's the door.

"Oh, my god, Mary! I'm so sorry. I can't believe I'm late on his first day. He was supposed to arrive tomorrow!" A familiar, sweet timbre fills my ears, sounding like she's talking around something in her mouth.

"Lucy, it's quite—"

"I tried to reschedule my appointment, but I was

already there, and you know how hard it is to get into the gyno. God, I hate being a woman."

Turning, my heart nearly stops as I see rich, russet, waist-length waves hugging an hourglass figure. She removes the tan paper bag clenched between her teeth and tosses it down before setting a drink carrier with two coffees on the desk.

"Lucy, if you'd just—"

"And of course, since I was already out, I figured I might as well stop and get his favorite coffee and pastry because I've already made a bad first impression by being late, so I wanted to sweeten him up a little. You know what I mean? Is he here yet? Tell me I didn't miss too much." As she stands straight, smoothing her olive-green pleated dress, I try to control the spark of irritation at her deliberate attentiveness to know Cameron's coffee order.

Mary's brows fall into a flat line as she points to me in the corner without saying a word.

Lucy turns, and whatever she's about to say dies in her throat as her eyes widen.

It seems too bizarre to be true. The odds of it being *her* who's my new assistant are slim to none.

But I haven't forgotten the way her chest heaves when adrenaline pumps through her veins. How her raspberry-painted lip always disappears between her teeth when she's nervous. Or how her hazel eyes have golden rings around the irises that become brighter when she's excited. All of which is happening right now, like beacons of light on a dark night.

It *is* her.

My rainbow.

# ELEVEN

IT SEEMS as if every higher power in existence is against me today.

Alarm going off late? Check.

Not having time to shower and barely having a few minutes to take a ho bath before dousing myself in perfume? Double check.

Missing my wax appointment last night and not having time to shave my lady bits before my appointment? Not reading the morning memo, even though Dr. Russo ran late, and I had more than enough time, but decided to scroll Iconic instead? Thinking the worst is behind me and that nothing else can possibly happen on this beautiful summery day?

Check. Check. Check.

*Fuck. Fuck. Fuck.*

I'm acutely aware that Mary is looking between Lawson and me like we're a strange sideshow at the circus, but I can't bring myself to speak, and he looks like he's seen a ghost.

Lawson Morgan.

A man I truly never thought I'd see again.

A man I've thought about at least once a day since graduation night.

A man who...

"You blocked me on Iconic?"

*Six years and that's what you say to him? Yeah, that's really gonna show him you've grown up. So smooth, Lucy.*

A flicker of a smirk pulls at his lips before he presses them into a flat line, eyes hardening as he looks at Mary briefly before turning the stormy gaze that I think about so often back to me. "Ms. Bradee, I wasn't aware you worked here."

Mary swishes her finger between us. "Do you two—?"

"Yes, we know each other," I interject, straightening as his subtle glance reminds me to remember where we are.

Professionalism drips from Lawson's clipped tone when he quickly adds, "She used to date my son. It's good to see you again, Lucy."

It should offend me, but one look at Mary's skeptical expression has me agreeing. "You as well, Mr. Morgan."

"Will this be a problem? I can arrange for Lucy and Anna to switch if you'd like?" Mary inquires, even though Anna's job is a step down from mine, and there's no way in hell I'm taking a pay cut after I've worked my butt off for this company for the last year.

"No. It won't be a problem. If anything, this is a blessing in disguise. Lucy has done some work for me in the past, and her organizational skills are impeccable." Lawson motions to the bookcase behind him. "And here's all the proof I need that she hasn't lost her touch. If you could go ahead and get that email sent out by the end of the day, I'd appreciate it." He dismisses her with a tight smile that doesn't quite reach his eyes.

Mary doesn't read into it and offers him a beaming grin before looking at me. "Great! If you need anything, let me know!"

"Will do. Thank you, Mary." My new boss ushers her out of the room with his hand hovering over the small of her back.

As he shuts the door, the tension visibly seeps back into his posture. He takes a few seconds to collect himself, expelling an audible breath before he turns around and bores those twin thunderclouds into my soul.

"I thought Cameron was taking over the Chicago office?"

*Again,* that's *what you say to him the first time you're alone? Get it together, girl.*

He bristles at my use of Mr. Crueller's first name, fists clenching at his sides as he goes to sit behind the desk. "*Cameron* wants to stay in New York to take Danvers' place when he retires. Sorry to disappoint you."

My face burns with embarrassment and something *else* as I observe him. The last six years have been kind to Lawson, as time usually is to men like him. His charcoal gray suit hugs his muscular body, which is still toned enough to tell through the fabric, and he's stopped dying his hair, allowing the silver to shine through at the temples and in the scruff of his short beard.

He looks good enough to eat—and I didn't have breakfast.

And I know firsthand just how appetizing he is.

"I didn't mean to sound put off that it's you instead. I just... I was... prepared for *him*," I offer lamely.

He arches a brow as he slides the coffee meant for Cameron toward himself. Removing the lid, he lifts the paper cup to his nose and inhales before huffing a short laugh. "You sure were. Even got a dash of cinnamon. Cam always likes his coffee sweet as shit."

As he places the lid back, I can't help but notice the absence of his wedding ring. Before I can say anything about it or even ask how Rhys and River are doing, he pushes the cup back my way and says, "For future reference, I take mine black."

Confusion screws my brows together. "Since when? Last I remember, you always took it with one sugar and a dash of milk."

"Well, I don't anymore. I'm going to need all the files on the current deals that haven't been finalized yet. And there's a conference in a few weeks that we'll be attending up north. I'll forward you the resort information, and you'll need to book a couple of rooms for us. You didn't miss much at the meeting this morning. I told the staff that I have an open-door policy, so I need to be made available to them at all times. Do you understand?"

The way he starts to spit out orders catches me off guard. There's no, '*How have you been?*' Or, '*What have you been up to these last six years?*' Lawson treats me like I assume he'd treat any new assistant, instead of with the warmth I've always associated him with.

I want to tell him, "*Yes, sir.*" Just to see his reaction. The memory of prom night is as fresh as if it happened yesterday.

Instead, I steel myself and go into work mode. "I understand. I'll also email your last lead and get a list of your preferences."

Gathering my purse, the coffees, and the cream cheese Danish that was supposed to be for Cameron, I try to will away the warmth in my cheeks.

"You can leave the coffee and whatever's in the bag. I can deal with it for a day." His tone is borderline teasing, and I find it highly annoying.

"Don't worry about it, *sir*. There's a small café downstairs. I'll go get you a regular cup of sludge since apparently, you're dull and have no taste now."

Those are the same words he once used to describe plain coffee drinkers.

A shock zips up my arm and throughout my body as his hand encircles my wrist. My head whips back around, eyes landing on where he's touching me.

"If it will make you more comfortable, we can tell HR to switch you and Anna." He pauses, trying to gauge my reaction. "Is that what you want, Lucy?"

The electricity that's been lying dormant for years sparks between us over the desk as we size each other up. Heat gathers in my belly, pooling in a small trickle to my center. I try to clench my thighs without him noticing, and out of habit, I bite the corner of my lower lip. His eyes snap down to track the movement.

My voice is breathy as I reply, "No. No, that isn't what I want, Mr. Morgan."

His answering nod is tight as he returns my gaze and lets me go. "Good. It's not what I want either."

I cross the room quickly, looking for something to prop

the door open with. Would he have still told the staff about his open-door policy if he knew it would give him a direct line of sight to my desk?

"I'll need your number, Lucy," he calls after me. "And you don't have to call me Mr. Morgan. Lawson is just fine."

My breath catches in my throat as I pause with my back still to him. Shifting slightly, I look over my shoulder. He's staring at me, the gray of his eyes darkening to the point that they match his suit.

"My number hasn't changed, *Lawson*. You'd know that if you bothered checking in over the last six years."

# TWELVE

*Lawson*

SQUEEEEAKKKKKK. Squeak. Squeak. Squeeakkk.

Is it too late to rescind the open-door policy?

It's bad enough that all I could think of yesterday and last night was the only woman I can't have. Instead of familiarizing myself with the work I'm taking over, I find the only things I can focus on are Lucy's wild mane of russet hair, her navy blue and white polka-dotted swing dress, and the soft grunts she's making as she attempts to turn her desk around.

As soon as she sat behind the heavy, wooden, L-shaped piece of furniture yesterday, she looked up and realized we'd always have direct eye contact if my office door stayed open. Now, she's spending her break attempting to turn her entire workstation around.

"Need a hand there, Lulu?" Justin, the blond man from yesterday's morning meeting, asks as he and the raven-haired guy, Mike, appear in the doorframe.

*Why the fuck do they keep calling her Lulu? What a stupid name.*

A smirk curls the corner of my lips as I grab my plain cup of coffee—the one that was waiting for me this morning—and focus on a building proposal. I wait for Lucy to launch into a tirade about being an independent woman and how she's fully capable of doing it on her own. I'm prepared for her to insist that she do it herself.

Instead, I hear her blow out a breath, and I look up to see her straighten and place her hands on her hips, gracing Justin and Mike with a beaming cherry smile.

"Would you guys mind? I'd be so grateful." She takes a step towards Mike and places a hand on his bicep. Something bitter and sharp rips through my chest that I haven't felt in a very long time. "I'm sorry about running out the other night, Mike."

I'm instantly reminded that she went on a date with this guy. I know I said no layoffs, but I think I can make an exception.

Just this once.

"Uh-huh," he drawls amusedly, not informing her that Anna let slip about her fake emergency. "I guess you'll just have to make it up to me."

Lucy blanches but quickly recovers with a noncommittal laugh as he and Justin pick up either side of the desk and position it the way she wants. Watching them eat up everything she says as she changes her mind multiple times before settling on an arrangement is fascinating. The Lucy I know—*knew*—would have just dealt with staring into my open office.

Anna appears at Lucy's side, handing her a stack of files, saying something I can't hear as the women watch the men rearrange her computer. The whole thing takes less than ten minutes. But when Justin and Anna break off to have their own conversation, Mike steps just a tad too close to Lucy to be professional, and I'm tempted to break up the little soirée.

Another sharp, bitter feeling blooms. It arcs against my chest like the very nickname I've given her. She throws her head back, laughing at something he says, and my skin feels hot as it sears through angry shades.

Pink. Red. Purple.

His head dips to say something in her ear—a whispered secret he shares for no one else to hear but her.

*Green.*

"What are you doing?" I'm surprised to find myself just outside the door. I don't even remember getting up from my desk.

Four sets of eyes snap to me, wide and alarmed like they've all been caught with their hands in the proverbial cookie jar.

Lucy recovers first, her tone saccharine as she replies, "Sorry, Lawson. Just doing a little rearranging."

They all look at her in surprise at the use of my first name. Her gaze swings to them and back to me before her deep hazel eyes widen in realization. "I mean, Mr. Morgan."

"Weak save," Anna mutters, trying to disguise it with a cough.

Mike steps closer to her, setting his hand on the edge of the desk so that it appears as if his arm is actually around her. "Do you two, uh, know each other?" He wags his finger between her and me as he presses into Lucy's side.

She's not stupid. She knows exactly what he's trying to do and takes a step closer to me to put a little distance between them. I'm ashamed that it makes me puff my chest up just a bit.

"I dated Mr. Morgan's son in high school."

Then it deflates like a balloon before the feeling of utter ridiculousness settles in my bones. What did I think she was going to say? That I finger-banged her on her graduation night after we'd been drinking together because she walked in on my son cheating on her?

"Interesting. It's kind of a conflict of interest, don't you think? Should at least probably report that to HR." Mike straightens and moves next to her again, and a feeling of possessiveness burns through my veins.

*She was mine first, little boy. Back off.*

If it shows on my face, he doesn't recognize it.

Lucy does, though. Even though we haven't spoken a word to each other in the past day and a half, other than me asking a few requests and her giving me clipped answers, she's still able to read me as well as she could six years ago.

"That's not necessary. Mary already knows. Besides, it's not like *we* dated or anything?" She motions between us with a high-pitched, forced laugh.

"Is that a question? Or..." Anna trails off, watching us both through shrewdly amused eyes. The chatter of the cubicles around us has died to near silence, and I quickly look around the room to find multiple pairs of eyes on us.

"Why doesn't everyone get back to work?" I calmly state, casually putting my hands in my pockets and refocusing on Mike. "Lucy, if I could have a moment?"

I'm being a total dickhead, and I know it. I have no claim on the woman who has plagued my thoughts for the last six years. My son's ex-girlfriend. What would I have done if she and Mike were actually dating?

She's off-limits. Always has been.

Yet, everything in my body relaxes as she steps forward, a familiar sense of home washing over me when our bodies brush as she walks into my office. Instinctively, my hand finds the small of her back as I turn to follow, not missing the way Mike's eyes narrow on the action.

"I thought you had an open-door policy?" he asks tightly as I begin to shut it behind us.

Smug satisfaction rolls through me, and I throw over my shoulder, "That means you can come to me with any questions or concerns. I didn't mean it in the literal sense."

Annoyance flashing over his face is the last thing I see as the door clicks shut, and I pivot to find Lucy staring at me —her arms crossed and full lips set in a frown.

I can't help the fucking giddy feeling that flutters in my chest and roars to life as we stare at each other. I feel like a goddamn woman, full of emotions I don't want to be feeling.

Her ponytail sways as she shakes her head and taps her white stiletto-clad foot. "We're allowed to take breaks, you know."

"Is this how it's always going to be? You're acting like you're mad at me, and I haven't done anything." I walk toward her one slow, calculated step at a time.

Not one hair is out of place, and her makeup is bolder than yesterday. Her navy swing dress is office professional, yet still somehow manages to make me think of all the dirty things I want to do to her while she's wearing it. When I arrived at the office this morning, a little zing of pride shot through my chest at the thought that maybe she'd dressed up for me, though I quickly squashed it.

Lucy Bradee is eighteen years younger than I am. And a mistake I made six years ago that changed my life forever. I can not and *will not* go there with her again.

But fuck if I don't want to bend her over my desk right now and have my wicked way with her. I'm ashamed to admit I jerked off to thoughts of doing precisely that— multiple times last night, not to mention this morning in the shower.

"I don't know, *Mr. Morgan*. I'm a little confused, if I'm being honest." She stands her ground as I approach, craning her neck up to maintain eye contact as I step closer than I should. I still want her just as badly as I did back then, regardless of her connection to my son. No matter how many times I've tried to remove her from my brain, she's stamped on my damn heart like a forbidden sin.

Images of her on her knees with my hand wrapped around her ponytail flash through my brain. Mentally, I swat them away.

*Pull yourself together, Lawson.*

"What are you confused about?" My fingers curl in my pockets as a cloud of the same vanilla-lilac perfume she wore when she was younger drifts up to tease my senses.

"Well," she starts, looking down at the floor as if suddenly unsure of her words. "...considering how we left things all those years ago, and how you always treated me, I guess you'd be a little more... nice?"

Her statement jars me. I blink down at her in surprise. "Nice?"

"Yeah, I don't know. You're... different." She blows out

a breath and tosses her hands up. "I get it. A lot of time has passed. I'm just used to you being a nice guy, and all you've done for the last day and a half is bark orders and make me feel like everything I'm doing is wrong. The Lawson I know—"

"The Lawson you *knew* is a very different man now, Lucy." Against my better judgment, I pull my hand from my pocket and grasp her chin, lifting it so she has to look at me again. Just like all those nights ago, a visible current of electricity sparks between us at the touch, drawing a gasp from her lips that I want to swallow whole before eliciting an entirely different sound from her mouth.

Her eyes darken, and her breath picks up, chest rising and falling rapidly as my fingers tighten ever so slightly. "I'm sorry if I've made you feel like you're not doing a good job. However, the Lucy I know wouldn't be so bothered by a man *barking orders*, as you so eloquently put it. The Lucy I know also wouldn't *sass* her boss so much."

She steps back, jerking her chin out of my hold with a smirk. "Well, I guess I'm a very different woman than I was back then. The Lucy you *knew* doesn't exist anymore," she throws her version of my words back at me. "Did you need something?"

*You—on my desk so that I can bury myself inside you.*
*Fuck. Lawson, knock it off.*

I move around the desk to sit in my chair, clicking at something random on my desktop to look indifferent. "It just looked like that Mike guy was making you a bit uncomfortable, that's all." She makes a little huffing sound, and when I glance back at her, she's wearing a giant smile. "What?"

"Nothing." She shakes her head, ponytail of bouncy waves flying to and fro. "You're just always looking out for me. Guess *some* things never change."

## Lucy

I really regret moving around my workstation now.

It's like I can feel Lawson's eyes burning a hole into my back at all hours of the day. My shoulders ache from sitting so stiffly since my body is not used to what is technically supposed to be "correct posture."

The bow at the base of my throat that ties the neck of my dress together feels suffocating. My entire body feels feverish, and the thing I want most in the world is an ice-cold bath.

After Lawson takes me on top of his desk.

Or against the bookshelf in his office.

Hell, can it be both?

I'm not ashamed to admit I've spent at least an hour between last night and this morning hittin' the kitten to thoughts of the man I could never seem to get out of my head. I know it's against company policy for executives to date employees—

*Whoa, no one said anything about dating, Lucy. No, we're just talking about that gorgeous specimen of a man fucking you until you see stars and pass out.*

I don't know how this will ever work.

I feel like I can't get my job done with him just feet away, staring at the back of my head like he wishes that act alone would get rid of me. Clearly, Lawson doesn't want to work together. And I can't figure out if it's because he's reminded of that night when he looks at me or because he just doesn't want someone as young as I am being his assistant lead.

He's been hot and cold, ordering me around with a tone suggesting his demands are too hard for me to handle. Yet, in moments like the one in his office earlier, the tenderness I remember him having shows itself, and a palpable heat reignites between us.

Am I being foolish?

Or does he feel it, too?

We haven't spoken since that night. I tried reaching out to him, but my messages went unanswered. I even went as far as trying to message him on Iconic, only to find that he'd blocked me.

We didn't have any issues before the night he saw Rhys and me, but everything changed after that. Lawson sent me off into the world feeling like a woman. He changed my life.

Does he regret it?

*Of course, he regrets it, Lucy. You were a child who came on to him. He said you couldn't, and yet you did anyway. He probably resents you for forcing yourself on him.*

My cheeks flush at the memory, and I can't help but wonder if that's how he feels—that I forced myself on him.

The adult Lunchable I ate earlier threatens to make an appearance all over my keyboard. Breathing deep through my nose and exhaling out my mouth, I nearly miss Lawson's sharp exclamation.

"Fuck!"

Turning abruptly to see what's wrong, I see him staring at his cell phone typing furiously on the screen with a frown.

"Lucy!" he hollers loud enough to make me jump even though I'm looking right at him.

Anxiety ripples through my body, and I scramble out of my seat, wondering what I could have possibly done wrong. "Yes, Mr. Morgan?"

Lawson scratches the back of his neck. I always thought it was an endearing habit, one Rhys picked up, and I always used to smile when they'd do it simultaneously.

"You're free to go for the day. I'll see you Monday morning," he dismisses me without even glancing up from his phone.

It's so quiet, the only thing I can hear is the sound of my blood rushing through my ears.

"Excuse me?" My eye twitches. "Look, I know I was late yesterday, but I had the morning scheduled off for months. I don't make a habit of coming late and leaving early."

"I'm letting you leave early for the weekend, and you're complaining?" He finally jerks his head up toward me before nodding to my desk. "I'm serious. There's nothing more for you to do today. Go home." His words are audibly stressed, and I see panic growing in his gray eyes.

"No." My tone is firm and resolute. "I still have to work on the reservations for the conference."

"You can do it next week, Lucy," Lawson nearly growls as he storms around the desk, gripping my elbow and leading me across the room. His fingers dig into my skin almost painfully.

"Lawson, let me go!" I whisper shout, yanking my arm out of his hold. Turning to face him, I narrow my eyes in a glare and wipe my faux side bangs out of my face with a huff. "What is *wrong* with you?"

"Nothing. I have a work acquaintance coming in from New York. I'm leaving early. You might as well, too."

"Work acquaintance?" I look at him skeptically. "Don't you need me to send a car to the airport? Book a restaurant for dinner? Those are all part of my job, you know."

"Oh, honey, if you have a good recommendation for dinner, we'll take it," a sultry, feminine alto rings out behind me. "Lawson may be a wonderful cook, but his taste in dining out leaves a lot to be desired."

Lawson's eyes snap above my head and widen, prompting me to turn around.

"Jules, how the hell did you get here so fast?" he asks as I take in the female who appeared out of thin air.

*Jules* is nearly as tall as he is, with a mass of sleek butter-blonde hair, a creamy, pristine complexion, and sparkling eyes that are neither blue nor green but a unique combination that takes my breath away. A chic, little black dress adorns her willowy frame, and I can't help but notice she bears a slight resemblance to Charlotte.

She's stunning, and the green little monster known as jealousy winds its slippery way up my rib cage to squeeze my heart.

*Work acquaintance, my ass. Lawson obviously has a type.*

"Darlin', I messaged you as the car was pulling up to the curb. I wanted to see M.I.G.'s newest acquisition," she croons, stepping forward to kiss his cheek.

His hand finds her waist as he takes her coat and purse, and all of a sudden, I feel like I've swallowed one of those shots where the liquor doesn't mix well, thickening and expanding in your mouth.

Charlotte is the only woman I've ever seen Lawson

with, and they were never overly affectionate, even before she cheated on him.

He still hasn't let go of Jules, paying me no mind even though I'm standing right here.

My chest constricts painfully, and I leave his office to gather my things. Turns out, I'm perfectly fine with going home early now. It's obvious Lawson didn't want me to meet Jules. That's why he was trying to get me to leave.

I don't know why he thinks he needs to hide his girlfriend from me. I don't care.

*Sure, you don't.*

"Hey, Lulu. Are you joining us for after-work drinks tonight?" Mike appears in my peripheral, leaning against my desk with his hands in his pockets.

It isn't that I don't like Mike. He's a great guy. He's just not the guy for me. He thinks that the way to a woman's heart is by trying to impress her with how much money he makes, and I've just never been one of those women who cares that much about a man's net worth.

I want a man who can make me laugh. Who will cook dinner with me and snuggle up on the couch to watch stupid reality TV shows before he takes me to bed when we can't keep our hands off each other. I want someone comfortable who pushes my limits and doesn't let me walk all over him.

I want the kind of relationship my parents have. And I know it exists out there somewhere.

Resisting the urge to look over my shoulder at Lawson's office, I meet Mike's gaze. "I don't think so. I'm gonna go home early and head to my parents' for the weekend."

"Aww." Mike pouts. "Come on. You owe me a dinner.

Buy me a drink instead?" He's being playful, but I'm not really in the mood for it.

I fix him with a disinterested stare, opening my mouth to reply, but his eyes snap over my shoulder as Jules' voice rings out. "I'm so sorry, honey. I didn't get your name."

Turning, I see her standing behind me. She beams a perfect set of pearly whites and holds out her freshly manicured hand. Hesitantly, I take it. "I'm Lucy."

"Hi, Lucy. I'm Jules. I work in the New York office. Sorry. I was so rude when I got in. I wanted to surprise Law." Her New York accent has a slight Southern twang to it. She seems genuine, which makes me hate her more than I already do.

"Consider me surprised," Lawson drawls as he walks out of the office.

Mike sidles up to me, close enough that his arm brushes my elbow. Lawson's eyes narrow at the contact, sending a petty wave of triumph thumping behind my ribs.

"Well, hi there." Mike sticks out his hand. "I'm Mike."

Jules unabashedly runs her bright eyes down his frame like a cat sizing up a mouse. "Well, hello there, handsome."

"Jules!" Lawson snaps.

"What? He's not *my* employee," she retorts.

Mike chuckles, and even though I'm not interested in him in that way, it irks me that his attention is so unloyal. He's been begging me to go on a date with him for months. Suddenly, Jules shows up, and I'm chopped liver.

However, the exchange makes me wonder if she really is just Lawson's work acquaintance.

Surely, Lawson wouldn't put up with another Charlotte.

"You two should join us," Mike offers.

"I don't really think—"

"Join you for what?" Jules asks.

Lawson grabs her elbow, gentler than he held my arm earlier. "Jules, no. Despite your distaste for my dining preferences, I already snagged us a reservation at The Overlook."

The Overlook is a romantic little restaurant at the top of a hotel by the river, which fuels my jealousy that it's the first place he thought of to take her. It also just so happens to be right around the corner from where we usually go for after-work cocktails.

"Perfect!" Mike claps. "Lauren's Fault is less than a block away. You can join us after your dinner. Since it's Friday, most of us will still be there."

It's true. Many weekends have started—and ended—at our favorite Friday night haunt.

Jules scrunches her nose. "Why is it called Lauren's Fault?"

"I don't know who Lauren is, but it's their fault that I don't remember how I got home after drinking there," Mike jokes lamely.

"Jules, we're not going out to have drinks with them. You know the rules," Lawson gently reprimands her.

"Oh, come on, Law. Live a little, darlin'." She reaches up and pats his cheek. It's an intimate gesture, and I hate how they look at each other while she does it—an unspoken conversation passing between them in a way only people who are incredibly familiar with one another can do.

"Okay, well, I'm headed out. Have a good weekend," I

say with a droll tone to no one in particular. "Nice to meet you."

"Nice to meet you, too," Jules replies to my back as I walk away without so much as another glance toward my boss.

"See you later, Lulu?" Mike calls after me.

Part of me wonders if Lawson and Jules will end up there after their dinner. I already told my parents I'd be driving out to their place tonight, but I can always go in the morning.

Making up my mind as I walk down the hall, I wave a hand in the air without responding. They won't be done with work for at least another hour. If there's a possibility of Lawson showing up at the bar tonight, I want to make him see me as a woman. Not his assistant lead, and certainly not the high school girl he last knew me as.

I know Lawson is attracted to me. I just need to remind *him* of that.

After all, if I fail miserably and make a fool of myself, I can always just blame Lauren.

# Thirteen

*Lawson*

My FINGER JAMS the lobby button of the elevator, and the annoyance I'm feeling seeps into the small steel box to wrap Jules and me in its angry cloud. "You should have given me more of a heads-up."

From my peripheral, I can see Jules lift her oblivious face from her phone to look at me. "Are you really upset? I don't see what the big deal is. You've been here for two days, and you already look as angry as a hornet. Is the office that bad?"

A vibrating *buzz* begins in my inner suit pocket before the familiar sound of my ringtone mixes with the jazzy elevator music. Pulling my phone out, I see it's a business call that should have come through hours ago.

"I have to take this."

Jules nods, her attention going back to her cell without another word.

The conversation takes longer than I anticipate, lasting the entire car ride to the restaurant and all the way through ordering our entrées. As I finally set down my phone, her bright eyes are glued to my face, a knowing smirk etched across her Botoxed lips.

"What?" I snap with more annoyance than she deserves.

She sips her sauvignon blanc slowly before responding, "We all knew coming back would be hard on you, Law. I just didn't expect it to take its toll so soon."

My filet melts on my tongue. It's possibly one of the best steaks I've ever had, but I can't enjoy it because all I can keep thinking about is the way Lucy looked when Jules arrived. When I agreed to return to Chicago, I never dreamed we'd run into each other again, let alone be working together. Our few stolen moments and one very big mistake on my part are set aside in a rainbow-colored box in my mind—part of my past, where it needs to stay.

Yet, it seems as if no time has passed at all. Lucy and I are both very different people now, and still, the attraction remains as strong as it was then—stronger because she's a *woman* now—a young woman, but not an eighteen-year-old girl anymore.

*Would it really be so bad, Lawson?*

I recognized the flash of jealousy in her eyes when she saw Jules, and fuck if it doesn't confuse the hell out of me. Why would she care? Is there a chance she's feeling what I am? The strong pull. That electric spark.

*Yes, it would be. You crossed a line back then and encouraged something you shouldn't have. She would have never thought of you like that otherwise.*

*Think of Rhys.*

My son barely speaks to me as it is. If he ever finds out that I'm even *entertaining* the thought of starting something with Lucy...

"Lawson?" Jules' voice cuts through my thoughts. Shaking my head, I realize I've been absentmindedly staring out the glass of the solarium.

My shoulders hitch in a noncommittal shrug as I focus my attention back on her. "I'm fine."

Being one of my closest friends for the better part of the last six years, she knows when not to push the subject. Candlelight bounces off her face as she cuts another piece of her herbed chicken, lips pulling wide as she glances at me from beneath her lashes. "You must be thrilled about your new secretary."

"Assistant lead," I correct automatically. M.I.G. stopped using the term "secretary" years ago. "And why do you think I'm thrilled?"

*Because where Lucy is concerned, you're too damn easy to read.*

"I think we both know why, Lawson." Her eyes narrow as she focuses on a random spot behind my head. "Lucy... She looks young. Maybe around Rhys' age?"

I can feel the sweat beginning to bead at my temple. And because Jules knows me too damn well, her eyes grow wide as she puts all the details together. She sets down her fork and picks up her wine, settling back in her chair while I reach for my water glass and down half of it in one gulp.

"It's *her*, isn't it? She's why you like the red wig so much," she muses, rubbing her glass along her bottom lip.

Jules and Cameron don't know all the details of what happened between Lucy and me, but they know enough. When I moved to New York, I was broken. I'd committed what I felt was a heinous crime, and I didn't even go after Lucy to try and rectify it. I didn't check on her to see how she was. I blocked her from my life and ran from my problems.

I don't know what type of life I would have fallen into if it weren't for them. They took me in and helped me learn a lot about myself, even though I was thirty-seven and should have had my shit together.

"It makes sense now, why you're so grumpy."

"Can we not talk about it?"

"She's beautiful, Lawson. And looks like she adores you. She wanted to stab me the second I walked into your office," Jules laughs. "I imagine she noticed how much I look like Charlotte, too. Oh, what I wouldn't give to be a fly on the wall when she realizes you prefer redheads."

"She isn't going to find out," I grit out derisively, motioning for our server to bring me another whiskey.

"Well, that's a damn shame. You two look positively edible together." Her tone drops suggestively, a recognizable heat filling her gaze as she licks her lips. "Can you imagine if Cameron *had* taken the job? You'd have never known she worked for us, and I guarantee he would have had her on her back in the first week."

The thought of Cameron touching Lucy instantly brings my blood to a roaring boil—a feral, possessive monster ripping through my chest in a way it didn't when I thought of her and Mike together. Lucy was prepared for Cameron to take over. She'd studied him. Knew his likes and dislikes. She was eager to please him, yet she keeps giving me so much sass.

If she sassed Cameron the way she does me, he'd have put her over his knee and punished her, company policy be damned. He'd throw caution to the wind in the same way I *want* to but can't.

Not with her.

Roughly, I push my plate away as the server appears with my new drink. "Thanks, Jules. I'm no longer hungry."

"Aww. Did the whittle baby lose his appetite at the thought of his friend bending the woman he wants over a desk?" she mocks in a child-like tone.

An abrupt cough flies from our server's throat as he clears the table silently. I glare at Jules while she beams a Cheshire grin back at me. "I can't wait to fill Cam in on all this."

"There's nothing to fill him in on. I've already decided I'm going to pass the office off to Randall once it's integrated. Shouldn't take more than a year." I fish my wallet out and pluck two hundreds and a fifty from it, handing them to the server. "Keep the change."

When he leaves with a thank you, Jules eyes me skeptically. "And then what? Come back to New York and go back to your old ways?"

"Sounds like a good plan to me." I knock back my whiskey.

New York helped me bury my sin before it taught me all the things I should have already known about myself. Charlotte and I had Rhys so young that I never had the opportunity to find myself after high school.

Now that I know who I am, it's even more reason to stay away from Lucy.

"Have you tried to talk to her about it?" Jules asks, setting her empty glass down. "She didn't appear frightened of you or uncomfortable. Perhaps you're making a big deal out of nothing."

"She was a child." My teeth clench together so hard I swear I hear my molars crack.

"She's not a child now, Lawson," Jules parries. "And what will you do when Rhys finds out? Or are you planning on keeping it from him for a whole year? Isn't he moving back in a few months?"

"Have you always been this much of a nag?" I deflect.

"Darlin', you know I'm only quiet and subservient in the bedroom," she teases.

While we wait for the elevator to take us back down to street level, Jules turns to face me full-on. "You know, I think I *will* join them at that bar for drinks."

"You can't fuck the employees," I remind her, though she doesn't need reminding. I happen to know she gets away with it in the New York office because no one blinks twice if a woman in power wants to dally with men who work under her.

"Like I told you earlier, Law. They aren't *my* employees."

FROM THE OUTSIDE, Lauren's Fault looks like a hole in the wall with a blue neon sign. The L and F are dimmer than the rest of the letters, and a bunch of newspaper clippings are plastered over the front window.

Inside the bar, however, it's all smooth black walnut,

with maroon and forest green vinyl booths and golden stools with tufted vinyl cushions. The establishment stretches far beyond the large bar and pool table area to a patio. And hanging on the walls are framed news articles from various major events throughout the years.

I recognize the flash of Lucy's wild mane at the end of the bar as she throws her head back with a shot of something clear lifted to her lips. She slams the glass on the table with the rest of the group as they all cry out, "It's Lauren's fault!"

Jules hears them before she sees them, grabbing my hand to pull me through the crowd toward a bunch of employees I haven't bothered getting to know yet.

"Whoo! Looks like you all got the party started already!" she shouts.

Many sets of eyes turn our way, but I can't pull my gaze away from the deep hazel ones currently glaring in Jules' direction before they fall to where our hands are still locked together. Untangling my fingers, I turn toward the bar without greeting anyone, sneaking glances at Lucy as she walks toward one of the dart boards, where Anna and Justin are having an animated conversation over a pitcher of beer.

Lucy's let her hair down from her ponytail, and the curls are tousled like she's just run her hands through them —or like she just got fucked roughly into a mattress. Her dress is a swatch of rainbow watercolor fabric that hugs her breasts and is only secured by thin straps around her neck. A cutout over her sternum shows a stretch of sun-kissed skin before the skirt ripples down, kissing the tops of her toned thighs.

It's both incredibly sexy and incredibly Lucy-like. I always wondered if she kept wearing her brightly-colored patterns or if she'd dull herself down to please the bleak monochrome masses of the business world.

*"Guess some things never change."* Her words from earlier haunt me.

"You made it!" Mike shouts over the clamor of the bar, coming over to us from one of the pool tables. He's removed his suit jacket, and his sleeves are rolled up to his elbows with the top two buttons of his dress shirt undone. Holding the pool stick out to Jules, he asks, "You play?"

"Oh, honey. I'm a lot older than you. I can probably show you a thing or two." She smacks my chest lightly. "Get me a vodka soda, would you?" As Jules walks away with Mike, I can't help but notice one of the guys I don't know hand Lucy a tumbler with amber-colored liquid in it.

*Thought you couldn't handle the amber ones, rainbow?*

She sips it before making a face, shoving it back into his hands before picking up a glass full of a pink drink while the guy laughs. The music changes from a song I've never heard of to a dance version of a popular hit from the eighties. Lucy lets out a whoop and grabs Anna, pulling the blonde from her chair abruptly and dragging her out to the dance floor. While Anna flounders around like she's never danced before in her life, Lucy twists and turns her body sensually, attracting the attention of multiple men around her.

None of the employees try to talk to me over the course of the next thirty minutes. I don't blame them. I don't exactly make myself look approachable while I watch Lucy bounce from the dance floor to a spot at the bar to take shots and back again. By now, Jules is on her third drink. She and Mike aren't even trying to hide the fact that they plan on going home together after this.

My little rainbow doesn't think I notice the way her eyes dart to me every now and then. She's trying to be discreet while she checks to see if I'm watching. Every time she knows I am, she sways her body just a little more, the skirt of her dress riding up as she entices me with her bare skin. Or she'll thrust her hands into her hair, lifting it as she dances before letting it fall slowly to hide the naked expanse of her back.

She's daring me to approach her. Tempting me like a siren luring a sailor out to sea.

I'm still nursing my first glass of whiskey when a random guy appears behind Lucy, caging her in by placing his hands on the bar top. He leans down to whisper something in her ear, and she makes a face before trying to get away from him. I'm out of my seat before I can even think about my actions—think about what it might look like to the rest of the employees—as I grab the guy's arm and yank him away from her.

All I see is red as I step into the piece of shit's personal space like an angry bull. "Keep your fucking hands off her."

"What the fuck, man?" the guy shouts at the same time Lucy grabs my bicep to stop me.

"It's fine, Lawson! I'm fine!" But her eyes are glassy, and her words are slow, and I wonder what would have happened if I hadn't been watching.

"I think you've had enough to drink." I pull the shot she's holding out of her hand and slam it back on the bar.

"Oh? You think I've had enough to drink?" she parrots.

"Why don't you go worry about your girlfriend, *Mr. Morgan*? She looks like she's had enough to drink for all of us." Lucy sloppily motions toward where Jules and Mike are now making out. "Besides, you're not my daddy," she sneers in a bratty tone, shaking her head saucily and crossing her arms.

*Oh, I'd very much like to be your daddy, rainbow. I'd love nothing more than to put you over my knee right now and punish that smart mouth so the whole bar can hear you scream for me.*

Instead, I grab her arm and haul her through the crowd to a long, empty hallway. The din of the bar finally dies down, and when I stop and turn around, it's only her and me in the pink-lit space.

"Is this how you spend your weekends? Getting blackout drunk and letting random men take you home?" I demand, tossing her arm away from me a little rougher than I probably should.

"What's it matter to you? Like I said, you're not my daddy. Go worry about your *girlfriend*."

"Jules isn't my girlfriend, and she's the least of my worries right now. I'd be more worried about Mike. He has no idea what he's getting himself into. Now answer my damn question, Lucy." My growl reverberates through the space, the acoustics expanding my voice even though I'm speaking lower than normal.

"Maybe I do, Mr. Morgan." She steps into me, probably thinking I'll step back, but I hold my ground as our chests press together. "Maybe I do spend my weekends letting random men do whatever they want to me. What are you going to do about it?" Her index finger jams into my chest. "You haven't cared enough to speak to me in the last six years. You blocked my number *and* blocked me on Iconic. So what. Do. You. Care?"

Each word is a new jab until I snatch her wrist mid-air and haul her against me, stepping forward until her back is pressed against the wall. I'm instantly hard, my erection pressing into her stomach. I know she feels it from the way her eyes widen and her mouth drops open in an O.

"You know damn well I'm not going to sit by and watch you make stupid decisions just to spite me, Lucy." In a softer tone, I say, "I'd never forgive myself if something happened to you."

With a huff, she slants her hips into mine, dragging her body against my cock as she whispers sultrily, "What? Do you want to take care of me now?" One arm winds over my shoulder, the other still firm in my grip as I hold it against the wall next to her head. "You always did like making sure I was taken care of, especially when Rhys wouldn't do it."

*Little fucking brat.*

Against my better judgment, molten desire claws down my spine, my body begging me to flip her skirt up and take her right here, even though anyone can walk by at any moment and see us. "You're acting like a child."

She smirks, lifting her chin. "You liked me better when I was a child."

My grip tightens, the flimsy material of her dress bunching beneath my fingers as I dig them into her side. My stomach twists at her words.

"Are you trying to press my buttons, rainbow?" My nostrils flare, my breaths becoming hot, shallow pants as my anger at the insinuation and my lust from her proximity increases.

Lucy pushes up on her toes, using my shoulder for balance as she brings her face close to mine. "Can your buttons be pressed, Lawson? You act like you hate me one moment, and the next, you look like you want to repeat graduation night. Which is it, *sir*? Where is the button I need to press to get my way?"

Our lips are nearly touching. This damn temptress is just daring me to close the distance and give her what she wants. Her wrist slips out of my grasp, and she lays her palm flat against my chest, sliding it downward to my painfully obvious erection.

She's always been this bold. From not freaking out when I saw my son fucking her to straight up looking at my cock. Not to mention that night, which she keeps bringing up, when she rode me like I wasn't her boyfriend's dad, pressing arousal-coated fingers into my mouth.

Lucy isn't shy about what she wants, and for a split second, I almost give in—until a breathy moan leaves her mouth and logic kicks me in the balls, reminding me of all the reasons it's not a good idea.

As much as I want to shove her against the wall and spank the sass out of her while fucking her, I unwind her hands from me and take a wordless step back.

Disappointment fills her eyes as she deflates like a popped balloon. "Message received, *Mr. Morgan*." Without another word, she turns and walks down the hall, disappearing into the crowded bar.

And I let her go.

Because that's the kindest thing I can do for her.

# FOURTEEN

*Lucy*

DAMN LAUREN.

*This* is what they mean by *Lauren's Fault*.

Nearly two days after that evening at the bar, I still don't know how I'm supposed to face Lawson at work tomorrow.

"Luce?"

Lawson, with his hard abs and chiseled jaw. I can't stop thinking of the way his moody gray eyes filled with raw desire when he pushed me against the wall, his hard length pressing into my abdomen.

The way his palm twitched like he wanted to spank me when I called him Daddy.

"Luuuucyyyyy? Earth to Lucy."

I called him *Daddy*.

Okay, well, technically, I said he *wasn't* my daddy.

"LUCY!" Lorraine's dream-like voice cuts through my thoughts, her fingers snapping in front of my face. Her pine-colored eyes come into view above me as reflections of what happened Friday night flee from my brain.

"What?" I snap, jackknifing into a sitting position on my childhood bed.

Even though I have an apartment in the city, I still like to come home on the weekends for brunch club. This particular weekend, I promised to help Lorraine finish the friendship bracelets she made for her entire graduating class since her ceremony is next week. But from the looks of it, she completed most of what was left while I abandoned my beads and elastic cord for memories of heated glances and the thin thread of Lawson's willpower that I almost managed to snap.

"My lighter is out of fluid. Where is yours?" If my little sister is upset at being ignored, she doesn't show it. Her expression has settled into her typical serene regard as she holds out her hand expectantly, gripping a frayed cord in the other. As I stretch out to grab the lighter I keep in my nightstand drawer, she asks, "Where have you been all day?"

"What do you mean?" I frown when my fingers brush an empty space where my pink and golden Zippo usually is. "I've been right here." I sit up to get a better look in the drawer.

It's filled with things like my old journal, colored pens, and annotation tabs for whatever books I was reading in high school. There's a small vibrator that looks like a tube of lipstick that Rhys got me for my eighteenth birthday and a few unused condoms from when he'd sneak into my room. But the lighter my aunt Kendall gifted me for my sixteenth birthday when I was going through a candle phase is missing.

"No, you haven't been." Lorraine sighs softly. "All through brunch, you were distracted. Does it have anything to do with Rhys' dad becoming your new boss?" She twirls a dark coppery lock around her finger with a dreamy expression like we're discussing her favorite couple in a romance novel.

"How do you know about that?" My cheeks instantly burn as I slide my feet into my slippers. I didn't bring up the Lawson situation at brunch because I didn't think it was necessary to tell my mother. At least not right now. I still remember how suspicious she was about graduation night, and I can't even speak Lawson's name without turning as pink as my favorite lip gloss.

"Rose and River were talking about it yesterday. Don't worry. I kept Mom distracted so she didn't hear them." My sister sends me a knowing smile as I head to Liam's room. "I'd tell her sooner rather than later, though, or else she's going to wonder why you kept it from her."

As I cross the hall and enter our brother's room, I contemplate my close relationship with my mother and wonder if, now that I'm older, she'd accept if anything were to happen between Lawson and me.

*Fat chance of that happening, Lucy. He made it clear he didn't want you.*

*No, he technically didn't say anything. You were drunk and threw yourself at him. Of course, he doesn't want a drunk, sloppy girl when he could have any woman he wants.*

My proverbial angel and devil on my shoulders argue while I search the top of Liam's dresser. It's cluttered with papers and random things that belong in a junk drawer. Big sister instincts kick in, and I take the chance to check anything that looks like he could be hiding any sort of paraphernalia in it.

Liam is only two weeks out of his second stint in rehab. I love my brother dearly, but I'll never understand how such an intelligent man let alcohol and cocaine ruin his early adult life. He's lucky our parents are so good to us. They sent him to a great facility the first time and an even better one the second. Now if he can just keep his shit together, he'll be golden.

A small maroon box appears as I flip over a piece of yellow receipt paper. Wanting to make sure he's not keeping anything he shouldn't be in there, I open it just as he appears in my peripheral.

"What are you doing?" he snaps angrily.

"What is this?" I ask simultaneously, plucking a small rose-shaped pendant on a dainty golden chain from the box. The gleaming rose-gold petals are edged in tiny sparkling diamonds that suggest the necklace cost a pretty penny.

Glancing up, I notice that Liam's jaw is clenched, his chest rising and falling heavily as he stares at the jewelry in my hand. Instantly, I recognize that he's counting in his head. It's an exercise he learned in rehab for when he gets overwhelmed or feels the need to rage at whoever he believes has earned his ire.

Not wanting to trigger him further, I place the necklace back in the box and continue searching for my lighter. "Do you have my pink Zippo?"

Without a word, he crosses the room to his nightstand. I don't say anything about the stench of fresh marijuana that permeates his room as soon as the drawer is open or berate him for taking my stuff.

"Who is the necklace for?" I want to hear him say it.

Not because I need the answer but because I'm afraid I already know.

He shoots me a flippant look, running a hand through his shaggy blond hair as he places my Zippo in my waiting palm. "It's not a big deal, Luce. It's a birthday present for Rose."

I'm equally shocked that he answered me truthfully and slightly disturbed by his admission. I don't know what happened when we were younger, but *something* changed between them when Rose was nine and Liam was seventeen. I've questioned both of them about it numerous times —hating that I had to mentally prepare myself to possibly hear that Liam had done something downright treacherous —but I believed them both when they assured me it wasn't like that, they just didn't want to talk about it.

"Rose's birthday isn't for another seven months. And that's a pretty intense gift for a fifteen-year-old. Especially coming from her twenty-three-year-old cousin."

"Eww, Lucy, don't go there. First off, it's for her sixteenth birthday, which is a milestone for girls. You know that. I saw it and thought she'd like it. It's really not a big deal. And second, we aren't cousins by blood. Just because Mom and Aunt Daphne are best friends doesn't make us related. Don't make it weird." He grabs my shoulder and turns me toward the door. "Now beat it. I'm gross from working with Dad and Uncle Henry and want to shower."

"Why'd you get her a present so early?"

Without missing a beat, his ominous reply comes as he closes the door behind me. "Because who the fuck knows where I'll be in seven months."

A heavy sense of sadness fills me. It's clear my brother

doesn't think he can stay clean, and evidently, he can't if he's already smoking weed to cope with the loss of his other addictions. I don't relay any of that to Lorraine as I return to my room, handing her the lighter before quickly finishing the bracelet I'd been working on.

"Your phone went off," she tells me as she lights the end of her cord and quickly blows it out, pressing the frayed ends to melt together before stringing more beads.

I grab my phone. My vision tunnels, and the air disappears from my lungs as I stare down at the screen, where I have a notification from Iconic.

**Lawson Morgan followed you.**

"Is everything okay? You look like you've seen a ghost."

Lorraine touching my knee startles me, and I jump. I can feel the panic settle over my features as it dips from my chest to my stomach, threatening to make friends with the blueberry pancakes Mom made earlier.

Worry is evident in my sister's doe-like eyes. "Luce?"

"He followed me," I whisper, unable to clearly focus on her face.

"Who followed you?"

My gaze snaps back to my phone, and I quickly open the app, pressing my notifications to go to Lawson's profile. He's barely updated it in the last six years. A photo of him, Charlotte, and Rhys from graduation day is still in the top six photos, but I don't pay much attention to the new ones as my fingers fly over the screen to open a message thread between us.

"No!" I cry pitifully, slamming my hand on my comforter like a child throwing a tantrum. "No! No! No! No! No!" Each outraged wail is punctuated by a slap against my bed as my sister asks what the hell is wrong with me.

I don't answer her as hot, angry tears cloud my sight, and I fall back against my pillows, sending Lorraine's beads flying through the air and all over my bedroom floor.

Lawson might have blocked me all those years ago, but Iconic still lets you message people who have blocked you. They just store the messages until the person unblocks you or you delete your profile.

Which means as soon as Lawson unblocked me, his inbox received an influx of every message I sent him before I left for college and my first semester away from home—and unfortunately for me, I sent him a lot of messages.

Grabbing my tangerine pillow, I hold it to my face and scream. "FUCK MY LIFE!"

### Lawson

**@lucybradee: Hey.**

**@lucybradee: I think maybe I do want to talk before leaving.**

I stare at my screen, reading the messages as they come through the second I unblock Lucy on Iconic. One after another, each one makes me more ill as her desperation reads clearly through the words.

**@lucybradee: Can I at least say goodbye?**

**@lucybradee: I'm pretty sure you blocked me. Can't say I blame you.**

My stomach twists, and my heart beats rapidly as I think of how alone she must have felt. I'm such a fucking jackass for blocking her because I didn't want the temptation of seeing her beautiful, smiling face every day as she went on living her life.

**@lucybradee: (picture of dorm room) All moved in! My roommate is pretty great. California is beautiful.**

**@lucybradee: You blocked my phone number too? I think that's a bit extreme.**

**@lucybradee: You know, the LEAST you could have done was talk to me before I left. I thought you were a nice guy?**

In some of the messages that span her first semester away, the words are jumbled and don't make sense. Clearly, they're a sign she was drunk when she sent them.

When did her drinking that much begin? Did I cause it? As far as I can remember, she never used to drink to excess.

But the fact that it was me she was thinking about while she was out having fun softens my resolve to keep her at arm's length the rest of the year I'm here. What we did on graduation night wasn't okay. I'm a sick man for letting it happen and an even worse one for cutting off all communication afterward.

**@lucybradee: Why won't you speak to me, Lawson?**

**@lucybradee: Are you mad at me?**

**@lucybradee: If you think I'm upset, I'm not. I don't regret what happened.**

The chicken salad I made for lunch threatens to reappear as her distress rings clear in the number of messages she sent.

**@lucybradee: I'm coming home for Christmas. Do you think we can talk?**

The dates of her messages are further and further apart. Where days used to separate them, it stretches to weeks, and the last two have nearly a month between them.

She sent the final one on New Year's Eve of that year.

**@lucybradee: I'm sorry for all the messages. You must think I'm pathetic. I won't bother you again. Have a nice life, Lawson.**

If I felt bad before, I certainly feel worse now.

I don't know what made me decide to unblock her. If anything, what happened on Friday night should justify my reason for keeping her blocked. All it did, though, was make me want to keep an eye on her.

And my instincts are screaming that she needs protection and someone to take care of her.

Scrolling until I find the last photo I recognize from graduation night, I scour through images of Lucy's life. I take in her smiling face in every snapshot of the summer before she moved, her first semester at Berkeley, every beach she visited, and all the taco plates she tried before claiming her favorite. There are pictures of her cheering and random fundraisers the team held. And as much as I try to convince myself I'm not searching for any images or hints of a boyfriend, I find myself relieved that the only men she posts about are her dad and brother.

"Hey, Dad! Whatcha doin'?" River startles me as he and Rose saunter into the kitchen, making me jump and causing my thumb to press on the phone screen. The result is "loving" the photo that's blown up, which just so happens to be one from nearly four years ago of Lucy in one of her 50s-style bikini dresses.

"Fuck," I mutter, clicking the side button to turn off the device. Looking up, I see them raiding the fridge. They both have swollen lips and mussed hair, yet neither seems to think it's a dead giveaway for what they must have been doing in the pool house.

"Nothing. Work stuff. Are you guys hungry? I can get dinner started?"

"Nah, I'm fine with leftovers." River pulls out a pizza box from last night. "Besides, Rose isn't staying."

"Nope," Rose agrees, popping the p. "My dad is on his way to pick me up." She chugs half a bottle of pink Gatorade before handing the rest to River. "Are you happy to be home, Mr. Morgan?"

"I'm happy to be closer to River all the time. Can't say I don't miss the city, though," I state honestly.

There's something about the hustle of New York that just feels more like home than Illinois ever has. Even Chicago doesn't sate my need for chaos. When things get too quiet, and I'm left alone with my disparaging thoughts, my demons have a better chance of winning.

"Well, *I'm* happy you're home," my son declares. "Honestly, I know I shouldn't say this, but it's kind of nice to have a break from Mom. Her drinking is really getting out of hand. And when she has her friends over, all they do is stay up all night cackling about the stupidest shit. Sometimes, I can even hear them past my headset."

"Be nice. She's your mom," Rose gently scolds. Her phone vibrates on the countertop, and she taps the screen before picking it up. "Gotta go. See you at school tomorrow!"

"Byeee." River watches her go with a fond expression.

"Are you two dating?" I gently inquire.

I've noticed he gets a little moody whenever someone brings up their friendship being the way it is, so I tread lightly and watch my hormonal teenage son for any reaction that might tell me the truth.

He laughs and shakes his head. "Nah. Rose and I are just best friends, Dad. Although, we did decide to experiment together so that when it comes time to do things for real, we don't look like idiots."

"Experiment?" I parrot flatly, not exactly excited that my fifteen-year-old is already thinking about sex. "Do we need to have a safe sex talk already?"

"Uh, Rhys already covered it." River laughs awkwardly, scratching the back of his neck like his older brother does when he's uncomfortable—a trait they got from me.

Furrowing my brow skeptically, I dip my head, trying to catch my youngest's attention. "Your brother had 'the talk' with you?"

He leans further into the fridge, searching for something besides last night's cold pepperoni pizza to avoid my gaze. "Yup. Got it covered, Dad. You don't have to worry. Besides, it's not like we're having sex or anything. Neither of us is ready yet."

Relief floods my veins at how he talks about Rose respectfully. "Just make sure to ask if you have any questions, okay? I'd rather you be honest with me than try to sneak behind my back. You know we've always had an open household."

"I know. I know. Hey, how is Lucy doing? I didn't get a chance to see her when I was at the Bradee's the other day." River changes the subject as he pulls out cottage cheese and closes the fridge.

As he moves to the cupboard for a can of pineapple, my thoughts wander back to my little rainbow, and I realize I can't really answer my son because I don't know how she's doing. I blocked her from my life and then nearly physically assaulted her in a dingy bar hallway. I keep telling myself that I can't think of her as anything other than a woman who's young enough to be my kid, but I sure as shit can't seem to keep away from her, either.

"She's doing good. I think it was a bit of a surprise for us both to be working together now, but we're figuring it out." I pick up my phone again and resume scrolling through Lucy's photos, careful not to "love" any of them, feeling like an idiot knowing she will get a notification that will clue her in to the fact that I'm stalking her profile.

"I'm sure Rhys will be happy they'll both be in the city in the fall. She was always the one who got away."

River's words don't sit right with me. The idea of my oldest son contacting her again bothers me in a way it shouldn't.

I hum noncommittally, but River doesn't pay me any attention as he finishes up in the kitchen and heads to his room.

"Goodnight," he garbles around a mouthful of pizza.

Lucy *should* be with someone her own age. But the thought of her and Rhys getting back together causes the little green monster known as jealousy to sear straight through my heart, eating away at the flesh like acid. And the more I think about it, the worse the pain feels.

There's no way in hell I'd be able to sit by and watch them reconcile. As selfish as it is, I can't have her be a part of this family.

*Not unless it's by* my *side.*

And it would destroy Rhys if he ever found out the truth about what happened between her and me on graduation night. Whether he wronged her or not... I wronged them both.

Willing those thoughts away, I reopen our message thread and read through them again. Disappointment at my actions settles in my bones. Regardless of whether I should act on my feelings, Lucy deserves an explanation.

And I know the perfect peace offering to start with.

# Fifteen

## Lucy

Come Monday morning, I'm feeling a little petty. Instead of getting to the office early to make sure he has his coffee, I arrive right on time—only to find my desk turned back toward his open office, complete with a familiar bag of cookies beside my keyboard.

During my meltdown yesterday afternoon, Lawson liked one of my pictures from my first year in college, giving away the fact that he'd scrolled back years to see what I'd been doing with my life once I left. Once again, giving me whiplash from his hot and cold actions.

Knowing his eyes are on me, I push the bag to the edge of the desk without so much as another glance before I settle in and act as though nothing is amiss—even though I want to attack the cookies like a feral raccoon because I haven't had them in years. No amount of time and memory ever allowed me to recreate the recipe.

"Good morning," Lawson greets.

I glance up to see his unbothered, perfectly tanned

features smiling down at me, looking like he doesn't have a care in the world.

"Morning," is all I offer in response as I power up my computer. When Lawson doesn't move, I flip my loose waves over one shoulder and look at him expectantly. "Was there something you needed, Mr. Morgan?"

"I was hoping we could talk. Why don't you come to my office?" The words are quiet as he surveys the area to make sure the few people who are in the office aren't within earshot.

"There's nothing to talk about. I'm sorry about Friday night. It won't happen again."

I don't miss the way his body tenses at my rudeness before his features morph to amusement. The corner of his lips quirks up before he nods amicably. "I'm sorry as well."

I want to ask him what he's sorry for. I want to know if he's sorry for ignoring me the second Jules arrived. Or if he's sorry for dragging me into the hall and pinning me against the wall like he was ready to take me right there. Is he sorry for getting hard when he had my body trapped? For getting turned on by our position? Or perhaps for not acting on it when he had the chance?

"If that's all, then I have work to do," I snip, crossing my ankles to stop my feet from bouncing on the toes of my sky-blue stilettos.

"Lucy—"

"Look... I'm sorry for all the messages I'm sure you got on Iconic, and I'm sorry for the way I spoke to you on Friday. It won't happen again," I repeat. "Now, if you don't mind..." I bite my inner cheek from saying anything else.

At the end of the day, Lawson is my boss, and I have to

respect that. I'm toeing a line with my attitude as it is. But as his jaw tics, and he looks like he's debating hauling me into his office with or without my consent, I'm tempted to scream and yell and throw a fit. I can't help but notice that when I give him sass, he seems to lose control over whatever is holding him back.

"I need you to set a budget for the quarterly morale party. I finished booking everything using the budget we had for last quarter, but I need to know exactly how much I have left to play with for catering," I inform him as he starts to head back to his office.

I can feel him watching me as I push back from my desk, notebook and pen in hand. Everyone else's assistants use the company-provided iPads. However, I like writing everything down and knowing I'm never at risk of losing notes due to a technology malfunction.

Following Lawson into his office, I don't miss that he veers to the right, stepping out of the way so he can close the door behind me. When I spin around, he's already in my personal space, nearly toe to toe, appraising me with a soft look that reminds me of another time—when we were different people.

"This isn't the time or place to have this conversation." His voice is a husky purr that makes my nipples harden and everything from my belly down to clench. "But I want you to know how truly sorry I am that I wasn't there for you after what happened."

He doesn't need to explain what he means. I'm already painfully aware, and as I crane my neck to look up at him, the memory of how isolated I felt rushes back. I had no one to talk to about what we did. I was confused and didn't understand why, all of a sudden, Lawson had taken up every inch of my brain and my chest cavity. I thought about him so often that I literally hurt my own feelings, thinking about how he must have hated me for what I forced him to do.

The unwanted feelings cause an unwelcome tingle to build in my sinuses, and I quickly blink it away before tears can form. Lawson's gaze keeps drifting down to my lips like he wants to kiss me, and I hate it.

"You're right. This isn't the time or place. *Never* is the time or place. As in, we never have to have this conversation." I take a step back and look down at my notepad. "Now, about the budget—"

"I don't care about the budget," he interrupts, hand flying to his neck to scratch a non-existent itch.

"Well, I don't want to talk," I snap back, fixing him with the best steely gaze I can muster. My right foot taps, my fists clenching around the notepad and pen as I set my hands on my hips. "So we can talk about the party, or I can return to my desk."

Lawson's jaw tics again. And I swear I see his palm twitch as he drops it to his side, but it could also be a trick of the buttery light filtering through the windows.

"What are these events for again?" he inquires, moving to his desk.

"We do them every quarter. It's good for morale. Shows the employees that you care about their mental health. We usually pick something fun to do on the company dime. Last quarter, we rented out a bowling alley. This quarter, we're doing an 80s-themed party at Sk8 Land."

"Sk8 Land?" His brows shoot into his hairline. "That place is still open?"

"They renovated it, so it's still pretty popular. The upstairs has an arcade and laser tag now."

Lawson shakes his head incredulously. "And a bunch of adults want to have their company party there?"

A smirk pulls at my lips. "We like to have fun. I think dressing up in brightly-colored spandex and roller skating while drinking sounds like a great time." When he doesn't reply and fixes me with a flat glare, I continue, "Not all of us are *old*, Mr. Morgan. Some of us like to do more than work."

Excitement flickers through me as his eyes darken at my playful words. Pressing Lawson's buttons has become a game I can't get enough of—one I want to become a champion at.

Triumph blooms throughout my chest as he says, "Oh, I know how to have fun, Lucy. Trust me, my kind of fun has nothing to do with glow sticks and rock music."

*I want to know what kind of fun that is, Lawson.*

Heat melts down my spine as he stares at me, dragging his eyes down my body suggestively. I'm aware that my bright pink shift dress isn't exactly office wear, but then again, most of my closet isn't exactly office-appropriate. Chadwick never had an issue with my wardrobe. But as Lawson takes in every dip and curve, I press my thighs together to try to quell the wetness gathering between them, and it occurs to me that perhaps I might need to go shopping.

His attention abruptly goes to his computer screen. "Use whatever you need for catering, within reason."

Whatever heat had been growing between us quickly dies as he dismisses me, making me wonder if I should just invest in a neck brace. I turn and leave his office without a word, leaving the door cracked so that we don't have to stare at each other.

I work until lunch, finalizing everything for the party and ordering the last piece of my outfit. Justin and Anna stop by briefly to ask if we're all still planning on going together. Mike hasn't spoken a word to me all day, and I bet he's embarrassed about how he acted with Jules on Friday, so I leave him to lick his wounds. According to Justin, Jules went to Mike's place and left right after they slept together, bruising his overinflated ego.

It's about time someone knocked him down a peg.

As soon as the clock hits noon, I grab my purse and shut down my computer. I don't feel like eating at the café downstairs, and I'm in dire need of groceries, so no packed lunch. What I need is fresh air and space from the man I can't stop thinking about, which means the little restaurant a few blocks away with the best pecan-crusted chicken and pear salad is the perfect solution.

"Will you grab me a sandwich when you go downstairs, please?" Lawson calls out as I walk past his door.

I pop my head in and state, "I'm not eating downstairs. I'm going out to grab lunch. I can bring you back something if you'd like?"

Lawson stands unexpectedly, grabbing his phone and slipping it into his pocket. "That sounds like a great idea. I'll go with you."

I blink. "That... that wasn't an invitation to join me."

I need space, not an entire uninterrupted hour with him.

But his hand is already on the small of my back as he ushers me down the hall, sparking tingles throughout my body. Being this close to him keeps me in a permanent state of arousal, and I hate it. It isn't fair.

In fact, it downright pisses me off.

"I don't get you, Lawson," I snap when we step onto the sidewalk. The sun beams down on us, warming my skin as a light breeze ruffles my hair. As we walk, I search for my sunglasses, thankful for something to shield my gaze because if looks could kill, Lawson would be fatally wounded by now.

"I know. I'm sorry for what happened on Friday. Jules is the one who wanted to join you for drinks. Trust me, I wanted to stay away."

His words send new angry and offended sparks through me. "Am I that disgusting to you?"

"What?" He grabs my arm to pull me to a stop. "Why on earth would you think that? I don't think you're disgusting at all, Lucy."

"Well, what *is* your problem then? You're rude, and then you... you act as if you want me. You act jealous of Mike and the guy at the bar, yet when you have the opportunity, you don't take it. You say you're a different man, Lawson, but whoever this man is..." I gesture down his body and pull my arm from his grip. "...I don't think I like him very much."

I resume walking, and he follows, hot on my heels. "What would you have me do, Lucy? You are young enough to be my kid, *and* you work for me now."

"You sound like a broken record. And if that was the case, then why unblock me on Iconic? Why like a photo from years ago?" When we get to the restaurant, I push the door open more forcefully than necessary and run straight into a solid block of muscle.

"Whoa there," a familiar voice rings out as warm hands encircle my biceps to steady me.

Looking up, I see Dr. Gavin Russo smiling down at me —my gynecologist. All my anger dissipates as I cordially greet the man I've entrusted my female health to for the last two years. "Dr. Russo, what are you doing here?"

"Same as you, I suppose. Grabbing lunch." He lets me go, and I take a step back. His eyes shift to Lawson, who comes up beside me, radiating annoyance. "Is this your father?" He sticks his hand out. "Gavin Russo."

### Lawson

*He's tall. Too tall. And why is he touching her? Why is she smiling at him like that?*

My face grows red as I take in the easy way the man puts his hands on Lucy, smiling at her adoringly before turning his attention to me and asking if I'm her father. Lucy's lips roll in as she tries not to laugh, and I reach out to take the man's hand, squeezing it with more force than necessary.

"Not her father. I'm her boss, Lawson Morgan." My head tilts to the side as I look at her questioningly. "And how do you two know each other?"

An uncomfortable expression crosses Gavin's face for a moment before Lucy explains nonchalantly, "Oh! Dr. Russo is my lady doctor."

My insides blow up like uncovered leftovers in a microwave.

*He's seen her naked from the waist down. His fingers have been* inside *her.*

Since she offered up the information, the doctor relaxes. "I have to return to the office, but it was good to see you, Lucy. And it was nice to meet you, Lawson." He quickly sweeps his eyes down my frame before disappearing out the door.

*Wait, was that my imagination, or did he just check me out?*

As if I asked the question out loud, Lucy laughs and rolls her eyes. "Calm down, *Daddy*. He's not into women."

"Into women or not, it's weird that men choose to go into that profession. There's no way in hell he's going to see you exposed ever again," I bite out.

She lets out a little huff that I find endearing before storming to the counter to order her lunch. After I order and pay for both of us, we take it to go and head back to the office.

As soon as we're outside again, she whirls around and jabs her finger into my chest, reminiscent of Friday night.

"You have to *stop*! Either we work together, and you stop getting jealous of every man who looks at me, or you *do* something about whatever this is!" She gestures between us before turning and walking away.

"I'm navigating this the best I can. It isn't exactly easy, okay? Do you think I *want* to be jealous of every man who looks at you? Do you think I want to feel the need to protect you when I see you making bad decisions like you were at the bar?"

"Oh, please," she laughs. "I wasn't making bad decisions, Lawson. It's called having fun. I don't need anyone to protect me from that."

"Yeah, well, that type of fun is going to get you drugged and raped. So forgive me if I won't stand by and watch that shit happen."

There were plenty of men who had their eyes on her that night. It's a wonder it hasn't happened already. And if it has...

A wave of sickness curls in my stomach, quickly turning to anger as she shouts over her shoulder, "You're not my father!"

We grow quiet as we enter the building, waiting to speak again until the elevator doors close behind us, and we're the only two in the enclosed space.

"I'm not trying to act like your father. I care about you, Lucy."

She turns around and faces me. "So you *are* interested in me?"

As I search her hazel eyes that shine with so much hope, my jaw aches from clenching it so hard. Finally, I whisper, "I would be stupid to lie and say I wasn't."

Her pink berry lips turn up in the smile I love so much. And I hate that my next words are going to take that image away from me so soon. "But you are half my age. And I am your boss. Nothing can happen between us."

As predicted, her smile falls as the elevator doors open. She turns and realizes we're not on our floor. Lucy gets pushed into me, her ass flush against my cock, as a large man, who is yelling about a lawsuit on his phone, enters the tight space.

Her scent surrounds me, and I'm instantly hard, reaching for her hip instinctively. Her pink dress bunches as I curl my fingers, pulling a little gasp from her throat with my touch. Leaning against the wall behind me, I try to put some distance between us, but she discreetly steps back, turning her head to catch my gaze in the mirrored wall next to us.

It's evident that my cock is rock-hard, and without drawing attention, I lean down to whisper in her ear, "I'm sorry."

Everyone else in the elevator fades away as she looks at me over her shoulder, our mouths nearly touching. Lucy's eyes deepen to a lovely shade of forest pine as her tongue darts out to wet her lips.

"Don't be," she whispers back, using the rail as leverage to push against me harder.

It takes everything in me not to let out a groan as she presses up on her toes, dragging her ass over my erection like a devious little vixen. "I'm not."

# Sixteen

## *Lucy*

"WHAT? What do you mean you aren't going to come? Aww, come on. We worked so hard. Mr. Benson always came and had a great time." Molly from accounting pouts in Lawson's direction, sticking her bottom lip out in a way she probably thinks is sexy but makes her look like a child.

The boardroom has nearly emptied after today's meeting. Molly is on the planning committee with me, though she's barely done anything besides complain about decorations and food. But did she offer up any other suggestions? No. It's par for the course for her, though. Always complaining, never helping, and trying to ride whatever new alpha male comes through the office.

Since Lawson is the new stallion in town, she's been after him all week. And I don't know if he's actively trying to piss me off or if this is just how he is now, but the easy smiles he sends her way and husky words of gratitude for the *excellent job she's doing* make me want to shove my pencil right into one of her bright blue irises.

*You sound like a psycho, Lucy. Get a grip.*

Lawson laughs—a deep, throaty chuckle that sends every woman who's still crowded around the table swooning. "I don't think so, Molly. The morale parties are for employees. How will you all talk about me behind my back if I'm there?" he jokes smoothly.

A loud crack audibly interrupts the conversation. The sting of wood and lead striking my fingers is sharp and slightly painful, but does nothing to diminish my annoyance. If anything, it heightens it as all eyes flick to me and the pencil that now resides in two halves in my grip.

"Besides. I'm not one for costumes," Lawson finishes, focusing his attention back on the blonde sitting across from me.

"That's funny," I muse in a tone I know will grate on his nerves. "I remember you used to love dressing up for Halloween." I gather my things as my coworkers share knowing glances.

It's common knowledge now that Lawson and I know each other, but since I dated his son, no one would ever suspect we have a past that was anything other than platonic.

When I swing a saccharine smile towards him, he clenches his jaw. "That was a long time ago, Lucy." He turns his attention back to the rest of the women. "You all have a great time. Be safe."

A round of sighs follows us out the door, and I can feel the tension radiating from Lawson in hot waves of energy that wrap around us as we return to his office.

"You just won't let up, will you?" he says under his breath, careful not to pick a fight too loudly.

"I don't know what you're talking about, Mr. Morgan," I singsong.

"You know damn well what I'm talking about, Lucy. Is this how our time here is going to go? With you pressing my buttons every chance you get?"

We stop in the space between his office door and my desk, peering at each other as casually as we can muster, though the tension in our eyes is hard to conceal. It dances over my skin, prickling like static electricity wrapping around my limbs.

"If you weren't so easy to get a rise out of..." I lower my eyes slowly to the buckle of his belt, making my double meaning crystal clear. "...it wouldn't be a problem, would it?"

His nostrils flare, and heady desire makes his pupils dilate. "Lucy..."

"Lawson..." I draw out his name the same way he does to mine, batting my eyelashes up at him expectantly.

A shrill ring from my desk breaks the moment. Without a word, he turns away, and I pick up the company phone from its cradle.

"Lawson Morgan's office, how may I help you?"

*Beep. Beep. Beep.*

The timer to remind me about Lawson's phone conference interrupts my concentration. Checking the time, I inwardly curse. I worked straight through lunch.

"Shit, Lucy. This is why you need to go to the damn grocery store," I mutter to myself, slipping into my heels and smoothing down my emerald silk shirt dress.

There's no time to run down to the café, so I head to the break room's snack bar. I'm a picky eater because certain ingredients set off a weird skin rash I've developed over the last year. But surely, there's a piece of fruit or something that will hold me over until dinner.

*If you hadn't eaten all the cookies Lawson made you already, you could have snacked on one of those.*

Cookies of any sort don't last that long in my apartment, though, let alone my favorite kind.

"...and it was the sweetest thing, I'm telling you. He got me a gift card to this swanky spa in The Radford and told me he was impressed with my work on the morale party," Molly gushes to a few women as they sip iced coffees in the break room.

Instantly, my skin prickles with irritation.

*Is she talking about Lawson?*

"Wow, Molls. That didn't take long," Jordanna, a middle-aged woman who works in her department, says.

"Of course, it didn't. Rumor has it that Mr. Morgan has a thing for blue-eyed blondes," Jennifer from Rentals whispers.

My fingers drum along the granite countertop while I decide on a selection of granola bars. Grabbing one to read the label, my attention pulls back to Molly's gaggle of geese.

"I asked if he was interested in getting dinner this weekend. Told him that I could use the card to make myself all pretty for a night on the town," Molly lilts with a laugh like it's already a sure thing.

*Don't say a word, Lucy. Don't say a word.*

"Oh, Lucy? Will you be a dear and clear Mr. Morgan's schedule for Friday evening?"

My left eye twitches, fingers clenching around the granola bar. Slowly, I turn to see her grinning at me like the cat that got the cream.

"Better yet. You should probably make sure Monday morning is slow, too." She laughs.

I think of one of my mother's favorite quotes from Ralph Waldo Emerson, *"For every minute you remain angry, you give up sixty seconds of peace of mind."*

I can sacrifice sixty seconds to put this cow in her place.

## Lawson

"Lucy, are you com—" My words die in my throat when she's not at her desk.

Checking my watch, I see there are only about two minutes before my conference call with New York. Usually, Lucy is ready before I am.

"There's about to be a catfight in the break room," a guy announces as he heads back to his cubicle. "Molly is on one again today."

"Is it Lucy? She looked like she wanted to rip out Molly's hair earlier," a woman whispers.

Before my brain catches up, my feet are already taking me toward the break room.

Molly's voice filters from the open door halfway down the hall as I round the corner. "...probably make sure Monday morning is slow, too."

I make it three steps before I hear Lucy. "You're kidding

yourself if you think he would ever be interested in *you*. He might have gotten you a gift card to say thank you, even though it was *me* who did all the planning for the party, like I always do, but I assure you, he's just being nice because Lawson's a nice guy like that. He probably got something for everyone on the committee. Trust me, you aren't special."

I stop just outside the room. Lucy sounds like she's trying to convince herself just as much as anyone else of what she's saying, her tone dripping with irritation and condescension. "And for the record, he is still very much *married*. So unless you want to be a homewrecker, I'd back off."

I grin. She sounds jealous, and I can't help the way it makes my heart skip a beat at the way she publicly claims me through the guise of my sham of a marriage. Lucy knows damn well there's nothing but a piece of paper between Charlotte and me anymore.

"He doesn't wear a wedding ring. I heard they're separated, and his *wife* lives in Florida now," Molly snaps back.

Deciding this has gone far enough, I enter the room and nearly run right into Lucy, who is just inside the door. Molly's eyes widen, and everyone in the room looks between the three of us like we're acting out a real-life soap opera.

"What's going on in here?" I demand more authoritatively than I've ever spoken in this office.

Lucy's body stiffens, while Molly's mouth opens and closes like a fish out of water. "Mr. Morgan... I..."

"My personal life isn't to be a topic of discussion in the office, do you understand?" I direct the question at her but meet everyone else's eyes as well. "Now, all of you need to get back to work and stop using company time to discuss your personal lives."

They all jump to their feet as I lower my voice for only Lucy to hear. "Let's go. I'm about to be late for my meeting."

She whirls around, refusing to meet my gaze as we return to my office, her heels clicking against the floor with angry clacks. She swipes her notepad off her desk and rips the wrapper off the granola bar before shoving half the thing in her mouth like a rabid animal.

Instantly, I wonder how much of me she can fit down her throat before my length makes her gag. How much she can handle before tears stream from her eyes and she has to tap out. How her hair would feel wrapped around my fist as I fuck her fa—

No. She's too precious to do such devious things to.

As she grumbles incoherently around a mouthful of granola, she stomps into my office and answers the call ringing through. I close the door behind me as Cameron's voice comes over the speaker.

While he talks about numbers and projections for next quarter, I stare at my computer screen and try to focus on anything other than Lucy's jealousy when she was talking to Molly.

I'm giving *myself* damn whiplash. One moment, I'm amenable to staying away from her, and the next, I want her more than I've wanted anyone in my entire life.

*Either fucking take her like you want to, or stop leading her on and let her live her damn life.*

I know I'm being selfish by giving her hope and then

taking it away all within a few seconds. My heart and head are at war with each other. All the bloody shrapnel flying from my eyes and mouth in the form of heated glances and things I shouldn't be saying to her.

My eyes drift to her as she reaches over and mutes our side of the line before pulling her skirt a little higher and slapping the skin of her right thigh roughly.

Every part of my body freezes except my cock. He jumps at attention like an eager puppy, watching its master prep a treat for him.

She does it again, turning her skin bright pink. Little sounds escape between her parted lips—something between a moan and an exasperated sigh. I want to hear her make those sounds when she's naked and quivering beneath me, moments from begging me to fuck her.

Would she let me strike her flesh in the throes of passion? Would she allow me to sensually assault other parts of her body purely for the pleasure of watching her writhe under my control?

Images of her spread out, baring herself to me before I sink my cock into her warm center. Hair fanned over my sheets, every limb tied to a bedpost, her wet—

"Lawson!" A snap of fingers in front of my face yanks me out of my daydream. Shaking my head clear of my thoughts, I realize the object of my fantasies is staring at me with a concerned look. "Did you hear anything he just said?"

*Not a damn word, rainbow. I was too busy thinking about what your reddened skin would look like painted with my cum.*

I hit the receiver's mute button before discreetly rearranging myself. "Sorry, Cam. Can you repeat that?"

Lucy is still itching her skin, where several hives have begun to bubble up. Alarm rises in my chest, but when she notices I'm staring at her with worry, she shakes her head and mouths, *It's nothing.*

By the time I'm off the call with Cameron, Lucy's skin has evened out, and the hives are disappearing from her thigh completely. "What was that all about?"

She sighs, smoothing the emerald fabric back down. "It's just something I've had for the last year. It only pops up when I eat certain foods." She lifts the wrapper of her granola bar and inspects the content label. "I was looking at the ingredients when Molly started talking about... Never mind."

"Lucy," I call her name to stop her from leaving. Opening my desk drawer, I pull out a white envelope, sliding it across the desk with a knowing look. "I did happen to get something for everyone on the committee. Yours might be a little more than everyone else's, though, so don't tell anyone."

Throwing her a wink, I hold her gaze as she reaches for the gift card. Silently, she slides the envelope back toward me without looking at it, a delicate copper brow arching toward her hairline. The corner of her raspberry-painted lips turns up as she leans over my desk, the top of her dress dipping low to reveal black lace that has my cock tightening all over again.

Her tone is throaty as she whispers, "Thank you, but no thank you. I don't need presents, *sir*. I'm more into praise."

The little tease straightens up and turns on her heels,

strutting out of my office without another word and leaving me with a whirlwind of emotions.

As she sits at her desk, I adjust my cock again. I grab my phone, not allowing myself to think too long about what I'm about to do. Shooting off a text, I watch her pick up her phone, and I can see her cheeks turn pink all the way from here.

## LAWSON

> You did a good job, rainbow. You're such a good girl.

Lucy's eyes meet mine through the doorway, and the heat in them is palpable as she licks her lips.

I am well and truly fucked.

# SEVENTEEN

*Lawson*

**@LUCYBRADEE: Roller skates, fanny packs, and glow sticks, oh my! #companymorale**

I huff an amused laugh at the photo Lucy recently uploaded on Iconic. Apparently, there's a way to make a private folder that no one can see without a password—which she left on my desk along with a note that said:

*In case you get bored and want to see what you're missing out on.*

Missing out, indeed.

In the photo, Lucy and Anna are wearing neon-colored spandex bodysuits with different-colored leggings and leg warmers. Both women have their hair pulled up in ponytails with sweatbands and an obscene amount of glowing jewelry.

Lifting my second tumbler of whiskey of the evening to my lips, I swipe my thumb and scroll through the photos that have been uploaded so far. It wasn't even a thought to go tonight, even if the idea of being able to sneak Lucy away into a dark corner was tempting. But image after image has me rethinking my decision.

It's bad form to attend these types of events. Morale parties are for employees, not their bosses. However, the fact that nearly everyone there right now is holding a drink makes my protective instincts kick in.

*What if she drinks too much?*

*What if someone tries to take advantage of her?*

I can hear her response to my agonizing internal questions. *Okay, Daddy.*

My palm twitches.

Another swipe shows a photo of some guy with his arms wrapped around both Lucy and Anna. Both women are leaning in to kiss his cheek, and Lucy's bright pink lipstick has left a mark on his skin.

"Put the phone down, Lawson. You're going to drive yourself crazy," I mutter to myself.

Darkening the screen, I toss my cell on a pile of file folders and pull up my email. I need a distraction, and even though it's the start of the weekend, working seems like the best choice.

Not even a few minutes go by before my phone lights up, and an image of Jules appears on my screen. Sighing, I slide the answer tab over. "Yes?"

"Well, that's no way to greet your best friend, now is it?" she sarcastically chides, clearly on speakerphone.

"I'm his best friend," Cameron argues. Apparently, this is a three-way call.

"Yes, well, the question would remain the same then, wouldn't it?" she sardonically replies.

"Can I help you two? I'm trying to get some work done." In reality, I've been blankly staring at my computer screen, not registering anything.

"How many drinks in are you, Law? And how many more will it take to convince you to get your ass to the rink to get your girl?" Jules asks.

As I put them on speaker and set my phone down, I can hear the clinking of glasses on their end, and for a moment, I miss New York *badly*. It's not just my friends, but also the fact that I could be doing the same thing in the city right now and not feel so alone. All I'd have to do is open my window, and the bustling of the people below, the sound of taxis honking their horns, and the smell of street food would surround me even if I weren't down in the middle of it all.

Here, it's just River and me, and my broody teenager is off somewhere with Rose and Nova tonight, leaving me completely and utterly alone to watch Lucy's night play out on a social media app.

It's like my life reversed right back to being that sad and pathetic man I was before I moved to New York.

"Stop pushing him. Lawson, why don't you come back for the weekend? We can go to the club and get your mind off your woman problems."

"Ooh, we haven't all been to the club together in a long time!" Jules says excitedly.

My screen lights up with another notification from Iconic. "I have a lot of work to get done. Plus, I can't just take off for the weekend, Cam. I've got River."

"Well, sitting at home in your office with a bottle of whiskey while you watch your pretty little assistant get drunk isn't going to do you any favors," he scolds good-naturedly.

"How the hell do you know I'm watching her get drunk?" I pick up my phone to look at the new photo.

"Mike might have shared the password with me," Jules singsongs.

"She's a pretty little thing. Kinda makes me wish I *had* taken the job in Chicago," Cameron jokes.

"Shut the fuck up."

They both burst into laughter while I pull up the app. Irritation prickles down my spine as a carousel of images pops up, featuring the same man holding Lucy bridal style as they gaze at each other with giant smiles.

"Ooooh, are you gonna let this guy paw at her all night, Law?" Jules asks. "You know, I'll bet the little cherry pop is trying to get a rise out of you. That's what *I* would do in her situation. Smart girl."

After the way we've been around each other, it wouldn't surprise me in the least. It's like Lucy is doing everything she can to make me snap. Especially since I called her a good girl.

Irritation bursts into feral possessiveness as another photo loads, and I find myself staring at the guy nuzzling her neck while Lucy grins at the camera like she's looking straight into my soul.

*Come and get me, Lawson. I dare you.*

I'm losing the battle with myself because all I want is to claim the little brat. Damn the company policy. Damn our age difference. And damn the fact that she used to date my son.

"You know, you're getting far too much entertainment out of this," I tell Jules as I stand to collect my keys and wallet.

"I heard the keys. He's going to get her. Jesus, man, it's about time," Cameron comments.

"Goodbye, you two." I don't wait to hear what else they have to say and hang up, already halfway down the hall.

*It's only because she's going to get herself into trouble. I'm just looking out for her.*

But as I get behind the wheel, even though I've had a few drinks, I know it's a hell of a lot more than that.

My tempting little rainbow just won this round.

EVERYONE AT SK8 Land is decked out in neon colors and glow stick necklaces and bracelets, so I stand out in my dark work slacks and white button-down. A few people peer at me as I walk by, but no one greets me or acknowledges that the boss has arrived.

Roving spotlights dance over the giant skating rink, and dim recessed lights barely illuminate the surrounding area where people gather around tables of food. A particularly enthusiastic group in one corner is doing karaoke despite the loudspeakers playing classic 80s hits.

I keep to the shadows, searching for Lucy's red hair and sky-blue bodysuit. Finally, I find her talking to the guy from the photos with a red Solo cup in hand. They are secluded from everyone else, half in the shadows of a row of lockers.

Lucy tips her head back and lets out a loud peal of laughter at something he says. Red takes over my vision, and it's not from the flashing spotlights. I pull out my phone and dim the screen as low as it will go before sending her a message.

### LAWSON

Excuse yourself to the bathroom. Now.

Her phone lights up in her black, paint-splattered fanny pack, and without breaking eye contact with the guy, she pulls the device out before her eyes finally fall to the screen. A smirk pulls at the corner of her lips, and I realize two things simultaneously.

One: She *was* goading me to come out, and I fell for her little plan. And two: Lucy will definitely receive the spanking she desperately needs tonight.

Without waiting to see if she obeys me, I turn and walk to the bathrooms by the entrance. I purposefully parked nearby in the parking garage so that I could easily grab her and haul her ass to my vehicle without anyone seeing.

If Lucy wants to act like a little brat, then a punishment from Daddy is exactly what she will get. The whiskey swims in my veins, enough to create that floating feeling but not enough to hinder my ability to drive or give Lucy an orgasm after she's slept off all the alcohol in her system. I know it's a bad choice, and I know there will be consequences I'll have to deal with in the morning. But it's a problem I can deal with tomorrow.

Tonight, the little brat is *mine*.

### Lucy

Triumph rushes through my veins as I see Lawson's message. Did I know what I was doing when I kept uploading pictures of my cute outfit? And with Joey—who wants to jump Lawson's bones as much as I do? Of course, I did.

Lawson might tell himself that something between us isn't possible because of whatever x, y, or z problem he wants to come up with on any given day, but the fact that he's *here* only proves that we still have an undeniable pull to each other.

He wants to be my protector, and I want to snap his resolve like a rubber band. Judging by the angry look on his face, the rubber band is fraying.

"Well, hi, Mr. Morgan! It's so good of you to join us! I'm sure everyone will be thrilled to see you." Liquid courage has me doing a little spin for him. "Whatcha think? Did I manage to pull off the 80s vibe?"

"What did I tell you about drinking so much in public places?" he growls as he grabs my arm and pulls me to the exit. "Let's go."

"Hey! What the heck, Lawson? Where are we going?" My efforts to get him to slow down are futile as he drags me toward his car. "I'm not ready to leave yet. Stop!" I have to use all my weight to pull my arm from his grip.

When he spins around, I can smell the whiskey on his

breath as he crowds me against the wall of the parking garage. "Aren't you, Lucy? This is what you wanted, isn't it? For me to show up?"

Every part of me ignites at his strength. The way he grabs my wrists—gently but firmly—reminds me that he's bigger. Stronger. *Dominant.* And the need that flows through me—the need to make him lose control—is so powerful that I feel like I'm turning to liquid beneath his stony gray scowl.

"Because you can't resist a damsel in distress, can you?" I taunt.

"Only when it's you, rainbow." His smirk is downright treacherous.

I'm not prepared for him to bend and effortlessly throw me over his shoulder like a sack of potatoes. "Lawson! Put me down!" He braces his arm around my thighs as I beat on his back and kick my feet. I'm still wearing my roller skates, for Christ's sake. "Lawson!"

*Smack!*

The sound reverberates through the parking garage as a sharp sting blooms on my ass. *Did he just…?* "Did you just fucking *spank* me?"

"Yeah, and it probably made you wet, didn't it?" He smacks my ass again before curling his thumb between my legs, pressing it directly over my clit. A sharp moan flies from my lips as my back arches.

"Lawson," I cry his name like a plea, fisting the back of his shirt as he swipes over me again and again, pressing harder each time. Arousal leaks out of me, drenching the thin spandex material of my bodysuit and leggings.

He chuckles darkly. "Just like I thought, fucking soaked."

When we reach his car, he walks to the passenger side and sets me down, rotating his hand to swipe along my center. As I wobble on my skates, I reach behind me for the car to steady myself, and his deep stormy eyes hold mine as he brings his fingers to his mouth and sucks them clean.

Without a second thought that someone might see us, I launch myself at him, holding onto the material of his shirt as I pull him down and smash my lips to his with a strangled moan. Lawson's hand finds my hip to steady us, and the other boxes me in against the car. Our lips mold together like they were created to fit that way, but I feel his hesitation, and all too soon, the kiss ends as he backs away.

"Fuck. We can't. Not like this," he whispers raggedly.

"I'm sick of hearing that. We *can*." I hate how needy I sound as I reach for him again. Just moments ago, I held the power, and now I'm back to being putty in his hands that he's just playing with, always warping and bending to his will, never forming something solid—something substantial.

He clutches my wrists, holding them between us, pressing his forehead to mine. "You're drunk. I won't make that mistake with you again."

Trying my best to feign indifference, I shrug. "Fine. Then I'll go back to the party."

"The hell you will," he growls before his lips descend on mine again.

Lawson drags me to the front of the car, which is thankfully facing away from the entrance to Sk8 Land. He hauls me onto the hood, knocking my body back with his sheer size as his hands and lips roam everywhere. It tickles when he nuzzles my neck, breathing hot air just below my ear before nipping my skin.

"You've been such a bad girl tonight, haven't you?"

Electricity hits my clit at his words, and a pleasing trill rumbles through my chest as he caresses my sides, thumbs flicking over my nipples before continuing down, down, down, between my legs to grab the spandex. Effortlessly, Lawson rips both my bodysuit and leggings, baring my most sensitive part to the cool night air.

It's possessive and feral and utterly savage. And I love every second of it.

"You gave me that password because you wanted to make your daddy mad, didn't you?" He sinks his fingers into me. One, then two. His thumb slides against my clit, stroking me repeatedly with circular patterns that generate pulses that drift down to my toes.

My skates are heavy on my feet, weighing my legs down as he moves between them. "Oh, fuck. Lawson!"

"You're lucky I don't bend you over and make that ass red, rainbow." His fingers thrust deeper before he pulls out and slams them back in. "Or maybe that's what you've wanted all along, is that it?"

Each pass hits a spot inside me I haven't felt in so long. Heat blooms throughout my whole body, coiling tighter and tighter, making my toes curl, and my fingers twist roughly in his shirt. The car shakes beneath us, and I know that at any moment, anyone can leave the party and see that two people are fucking around. *Hear* the wetness that Lawson pulls from me with each stroke. I sink my teeth into the muscled flesh of his neck, muffling my screams so I don't cry out his name again.

"That's it." I open my eyes, pulling back to see him staring at where his fingers are inside me. "Come for me like a good fucking girl. Drench my fingers and make a mess for me, Lucy."

"Fuuuuck, Lawson!" My keening wail is muffled as he slams a palm over my mouth.

My body convulses as I come. Wave after wave crests through me as he continues pumping, my hips chasing his hand, prolonging my orgasm. Bright white spots explode behind my lids as I squeeze my eyes shut and yell my release against his warm skin.

Through it all, he murmurs in my ear, "Such a good fucking girl. Keep giving me more, rainbow. You're doing so good. You're making Daddy so proud."

Somewhere in the back of my mind, it registers that at any other time, calling a man other than my father "*Daddy*" would be a huge ick for me. But hearing it come from Lawson's lips makes me preen beneath his lusty gaze. I want to be his good girl. I also want to be his bad girl, pushing him to punish me in a way I crave—a way that only *he* can satisfy.

When my whimpering ceases, we stare at each other, breathing heavily as reality settles around us. I see it, the *oh shit* moment he has before he starts to panic.

"Fuck." He slides his fingers out of me and backs away from the car. "Fuck!" he shouts as he storms to the driver's side, causing me to jump as I attempt to cover the hole in my clothes as I stand.

"Lawson—"

"Get in the car."

Quietly, I do as he says, and he whips his suit jacket onto my lap. All the earlier dopamine fades as an unhealthy amount of uncomfortable adrenaline surges through my veins. "What's your address?"

"*Lawson*—"

His eyes snap to mine, causing me to shut my mouth. "Address, Lucy."

Tears sting my eyes as I clutch his jacket and relent. The smooth fabric feels cool between my fingers while I play idly with the edge of a lapel. "Why do you keep fighting this?"

A deep sigh leaves his chest. He runs a hand over his face before bracing an elbow on the edge of the window, propping his head against his fingers. "Because everything about it is wrong."

I blink away my tears. "Why is it wrong? We're two consenting adults who *want* each other. What is the problem with that?"

"Because you shouldn't want me!" he shouts, the loud exclamation booming through the car. "You should be at the party right now, with guys your age, not with your boss." I open my mouth to interrupt him, but he cuts me off. "The only reason you feel this way toward me is because of what happened on graduation night."

Confused, I shake my head. "I mean, not really. Things started happening before then."

He barks out a dry laugh. "No shit. And they shouldn't have. We should never have gone there. *I* should never have entertained it. And now, you *think* you want to be with me, but trust me, Lucy, you don't."

"Why?" I cry incredulously. "Why are you being so

stubborn about this? I think I'm capable of knowing what I want, Lawson!"

"But you didn't then! You were a child. And I knew better!"

"I was eighteen! That is considered an adult, isn't it? I mean, the consenting age in Illinois is seventeen, right? It could have been worse."

"God, Lucy, don't try to justify it that way. What happened was wrong. No matter how you look at it." As we stop at a light, he whispers, "It was so fucking wrong. Every single message you sent me, the need to see me and talk to me, it was all a trauma response."

*A trauma response?*

"What trauma? Lawson, you didn't traumatize me. You aren't making any sense," I argue, slapping the center console to try and get his attention. The light turns green, and he presses on the gas pedal.

"I did, though! And it wasn't fucking okay! What I did to you—" He roughly runs his hand through his hair, an exasperated huff expelling through his nose. "It was assault, Lucy."

An incredulous laugh erupts from my throat, and his storm cloud eyes snap sideways to look at me with an unapproving gleam in their depths. The skin around his knuckles turns white from how hard he's gripping the steering wheel.

"You're not... Are you serious? You think you *assaulted* me?" Utter disbelief shatters my composure. "You definitely did *not* assault me! If you don't remember, you tried to stop it. *I* didn't want to! If anything, I forced *you*."

"I was a grown-ass man. You didn't force me to do shit.

I willingly fucked around with you, knowing you were too young, knowing you were dating my son, and I didn't fucking care. I was selfish, and you were scarred because of it."

"Stop telling me I'm damaged," I snap, crossing my arms with a huff as I turn away from him. "You didn't *scar* me. I messaged you because I missed you. Because we had no time to explore our very obvious connection. That's it. End of your ridiculous excuses."

Another deep sigh sounds from his side of the car. He pulls onto my road as the honey locusts begin to sway in the wind, the rain clinging to their branches with the sudden downpour. Lawson turns on the windshield wipers, then the heat up a few notches as his gaze takes in my shivering body.

Always trying to make sure I'm comfortable.

We remain silent as he pulls up next to the curb, the only sounds coming from the whir of the heater and the wipers' rhythmic swipes as they chase the rain away.

After what seems like hours, he finally turns to me, remorse heavy in his eyes. "I wasn't trying to say you're damaged, Lucy. I just think that your attraction to me stems from an unhealthy place. I don't think you would have even given me a second thought if everything that happened hadn't."

"Well, it did, Lawson. It happened, and I don't fault you for any of it. I don't think you assaulted me, and I'm sorry that my age bothers you, but there's not a teen at the end of it anymore. I'm an actual adult with adult feelings, who makes big adult decisions. And I'm telling you that I want to explore this. Explore *us*." I plead with my eyes, my voice, my body language—everything to try and show him how serious I am about this... about *us*.

His remorse turns apologetic. Ice grips my heart, as cold and brutal as the storm picking up outside. "You've always been so gray and moody, like a storm. Beautiful in its ability to wash away the bad but still leaving devastation in its wake if it chooses to." I reach for the door handle, pulling it open as I lay his jacket on the seat behind me. "But you know what comes after a storm?" His eyebrows dart into his hairline briefly as he waits for me to answer. "Rainbows. We'd make a good pair if you'd just allow us to explore it."

His gaze drops to the console, his resolve firm as he stays silent.

I expect to be angry but find myself melancholy instead. "Goodnight, Lawson."

"Goodnight, Lucy." I exit the car and enter the storm, taking my time to let it wash away the desperation I always feel when I'm near him.

*It's time to let it go, Lucy. It's time to move on.*

After all, when a woman decides she's done with a man's shit, it's usually when he gets his act together.

Right?

# EIGHTEEN

*Lawson*

**USER NOT FOUND.**

My brows stitch together as I frown at my phone's screen. I type in Lucy's name again, but Iconic keeps saying the same thing.

**USER NOT FOUND.**

*Did she block me?*

Honestly, if she did, I don't blame her. I can probably win the Flakiest Person of the Year award without even trying.

I'd intended to make her mine, the whiskey swimming in my veins leading me to not make the most rational of decisions. But as she screamed her release into my hand, I had a startling realization that anyone could have heard us. Anyone could have *seen* us.

And that sobering thought had me running with my proverbial tail tucked between my legs once more.

Glancing up, I see she's engrossed in whatever she's working on at her desk. I was prepared for things to be awkward this morning when we got to work, but my usual coffee was waiting for me on my desk, and she politely asked if there was anything I needed her to move to the top of her task list like it was just another day between a typical boss and his assistant.

As if she can feel my stare, her eyes lift from the paper she's writing on, not to meet my gaze, but to focus on something random—as if she's assessing her surroundings like a rabbit who caught the scent of a fox upwind.

Gathering her things, she reaches for her coat as she powers down her computer. There's still an hour before work is over, but she looks like she's planning on leaving early anyway, which is odd given her normal work ethic.

I pretend to be busy with a file when she raps her knuckles on the door.

"Mr. Morgan? If you don't mind, I'm going to leave a little early today. I finished booking the hotel for the conference this weekend and finalized your attendance at the forums you wanted to sit in on." She approaches my desk and sets a folder down before slipping an emerald green trench coat over her garnet swing dress.

As she flips her hair out of the collar, I muster a smile and ask, "Hot date?"

It's a joke—a poorly timed, inappropriate, and absolutely downright disrespectful joke, given our circumstances.

Lucy doesn't find it amusing.

She purses her lips, staring at the papers on my desk instead of gracing me with her beautiful hazel irises.

"I'm sorry, that wasn't—"

Her tone is soft and a little unsure when she cuts me off. "Yes. As a matter of fact."

A fist curls around my chest. Large and icy, yet full of heat at the same time. The type of cold that burns and takes your breath away.

Her brows knit together as I cough to dislodge the horrible feeling. "Are you okay? Would you like me to go get you some water?"

Beating my chest, I shake my head. "I'm fine. Go ahead. I'll see you tomorrow."

A brief flash of disappointment dances across her face, as though she expected me to inquire more about it. "See you tomorrow, Mr. Morgan."

I don't ask her why she blocked me. Or why—if she is so adamant about giving us a try—she's already got a date lined up with another guy.

But I do message Jules and ask her if she can still see Lucy's account.

**JULES**

> The little cherry pop blocked me, too.
> Want me to get Cam to follow her?

*Fuck no.*

Am I really this desperate? This is what I wanted all along, isn't it? To dash any hope of a future for us?

*Then you probably shouldn't have finger-banged her on the hood of your car Friday night like a fucking asshole.*

I breathe deeply through my nose before letting it out in a long exhale.

Like I said, the Flakiest Person of the Year award goes to me.

## Lucy

"It was nice of Mr. Benson to let you leave early. I could have waited, sweetheart." My mother is all sunshine and smiles as she greets me.

For as long as I can remember, she's always been this ball of bright, bouncy energy. I've only seen her get truly upset a few times throughout my life, and as I remove my jacket to take a seat across from her at a cute little restaurant called Lotus, I wonder if this will be one of those times.

"Mr. Benson retired, remember? Do you remember Rhys' dad, Lawson? He's my boss now—or at least he will be for the next year while his company integrates us into its business model."

*There. The best way to deliver the news is by ripping off the Band-Aid.*

Surprisingly, Mom just continues browsing the wine selection as if we haven't been coming here for years. After all, my Aunt Charleigh's long-time boyfriend, Michael, owns the place. "I thought he moved to New York?"

Since I already know what I'm getting—because it's the same thing I get every time we're here—I pick at the edge of my napkin. "He did. Like I said, he's only going to be back for a year."

Mom waits until after we order a bottle of wine and our entrées to ask, "How do you feel about working for him?"

I blink, desperately trying to calm the pink hue I can feel warming my cheeks. "It's fine. He's a good boss. Everyone really likes him."

*Some of us a little too much.*

My mind drifts to how Lawson reacted when I told him I had a date. His abrupt and sudden changes in mood are getting tiresome, and a tiny evil seed unfurls in my brain—a twisted little thought of how I should compile a list of therapists and leave them on his desk in the morning.

A smile pulls at my lips that doesn't go unnoticed by Mom. "Are he and Charlotte still together?"

With a groan, I roll my eyes as our server returns and pours our syrah. "Married, yes. Together, no."

"How unfortunate for him to still be shackled to that absolutely horrid woman." Mom swirls and sniffs her wine before sipping it. She tucks her long, coppery locks behind an ear and fixes me with a knowing gaze. "Is he still good-looking?"

"Mom!" I laugh, reaching across the table to swat at her with my napkin. "I thought you had an issue with us being... friendly, for lack of a better word."

"I mean, yeah, you were a child, Lucy. I just wanted to make sure things were all appropriate over at the Morgan household. You're an adult now, though. Not that I'm saying it's appropriate *now*, but we can appreciate how handsome he's always been without it sounding like I condone pedophilia." She shudders and takes a long sip from her glass.

"Eww, Mom, gross."

She peers over the rim of her glass at me with an unreadable expression. "Didn't you say you'd be out of town this weekend for a conference? Does that mean you two will be going away together for the weekend?"

"Yes, but it's not like that. And honestly, it's weird to be talking about this with you. You're my mom. He's my boss. End of discussion." I wonder why she's acting like she wouldn't be entirely against the idea. She certainly hadn't liked the thought of Lawson and me being in the same room while I was in nothing but Rhys' jersey.

Mom sets her glass down as our pre-dinner salads arrive and raises her hands in mock surrender. "Okay, then. Have you talked to your brother lately?" she asks, abruptly changing the subject.

I nod, and she launches into a tirade about something new Liam has done to upset her and my dad. Having heard it all before, I let my thoughts drift to how the weekend will go. It's a short plane ride to the northern shore of Lake Michigan, and the weekend is packed with forums and meet and greets, networking opportunities, and dinner on Sunday that everyone is expected to attend.

I don't think it's normal for people to bring their assistants, but I've already packed a few new outfits—classic cuts and mostly bland colors—so I won't stand out and embarrass Lawson amongst his peers. But an entire weekend away together?

Lord, give me strength.

# Nineteen

## *Lucy*

As I navigate through the crowd of business suits and office-appropriate dresses cluttering the hotel lobby, I see Lawson right where I left him, arguing with someone on the phone.

His attention is laser-focused on grilling whoever is on the other end of the line, so he pays no attention to the appreciative glances he receives from random women as they pass—women his age who probably know exactly how to please him.

His navy suit is impeccable, clinging to every muscle without looking ill-fitted. He's clean-shaven, and though I prefer him with a short beard, the new grooming routine shaves years off his appearance.

Rumor around the office is that everyone hooks up with everyone at these conferences. Is that why he cleaned up? Is he trying to look more desirable so he can spend his weekend evenings shacking up with a pretty face?

Irritated with my self-imposed spiral, I patiently wait for him to finish his call, pasting on a smile for anyone who bothers to make eye contact with me. Chadwick never attended these conferences, and I want to make a good impression. I like the industry, and if I don't stay with M.I.G., this will be a good networking opportunity for me.

"Sorry about that." Lawson shakes his phone in frustration before pocketing it. "Charlotte is up to her usual bullshit."

Typically, I would ask what she did, but I've been doing exceptionally well all week in keeping our relationship strictly professional.

"I'm sorry to hear that." I extend my hand to give him his room key. "A suite, as requested. Since the welcome party is tonight, I didn't make you a dinner reservation, but if you'd like to message me which restaurant you'd prefer for dinner tomorrow, I can set that up right away. I'm a few floors down from you on the other side of the hotel, but if you need anything tonight, let me know. Otherwise, I'll see you in the morning."

"In the morning? You're not going to the welcome party?"

Butterflies erupt in my stomach at the way he looks at me. It's wholly innocent, yet sensual, as he steps into my personal space. "I wasn't aware you wanted me to attend."

His lips curl up in a smile, and my insides melt despite my every silent wish for them to remain very much intact. "Did you think I wanted you to come away for the weekend only to make you sit in your room the whole time? Did you bring a dress?" I nod, not trusting my mouth. "Good. Meet me back down here at seven."

After another silent nod from me, he strides toward the elevators for his side of the hotel without another word, greeting various people and even shaking hands with a few of them as he stops and talks for a few seconds. I glance at my phone and realize it's already five-thirty. That barely leaves me any time to get ready. I hightail it to my room to get started on hair and makeup, incredibly thankful that I packed my travel steamer.

The welcome party's dress code is cocktail attire, and though I wasn't expecting to go, I did pack a dress.

You know, just in case.

### Lawson

Lucy's late.

To be fair, I know most women take a long time to get ready for an event like this, and I didn't exactly give her a heads-up that I wanted her to attend. So that's on me.

Even among people I've known from the industry for years, though, it feels wrong knowing she's somewhere in the hotel and not here by my side.

"So, Lawson, back to Chicago, eh? Missing New York yet?" Richard Dorsen asks, clapping a hand on my shoulder as he and a group of guys from the Minneapolis branch gather around. Richard is a few years younger than I am and damn good at his job, though I'd never tell him that. Humble isn't in his vocabulary, and he'll tell anyone who listens that he's their branch's top executive.

"Bet you're missing Jules, aren't ya? She's a fine piece of ass. Too bad she didn't come this time," Luke Pierce, a man as greasy as his slicked-back hair, states with a smarmy smirk.

I ignore his taunt, addressing Dorsen instead. "Chicago

is more welcoming than I remember. The office has been great. I'm in no hurry to return to the city."

"I can't believe you turned down Danvers' position, man. That would have been one hell of a raise."

I'm about to tell him I don't need the money when he chokes on his drink. "Jesus fucking Christ. Who's the lucky bastard that landed *that* piece of artwork?"

The entire group glances toward what's caught his attention, and my blood warms in my veins as I see Lucy walking through the door. Her late arrival is well the fuck worth it. She's styled her hair in glamorous waves and darkened her makeup slightly. The only bright color she wears is a ruby red shade of lipstick, and I feel the slightest twinge of disappointment seeing her without her typical color palette. The black silk of her one-sleeve, asymmetric dress hugs her curves, and the slit in the skirt borders on indecent, making me imagine all the ways I can peel the dress off her body later.

Our gazes connect across the giant space, and her lips widen just a bit with an unsure smile as she takes a step toward our group.

"Please tell me she's single. Does anyone know who she is?" Dorsen asks.

Numerous murmurs break out, signaling that none of the men saw us arrive together earlier. Swinging my gaze his way, I frown as he watches Lucy with a predatory glint in his eyes, every protective instinct in me firing off at once.

"She's min—" I catch myself before finishing my abrupt response, "My assistant."

"Hook a guy up, why don't you?" Dorsen mutters before Lucy reaches us.

"Everyone, this is Lucy Bradee. Lucy, this is Luke, Richard, Brant, and Tyson." I introduce her and point to everyone in the group.

"Hello." She looks fucking adorable as she gives a little wave. "I'm Lucy." She's nervous, and it probably doesn't help that all of them are salivating over her like a hungry pack of hyenas.

Dorsen steps toward her, hand outstretched as a charming smile takes over his face. "Richard Dorsen. Nice to meet you."

Lucy blushes a pretty rose under his attention, making my insides roil with disgust. "Nice to meet you, too."

"A beautiful lady like yourself shouldn't be empty-handed. Would you like a drink?"

I inwardly kick myself for not being the first to offer because now I'm going to be worried about her drinking around these wolves all night.

"Oh!" Her eyes dart to me. "I would love one, actually."

As he offers her his arm, someone behind us yells out his name. A wave of relief washes over me. Turning, I see his boss and silently thank the old man for unknowingly keeping my rainbow out of trouble.

"Come on, I'll take you." My hand settles on the small of her back. "Better run along, Dorsen."

He laughs awkwardly, still showering Lucy with all his attention and his stupid, charming smile. "Duty calls. Maybe I'll see you around this weekend?"

To my displeasure, she returns his smile and flirtatiously replies, "Maybe."

As I lead her away, she peers up at me. "He was nice."

"They're all nice when they want something." I refuse

to look at her for longer than a second. I don't want to get wrapped up in her hazel irises. They're glowing with mirth and drawing me in like a moth to a flame. "A few of the higher-ups brought their assistants, too. I figured I could introduce you, and maybe you could mingle with them."

"That would be great, actually. I know you have other things to do, and while I normally don't have any problems making friends, for some reason, I'm really nervous," she admits as we step up to the bar.

She orders a shot, but I shake my head and tell the bartender, "No shots for this one tonight. Get her a Paloma."

Lucy flattens her brows. "Thanks, Dad."

My cock twitches at the same time she realizes her mistake, and horror crosses her face. "Shit. I'm sorry."

"It's fine." After a few moments of silence while we wait for her drink, I say, "You look beautiful."

She doesn't look at me. No, she keeps staring at the bar top, fingers playing with the edge of a drink napkin. "Thank you." Her voice is filled with so much self-control that I have to applaud her.

Lucy's trying not to trigger me—to start something between us that I keep saying I don't want but still continue pursuing her for. And not once, until now, have I realized how hard it might be for her—to have to dull herself down so our playful natures don't tempt and tangle the way they naturally do so easily.

After the bartender hands her a pastel peach drink, I lead her to a group of people I recognize as assistants from past conferences. With them, she seems much more like herself.

And she doesn't even blink when I'm called away to talk to someone else.

Lucy's laughter rings out through the room as she parts ways with a few other women, and I catch the tail end of their conversation—something about meeting up at the spa tomorrow.

"You seem like you had a good time tonight." I brush my fingers against the small of her back as I lead her out of the conference hall. "Come on, I'll walk you to your room."

"I had a great time! The girls and I are going to have a spa day tomorrow while you are stuck in stuffy forums all day." She shoves a finger into my chest while we wait for the elevator, and her traitorous lilt gives away the fact that Lucy is, at least, a little buzzed.

Snatching her finger before she can pull away, I slip into the elevator with her and slam my hand against the close button before anyone else can grab this one with us. With my fragile hold, I back her up against the side of the compartment.

"Whatever you want, charge it to my room."

Wide hazel irises gaze up at me in awe as pink spreads from her cheeks to her neck. "I'm not going to argue with that."

Unfairly, I whisper, "Good girl."

A small whimper escapes from between her lips. Her eyes drop to my mouth, and I so badly just want to say,

"Fuck it." Slowly, I brush some hair off her shoulder, lightly running my fingertips against her bare skin. She shudders, and my cock hardens.

Something unrecognizable flashes over her face as the elevator dings and the doors open—something that makes her remember that we shouldn't be in this position. Yanking away from me, she storms out and down the hall toward her room.

I calmly watch as she fumbles with her purse to retrieve her key card, and just as the green light flashes after she swipes it, I catch her around the waist, forcing her to turn and look at me.

"Hey."

When she refuses to look at me, I bring my fingers under her chin to lift her gaze to mine. "Lucy?"

She swallows, batting those thick lashes of hers up at me, and her ruby-painted lips part as she breathes, "Yes?"

I allow my eyes to drift down her body slowly, taking in every single inch of her that I want to devour—want to lay claim to like the monster I am. "I don't ever want to see you wear black again. While you look beautiful, it's not *you*. Do you understand?"

Her pretty blush deepens to a cherry red, breaking out along her cheeks and the bridge of her nose. "Y-yes, sir."

Flashing her a fiendish smile, I slide my hands into my pockets to keep myself from backing her into the hotel room and painting every inch of her flesh with *me*.

"Such a good girl," I whisper, loving the way her breath hitches and her breasts heave against the tight fabric encasing them.

With every ounce of strength I possess, I turn away and

don't look back as I wait for the elevator to take me far away from the tempting woman.

Heaving a sigh, I step into the metal box and wait to turn around until the doors shut behind me. One thing is very clear: This weekend will either end with my balls as blue as a Smurf or as deep inside her as possible while my resolve goes on an extended vacation.

# TWENTY

*Lawson*

As a forum about the trending market report on rental increases comes to a close, Dorsen approaches me with a look of uncertainty. "Hey, so uh, I hope this isn't weird or anything, but I was wondering if you knew if Lucy is seeing anyone?"

Irritation prickles down my spine, licking at my nerve endings, and I surprise myself when I answer him honestly. "To my knowledge, no, she's not seeing anyone."

"Damn lucky for me then, eh?" He waggles his eyebrows. "Do you mind if I take her to dinner tonight?"

"Didn't realize you were into teenagers, Dorsen," I grumble, lifting my gaze to catch a pretty blonde peering at me over his shoulder. She's talking to a brunette, and they're both looking at me like they're deciding who will approach me.

"Aww, come on. You have eyes, Lawson. She's a total knockout. If Clemmens hadn't kept me wrapped up all night kissing the Los Angeles branch's ass, I'd have taken her back to my room."

My eyes veer to his slowly, an unamused glare settling over my face. "Lucy isn't that type of girl. So, if that's what you're looking for—a quick conference fuck—you can forget it."

"That's not the type of girl you fuck and leave in a hotel room on a weekend. That's wifey right there, Law." He chucks my shoulder like we're pals. We aren't good enough friends—merely work acquaintances—for him to use a nickname with me. And I find his definition of Lucy extremely bothersome.

Like I don't know she's wife material? Any man would be fucking lucky to have her on his arm.

I've been replaying last night over and over again in my mind. I could have pushed her into that hotel room, and she would have let me have my way with her—let me ravish her body until she was a puddle in the middle of the bed. But I know myself. I would have left and tried to say it didn't mean anything.

I would have fucked things up between us for good.

I'm confusing *myself* with my conflicting emotions. I can't even begin to fathom how she's feeling.

One thing I know for certain, though? She won't give Dorsen the time of day.

"Put in a good word for me, eh?" He elbows my ribs. "Maybe I'll be taking her off your hands by the time the next big party rolls around."

As he walks off, the blonde approaches me. "Lawson Morgan! It's so good to see you!" She presses up on her toes to kiss my cheek as she grips my bicep for balance.

"You as well..." I nod politely, unsure if I'm supposed to know who this woman is.

"Judy Bell, we met in New York last summer. I'm an acquaintance of Jules'."

Quickly, I search my memory, but come up short, so I lie, "Ah. That's right. How are you?"

"Dying to finish that night we started... if you know what I mean?" She runs a finger down my chest. "I'm in room 1375 if you want to... catch up."

The insinuation that anything happened between us last year makes me queasy. I have better taste than a box-colored blonde with bubblegum lips and lashes thick enough to look like caterpillars hanging over her mousy brown eyes.

Being the gentleman I am, though, I flash her a suave smile. "Kind of you to think of me. Perhaps I'll see you later."

I don't wait for an answer before fleeing, rushing toward the lobby. It's fate that I happen to run into Lucy halfway to the elevator. She's wrapped in a fluffy robe, her hair tied up in a large white towel, fresh-faced and looking downright fucking beautiful with her glowing skin and bubbly aura.

"Hey! How was the forum?"

"Boring. Honestly, nothing I didn't know already." I nod to the towel. "How was the spa?"

"Heavenly." She grins mischievously. "I might have given your credit card a workout."

With a laugh, I wipe a stray strand of copper hair off her forehead. "That's good. You deserve it. Besides, you might have dinner plans tonight. Dorsen wants to take you out." I don't know what makes me say it because internally, I scream at myself as soon as the words are out of my mouth.

Her face turns pink, and it's not a side effect of her facial. "Well... how would *you* feel if I went to dinner with him?"

*What the actual fuck?*

Furrowing my brows, I frown at her as I place my hands on my hips like a disapproving father. "You're actually interested in that guy?"

With a slight shrug, she coyly peers up at me through her lashes—they're perfect, naturally thick, and not at all like caterpillars. "Sure. Why not?"

Rage floods my system, setting every warning bell in my body off. My brain flashes a big, red "*NO*" symbol, telling my body to cool off and remain calm. I count to ten, focusing on my breathing as she analyzes my face, no doubt searching for my reaction.

"You're a grown woman." I finally relent. "You're free to do whatever you want. I don't care."

Her shoulders drop slightly before she catches herself and draws her body up to full height. "Okay, then I'll go," she informs me in that bratty tone that has my palm twitching. "Have a good night, Mr. Morgan."

She brushes past me, and even though I want to yell at her to come back so I can tell her I don't want her to go, I remain silent, inwardly chastising myself for delivering her to Dorsen on a silver fucking platter.

## Lucy

I check my appearance in the mirror one last time before I head downstairs. Sometime between running into Lawson in the lobby and my next appointment at the spa—

hello, hot stone massage—Richard asked the front desk to patch a call to my room, leaving a message asking me to dinner at the hotel's fancy Greek restaurant.

Do I want to go on a date with Richard Dorsen? No.

Am I going just to get under Lawson's skin? Abso-fuck-ing-lutely I am.

I've been damn good all week, and then that fucker goes and pulls the shit he did last night—walking me to my door, calling me a good girl like he doesn't know it makes my panties flood, and touching me the way he did.

Lawson Morgan is the ultimate definition of the word "whiplash." The man has no fucking clue what he wants. Well... he does. He wants me. I *know* he does. But the constant back and forth, the let me get intimate with you only to push you away afterward?

That shit stops now.

Time to put up some fucking boundaries, Lucy.

I primp in the elevator, pushing my hands through my tousled curls to make them look extra mussed, ensuring my red lipstick isn't out of place or smudged on my teeth, and adjusting the sweetheart neckline of my mini emerald-colored dress to make sure my boobs look incredible.

Lawson won't see me tonight, but it doesn't mean Richard won't brag about it to his friends later.

My date is waiting for me in the lobby. He turns when I call his name, and his crystal blue eyes darken as they inch down the length of my body. I give him a little show, tensing my thighs at his perusal, knowing he'll notice and think his attention turns me on.

Men like Richard don't interest me. He's handsome

and charming, but he's a damn cocky bastard who thinks I'm a sure thing.

"Wow, you look incredible," he compliments me as he kisses my cheek.

"Thank you. You're looking dapper yourself." He does, and his easy smile tells me he knows it, too.

Richard is as tall as Lawson, built like a model, with a trim figure but not overly muscular. But my breath doesn't quicken at the thought of what his powerful arms would feel like wrapped around me—of what his strength would feel like in bed as he forces me to my knees to take his length.

No, those are thoughts reserved only for Lawson, apparently.

Stupid hormones won't listen to my stupid heart.

Or maybe they are, and they just know that the heart wants what the heart wants.

"I hope you're hungry. This place has amazing moussaka." Richard wraps his arm around my waist, and I immediately do not like his touch. It's possessive and heavy, and we've barely known each other for twenty-four hours. It's unwelcome and nothing like Lawson when he guides me by lightly touching my back, but I do nothing to remove it.

"Starved," I lie.

Honestly, I ate a lot of snacks in the spa relaxation center and drank a lot of champagne. Even though I chugged copious amounts of water—as you should on a spa day—and took a nap before getting ready for tonight, my head is still fuzzy, and my stomach is in knots.

Richard opens the restaurant's glass door with OPA! sprawled across it in elegant, frosted script before giving the hostess his name for our reservation. The establishment is cute. It's dimly lit and covered in greenery. A heavy garlic scent permeates the air, laced with a slightly acidic fragrance, and it smells good enough to make me wish I were hungry. Honestly, I'm bummed I'll have to miss a full meal at this place.

*I wonder if I can eat here tomorrow while Lawson attends the goodbye dinner.*

The hostess leads us to a double-sided, leathery, eggplant-colored booth. It's near the back and out of view from most of the other tables—something Richard probably asked for when he made the reservation.

"Well, this is cozy," he exclaims with glee, as if he didn't already know we would be sequestered away from the rest of the restaurant.

I expect him to sit across from me, but to my surprise—and slight annoyance—he slides in next to me until our thighs are touching, swinging his arm around me to rest on the back of the booth.

"Whatever you want to get, get it. Don't be afraid to eat in front of me. I like a woman with an appetite." Richard flips open a menu, nudging it between us to share like I'm incapable of looking at my own. "Hmm... I'm thinking something light. I wouldn't want to get too weighed down." He flashes me a wicked smile. "Want to keep our energy up for whatever else the night brings."

"And what exactly do you think you're getting out of me tonight?" I ask in a thick, saccharine-laced tone with a sweet smile. "Because if it's what I think you're implying, I'm not that kind of girl."

Richard laughs and turns all his attention to me. "I'm sorry. I'm probably coming off a little strong, aren't I?"

*Gee, buddy. You think?*

I blink my lashes at him expectantly, waiting for him to continue.

"Look, all I'm saying is that when I see something I want, I go for it. And I know I can be a little overbearing about it, so forgive me. I just know that you're special. And I want to get to know you. Beyond this weekend, you know? Minneapolis isn't that far from Chicago. We can make it work," he explains like it's already a sure thing.

"Wooow." I draw out the word while he starts perusing the menu. "You got all that from one little old, '*hi, my name is...*' huh?"

*Why am I smiling? This isn't cute behavior.*

Richard's hand flexes where it rests on the table, and a moment later, he pulls his arm away and downs half his water in two gulps.

*He's nervous. And dammit, why am I finding it endearing?*

To be fair, it's in a pitying sort of way. Like how you feel bad for the little guy who just wants to get the pretty woman's attention, but she's more interested in the muscle man even though she probably knows he'll be disappointing in bed, and the other guy will probably rock her world.

Not that I think Richard could rock my world.

*Coooool. Cool, Lucy. Now you're internally rambling. Why did I agree to this?*

I'm about to open my mouth and tell him there's nothing to be nervous about when a man clearing his throat interrupts me. Lawson is standing near our table, his hand on the back of some pretty blonde woman.

Jealousy curls its evil, green talons into my lungs, filling the holes they create with a poison so thick and noxious I have to reach for my water to dilute the bile that rises in my throat.

"Well, funny we should run into you guys tonight," Lawson drawls. The blonde looks between us, him, and the hostess waiting for them four tables away.

"Yeah, funny, eh?" Richard bites out. He leans back against the booth, swinging his arm around me once more, and Lawson's gray eyes darken to storm clouds as he tracks the movement.

"Why don't we all have dinner together?" My boss suggests, already ushering the blonde into the booth across from us.

"Well, u-uh... I mean... it's kinda weird, isn't it?" she stammers.

Richard makes a sound of agreement, narrowing his eyes at Lawson like he's trying to pierce his soul with his gaze—a silent, *what the fuck are you doing*, etched across his features.

"Oh, I don't think so. Lucy and I have dinner quite often back in Chicago. She's fond of my parmesan potatoes." He signals to the hostess. "We'll be dining with them."

*Is he for fucking real?*

I haven't had his parmesan potatoes since high school. And we *don't* have "dinner quite often," as he so shamelessly puts it, trying to imply that we're close—which we *are,* but... he's doing this on purpose!

Lawson ignores my glare, beaming his gorgeous smile at each of us before focusing on the menu. The blonde woman peers at me across the table, her brown eyes flitting over my neckline before darting back to Lawson, no doubt assessing our relationship regardless of company policy.

Suddenly, I realize I'm even less hungry than before.

When our waitress arrives, I smile sweetly up at her and ask for a shot of tequila, delighted that Lawson doesn't object with words—only his disapproving stare and an arched brow.

"And please, keep them coming."

THE WAITRESS DOES NOT, in fact, keep them coming.

Lawson cuts me off after two, even though Richard seems more than willing to let me drown myself in Patrón, and makes sure I order more than just the salad I was prepared to pick at.

Richard and Marilyn Monroe seem to be hitting it off spectacularly, though. If I have to listen to another one of his ice fishing stories, I'm going to bang my head against the glass table.

As it is, Lawson is currently telling Richard all the reasons he's wrong for using artificial bait, and I want to plug my ears because I hate fishing. I hate how this evening is going, and all I want to do is climb back into my fluffy robe, spread out on my big, comfy bed, and fall asleep to a rom-com.

Marilyn—yes, I'm aware her name is Judy—bats her falsies between them like she wants to drizzle chocolate on them both and eat them for dessert.

Richard nudges my shoulder to pull me into him, and his lips ghost over my ear as he whispers loudly, "Why don't we take this party away from your overbearing boss?"

Marilyn pouts and glances at Lawson, who looks like he's about to leap over the table and shove my date's face down into what's left of his moussaka. I play into it, turning my head, which brings our faces so close together that his lips could brush against mine with the slightest movement.

"Okay."

A flash of excited surprise fills his blue eyes before he lifts his hand to try and signal our waitress for the check.

Continuing to ignore Lawson, I place my hand on Richard's thigh. "Would you mind letting me out? I'd like to freshen up before we leave," I state with the sultriest lilt I can muster.

The man nearly trips over himself as he scrambles out of the booth so fast it's comical. I press my hand to his chest and give him a demure "thank you" before walking toward the bathroom, making sure to put a little extra sway in my hips for Lawson to stare at.

I figure I have about two to three minutes to think of an excuse to go back to my room—*alone*—before it looks like I'm taking a poo instead of checking my appearance.

*That's actually a good excuse! Tell Richard your souvlaki isn't settling right, and you aren't feeling well.*

When I open the door, no one else occupies the bathroom. It's small, with only two stalls, but clean.

Leaning against the vanity, I check that my lipstick isn't smudged or worn off too badly. And a few seconds later, my heart jumps into my throat as the door slams open. Lawson storms in, locking the door behind him.

"Lawson! What are you—" My words die in my throat as he lifts his hand to collar my neck, walking me backward until I'm pressed against the wall.

"Are you *trying* to piss me off?" Fire and brimstone fill his gravelly tone with so much heat it sends a slick wave of arousal between my legs.

His reaction fills me with something I can only describe as immense power. Like it doesn't matter what I say. This man is ready to drop to his knees to prove that he's the only one I should be leaving this restaurant with.

"I thought you didn't care?" I arch a brow, relishing how his nostrils flare at my daring question.

"I didn't want to, but it turns out that I do. I very much fucking *do*," he growls. "Now, you don't want to be here anymore than I do, isn't that right, rainbow?"

Lawson's so authoritative, demanding my compliance with a squeeze as his other hand drifts down my belly to the hem of my dress. Silently, I shake my head slightly.

"That's right. You'd rather be naked, spread out on my bed, waiting for me to spank your ass so hard you won't be able to sit for a week." He presses against me, swiping his fingers up the center of my thong, where I'm wet and needy and desperate to feel his touch. I whimper as his lips ghost my skin. "And then, when you've been thoroughly punished, I'm going to spread those thighs and eat your pussy for dessert before I fuck you bare and fill you so full of my cum, you'll never forget who your daddy is because I'll be dripping between your legs for the rest of your life."

*God, yes.*

My body screams for his touch, but my heart shudders at his words. *For the rest of your life.*

So possessive. So final. But at this point, he's primed me to expect his immediate dismissal whenever we get intimate, and it isn't fair.

My voice is hoarse when I reply, "You can't keep doing this, Lawson. You can't keep saying you want me and then telling me we can't."

I feel betrayed when tears prick my eyes, but he leans forward and kisses them away. The touch is so featherlight I barely feel it.

"I'm done fucking around, Lucy." He shoves my underwear to the side and plunges two fingers into me.

A gasp flies from my mouth and into his as he lays his lips over mine, swallowing every sound I make as he pumps in deep, quick, hard, and so fucking good that he has me coming in under a minute.

I don't even register what's happening as he pulls his fingers out and shoves them in my open mouth.

"Do you taste this?" Instinctively, I close my lips around them and suck my essence off him. "This is what only *I* can do to you."

Lawson kisses me once more, then releases my throat and steps back to fix my dress. He pulls out his room key and hands it to me. "You have five minutes to go upstairs and get ready. I'll tell your *date* you aren't feeling well."

*Ready? Ready for what? Is this finally happening?*

My internal questions must be obvious on my face

because his gaze softens, and he reaches up to brush his knuckles along my cheek. "Tonight, I'm going to finally make you mine, Lucy Bradee. Tomorrow, you will still be mine, and I plan on spending as much time as possible fucking that fact into you until it's engrained on your fucking soul."

So poetic, and downright fucking filthy, and utterly romantic.

His voice is low and husky. "Clock is ticking, rainbow. Get going before I fuck you right here. My self-control is close to snapping, and you deserve better than being fucked on a dirty restaurant vanity."

I've never power-walked so damn fast in my life.

# TWENTY-ONE

## Lucy

By the time I make it to Lawson's room, I'm hot and bothered.

A million questions race through my brain.

*Should I wait on the bed?*

*Should I take off my clothes?*

*Will he change his mind in the next five minutes?*

I swear to god if Lawson changes his mind, I'll submit my resignation and move out of state. I can't continue this back-and-forth game of cat and mouse. It reminds me of a movie I watched once where a girl drunk-dialed a man she interviewed after they shared an obvious connection.

*Come here... no, stay away.*

Story of my life lately.

I'm so lost in thought that I don't even hear the door open. As it clicks shut, I spin around, mouth open in surprise. Lawson stands just inside the door, chest heaving like he ran up the stairs instead of using the elevator, hair disheveled as though he's been running his hands through it. Just the sight of him sets everything on fire all over again.

We stare at each other, the liquid pool between my legs igniting from the heat in his eyes. The *hunger.*

"You have ten seconds to change your mind about this, Lucy," he warns.

Taking a step forward, he undoes the button on his suit jacket, removing it and flinging it onto an armchair.

"Why would I want to change my mind?" My voice is breathy. Hoarse. *Needy.* There's no mistaking my feelings.

"Because you don't understand what you're getting into. I'm not the same man I was." His statement intrigues me. With every step, he pops a button on his dress shirt, slipping his shoes off and kicking them to the side. "There are many reasons I keep saying we can't be together. I feel so fucking feral when you're in the same room as me, and I don't want to scare you with my intensity."

Slipping out of my heels, I reach for the zipper on my dress, and a shiver runs through me at the low growl that emanates from Lawson's chest as I slowly pull it down. "Have you thought that maybe, instead of frightening me, it would be exactly what I need? What I *want.*"

With his shirt fully unbuttoned, he removes his belt, and I can't help the low whimper that escapes my throat at the promise of what the thick, dark brown leather will feel like against my skin. He said he'd spank me. The mere thought of being completely naked and bared to him while he paints my skin pink has me so swollen with desire that the slightest movement of my underwear against my clit sends a jolt through my center.

Still, I voice my fears when he doesn't answer me. "I'm afraid that if this happens, you will turn me away afterward. I don't know if I can survive it again, Lawson."

His eyes soften for a fraction of a second, and he stops approaching. We're at least ten steps away from each other now, the space between us filled with so much thick tension I can feel it licking across my skin in searing hot waves.

"I have fucking *tried*. So help me, God, I have tried not to want you. Tried not to think about you. I have told myself over and over again that this can't happen. But no matter how hard I try, I can't stay away from you. And I'm done trying to fight it. I'm so fucking done."

It's everything I've wanted to hear from him since that night in his office. I can hear that he means it this time. There will be no turmoil once the post-release bliss fades away.

I let the dress slide from my body, revealing the set of lingerie I wore for no one but me, but bought with him in mind. It's all black lace and satin, and the bodice is strapped to the band of the matching thong.

Lawson's eyes rove over my body as he removes his shirt, throat bobbing thickly as he takes me in. "I thought I told you I didn't want to see you in black again?" His voice is so low and husky. So incredibly fucking sexy.

A smirk pulls at my lips, instinct taking over as I turn and lift a knee onto the mattress, slowly climbing on as I hold his heated gaze and arch my back, poised with my ass pushed out. "Are you going to punish me, *Daddy*?"

"Little fucking brat," he growls in an amused whisper.

The outline of his cock is large and straining against his pants, and he palms it to adjust himself as he closes the distance between us, belt in hand.

My skin breaks out in goosebumps as he positions himself behind me, collaring my neck to force my head up until I'm looking at him upside down. "You're so beautiful, Lucy. I'm going to enjoy making a mess of this perfect image you painted for another man."

I don't correct him. Don't explain that I had no intention of letting Richard see what was underneath my dress. Lawson dips his head to capture my mouth, ravishing me with hungry lips as his other hand reaches around to palm one of my breasts.

His thumb flicks over a hardened nipple, and our tongues caress for a few seconds before he abruptly lets me go and shoves me down to the mattress, grabbing my hips to lift my ass in the air.

"How many do you think you can take, rainbow?" His palms are warm as they massage my cheeks before spreading them apart to view the glistening mess between my thighs.

It's dirty and depraved, and I've never been more turned on in my life. "I don't know. I've never been spanked before."

A low, dark chuckle sounds behind me. I can just imagine him staring at my pussy, and the image makes me squirm in his hold. Suddenly, something lands on the bed next to my head. His belt.

"Did you think I'd strike you with that the first time I get to taste your flesh?" A thumb dips between my legs to gather my wetness and smear it along my center.

Fire. Everything feels like it's on fire as he kneads my skin roughly—his grip tightening with each pass.

*Smack!*

A keening wail thrums in my throat. It's only a light slap against my left cheek, but it makes everything low in my belly tighten.

"I asked you a question, Lucy. I expect an answer."

This time, when his palm meets my flesh, it's sharper. More intentional. And he groans as I whine, "Yes."

"Yes, what, rainbow? Yes, you thought I'd use the belt? Or yes, you want more?" There's a tearing sound and a sharp tug as he rips my underwear off.

"More. Fuck, Lawson. Give me more." I arch my back and push my ass up higher in the air.

"God, you're perfect. So fucking needy and so fucking soaked, just waiting for me to drink you down." Another smack against my ass, closer to my throbbing pussy. I widen my legs, shamelessly begging for my punishment.

I never in a million years thought calling him *Daddy* and begging to be spanked was what would get me going. How do people even find out they're into this kind of stuff?

Lawson delivers one final slap—harsh and stinging—to my backside before spreading my cheeks and bending down to lick up my center.

"Oh, fuck!" I cry out, fisting the cloud-like duvet as I press my forehead to the bed. "Lawson." I beg for his mouth. For his tongue. He strokes every part of me languidly, closing his lips around my clit, and sucking as he swallows everything I have to offer.

"You taste better than I imagined you would," he murmurs against my wet flesh before devouring me again. "And I've thought about this so many times."

My release coils tighter and tighter, winding me up so intensely that I writhe against his face and the bed, chasing my orgasm as he licks and nips and sucks, and eats me with a fervor I've never experienced before.

"Lawson! I'm gonna... fuck! I'm gonna—"

"Come for me, baby. Be a good girl and give Daddy what he wants. Make a mess for me, rainbow."

His teeth graze my clit, and it's my undoing. Like a dam breaking loose, a flood of warm wetness releases from my body into Lawson's mouth. Crude, wet sounds join his moans as he eagerly laps at me like a cat with cream, cleaning every inch of my skin until I'm a boneless pile on the bed.

Low chuckling fills the air as he stands and flips me over, pulling my lingerie from my body. My ass is only a little sore from the spankings, but I have no doubt I'll feel it worse later.

"What a good fucking girl you are. So wet and ready to take every single inch I give you, aren't you?"

I don't even know how it's possible to still be this turned on after coming like that. But watching Lawson take in my naked body as he removes his pants, his impressive length springing up between us, long and hard and shining with precum—knowing it's about to be *inside* me—has my legs pressing together as a new wave of need washes over me.

"Oh no, rainbow. There's no hiding this glorious pussy from me any longer. Spread those legs and show me what you're about to give me." He wraps a hand around himself, pumping once... twice... A hot flush scorches every inch of my skin as I do what he says.

"That's it. Now tell me what you want." He doesn't remove his thunderous gray eyes from my glistening body, slowly pumping himself with such impressive, measured control.

"I want you," I state shyly. I've never had a man stare so much. It's enough to make a woman self-conscious.

"You can do better than that. Use your words." He releases his cock to hoist my legs into the crook of his elbows, spreading me wide as he uses pure expertise to line himself up with my entrance without using his hands. "Tell me what you want, Lucy."

During the times we have been intimate, Lawson has always made me feel like I'm the one with the power. Even though it seems like he's the one in control, he's always let that honor be mine.

I realize he's asking me for permission, testing my limits to see if I'll change my mind. Something else warm and satisfying blooms in my chest as I reach down to run a hand up his arm.

"I want you to fuck me, Lawson."

His grip tightens, and his hips surge forward. One inch pulls a gasp from my lips, my back arching to accommodate his size. Two inches, and his gaze falls to where we're joined —to where he's stretching me and making me his.

Inch by inch, he claims me, making me feel so full to the point where I almost need to tell him to stop. But just as I reach that point, he bottoms out. "And how do you want me to fuck you?"

His cock twitches inside me, and my eyes flutter shut. I try to undulate my hips, but his grip keeps me still as he awaits my answer. He tests my flexibility, pushing my legs into my chest as he bends to lay a kiss between my breasts. Twisting my fingers into his hair, my eyes shoot open to lock with his as I try to fight him—to try and get the friction I so desperately need.

"Tell me how you want me, Lucy. Slow and deep? Shallow and rough? Do you want me to bring you to the edge of climax only to pull back when you're ready to break?" His tongue traces patterns on my skin as he makes his way to my breast, pulling my nipple between his teeth.

"Fuck, Lawson. All of it! I want all of it! I need to feel you. I need you to move!"

Another round of deep, sinful laughter skims my skin. And then he's pulling out and slamming back in with such force it rocks me back on the bed. Moans, gasps, and cries of ecstasy fly from my mouth as he alternates between spearing me deep and stroking my walls slowly, rotating his hips to deliciously caress against parts of me I didn't even know existed.

Higher and higher, we soar, and the whole time, Lawson watches where he disappears inside me as if he's so fascinated with the way we fit together he can't bear to look away.

But when he finally lifts his eyes to mine, I can see it shining so clearly—his need for me, utter devotion and reverence, and a determination that's so close to shattering.

"Fuck, I'm so close. I'll pull out, don't worry." His words are thoughtful and considerate of my feelings, even though I made no resistance to him entering me bare.

"I don't want you to." My admission has his hips faltering, a low groan leaving his lips with a heavy sigh. "I want to feel you, Lawson. Every part of you. Please."

Maybe it's the *please* or the way I squeeze around his length when I beg for him to come inside me, but he falls over the edge, roaring his release.

I can feel it, burning hot and thick as he empties himself inside me. His thumb finds my clit, and after only two firm strokes, I'm shattering around him once more. "Lawson!"

He continues to move his hips slowly, releasing my legs to cover me completely, rubbing his pelvis against my sensitive clit as he cradles my face in his hands and kisses me savagely. Tongues and teeth and our very *souls* intertwine so thoroughly that I feel like I'm having a religious experience.

Our breathing slows as our frantic kissing turns into a lazy caress of lips. When he slips from me, I can feel the warm wetness dripping between my thighs, and I remember what he said earlier.

*'...fill you so full of my cum, you'll never forget who your daddy is because I'll be dripping between your legs for the rest of your life.'*

I'd say mission accomplished.

Lawson draws back, concern shining in his eyes, now bright again and full of uncertainty. "Are you okay?"

"I'm more than okay," I tell him as he wipes sweaty hair off my forehead. "Are *you* okay?"

His genuine, beaming smile lights up his face, a positive sign that tells me this time things are going to be different between us. This time, he isn't going to run.

"I don't think anything can top the way I'm feeling right now," he admits, thumb stroking a gentle pattern against my cheek. Tears line my eyes as a whirlwind of emotion crashes through my chest.

Alarm fills his eyes. "What's wrong? Did I hurt you?"

"No." I shake my head frantically, laughing as the tears fall down my cheeks. "I'm just really happy. Even though I'm wondering when you'll kick me out and tell me we can't do this again."

Lawson kisses me softly, relaying years' worth of

longing through such a simple touch. "I promise you, rainbow. I'm not going anywhere."

This time, I truly believe him.

"Mmm, this is nice," I sigh, cuddling further into Lawson's embrace as we soak in a cloud of bubbles in the suite's large soaker tub.

Husky laughter fills my ears as he sweeps a stray strand that's escaped my messy bun off my shoulder before he kisses my temple. "Are you sure you're feeling okay?"

Stretching like a lazy cat who's been napping all day, I make a sound of contentment and pull his arms tighter around me. "I'm more than okay. That was... indescribable. Amazing doesn't even do it justice."

A tickle, the tiniest nagging feeling, pulls at my stomach, and I turn my head to meet his gaze over my shoulder. "How do you feel?"

He presses a chaste kiss to my swollen lips. "Like I should have said *fuck it* a lot sooner." His fingers draw slothful patterns against my slippery skin, his cock remaining half-hard against my back, but he makes no move to use it, simply enjoying this time together. "I'm going to spend every moment we're alone making up for lost time and fulfilling your every fantasy."

"Hmm," I muse. "Besides this right here, there's only one other fantasy I've ever had, and I doubt you'll want to fulfill that one." In any other circumstance, this would be an embarrassing conversation to have with someone who you just had sex with for the first time. But at this point, I don't think anything will make me feel uncomfortable when it comes to Lawson.

"And what's that, rainbow?" His hand slides up to palm my breast in a comforting manner. He circles his thumb around my nipple until it forms a stiff peak, then runs his thumb over it again and again—and it's remarkable how his touch remains soothing and sensual.

"Well... I've always wondered what it would be like to have sex with two guys at once."

Lawson stiffens behind me, his thumb pausing in its ministrations. I laugh and squeeze his forearm. "See? I told you."

After a moment, he relaxes, shifting us in the water so we're lying down. He presses my cheek against his chest before running his hand lightly up and down my arm.

The sweet scent of coconut fills the air as the bubbles settle again, and then Lawson asks, "What is it about being with two guys that appeals to you?"

A gentle question. Curious and not at all judgmental.

My cheeks grow warm. "My roommate in college did it once. She forgot to lock the door, and I happened to walk in on it. And while I couldn't look her in the eye for a whole week afterward, I also couldn't help but think about what it would feel like to be that... *full*."

His cock hardens completely, the steel strength of him poking against my belly. It would be so easy just to lift myself up and sink onto him. So easy. But his arms remain firm and unyielding, even as a slickness gathers between my legs.

"If that is something you really want to experience, I'd do it... for you." His voice is strained, a clear indicator that he isn't exactly fond of the idea, but he means what he says when he tells me he wants to fulfill my fantasies.

I tilt my head up to catch his eye. "Earlier, you said you aren't the same man you once were. That I didn't know what I was getting myself into. What did you mean?"

He groans, rubbing his brow with a bubble-covered hand. "We don't need to talk about it right now."

"I want to, though. I want to understand you, Lawson," I tell him, propping myself up on his chest.

With a sigh, he relents. "Well, you know Charlotte and I were together since high school. She got pregnant with Rhys, and then we got married and had River. We didn't really get to experience life as young adults because we were too busy being parents. And I'm not saying you can't learn what you like as a young adult, but you certainly don't understand much about sex, or what it means to please someone, let alone what true pleasure feels like. Honestly, the majority of people never get to experience that."

I think about my sex life thus far. No one has ever made me feel the way he does. And I wonder if that's what he means.

"When I arrived in New York, I was a mess. I felt guilty for what happened between us. I couldn't reconcile my feelings with my actions, and honestly, I felt like a fucking predator." His words make me wince, and he kisses my forehead before continuing. "That's when I met Cameron and Jules. They took me in and brought me to a place where I could freely explore myself and recover from the way I felt about us."

"What do you mean? What type of place?"

"Technically, I'm not supposed to say, but I'll tell you. Just don't mention it to anyone else."

At my nod, he continues, "There's a club in New York where you can explore sex. Everything about it, everything you could ever dream up, you can do it there. Everyone has to wear masks, and there are different levels you can... *subscribe* to. It was like therapy and an awakening all at once," he explains.

Jealousy prickles down my spine. "So, you frequented a sex club and figured out what you liked sexually... with lots of women?" I know I have no right to be jealous. Lawson is an adult, and we weren't together—I don't even know if we *are* together—but I can't stop the green monster from taking root in my chest.

"Does that bother you?" I can feel the heavy thump of his heart against his chest when I lay my head back down. It echoes in my ear while I come to terms with what he's told me.

It's not like I didn't sleep with guys while I was away in college. We have pasts. And right now, we're in the present. If we get our feelings hurt about things we did back then, there's no healthy way to move forward.

"I guess not," I sigh. "So, does that mean you had other girls call you Daddy?" The question sounds so stupid as it falls from my lips, and I hate how childish my voice sounds as it echoes throughout the bathroom.

Lawson chuckles, tilting my chin up so I have to look at him. "No, rainbow. That's only ever been for your bratty mouth."

Warmth floods my veins even though the water is beginning to get cold. "Well, I told you one of my fantasies. What's one of yours?" I prop my chin on my hand as I stare at him.

He looks at me for a long while before he admits, "I want to film you."

*Film me?*

My brows furrow, making him release a deep, rumbling laugh. "I know it sounds creepy, but I promise, there's something about having a video to pull out and watch when you're alone."

He gently pushes me back and leans forward to pull the stopper from the drain. "It sounds narcissistic, but I wouldn't do it to watch me. I'm sure there will be nights where we can't be together, and I want to have something to remind me of the way your pussy swallows my cock when I don't have the real thing."

His crude words send a fiery blaze through my bones. Dirty talk gets me hotter than anything else, but coming from Lawson? I might as well just be a permanent puddle of goo.

"I would be okay with that," I admit shyly.

The idea of him filming me—filming us—is interesting. I don't exactly see the appeal, but as Lawson pulls me back against his chest, pointing to the giant mirrored wall across from us, I have a feeling I'm about to find out. He pulls the removable showerhead from its stand and turns the water on, ensuring it's a comfortable temperature.

"Your face when you came apart earlier is now permanently branded on my retinas." He begins to move the nozzle over me, washing away the tropical-smelling bubbles. "But having that immortalized on film? Having that memory any time you aren't near?" He moves the nozzle lower, inching toward that spot between my legs that's now aching for him. "I'd give anything to have that, Lucy."

"Ahh!" I cry out as he flips the spray to a steady, firm stream and sweeps it over my clit.

A hand cups my breast as he nips at my ear and whispers, "Watch the water." He lowers the nozzle again until the stream spears open my pussy lips, and a foreign, warm feeling floods my insides. My head rolls back on his shoulder, and he chuckles. "Be a good girl and watch, rainbow."

Wanting to please him, I do as he says. My breasts heave as he moves the water back to my clit. "Look how swollen you are for me. Look how pink, perfect, and needy you are." His tongue traces a line along the column of my neck as he presses the stream directly against my center before moving it away again. He flicks the pressure button, and the water changes to a series of strong pulses. "We are visuals, rainbow. Watching something creates an understanding that heightens the pleasure."

My fingers are white from gripping the tub so tightly. "Lawson," I whine as he presses the pulsing water to my clit and doesn't move it. My lower belly cramps, the pressure winding tighter and tighter.

"Watch," he commands when my head falls back again.

The pressure is too much, and I feel myself careening over that blissful precipice. "I can't! I'm going to come!"

My eyes snap shut, but his hand flies to cradle my face. "Open your eyes and watch yourself in the mirror as you come." He wiggles the nozzle, forcing the pressure of the water to hit that desperate, needy part of me, and I watch myself come undone. My mouth falls open, and Lawson's eyes darken as he observes. "Give it all to me. Be a good girl. Keep coming for me."

Wave after wave of white-hot scorching pleasure burns through me. When he removes the nozzle, I am breathing heavily, and a creamy white trail leaks from between my legs. It's a visual that does things to my body.

"See?" I can hear the smile in Lawson's tone as his cock strains long and hard against my tailbone.

I slam the water off and turn, climbing onto his lap and seating myself on his proud length. All his mirthful amusement dissipates as his eyes roll to the back of his head, and his hands grip my hips. He stretches me, and I can't help but feel a warm, fuzzy feeling that flows through my chest.

We fit together so perfectly like we were made specifically for each other.

In an impressive show of strength, he rises, effortlessly lifting me while still sheathed inside my tight, warm walls. Carefully, he steps out of the tub, and I smash my lips to his as he carries me back to the bedroom.

We tirelessly worship each other's bodies throughout the night, and when the next day rolls around, Lawson misses the rest of the conference and the goodbye dinner— choosing me for the rest of his weekend meals instead.

# Twenty-Two

*Lawson*

*Smack!*

Lucy discreetly slaps her thigh, bunching up her long skirt to reveal an irritated stretch of skin where a spot is beginning to bubble up. The sound isn't loud enough for anyone to hear over Mike's presentation, but since she's sitting right next to me—and my attention is already on her, dreaming of the way her lips would look wrapped around me instead of her pen—the action snaps me from my daydreams.

As she scratches, more spots bloom around the area, and she frantically reaches for the protein shake she brought into the conference room. After checking to ensure no one is paying attention to us, I slip my hand beneath the table, reaching over to gently push her hand away from the patch of aggravated skin.

Giving her a look that silently tells her she's making it worse, I rub my thumb along the area with long, deep strokes, trying to suppress the itchy feeling without spreading the hives. Her beautiful eyes fill with gratitude, then mischief, as my hand roams higher. She releases her skirt, trying to prevent me from going any further, as she nervously looks around the room. Instead of removing my hand, I capture her fingers, tangling them with mine to rest on her thigh as I flash her a warm smile.

It's been nearly a week since we returned from the conference, and I can't keep my hands off her. Days of berating myself for waiting so long—for denying us the immeasurable pleasure we've brought each other every second we can get alone.

Every single night I fuck her into exhaustion, and when she's fallen asleep, I go home to my fatherly duties. I've had Lucy on every surface of her apartment and every inch of my office at work. The pharmacy down the street from her place has made enough money from the amount of condoms I've been buying to fund their rent for at least a month.

With the exception of that first night, I haven't had her bare again. Birth control is only so reliable, and my kids are nearly grown. So, we've shelved difficult discussions for a later day. That conversation would only highlight how she's always wanted to be a mom and how it would be weird for me to have more kids so late in life. Not to mention, I'd be impregnating my son's ex-girlfriend.

For now, we're focused on enjoying our time and making up for *lost* time.

As Mike brings his presentation to a close, we untangle our fingers and gather our things. If anyone wonders what happens between us when I close my office door, they do a good job of keeping the gossip from reaching our ears because it seems like no one has caught on to the fact that my open-door policy has been rescinded.

"Lawson!" Lucy whispers as soon as the door clicks shut behind me. "We can't keep doing things like that in public. Someone is going to see!"

"It's not my fault you parade around in these damn outfits." I gesture to the blue and purple gradient-colored maxi dress that hugs her curves, before grabbing her hips. "Come here."

She doesn't argue as I sit in my chair and position her in front of me, sliding her dress up to expose her thigh once more. I grab a tube of hydrocortisone cream from my bottom desk drawer. As soon as I saw her have that first outbreak, I bought some and stored it away for times like this.

"I thought you liked my outfits?" she teases with a smirk. "In fact, I remember you picking out this specific dress and laying it out for me before you left last night." She nudges her foot forward, the toe of her bright pink pump rubbing against my semi-hard cock.

As she stands there, foot hitched up with the smooth expanse of one leg exposed and her hair hanging in full waves over one shoulder, I realize that there is absolutely nothing I wouldn't do for this woman. Lucy Bradee has me bewitched, body, mind, and soul. And now that she's captured me, I fear that even if she tries to cut me loose, I will remain tied to her for the rest of my life.

Smoothing the balm over her skin, I lean forward and press a kiss to the inside of her knee. "I adore your outfits." Another kiss. "And the sexy little things you wear beneath them." Pushing her skirt further up, I reveal a periwinkle scrap of lace, letting out a groan when I see the spot over her center is already wet with need.

"Lawson." Her voice is raw as she tangles her fingers in my hair when I make my mission clear. I maneuver her foot to the chair and drop to my knees. "Anyone could walk in."

"Then you'd better come quickly, rainbow." Cupping her ass, I pull her underwear to the side and sink my tongue into the depths of her warm, wet heat.

"Oh, fuck." She shoves a palm against her mouth to stifle a cry as I suck her clit and eat her like a starved man. When I plunge two fingers in deep, using the hand on her ass to rock her against my face, it only takes seconds before she comes with a strangled moan.

I love watching the pure pleasure she gets from me. It has my chest humming with pride, knowing it's *me* making her feel that way. I lick up every last drop she gives me before pulling her skirt back down.

"You're insatiable," she breathes, smoothing my hair back as she stares at me affectionately.

Wiping my mouth of her glistening release, I rise to lay a chaste kiss against her lips. "I have a lot of time to make up for."

Voices sound just outside my door, and we spring apart. Lucy goes to the other side of my desk as I sit back in my chair.

"River is going to his mom's tonight. He'll be gone for a week."

Lucy's cheeks turn a deeper pink than the already flushed hue from her afternoon delight. "Oh?"

"I was thinking... if filming is still something you think you might be interested in, it will be the perfect time for it."

I rub my thumb along my lower lip, feeling the wetness left over and smelling the intoxicating scent that is uniquely her.

To my pleasure, she nods eagerly. "Yes." Her voice is breathy, needy once more, and filled with a hunger I wonder if we'll ever satiate. "If that's what you want, I'll do it."

"I want you to do it because *you* want to, Lucy. Not because it's something I want. It's important to me that you know that."

She smiles, and goddamn, if it's not the most breathtaking thing I've ever seen when Lucy lights up like the rainbow she is. "I know. I want to. It sounds... *hot*, from the way you've described it."

Something indescribable takes root in my chest at the thought of having her in a way no other man has before. Of giving her a first experience—hopefully, the first of many more to come.

"River has to be at the airport at six. Why don't you come over tonight around seven thirty? Bring a bag, and stay the night. I can drop you off around the block if you're worried about someone seeing us arriving together tomorrow morning."

Her eyes warm, the hazel turning to a brighter shade of gold-flecked moss as she nods. "Okay."

"Okay."

Her fingers twist together nervously. "Should I, uh... should I bring anything specific?"

Shaking my head, I drag my eyes over her body shamelessly, imagining what every inch of skin will look like, bare and at my mercy tonight. "No. I have everything I need. I'll cook you dinner. Does salmon sound good?"

"Mmhmm," she hums as she opens the door. "That sounds great."

## Lucy

Returning to the Morgans' home is like walking into a fever dream. Nearly everything is as I remember it, with the exception of a few added photo frames on the walls—pictures of Lawson with River in New York and Rhys with Charlotte at Ole Miss games. It doesn't look like there's been one with all four of them since graduation day.

I follow the scent of pan-fried salmon to the kitchen. There's an undercurrent of my favorite cookies wafting through the house as I refamiliarize myself with the space I spent so much time in during my senior year.

"Lawson Morgan, did you make me cookies?" I singsong in my best Southern accent as I step into the kitchen to see him doing a million things at once at the stove. He's changed into dark gray joggers with a tight black t-shirt, making my mouth water at the sight of his rippling muscles.

"Maybe." He smirks and leans over for a quick kiss before resuming his cooking. "But you only get them if you're a good girl tonight."

Quickly, I reach around him and pluck an asparagus off the broiler pan. "Hey!" He swats at my hand with a black spatula. "Not off to a good start there, rainbow."

Lemony, buttery goodness floods my mouth as I bite off the end of the stalk. "Mmmm. God, I missed your cooking.

My parents are great, don't get me wrong, but I always loved having dinner over here." Muscle memory takes me to the cabinet, and I fill a glass with crushed ice and water from the fridge dispenser.

"I'll cook for you every night while River's gone if you want a staycation."

It's such a casual suggestion that it catches me a little off guard. I choke on my bite, taking a moment to clear my throat before I'm able to swallow correctly. "You mean, like, move in for the week?"

"Yeah. Only if you want to, though." He sounds a little more unsure than he did just a few seconds ago.

I'm silent for a while. I didn't really think about where we'd be sleeping tonight. I assume in his room, in his bed— a bed he shared with Charlotte for years. Suddenly, I don't feel the giddy excitement that I've had since we made our plans this afternoon.

As if he can sense the direction of my thoughts, Lawson looks at me over his shoulder. "I haven't slept in Charlotte's room in years. I sleep in one of the guest bedrooms, even when she's in Florida."

I find myself nodding and saying, "Okay. That would be nice then." My eyes flick to the island, where he's already laid out plates and silverware. "I remember you saying once that these aren't for eating meals," I tease, sliding onto one of the stools as I knock my knuckles against the quartz.

Turning the burners off, Lawson replies, "The dining room table is set up for other things tonight. While eating may be one of them, it's not for dinner."

There is so much heat and promise in his tone that I'm instantly wet. Turning to look over my shoulder, I can see three different cameras on tripods at varying heights pointed at the table in the dining room.

*Holy shit. This is really happening.*

His hands find my hips, large and warm and possessive, as he drags me forward on the stool and steps between my legs. His kisses are hungry as he devours my lips.

I'm all liquid desire as he cups my neck, angling my head back to kiss me deeper. His lips break from mine, roving down the side of my throat to the spot he knows makes me so weak. I can't help the little laugh that escapes. "Are we starting with dessert tonight?"

Lawson chuckles against my skin, nipping me lightly before pulling back. "No. Fish always tastes better straight from the pan." I roll my eyes. "One of these weekends, I'm gonna take you up to the lake house, get you out on the water, and you're gonna catch a fish."

Shaking my head vehemently, I wave my hands back and forth. "Nope. Too slimy. Not my thing. You can fish. I'll just lay out and soak up the sun."

Lawson genuinely seems to think about it. "You in a bikini, spread out between my legs while I fish? I'll take that as a win." He kisses the tip of my nose. "Now, let's eat."

"Remember, you don't have to do this if you don't want to. If you feel uncomfortable at any time, just say the word, and I'll stop." Lawson's words whisper along my neck, and my fingers twitch as I hold up my hair for him to unbutton the back of my dress.

Dinner was as good as foreplay with the way Lawson kept feeding me and telling me all the hypothetical things he'd do to me in the boat if there was no one else out on the water—if our lake house weekend ever happens.

"Is it weird that I'm actually a little excited?" I hate how childish I sound. I'm about to let this man record me naked, doing whatever he pleases so he can rewatch it later. Yet, I'm as eager as a puppy whose owner just returned home and is about to let it out of its kennel.

Lawson dips his head to press a kiss against the side of my throat. "The fact that you're into it turns me on, Lucy." As I drop my hair, the soft fabric of my dress slides off my shoulders, gliding slowly down my body until it pools around my feet.

He presses his erection against the small of my back as his hands slide around my body. One large palm slips beneath the band of my underwear, caressing my dripping center.

"Fuck, baby. Already so wet." He slips one finger into me, and the other hand drifts up to collar my neck and draw my head back against his shoulder. "Always so willing to please Daddy, aren't you?"

Before I can answer, he pulls away, sucking my juices off his finger. "Remove your bra and underwear," he commands in a raspy tone, like he's holding himself back from just bending me over in the archway between the kitchen and the dining room.

Quickly, I follow his demands. I'm too wound up to

speak without stammering and too horny to be a brat and face punishment.

I've learned quickly that orgasm denial is not something I'm partial to.

Naked and flushed, I wait for more instructions. When they come, the words caress my skin like molten lava. "Climb onto the table, face the cameras, and spread your legs."

There's a pang in my lower belly, a cramp of hunger for something other than food—a longing to be filled as I obey.

"Lawson." His name is like a desperate cry on my lips as I sit on the table that I've eaten dinner on, that his son eats dinner on, and bare my naked pussy—glistening and dripping with evidence of how much I want him.

"That's right, baby. Show Daddy how much you want to please him." Lawson presses a button on the nearest camera, the one level with the table's surface. A bright red light flashes, signaling the start of our little video, and I'm already starting to see the appeal. I can understand how watching this back would let you relive everything you felt in the moment.

"Fuck, your pussy is so pretty. Do you know how many nights I thought of filling you up?" He turns the next camera on. "Of fucking you so full of me there'd never be room for any other man?"

I squirm. My nipples stiffen to impossibly hard peaks, the desire in them pulsing with my heartbeat as the organ pumps blood and lust downward into my puffy, swollen clit. My knees draw in, dying to relieve some of the pressure.

"Keep them spread," Lawson commands sharply.

A whimper escapes from my throat as I stretch my legs

back out as far as they'll go, to the point where the ache in my pussy extends down my inner thighs to my ankles.

"What are you going to make me do?"

He smirks. It's villainous, corrupted with pure, crazed passion. It sets my blood on fire, and my breathing shallows as he turns and walks away, only to appear a few moments later, holding up a familiar phallic-shaped food.

"I want to watch you ride this until it's covered in your sweet honey, rainbow."

My eyes widen. That went from zero to sixty real fast. "You want me to... to... *fuck* myself with that?"

He saunters closer, cock straining against his sweats. "I want to record you taking every inch."

"Why a cucumber? Why not a dildo?"

Lawson grips the table between my spread legs as he leans forward and whispers, "Because when I eat this with my salad for lunch tomorrow, I want to see your face while you watch me consume your juices in front of everyone. Consider it my personal salad dressing."

If I heard anyone else say those words, I would have gagged. But coming from *him*, it's like the hottest thing a man has ever said to me.

The cool flesh of the cucumber presses against my opening, and my mouth gapes as I watch the blunt end spear my lips, spreading them wide.

"Now take this from me and fuck your pretty pussy until I tell you to stop."

His words already have me gushing around the vegetable... or is it a fruit? Whatever it is, he leaves me to it, walking back to the last video recorder to press play.

"Fuck it, rainbow." His demand is thick with lust,

stuffed full of decadent promises of what's to come as soon as I fulfill his request.

My face feels like it's on fire. Slowly, I begin to undulate my hips, every pass taking more of the cucumber. It's thick and lined with bumpy ridges, and the friction feels amazing along my inner walls. I tip my head back to the ceiling, and a moan of pleasure falls from my lips as I give the camera everything Lawson wants.

"That's right, baby. It feels good, doesn't it?"

"Mmhmm." I'm so fucking wet. The sounds fill the room, mixing with my sighs as I move faster, embarrassingly enjoying how the vegetable makes me feel so full.

Lawson removes his clothes. "Such a little slut for me, aren't you?"

I nod and whimper, loving the way the filthy words sound on his tongue. There's something about a man whispering sinfully degrading things in your ear while you're debasing yourself for him. I love when he gets like this—when he gives me exactly what I need without asking.

"Only for you."

Lawson approaches the table, taking over the rhythm I've set with the cucumber and gently pushing me back. "That's right, only for me. And you love being my little slut, don't you, rainbow?" He leans over and spits on my pussy.

"Yes!" I cry wantonly, arching my back as his mouth descends on me, sucking and biting at my clit while he keeps fucking my body with the cucumber. "I love being your little slut."

"What a good fucking girl you are." The praise caresses my skin like silk. My chest feels like it's about to explode.

I'm so close to that precipice, but not ready for the pleasure to end yet. My fingers fly into his hair as he moans against me, "Fuck, Lucy, baby. Come for Daddy. Give it all to me, you perfect fucking girl."

"Oh my god, Lawson, I'm about to come."

"Yeah?" he moans before licking my clit harder and angling the cucumber so that it hits my G-spot.

My orgasm bursts, hot and heavy, as the pressure explodes between my legs. Lawson stands, replacing his tongue with his thumb as he keeps stroking me through it, murmuring words of encouragement. "That's my girl. Keep coming, rainbow. Give me another one."

It feels like my soul literally flees my body as he pulls wave after wave of rippling release from me. My body shakes uncontrollably, my hips jerking when he doesn't let up. I didn't think it was even possible, but I count at least three real orgasms before he pulls the cucumber from my body and holds it up for me to see. Streaks of white and remnants of cum cover the bumpy, green vegetable. What should be a weird and embarrassing image looks more like the cover of a pornography magazine.

I am utterly spent and preparing myself for another round because Lawson hasn't even fucked me yet, but he keeps me waiting.

"Be a good girl, and keep those legs spread." He places the cucumber in a waiting Tupperware before grabbing a condom and ripping the wrapper with his teeth.

By the time he makes it back to me, my release has cooled on my thighs. Lawson scoops it up with his fingers and pushes it back into me before he thrusts in all the way to his base. His arms wrap beneath my ass, hoisting my legs around his hips.

"How many more do you think you can give me tonight, rainbow?"

When he moves, it's like a waterfall of heat. I grip his shoulders, pulling him as close as possible. "However many more you want to give me," I moan against his mouth before pressing my lips to his.

"Fuck, you're such a good girl."

I will never, *ever* get tired of hearing him call me that. When we're in the moment, I live to see how much praise I can receive from him. How well I can please him.

Yes, I've become one of those women who loves to please their partner. Because at the end of the day, Lawson lives to give me as much pleasure as he can.

"So fucking good," he groans as I squeeze my walls around him. "Such..." *Thrust.* "...a good..." *Thrust.* "...fucking..." *Thrust.* "...girl!" Lawson's movements become erratic, pumping into me with such frenzy that the kitchen table begins to squeak as it slides across the floor.

"Lucy!" he roars my name as he comes, fucking me fast and hard with his face buried against my shoulder. The familiar flutter of my walls milks his cock as I hug him to me, grinding my hips up into his as I continue to fuck him, even when he's gone still.

And his whispered, "Good girls," last long into the night as we fly through an entire box of condoms, worshiping each other until the sun comes up.

"Lulu, are you okay? You look red as a tomato. Are you coming down with something?" Anna asks, pressing the back of her hand against my forehead. "You're burning up."

*Crunch. Crunch. Crunch.*

Lawson smirks at me from his end of the conference table, deliberately sticking the entire end of the fork that has chopped cucumber pieces on it in his mouth and slowly pulling it out, giving me a private—yet very public—show of him sucking the vegetable and dressing off his silverware. The creamy vinaigrette makes me think of what we did last night, and no matter how hard I try, I can't stop the flush taking over my face.

"I'm fine." I wave her off before rubbing my temple with my middle finger and turning that side of my head to Lawson. When I glance at him again, he's silently laughing into his salad as he picks up another piece of cucumber.

*Crunch.*

# Twenty-Three

*Lucy*

HAVING sex on film is actually quite comfortable.

Once Lawson presses record, it's like the cameras aren't even there. At this point, we've made so many videos I keep joking that we could start one of those online accounts where people pay to watch you have sex.

Lawson doesn't find that amusing... and I think he's slightly concerned about how I don't even sound like I'm joking when I suggest it.

And living together–albeit temporarily–is like a dream. We've easily fallen into a routine that feels like we've already been doing it for years. Lawson drops me off around the block before work, and I grab us coffee in the café, only to meet back up *randomly* in the elevator. Then, once work is over, I walk home, where he's already waiting for me, and we go back to his house.

In the week River is in Florida, we become experts at the three c's—conversation, cooking, and coitus.

But the future still hangs over us like a heavy cloud,

ready to burst and drench us with heartache the second we start poking at it.

Lawson is hell-bent on returning to New York. I don't know if it's because he still wants to avoid the possibility of something more serious happening between us or because he genuinely hates Chicago that much.

We're just going through a honeymoon phase, right? Eventually, it will burn out. He'll move on, and I'll be left to wonder how I'll ever find someone to share my life with who makes me feel the way he does.

"We have dinner plans Saturday night," Lawson whispers into my ear, his minty pine scent surrounding me as we ride the elevator up to our floor Wednesday morning.

"Oh?" The doors open, and the rest of the people get off, leaving us alone for the remaining floors.

Lawson spins me by the waist, pressing me against the wall to kiss me fervently. His fingers dig into the plum-colored velvet of my dress at my waist, thumb caressing my cheek as he sensually assaults my lips in a way that won't leave them swollen once we step off the elevator.

*This* doesn't feel like a honeymoon phase. It doesn't feel like we'll burn out anytime soon. If anything, it feels like the longer we're together, the hotter things become.

As he reluctantly pulls his soft lips from mine, he smiles. "I have a friend coming into town. And River will be over at his friend's house, so I booked us a hotel."

"A hotel?" My brows furrow. "Lawson, I live here. We don't need a hotel."

"And while I don't mind spending time in your apartment, I'd like to treat you to a fancy weekend with room service, a spa day, and whatever else I might want to surprise you with." His tone is devious, with a matching smirk that has my panties wet, and it's not even noon.

"You spoil me," I murmur against his lips as he steals one last kiss before the doors open.

An ominous chuckle follows me as we get off the elevator. "You have no idea just how spoiled you'll be this weekend, rainbow. No idea."

———————— ∽◦∼ ————————

"TRUST ME, as much as I want to keep fucking you all day, you're going to be late for your massage." Lawson pulls me from our ridiculously comfortable king-sized bed as I pout.

"But, Daddy..." I whine teasingly, allowing him to pull me to the bathroom. "...you only got me off twice this morning. You promised me multiple orgasms."

I love the way his eyes drop to my lips as I stick the bottom one out. I think Lawson is obsessed with my mouth, and for all the time we've spent having sex, I still haven't given him a blow job.

Not for lack of trying on my part, but every time I initiate oral sex, he turns it back around and makes it all about me. It's always all about me. It's like Lawson's personal mission is to bring me pleasure.

Maybe I should tell him it would please me to suck his dick. It's such a nice one.

Lawson spanks me lightly before he starts the shower, testing the water before grabbing one of my hair clips from the bathroom vanity. "What do you call all the ones I gave you before I fucked you to sleep, rainbow?"

"True..." I shrug as he begins to gather my hair. Do I need a man to pull my hair up for me? No. Do I love it when Lawson does little things like this to pamper me? Absolutely. "We did have some pretty amazing sleep sex, too, I guess."

He pulls me into the shower, holding me beneath the spray as he runs his soapy hands everywhere along my body. "And don't forget the training. God, we are going to enjoy that later," he hums the last part more to himself than to me as he kneels and pays extra attention to my behind.

Ah, the *training*. I never thought I'd hear the expression *anal training*. But Lawson wants to make all my fantasies come true, so the last few days have been full of gentle fingers, small toys, and lots and *lots* of lube.

I'm fairly certain he's going to fuck me in the ass with a dildo while taking my pussy with his cock this weekend. Just the thought of it sends a shiver through my body that makes my nipples hard. I like the feeling of it, of something penetrating back there while Lawson pays extra attention to other parts of me. And every step of the way, he's made me feel relaxed and not at all embarrassed.

Lawson's a caretaker, and I love that about him. In fact, I'm afraid I'm beginning to just simply love *him*. That realization is scary. After he stands and wraps his arms around me, we stare at each other in silence while I play with the hair at the nape of his neck. The words hit me like a freight train.

*I love you.*

I want to tell him so badly, but I'm afraid this isn't as

serious for him. Ever since he gave in to this attraction between us, it's been easy and comfortable. But his off-hand comments about leaving after a year fill me with the sense that he'll have no problem walking away from us. There's been no mention of me going with him, of having a life together outside the confines of my apartment or his home when River isn't there.

He's still married, for Christ's sake.

The reminder is sobering.

"I'm going to be late," I whisper into the space between us.

Lawson shuts the shower off. "I have something I want you to wear while you're down there."

"Wear? I'm getting a massage. You're supposed to be naked." I laugh as he pulls me out and towels me off.

"You will be." He disappears into the bedroom while I grab a fluffy white robe from the closet. Before I can pull it on, though, Lawson reappears, holding a small white box with a matching ribbon.

"What's this?" I take it and appraise his fiendish smile.

"Open it," he prods, leaning a hip against the counter as he crosses his corded arms over his ridiculously fit chest.

My cheeks heat to a blazing inferno as I do as he says, opening the lid to reveal a shiny steel butt plug gleaming with all the different colors of the rainbow.

"You want me to... *wear* this?" My question is more of a squeak.

"All day. You'll be a good girl and keep it in until I remove it later." His voice is so damn husky that I'm instantly wet between my thighs. Lawson reaches for me, taking the box and turning us so I'm facing the mirror with

257

him at my back. "Tell me you're going to be a good girl and keep it in, rainbow."

I can't answer as I watch his reflection. The words dry up in my throat every time I try to speak. Lawson removes the plug from the box and hands me a bottle of lube, locking eyes with me in the mirror as he sucks his fingers before probing my back entrance. My lashes flutter at the intrusion.

"Tell me, Lucy." He leans forward, kissing the side of my neck before holding the plug in front of my face.

In answer, I open the lube and pour the jelly onto the toy. Once it's fully covered, he gently inserts it, spreading me so fucking slowly—he's always so careful with me. My clit pulses with need and the desire to be touched is a hot and heavy thing. The plug is bigger than two of his fingers, making it the largest size we've experimented with so far.

"I'll be a good girl," I whine as he draws lazy circles around my clit.

"That's right. You'll be such a good girl for me, won't you?" His thumb replaces his fingers as he slides two of them into my pussy. The sensation lights my body up like I've been shocked, and it takes less than a minute before I'm coming on his hand.

When we lock eyes in the mirror again, he looks so proud of himself that I smile.

"That's my girl." He kisses my temple as he slaps my ass, causing a sensation I've never felt before to ripple through my body.

*Well... that's different.*

"Fuck me," Lawson groans as I step out of the closet. "Where have you been hiding that dress?"

I look down at the forest green thirty's-style fishtail dress and shrug. "I forgot I had it."

There hasn't been a chance for me to wear it out since I bought it, but the ruching and the light, fluttery sleeves are flattering for my body shape, and while I was rummaging through my closet for something that would make a good impression on Lawson's friend, I came across it and knew it was perfect.

Besides Jules—who I *now* know is his best friend and am only *slightly* bothered by the fact that they've slept together—Lawson hasn't introduced me to any of his other friends. For him, tonight may mean nothing but dinner and drinks with a colleague, but to me, it's a huge step I'm not sure he even realizes he's taking.

"Well, you look positively edible." He kisses me, and though it's chaste compared to our usual lip-locks, it's still full of a possessiveness I'm obsessed with.

"You look good, too," I offer lamely. I'm not as good with the sinful compliments as Lawson is. "You still haven't told me who we're meeting."

The vulpine smile he gives me hides a multitude of secrets that send a flutter of nervous hummingbirds to take flight in my stomach.

When he doesn't answer me, I narrow my eyes. "Lawson, who are we meeting?"

As the elevator dings, he wraps an arm around my waist. "My other best friend."

The doors open, and my eyes slowly drift over to see a familiar-looking, devastatingly handsome, bright blue-eyed, brunette man in a charcoal suit standing there with a devilish smile—as though he were waiting for us.

"Lucy, I'd like you to meet Cameron Crueller."

Cameron's eyes rove unabashedly down my body as we exit the elevator. He sticks out a hand. "Nice to finally meet you, Lucy. I have to say, your Iconic photos are beautiful, but nothing compared to the real thing."

There's a slight accent to his cadence—Texan, maybe? And he's gentle as he shakes my hand. Lawson seems unbothered by his forward compliment. "Nice to meet you, too."

He looks like a guy from a TV show my mom used to watch—the brother-in-law of a woman who ends up working at a happy-ending massage parlor when her husband leaves her suddenly. He's handsome and charming without seeming to put in too much effort. And as he and Lawson greet each other, my mind goes wild with the image of them together—because I know that Lawson and Cameron have had a threesome with Jules and likely other women, too.

Would I have slept with Cameron if he'd been the one to take the Executive Director position like he was supposed to? I'm slightly ashamed to admit that I probably would have. Guilt courses through my body, but Lawson tucks me into his side like he can sniff it out like a dog with a bone.

"It's okay if you're attracted to him," he whispers into

my ear as we follow Cameron to the hotel restaurant. "It will make tonight go a lot smoother."

"What is *that* supposed to mean?" I ask, body jolting in surprise with his suggestive purr.

But Lawson and Cameron fall into a conversation about New York while we wait to be seated, not exactly ignoring me, but I suspect they're having a deeper conversation—one I don't follow—from the intensity of how they stare at each other.

Lawson is only into women. And I know Cameron swings both ways but prefers women. Even though he doesn't mind being intimate with men, I also happen to know that regardless of their shared experiences, the two of them have never been intimate with each other.

So, I stand between them, utterly confused about what the hell is happening.

To add to my confusion, the hostess leads us to a curved booth in the back of the dimly lit restaurant, away from the majority of prying eyes. When she goes to set the menus down on the black and gold marbled surface of the table, Lawson waves them away and shakes his head.

"We're just having drinks."

Earlier, he told me specifically not to snack in the spa so I could save room for later. I thought later meant a delicious meal, but evidently, it means two whiskey neats for them and a shot of Patrón for me—which addles me further because Lawson doesn't like it when I drink.

"She's beautiful, isn't she?" He's smiling like he's admiring a prized mare he's about to buy.

I look past Cameron, trying to see the woman who caught Lawson's attention. My cheeks grow hot with rage at the callousness with which he speaks about another female in front of me.

Cameron chuckles, leaning into me, his cerulean blues lit up with mirth. "Absolutely adorable. But are you sure you'll be able to share this one, Law?"

Wait, what?

*Me?*

*They're talking about me?*

*Holy shit. They're talking about me!*

"I'm sorry. W-what?" I manage to stammer.

A shiver runs down my spine, making me extra aware of the added piece of *jewelry* Lawson so generously gifted me this morning. Cue naïve, young Lucy, because how the fuck did I miss all the signs?

Cameron flashes me a devilish smile as Lawson comments, "She finds you attractive. You should have seen how eager she was to work for you the first day I took over."

My head snaps to him in astonishment. "Hey!"

Cameron laughs, his gaze turning to his friend. "Even so. Something tells me you want to keep this one. Can you live with that?"

"Do I get a say in whatever you two are talking about?" I huff, irritated that they're talking about me like I'm not even here.

"No," both men answer simultaneously in authoritative tones that instantly create heat between my legs.

"It's what she wants. I trust you to be respectful."

"Are you *pimping* me out?" I ask incredulously.

Cameron's gaze finds mine again. "No, Lucy. He's not *pimping* you out. He's trying to make one of your fantasies come true."

"And what exactly is that?" I'm annoyed that Lawson didn't bother to ask if I'm okay with whatever it is they're talking about. With whatever they've clearly discussed beforehand.

Lawson leans closer, his lips ghosting the shell of my ear as Cameron reaches beneath the table, slipping past the slit in my skirt to find the skin just above my knee. "You're going to get fucked by us both tonight, rainbow."

A gasp escapes my throat as he kisses just below my ear. Cameron slides his hand upward, pushing my skirt up as his fingers dig into the flesh of my inner thigh. My eyes dart around the restaurant, but there's no one in the booths around us.

No one nearby to watch as these two men fondle me like I'm their plaything. No one to see my eyes roll back in my head when Lawson grips my chin and devours my lips as Cameron's hot breath ghosts over my shoulder, placing a chaste kiss on the suddenly sensitive skin.

Lawson's hungry, gravel-filled words caress my lips. "You're going to do exactly as we tell you. Tonight, you're our little fuck doll. You're going to take every inch of both of us at the same time, and you'll say, *'Thank you, sir. More, please, sir.'* Won't you, rainbow?"

*Holy fuck.*

I'm speechless.

My breathing becomes labored pants as Cameron's finger traces the seam of my center over my underwear. "She's already fucking soaked. What a good little toy, all ready to be used up."

Lawson swallows my moan as Cameron strokes me

softly. A man I just met ten minutes ago is already playing my body like a fucking instrument, and in public, no less.

"The decision is yours, Lucy. I wanted to gift you your fantasy, and there's no one I trust more than Cameron," Lawson whispers between kisses.

"We don't have to if you don't want to," Cameron continues as Lawson's tongue sweeps against mine, dominating my mouth as he rubs against my clit. "But if you say yes, we're going to take you upstairs, and by the end of the night, you'll be so thoroughly wrecked that you won't remember your own name."

What the fuck do they put in the water in New York?

Lawson pulls back, staring at me with so much hunger in his eyes. One of his hands wraps in my hair, the other flicking a thumb over one hardened nipple. "It's your call, rainbow. You've been fulfilling my fantasies since your graduation night. It's time I satisfy one of yours."

The storm clouds that usually reside in his eyes are deep and dark—a maelstrom of intense lust and desire.

"Would you be okay with sharing me?" I ask, even though he's initiated everything. I've heard things like this can make or break couples, but are we even in a relationship?

"I want you to have every experience I didn't get at your age, Lucy. I don't want you to regret a single thing regarding us." His words hint at a future—at least, that's how it feels to me.

Turning my head, I meet Cameron's intense blue gaze as he continues to stroke the apex of my thighs. Lifting a hand to brush my fingertips along his clean-shaven cheek, I bravely cup his chin and draw him closer. He kisses harder than Lawson, and his lips are thinner but no less enticing. He tastes like the whiskey in his glass and smells like a spicy, sweet soap.

As we part, I look back at Lawson. "Okay."

The vortex of emotions in his eyes unfurls just as Cameron draws a small orgasm from me and groans into my ear, "This is the first of many, little Lucy."

THE NEXT FIVE minutes are a blur, from leaving the restaurant, entering the elevator, and returning to the hotel room. The door isn't even closed behind us before Lawson and Cameron are working in tandem to remove my dress, my heels, my bra, and underwear—which I'm pretty sure Cameron rips as he yanks them down with his teeth while undoing the buckle of my heel.

"Looks like you already got her started, didn't you, Lawson?" Cameron grips my butt as he stands, sliding his fingers through my dripping center to touch the plug still lodged firmly in my ass.

I whine as Lawson rips his mouth from mine as we both unbutton his dress shirt.

"We've been training all week," he murmurs before claiming my lips again.

Cameron grips my chin from behind, pulling my head away from Lawson so he can take my mouth for himself. "What a lucky girl you are, little Lucy. With two men just dying to fill you so full, you'll ache for us when you're empty again."

A strangled moan passes between my swollen lips. My breath comes in harsh, ragged puffs as Lawson rids himself of his pants before dropping to his knees. "Just wait till you taste her, Cam. Best fucking thing I've ever had the pleasure of devouring."

"I can't fucking wait." Cameron chuckles in my ear as Lawson's mouth closes over my clit, sucking softly as he pumps two fingers into me. I'm so wet it's almost embarrassing. My body is wound so tightly I'm not sure I will last long at all between these two God-like men.

Lawson looks up at me from the space between my legs, so much tenderness shining in his eyes as he watches me take pleasure from him. I tangle my fingers in his hair, messing up his perfectly styled coif as I undulate my hips against his face.

The heat at my back disappears as Cameron rids himself of his clothes. When he returns, his hands graze down my arms. A swirl of ink in a smoke pattern surrounds his right wrist, climbing up his forearm. I focus on the patterns as he disentangles my hands from Lawson to draw them around his neck. Looking over my shoulder at him, I welcome his kiss as he reaches down and grips my thighs, lifting me into the air and spreading my legs to give Lawson better access.

"Fuck!" My high-pitched hoarse cry fills the room as Lawson rips my climax from me. The intensity leaves me in a drunken state of contentment.

"Such a good girl for Daddy, aren't you, rainbow?" He helps Cam lower me to the bed, and I'm boneless as I stare up at them.

Cameron's sun-kissed skin is a lighter shade than Lawson's. His muscles are slimmer, and he stands maybe two inches shorter, but they're both beautiful. A warm gush of arousal spills from between my legs as they both pump themselves while watching me.

Lawson's cock is longer and thicker, but Cameron's is still impressive, and my mouth salivates at the sight. Without being told, I move to my knees, crawling toward them with my intentions clear as I stare up at them through my lashes.

"Fuck, sweet girl, you don't even need to be told, do you?" Cameron croons as I reach for them both, wrapping my hands around their cocks.

Lawson sinks a hand into my hair. "No, she's such a good, obedient girl." I preen beneath his praise, leaning my head into his touch. His fingers slide down to my chin, swiping along my bottom lip. "But this mouth is mine only."

"That's fair," Cameron relents as I continue to jerk them off. "Such a shame, though."

As he climbs onto the bed behind me, I try to lower my mouth to Lawson's cock, but he stops me. "No, rainbow. Tonight is about you."

I can feel one of Cameron's hands on my backside as the other grabs the plug and slowly, with gentle pressure, pulls it from my body. It makes me feel empty, even as a ripple of pleasure rolls through me.

"Cam is going to take that precious hole tonight." Lawson tosses a condom and a bottle of lube to his friend. "Is that okay?"

"I hope it's okay. I wouldn't want to take Lawson's monster cock in the ass," Cameron jokes.

Words still feel foreign, getting caught in my throat whenever I try to speak, so I just nod and reach for Lawson, drawing him down to tangle our tongues together again. In just a few moments, I'm going to be fucking both of them, and my emotions—as well as my adrenaline—are all over the place.

Lawson seems to understand my need for affection, for something soft to ground me, and he gently grips my face, moving his mouth over mine. Cameron's arm encircles me from behind as he kisses my neck, still probing at my back hole.

They work together to get me into position, laying me over Cameron's lap until his cock nestles between my ass cheeks. Lawson strokes my clit lazily, watching my face for any sign of discomfort as Cameron starts to slowly buck his hips, sliding himself against me until the head of his cock finally fills me.

A sharp breath escapes my throat at the pressure, accompanied by a low whine as Cameron pulls out and pushes back in, over and over, little by little, easing his way into me.

"Look at you. Look at my good girl," Lawson murmurs against my lips. "You're taking his cock so well, rainbow. My little slut can't wait until she has Daddy's, too, can you?"

"Oh my god," I cry out when Cameron is fully sheathed inside me. The feeling is so intense and indescribable that I start to panic. "I don't... I don't know if I can take you both."

How the fuck is Lawson also supposed to fit inside me? Surely, they'll tear me apart.

"Shh... Shh. We've got you, baby," Lawson soothes as he rolls a condom over his length.

Cameron reaches around me, rubbing my clit. "God, you feel incredible," he whispers into my hair. "Kiss me."

I turn my head to let him consume my lips. One of his hands pinches and pulls at my nipple while the other continues his ministrations, and Lawson watches the whole thing like one of the films he likes to make.

"You two look good together." There's a hint of *something* in his voice I can't place. It's not anger. Not jealousy either. Perhaps it's something closer to anguish.

But when he climbs over me, lining himself up with my pussy, I pull away from Cameron and hold Lawson's gaze as he fills me. My mouth falls open—hoarse, strangled gasps of air leave my chest as he pushes forward until he bottoms out and freezes.

"Are you okay?" His teeth grit together as though it's painful for him to be inside my body. Cameron's breath is also strained as he huffs against my ear, his fingers digging into my hips to anchor me between them.

It's painful—a sharp, needle-like sting that momentarily spears through my lower body before something heavier takes over. Something that has my skin breaking out in goosebumps.

"I'm okay. I need... I need you to—"

"Tell us what you need, baby," Lawson coos so softly, so reverently, that it brings a tear to my eye.

So many emotions wreak havoc on my body, but the

one that tops them all is the love I feel for the man above me. "I need you to move."

"Shit," Cameron curses.

"You feel so fucking good, rainbow. How do you feel? What do you feel?" Lawson asks as he gradually drags himself out before pushing back in. Cameron's hips begin to move against my butt, both of them finding a pace that works for them.

As Cameron's cock drags out of my ass, Lawson's pushes inside my pussy—back and forth, in and out, winding me higher and higher as they pick up the pace, and the sound of flesh slapping against wet flesh fills the room along with a symphony of their grunts and my cries of pleasure.

"It feels so good," I whine. "I feel so full." One of my hands cups Cameron's head behind me, and the other grips Lawson's bicep as they fuck me.

With every pass, they loosen me up until it no longer feels even the slightest bit painful. Eventually, I lay back against Cameron's chest as Lawson covers us, and I move my body in time with them, undulating my hips against them both as I fuck them back.

"That's our girl," Cameron praises, hands moving to cup my breasts and play with my nipples. "Holy fuck, you were right, Lawson. She's such a good girl."

The praise has me preening, wantonly arching my back as I fully give in to being their toy. "I like being your good girl. I want you to use me. Fill me up. Brand me."

"Fuck, baby. You love being our little slut, don't you?" Sweat beads along Lawson's temple. "Look at you, writhing like a whore between the two men who are worshiping your pussy and ass."

His dirty talk spurs me on, making little electric sparks ignite at the base of my spine. "Yes, Daddy. I'm your whore. Treat me like it." I don't even recognize the sound of my own voice, raspy and filled with a need for release.

"Fuck, I'm gonna come," Cameron grunts at my back, pinching my nipples so hard that I cry out.

Lawson swallows the sound, picking up his pace as he fucks into me rougher. One of Cameron's hands drifts down to rub quickly over my clit, and my walls tense, my orgasm ripping through me as the coil in my lower belly breaks.

The three of us cry out simultaneously, all coming together. A small part of me wishes there were no barriers— so they could fill me with their cum until it's spilling out of me. I like being dirty. I like being used. In the bedroom, I want to be Lawson's dirty little slut.

I can feel them both twitching inside me, my walls contracting to milk them dry as we all drift down from our highs. Slowly, Cameron pulls out, his head dropping to the bed as he lets out a string of soft curses.

Lawson and I continue to stare at each other. I think he's silently appraising me, trying to gauge how I'm feeling.

So I show him.

As he slips out, I spread my legs, letting him see just how messy they've made me. "That was..."

"Incredible?" Cameron supplies, his hand lazily stroking my side.

"Mind-blowing?" Lawson offers with a smug smile, cupping my face in his hands.

"All those things and so much more," I breathe into his mouth as he kisses me. "Thank you for that amazing experience. Consider my fantasy well-fulfilled."

Lawson smirks, and his eyes glance over my shoulder. "Isn't she cute? She thinks we're done with her."

I blink confusedly as his friend kisses his way down my shoulder. Lawson lowers himself between my legs as Cameron once again spreads them wide. "What are you—?"

Lawson closes his mouth over my sensitive clit.

"Oh, sweet girl," Cameron sighs. "We're just getting started."

# TWENTY-FOUR

*Lawson*

"WHAT WOULD you do if you didn't work for M.I.G.?" Lucy asks as she ties her russet waves in a messy pile on top of her head. The motion makes my dress shirt ride up on her naked body, giving me a peek at what else is bare between her thighs.

"Probably stick with landlord and tenant representation and focus on the low-income housing market. Rent is getting ridiculous, and these property owners are making money hand over fist while hard-working families can barely afford to keep food on the table." I finish the last sentence of an email before sending it off and placing my laptop on her nightstand. "It should be a crime to look that good in my clothes."

Her lips pull up in a smile as she crawls onto the bed and settles between my legs, wrapping her arms around me as she lies on my chest. "I think that's very admirable of you —wanting to help families in need."

Smoothing the stray strands that have already fallen out of her hair tie, I repeat her question, adding, "Do you want to remain an assistant lead? Or were you planning to move up in one of the departments?"

"I don't know. I like my job." Her brows scrunch together as she props her chin on my pec. "I like organizing things, keeping the chaos controlled. It brings me peace." She grins. "If I took your job, I think it would be too stressful."

"Oh?" I cock an eyebrow. "You're shooting from assistant to executive director in one fell swoop, huh?" My hands smooth under the shirt to tickle her sides. "It's a good thing we provide excellent stress relief at the company, isn't it?" I chuckle as she starts wiggling around, screeching for me to stop between bouts of laughter.

Rolling her over, I capture her lips as her legs come up to cage my waist. It's a slow kiss, full of purpose and something thicker than lust. Another L-word that's been bouncing around in my brain for weeks now. When I pull back, glowing golden sunlight filters over her face.

*This* is what brings me peace. Lazy Saturday mornings with the woman I adore so much it makes my chest hurt just thinking about it.

I'll admit, I was worried about what our night with Cameron would do for our relationship. Even if the thought of them together at one point drove me to jealousy, I knew I could trust him to help me give Lucy her fantasy, and I can honestly say that I loved watching them together. But part of me was afraid that after that night, I wouldn't be enough for her anymore—that once she got a taste of what else is out there, she'd want to explore on her own.

However, that night strengthened us in a way I never thought possible. Lucy feels like mine now in every way imaginable. And I hope she knows I'm hers. I hope my actions and words speak loudly enough to tell her what I haven't spoken out loud yet.

*I love you.*

*I want to stay in Chicago with you.*

There's only one last thing holding me back—well, two: Rhys' reaction and my marriage.

"Lawson?" Lucy reaches up to brush back the hair that's fallen into my eyes.

"Hmm?" I brush my lips against hers again, unable to stop touching her—to stop kissing her—just to remind myself that this is real. That *she* is real and that I'm the lucky bastard who has the privilege of being with her.

A flash of vulnerability lights up her hazel eyes as she opens her mouth, but before she can say anything, her phone starts ringing from its place on the nightstand. Her cheeks flush a deep rose, and she rolls out from beneath me to grab it, rising from the bed and turning her back to me.

"It's my mom. Give me a second," she says before answering the call. "Hey, Mom. What's up?"

I can hear Bree speaking on the other end of the line, but not clearly enough to make out what she's saying. Lucy answers with affirmative hums, pausing to look back at me for a second with a slight smile as she nods. "Okay, I'll do that. Yep, I got it. Okay, see you in a few hours."

Moving to sit on the edge of the bed, I wrap my arms around her as she hangs up and steps between my legs, winding her arms around my neck. "Sounds like Rose is bringing River to our Fourth of July BBQ today. My mom told me I should invite you, too."

Shock lances through me. Did she tell her parents about us?

Lucy reads the question on my face and shakes her head with a soft laugh. "No, my family doesn't know about us. I think she just thought it would be a nice gesture so you weren't alone, or in case you don't have other plans."

Her statement is more of a leading inquiry as she breaks eye contact to look at the floor between us. "You don't have to come. I know it might be... awkward to spend time with my family but not be able to be... *us*."

I pull her flush against me. "Do you want me to come?"

The little vixen smiles mischievously. "I *always* want you to come."

Laughing, I roll my eyes, even though my cock hardens at her innuendo. "If you want me there, Lucy, I'll be there."

Something warm shines in her gaze as she nods slightly. "Yeah. I want you there."

One of her hands slides down my chest and lowers to unfasten the button of my pants. Her free hand curls in the hair at the nape of my neck, pulling me in for a kiss full of heat and passion and intent. She breaks our contact to rid me of my pants, then climbs onto my lap.

"I also want you here." She lines my cock up with her entrance.

"We need a condom," I say, but I make no move to stop Lucy as she slides down onto my length. Warm, wet, and so fucking *right*. A groan escapes my throat as her mouth falls open, brows drawing together in satisfaction.

"I want to feel you," she moans as she begins to ride me. "I want to feel what's mine."

Her words rip a feral growl from my chest—a bestial

feeling as I hear her claim me for her own. Holding her to me, I flip us around, driving into her with heavy, deep thrusts. "If I'm yours, you're mine, rainbow."

I recognize the emotion in her sun-kissed irises, the love, as she takes everything I give her with equal fervor. Her nails dig into the skin on my back, hips rising to meet every sensual roll of my own as she whispers into the space between us, "I've been yours for a long time, Lawson Morgan."

ONCE UPON A TIME, I imagined what being part of this circle of friends would be like. In another life, where Charlotte didn't cheat, Rhys stayed true to Lucy, and they made it through college long-distance.

Now, I'm so fucking thankful it never worked out that way.

Because this? This is a dream I never allowed myself to ever imagine.

Lucy's parents and their friends welcome me with open arms... *literally*. Bree hugs me when I step over the threshold with River in tow, and her husband, Will, shakes my hand with a warm smile as he hands me a frosty bottle of craft beer.

"Thanks for taking care of my little girl, Lawson. She loves her job at M.I.G.," he tells me as he leads me to the backyard where Lucy's pseudo aunts and uncles are.

*I don't think you'd be thanking me if you knew* how *I take care of her.*

Part of me feels guilty for taking advantage of their hospitality because I know for a fact if they knew I just fucked their daughter a few hours ago, they wouldn't be so friendly.

"Well, she's great at her job. We're lucky to have her." I lift the beer to my lips just as Lucy appears between the open French doors. She's twisted her hair into a more complicated updo after I fucked her six ways from Sunday, and it was too tangled to leave down. Her distressed white denim shorts are so tiny they have me thinking of how badly I want to bend her over again, and her emerald top reminds me of the dress she wore a few weekends ago.

Everything about this woman always has me so wound up it's a miracle I don't get hard—and that no one notices how our eyes remain locked across the yard as she saunters over to her aunts.

"So, Lucy says you're returning to New York next year. I thought you took a promotion for this office, though?" Mark, Kendall's husband, inquires.

"Yeah, I did. If I went back, I wouldn't be an executive director. But I'm actually thinking of staying now." My eyes stray back to Lucy, who's laughing with her sister Lorraine about something.

Will flips a few burgers on his grill. "Oh, yeah? Lucy will be happy to hear that. She likes working for you. Does that mean Charlotte is gonna stay in Florida?"

"Honestly, I don't really know what Charlotte is going to do," I answer truthfully. Before my brain can catch up with my mouth, I add, "I'm having divorce papers drawn up at the moment, so I'm sure she'll take the house in Boca and whatever else she can get her hands on."

It was only really a thought, not a concrete decision. Yes, I'm having papers drawn up, but I haven't decided whether to send them. Charlotte will cost me a lot more post-divorce than she does now but with things changing between Lucy and me...

"Good for you." Henry, Rose's father, tips his beer in my direction. "That woman is bad news, no offense. I'm sure Charleigh has some suggestions for divorce lawyers if you need them."

"Thank you. I might just have a talk with her about it."

First, though, I need to discuss it with Lucy. We need to think about what the future will look like, what it will do to my sons, and what it will mean for *us*.

As the guys fall into a conversation about work, my eyes find hers again. All the difficult discussions we shelved for a later date need to be had now. We're at a crossroads where we either make a go of this or we don't.

At this point, I don't think I could walk away, even if she wanted me to.

———————⌒∽⌒———————

"LUCY! You're not at work. You don't have to serve him! Is this what you have her do, Lawson? Have her bring you food and drinks like some sort of servant?" Charleigh's teasing tone rings clear across the yard as Lucy hands me another beer and a plate of Kendall's ambrosia salad.

She laughs, "Aunt Daphne was doing the same for Uncle Henry! I thought I'd be nice!"

"Thank you, Lucy. I appreciate it." Our fingers brush as she hands me the cold bottle, lingering for a few seconds under the guise of grabbing my empty one. The women are still soaking up the sun on lawn chairs while the guys sit in a circle around the unlit fire pit.

"You're welcome. Does anyone else need anything?" Her uncles shake their heads as they continue talking about fishing lures—a conversation I'm interested in. However, I'm more interested in the daring smile Lucy flashes me when no one is looking before she heads into the house.

I wait a few moments, placing my beer on the ground and my plate on my seat as I get up. "Bathroom is down the hall, right?"

Will nods in confirmation, too distracted with their discussion to realize his daughter also went inside. Once again, I feel guilty, but getting Lucy alone for a few moments is worth it. I close the doors behind me as I enter their home. It's a large open concept with a joint dining room and kitchen, and the object of my affection beams at me as she puts food away.

"Having fun?"

"I am." I lean against the kitchen island across from her. "Is it weird for you that I'm here?"

"Lawson..." She looks behind me to make sure the doors are shut and no one can hear us. "...you came inside me multiple times this morning. I think... it wouldn't be such a bad idea if we came clean about what's going on between us."

My chest fills like a balloon with anticipation and

happiness, and a little bit of anxiety swells beneath my lungs as her suggestion tells me we're on the same page.

I open my mouth to agree with her, but the sound of pounding footsteps coming down the stairs interrupts me as my son enters the kitchen. His face is flushed with mussed hair and a wild look in his eyes.

"River? Are you okay?"

His light blue gaze darts to mine before he looks at Lucy and then back to me. "Yeah. I'm fine." His voice hitches like he's lying with an undercurrent of anger.

Lucy catches it, too. "River, where's Rose?"

"Upstairs talking to Liam," he answers in a rush, opening one of the doors and disappearing outside before we can ask any more questions.

"Liam?" Her face scrunches in confusion. "I didn't even know he was here. Liam!" she shouts from the bottom of the stairs.

After a few moments, I watch her face morph into curiosity as the heavy sound of her brother's footsteps resonates through the air, and Lucy steps back into the kitchen as Liam appears, looking pissed off and worse for wear. His skin is ashen, and his eyes, which are rimmed with red, narrow on me.

"Why haven't you come outside? Mom didn't think you were coming today. And where is Rose?" Lucy resumes putting away the food. Feeling like an outsider for the first time today, I busy myself with helping her to avoid Liam's glare.

"She's in the bathroom upstairs." He finally looks at his sister. "I'm not staying."

From my conversations with Lucy, I know Liam is

struggling. I know he's an addict, and it's a damn shame because the boy is sharp as a tack. He looks lost, like he's not sure he belongs here, even though it's his home and this is his family.

I know that feeling all too well. "Come on, Liam. Stay a while. I think your father was just about to start a fire."

Lucy shoots me a grateful smile, though it's tinged with a bit of sadness, as she turns back to her brother, who is now openly sneering at me.

"Gee, thanks for inviting me to stay in my own house, Lawson. What, you think because you're fucking my sister, you can play house here now?"

Lucy whirls around, mouth open in shock as she pales. "Liam!"

An icy wave of dread crashes over me. Before I can say anything, a movement in my peripheral has my head swinging in slow motion to see Kendall frozen just inside the door. Her eyes dart between us before she quickly looks over her shoulder and shuts the door. Instantly, I'm thankful that she doesn't march out and spill our secret to Bree and Will.

Liam has the grace to look remorseful for about half a second before he turns for the front door.

"Liam!" Lucy yells as she runs after him.

Rose appears at the bottom of the steps, eyes wide and skin flushed a deep pink. She watches the siblings before turning to look at me for a brief second, then she races past Kendall to go outside.

Neither of us speaks, avoiding eye contact as Lucy reappears. "Aunt Kendall..."

The blonde holds her hands up. "It's not my business.

You're both adults." Her blue eyes settle on her niece. "But if I were you, I'd tell your parents." She looks to me next. "And if I were *you,* I'd have that conversation before someone else tells them... or your *wife.*"

She turns and goes back outside, leaving Lucy and me alone in the kitchen.

"Well, that was..."

"Awful?" Lucy offers.

Every fiber in my being wants to go to her. To wrap her in my arms and tell her it will be okay.

Instead, I place my hand next to hers on the island. The tips of our fingers brush, and she closes her eyes, taking a deep, centering breath as she draws whatever comfort she can from our touch.

I rub my index finger along hers. "I think it's time for us to talk about the future. What do you say to that lake house getaway?"

# TWENTY-FIVE

*Lucy*

THE LAKE HOUSE is a few hours south of Lawson's primary home. In the two years I dated Rhys, he'd never brought me down here, but I know it's his favorite out of the three—now four—houses that the Morgan family owns. It's also the one place where Lawson and Rhys shared their love of fishing despite whatever animosity was brewing between the two of them.

It looks like any other typical home from the outside—with bluish-gray side paneling, white trim, and a speckled gray shingled roof. But the inside is massive—with oatmeal-colored walls and cherry-stained hardwood floors.

"Wow, Lawson. This place is gorgeous."

We drop our bags off in the living room. The open design flows into a large kitchen that boasts polished mahogany cabinetry with bright white quartz countertops and stainless steel appliances.

"Come here." Lawson summons me into a sunroom that sits off the living room.

French doors lead to an enormous deck and a staircase

that takes you down to the sloped backyard. He points to a small dock with an old wooden lake boat that looks like it's seen better days. It seems out of place against the well-kept house, but it reminds me so much of Lawson, and I love that he owns it instead of a flashy, newer, motorized one.

"I'm gonna get you out on the water tomorrow." His arms wrap around me, and he chuckles against my neck.

I jerk my thumb toward the dock. "As pretty as it is, this house screams Charlotte. It's nice to see there's still a touch of you here."

He kisses the spot below my ear before grabbing my hand and pulling me back inside. Grabbing our bags, he leads me down a hallway.

"Yeah, I've been thinking about redecorating the place for a while now. But it's hard to get down here with work. Rhys comes here more than anyone."

"What is the point of having all these houses if you can't enjoy them?" The walls are lined with family photos of their time here. Pictures of Lawson with the boys out on the lake, the four of them around the fire pit in the backyard, and even a Christmas photo where they obviously spent the holiday here.

We pass a bathroom and a guest room, and at the end of the hall is the large primary with its own en suite. I know Charlotte hasn't been to this house in years, and for some reason, the idea of sharing this room with Lawson doesn't bother me as much as it did at his other home.

"Well, like I said, Rhys comes here a lot. When River is older, I won't mind if he wants to come out here with his friends, too. I'm surprised Rhys never brought you here..."

Lawson trails off as he brings up our past, awkwardly scratching the back of his neck as he realizes what he's said.

Ignoring it, I wrap my arms around his middle and lay my head against his back after he sets our stuff down. "I'm happy to have another first with you."

He beams a smile over his shoulder before twisting to pick me up and lay me on the dark gray duvet. "Oh, rainbow, this weekend will be full of firsts for us."

A giggle escapes my throat as he kisses his way down my chest, pulling my shirt up to lay his warm lips against my belly. His fingers work the tie on my linen shorts, yanking them and my underwear down in one pull before hitching my legs over his shoulders.

"I thought you said we needed to go get groceries." My fingers tangle in his hair as he runs his tongue against my aching center.

"I've got a meal right here. I'll worry about feeding you later," he remarks before sucking my clit into his mouth.

I've never been with a guy who likes to go down on a woman as much as Lawson does. He takes his time, eyes closed as if he's savoring every drop of me, worshiping every inch of the flesh between my legs. His soft moans send vibrations through my lower body.

There's something about a man letting you know just how satisfied it makes him to please you—and Lawson doesn't just stop at pleasing me once.

My orgasm surges through me, and I come with a strangled cry as my back arches and my hips chase his mouth.

He grins against my soaked flesh. "Give me another one, rainbow."

Lawson likes to remind me that no other man will ever be able to bring me pleasure the way he does.

He works me slowly, adding two fingers as his tongue laps against my clit, making my body convulse as it nears another release.

And holy shit, I am *not* complaining.

"Are you making a gourmet meal for dinner?" I laugh as Lawson pushes the grocery cart down the baking aisle.

He grins, scanning the shelves. "I was going to surprise you."

"Surprise me with what?" I look over the things he's grabbed, unable to tell what meals he is planning. The cart is nearly full, even though we're only staying until Sunday afternoon. I know he wants to fish tomorrow, so that means bass for dinner, but I can't make heads or tails of the other ingredients.

"If I tell you, it won't be a surprise." Lawson pulls me in to kiss my temple. "Stay here a moment. I forgot something in the last aisle. Will you grab a bag of chocolate chips, please? Semisweet."

Giddiness flutters from my chest to my lower belly. There's only one reason I can think of for chocolate chips.

I browse the shelves for the brand I remember always seeing Lawson use. When I find them on the very top shelf, just out of reach, I debate waiting for him to come back before deciding to step on the bottom shelf to give myself a bit of a boost.

It tips slightly as I step on it, and a hand braces on the small of my back as I jump back in alarm, preparing for the whole thing to come tumbling down on me.

"Hey there, that could have been bad," a warm, friendly male voice says.

Looking up, I see a pair of brown eyes and the thin smile of a guy I don't know. He is basically caging me against the wall of chocolate.

"Hi." He reaches for the bag I'd been trying to get. "Was this what you needed?"

"Thanks," I mumble as he steps back. The whole interaction is innocent, but my body shivers in revulsion at the stranger's touch.

"No problem." He glances toward the end of the aisle. "I know this is probably really random and will sound weird, but I saw you a few aisles over and haven't seen you around before, and, uh... I'm just going to shoot my shot here. You're gorgeous, and if you're here for the weekend, I'd love to take you to dinner."

A throat clears behind me, and I startle, looking over my shoulder to see Lawson piercing the guy with a lethal gaze. If looks could kill, this man would be dead a hundred times over.

"Hi there, I'm Kip." *Kip* holds his hand out to Lawson. "At the risk of sounding like a real creep, I was just asking your daughter here if she'd like to get dinner this weekend."

I try and fail miserably to hide my erupting laugh behind a cough. Irritation rolls off Lawson in waves. He ignores the proffered hand and wraps his large, muscled arm around me, pulling my body into his side possessively. "She's not my daughter. She's my girlfriend."

Kip's eyes widen comically. "Oh, wow. Dude, I'm so sorry." He backs away, eyes darting between us as crimson stains his cheeks. "I'm just... gonna go now. Have a great weekend."

Lawson glares down at me when I turn my eyes to him, causing me to jump in shock. "What? I couldn't reach the chocolate you wanted, so he was just helping me."

"Uh huh," Lawson hums dryly, clearly not amused.

With a shrug, I push the cart further down the aisle, ignoring his pointed glare. "I can't help it if men want to help a damsel in distress."

Suddenly, Lawson's hands grasp the handle on either side of mine, his chest pressing against my back with a heavy heat that has me instantly wet.

Nuzzling my ear, he whispers, "You are neither a damsel nor in distress. What you are is a devious little brat who is going to get a spanking when we get home."

Everything he says sends sexual electricity down my spine, and I look at him over my shoulder, brimming with a need to get the fuck out of this grocery store and back *home.* "Yes, Daddy."

"DINNER WAS AMAZING. Thank you for cooking."

Lawson starts getting out bowls, mixing spoons, and a few different pots before pulling the remaining grocery bags toward him on the kitchen island. "Of course. I enjoy cooking. And you make a pretty good sous-chef."

"Please," I snort, "I nearly burned the rice. Who burns rice?" I am not a bad cook and will die on the hill claiming it's the type of pots he has here—that and the fact that I always use a rice cooker at home.

He pulls me to him. "You did fine. I'll just do all the stove work for these," he teases.

"'These?'" I ask, even though I'm well aware of what all the ingredients scattered on the island are for.

Lawson nuzzles my neck. "I think it's time I teach you how to make my cookies."

Curling my lips to stop the squeal that wants to leave my throat, I grip his arms. "I thought it was a *family* recipe?"

Butterflies and hummingbirds and every creature with little fluttering wings multiply in my stomach as he kisses the spot that drives me wild, murmuring in my ear, "Exactly."

### Lawson

"Tell me something true. Something I don't know about you," Lucy calls from the bathroom.

"That isn't a question, rainbow." I stretch out, settling back against the pillows. My skin is sticky with our combined sweat, and I debate pulling her into the shower to clean up before I get her dirty all over again.

I don't think I'll ever get tired of fucking Lucy. Each time feels like the first time, full of passion and hunger, and if I could make a job out of giving her orgasms, I would.

"I know, but I need more time to think of more questions." She laughs as she appears in the doorway of the en suite. Her hair is a mass of tangles giving her that freshly fucked look, and all she wears is one of my button-downs and a pair of tall, fuzzy cream socks.

The inner curves of her bare breasts peek out behind the buttons, full and begging for my mouth, perfectly on display.

"In New York..." I relent as Lucy stares at me, clearly not coming back to bed until I answer her. "...when I'd go to the club, I'd have—" a laugh breaks my words as I shake my head, amazed that I'm about to admit this. "...I'd have the women wear a red wig."

She arches an eyebrow, giving me a flat look.

"Think about it, Lucy."

After a few moments, realization flashes in her eyes. "A red wig... because of... me?"

I nod. "Does that freak you out?"

She shakes her head and replies with a soft, "No."

I want to ask what's going through her mind, but she lets it go and moves on.

"Hmm..." As she saunters toward the bed, she presses a pointer finger against her lips in mock contemplation. "What's your favorite body part?"

Without hesitating, I answer, "Your lips. God, I fucking think about these lips all the time." I swipe a thumb across the lower one as I cup her cheek. "I think about kissing them until they're swollen and branded." Tilting her head, she smiles before sucking my finger into her mouth. "I think about what they'd look like wrapped around my cock."

Soft, delicate fingers grasp my length as it hardens between us. As she continues to suck, Lucy swipes the precum already leaking from the slit around my swollen head. It jumps in her hand, responsive to her touch and eager for what's coming.

Her lashes flutter as she pops off my thumb. "Why haven't you let me suck your cock yet?"

A groan leaves my lips at hearing her talk so dirty. "I've always... had trouble... controlling myself." At her questioning look, I explain further, "I usually grab onto the back of a woman's head and... lose myself in the feeling. In the moment. It wasn't a big deal in New York because that's what the club is for—to find people who like the same things you do. But Charlotte always told me it made her feel like a cheap whore." I rub the back of my neck. "I never wanted to make you feel that way."

"You never do, Lawson." My breath catches as Lucy positions herself on her belly, lowering her head to kiss my tip before she looks back up at me. "I like it when you treat me like your dirty little slut." The words are teasing, but they quickly turn serious as she continues, "You praise me, and I love it. I like you telling me when I do a good job. It pleases me to please you. And afterward, you care for me and make me feel loved."

"But I don't want to hurt you." I grit my teeth as she drops her head again, swirling her tongue to lick up the glistening mess I've already made.

One of my hands moves to her hair, and she stares at me through her lashes. "Maybe we should get a pair of handcuffs. That way, I can maintain whatever pace *I* want."

A growl rumbles in my chest when she sucks the first

few inches as she laves her tongue against my crown. "You'll never get me in a pair of handcuffs, rainbow. The need to touch you is too strong. I'll never deny myself that privilege."

"Never say never," she whispers before sliding her mouth down as far as she can take me.

I fist the sheets, wanting so desperately to grab onto her head and force my length down her throat. I watch in awe as she bobs, taking more of me with every pass as she relaxes her throat.

"Fuck, baby. Show me what those pretty lips can do."

"Do you want to film me while I do it?" She settles into a role as she pulls off my cock to kiss my abs. "Do you want to film your good girl taking your cock so deep that I choke? Do you want to be able to replay the moment when you fill my mouth and watch it coat the lips you love so much?"

My insides tighten, and I have to steel myself before I answer. It's the first time she's willingly asked me to film her. I jolt back to reality when her tongue darts out to slowly lick the slit on my head.

"Grab your camera now if you want the memory."

Warmth blooms in my chest as she wraps her lips around me again. I widen my legs to make more room for her and gently—so fucking gently—wrap a hand in her hair as I guide her head. "Some things are meant to be savored in the moment, rainbow."

Her full, berry smile around my cock is the most rewarding vision. She makes little noises that vibrate up my shaft, gagging when she takes me too far and purring with pleasure as she starts to undulate her hips against the bed.

"Do you feel empty right now, Lucy? Would you rather my cock be deep inside your pussy instead of your mouth?" I'm giving her an out before it's too late and I come down her throat.

She stares at me defiantly, moving over me so slowly and pulling back all the way with every pass. Saliva pools from the corners of her mouth when she gets to my crown, where she pays extra attention to the flushed skin that's angry, purple, and so fucking hard I'm ready to burst.

"God, you're such a good fucking girl. I wish you could see how well you're taking my cock. I am so fucking stupid for not doing this sooner."

I burn the image to my memory, wishing I hadn't waited so long to let her do this. Lucy takes my cock like a pornstar, making love to it with her mouth and giving me a high-definition cinematic experience to replay in my brain over and over in the moments when she doesn't warm my bed.

"Lucy, I'm about to come," I warn, delicately smoothing her sweaty hair away from her face so I can watch without anything obstructing my view.

She nods, humming her approval just as my balls tighten and an explosion of heat flows out from the base of my spine. My hands shake, wanting to force her head down, but I have other plans for her this time.

"Don't swallow," I command as my cock twitches. I flood her mouth, and she moans while my creamy release leaks out, more than she can hold. After I finish, I help her to her knees and rise. "Open your mouth and show me."

Lucy's lips part to show me my cum. More drips out, spilling down her chin and onto her breasts.

"Good girl. Now, give it to me."

When her eyebrows draw together in confusion, I move my mouth to hers, and her eyes widen in understanding, cheeks growing even more red. A little moan leaves her lips, sliding into my mouth along with my salty release. When I take it all, I maneuver her back against the pillows and roughly jerk her legs over my shoulders.

"Lawson!" Lucy cries out in surprise, lips still painted milky white. "Holy fuck." She releases a breathy whimper as I feed my cum into her glistening pussy.

"That's right, rainbow. This pussy is mine. It's meant to take every ounce of my cum so you can be full of me all the time. I want you dripping *me* everywhere. At the office. At home. At your fucking parents' house. Whenever we're out, and some asshole thinks he can approach you like he has a chance in hell with my girl. This pussy stays full of me. Do you understand?"

I watch my essence disappear into her body. I don't release my hold, wanting it to travel as deep as it can before I fuck more into her. I lower my tongue to her center as she writhes and moans, twisting in pleasure as I eat her with vigor.

"Lawson!" she cries out as she comes.

I shove it all back inside her with my tongue, waiting until her breathing has calmed before I lower her legs and position myself at her entrance.

Slowly, I push my way inside her. "Do you understand?"

Lucy lets out a keening wail, nails clawing at me as I rub against her clit, smearing our combined releases. "Fuck, yes. Yes!"

"Good girl." I kiss her long and hard, just like how I fuck her. "You're so fucking perfect, baby. Such a perfect fucking girl." My hips snap forward, driving into her at an angle I haven't achieved with her yet.

"Yes. I'm your good girl. I'm your good girl," she whines over and over.

I can feel her walls tense around me, and as another orgasm crashes through her, I keep praising her, and we go back and forth like a beautifully broken record.

A record we play on repeat as I make love to her throughout the rest of the night and into the early hours of the morning.

# Twenty-Six

Lawson

"I swear to god, Lawson! Don't you—! Lawson! Don't you dare!" Lucy squeals as I hold a white bass over her.

"Come on, baby, he just wants a little kiss!" I laugh as slimy lake water drips onto her chest, and she scrambles to get away.

Throwing herself to the other end of the boat, the old frame pitches back and forth as she cries, "Lawson Morgan, I hate you!"

Her words are filled with faux contempt as she wipes off the fish water, but a smile stretches her swollen lips. Her little yellow bikini does nothing to hide the love marks I gave her last night, and I take great pride in seeing my brands on her flesh as she stretches out again.

"Aww, you don't hate me, rainbow. As a matter of fact..." I secure the fish in the cooler and grab another piece of bait. "...I seem to remember you telling me over and over again how much you *loved* all my parts last night—and this morning." I grin at her before casting my line out.

Last night would have been the perfect time to tell her that I love her, and Lucy caught herself almost saying it multiple times, covering it up with remarks about loving my mouth, my fingers, and my cock. We're both ready to say the words, yet we're both holding back. That damn conversation we still need to have hangs over our heads like a cloud full of rain.

Lucy flips me off and pulls her sunhat further over her eyes. "You're impossible."

I don't respond, letting the sounds of the lake and nature fill the space between us. For a Saturday, there aren't many boats out, and the ones who have passed by are mindful not to send huge waves our way. The birds chirp from the tree branches that line the shore, and there's laughter from children playing on the banks in the shallower water.

It's peaceful, and as I look at Lucy, it feels right—like *home*.

"We should probably talk about everything," I softly state, reeling in my line so I can focus on her.

As she sits up, Lucy lifts her hat and peers at me from beneath the brim. "Yeah."

"Where is your head at?" I hate how vulnerable I sound. It's a big decision to make—coming clean to everyone.

"I mean, you know how I feel about you, Lawson." Lucy reaches for her discarded sundress to play with the hem, something I've noticed she does when she's deep in thought or nervous.

"Come here." I motion for her to sit between my legs, where she'd been before I teased her with the fish. She does

—but only after I lay my shirt over the fish water so she doesn't have to sit in "*fish goo.*"

"This is nice." Lucy sighs, settling against my chest. "I love it here."

I'm sure she can feel the rise in my heartbeat as I take a deep breath, preparing to bare my soul. Hugging her to me, I settle my chin on her shoulder. "We can come out here every weekend if you want."

She hums with approval, fingers tracing idle patterns on my forearms. "And what about New York? Are you still thinking about returning once the office is fully integrated into M.I.G.?"

"I won't lie and say I don't miss the city. But I think my future is here in Chicago with you." My voice is husky as the words tumble from my lips. "We started something all those years ago, rainbow. Something that's turned into a whirlwind of emotions I didn't think I could feel again. And it's going to be hard... telling everyone. If I'm being honest, I don't know that we're quite ready for that." Lucy tenses in my arms, and I reach for her hands, lacing our fingers together as I kiss her temple. "Do you think you're ready to come clean to your parents?"

"Yes." Her answer is immediate, and she twists in my hold, climbing into my lap to wrap her arms around my neck. "Yes, Lawson, I *am* ready. Aren't you? Don't you want to stop sneaking around? It's getting exhausting. I don't want to hide anymore."

"I'm still married, Lucy. There's a lot to figure out... and Rhys... Fuck, when Rhys finds out—"

Her eyes have become glassy. "It's okay, Lawson."

"Baby, don't cry." I cradle her cheek as her eyes fill with tears that she tries desperately to keep at bay.

"No, it's stupid, I know." She shakes her head, pulling from my grip to wipe at her face. "You're not ready. It's fine." Her voice hitches, cracking like the little fissures her tone puts in my heart.

"Lucy." I pull her face to me again. "Lucy, look at me." Holding onto my wrists like a lifeline, she does, and I capture her lips, pouring every ounce of what I'm feeling into our kiss.

"Baby, I love you." My declaration pulls a gasp from her chest. "I love you so goddamn much it hurts not to be able to show you off in public." I kiss her again. "That's why I want to do this the right way. I don't want to tell your parents while I'm still married to Charlotte. And I don't—" I turn away to look out at the water as I think about all the times I took Rhys fishing in this same boat on this same lake. "I don't know how to tell Rhys. That is going to be a fucking nightmare I don't want to put you through."

Lucy is silent, and when my eyes slide back to hers, her lips are parted in surprise. "You... you love me?"

Chuckling, I draw her in for another kiss, whispering against her lips, "I don't think love is a strong enough word for what I feel for you, rainbow. You make me fucking crazy. Whenever I see another man look at you, I want to take you right there just to show him that you're *mine*. I can't get my fill of you, and I suspect I never will. You're it for me, Lucy Bradee. If you want me, I'm yours."

"Of course, I want you, you idiot!" she exclaims before pressing her lips to mine. "I love you, too." Another kiss.

"So fucking much that I feel like I'm going to explode sometimes."

Abruptly, she jolts from my lap, pushing back so roughly that the boat rocks with her movement. Grabbing the oars, she shoves them into my hands. "Take us back home right now before I get us a ticket for public indecency."

At my raised brow, she fixes me with a heated stare. "You just told me you love me, Lawson. Now I want you to fuck me while you say it."

"Yes, ma'am."

Her cheeks grow pink as she shoots me a saucy smile. "I think I like the sound of that."

I double-time it back to the shore. "Don't get used to it, rainbow. I'm still your daddy. I'm still the one in charge."

"For now," she singsongs as her grin turns devilish. "Because you love me, I'm sure you won't mind giving up control every once in a while."

Lucy sinks to her knees, flattening out on the deck of the boat as she reaches for the drawstring of my shorts. "What are you doing?"

Her hazel eyes are dark, the gold rings around the irises so fucking bright as she looks up at me and pulls my cock out. "Keep rowing, Lawson."

As she takes me in her mouth, I nearly come right there. *Sassy little brat.*

AFTER SPENDING the rest of the afternoon in bed, continuing our discussion between rounds of sex, Lucy falls asleep. I leave her naked and tangled in the sheets as I begin dinner so it's ready when she wakes up.

Oil sizzles and pops in the pan as I lay a piece of fish down. Garlic permeates the air as I open the oven to check on the parmesan potatoes, and the green beans have the perfect amount of crunch to them as I bite into one before removing their pot from the stove.

Everything couldn't be more perfect.

I have a plan. First things first, I need to finalize my divorce. I didn't admit it to Lucy during our earlier discussion, but I already called Charlotte the night I got home from the BBQ and told her we needed to talk. I need to show Bree and Will that I'm serious about their daughter—show Lucy that I'm serious about *her*—and I can't do that if I'm still legally married.

Next comes the bigger problem. *Rhys.*

Over the years, things have remained strained between me and my oldest son. I'm not sure how I missed Charlotte sinking her claws so far into him, filling his head with absolute bullshit about how I never wanted him and how I love River more.

It's all a fucking lie, but I've never been able to convince him of that. He's always felt like he's a burden, and now? What the fuck am I supposed to do *now*?

No matter how I present it, Rhys will take this as the ultimate betrayal.

And I'm stuck in the middle, having to choose between my son and the woman I love.

Lucy is worth it... I just need some time to figure it all out.

"Dad?"

*I'm thinking about it to the point where I'm hallucinating his voice now. Get a grip, Lawson.*

"Dad!"

My son's voice echoes through the kitchen, startling me as I drop the fish in the oil, causing the hot liquid to splatter on my hand. "Shit!"

"Fuck, sorry. I didn't mean to scare you. You were off in your own little world there," Rhys says as he strolls in, dropping his bag on the floor before sliding onto a stool. "What are you doing here?"

"What are *you* doing here?" I move to the sink, turning the water on lukewarm before placing my hand beneath the stream.

"Just wanted to get away for a little bit. Looks like you had the same idea. Or are you working?" Rhys tilts his head curiously as he takes in the dinnerware I laid out earlier. "Are you here with someone?"

Before I can reply, Lucy's voice rings out from down the hall. "Mmmm, something smells good!"

Fuck.

Rhys' head snaps toward the hall, no doubt recognizing the sweet timbre of his ex-girlfriend.

*Please don't be naked. Please don't be naked.*

My heart hammers against my chest, and I'm sure Rhys can hear it as he stares at the spot where the hall opens into the living room.

"Lucy?" His voice is barely audible.

"Rhys?" There's surprise in her tone, but underneath, it's tinged with...*joy?*

They laugh as they greet one another, and I turn to look over my shoulder to see Lucy wearing a sky-blue linen romper, her hair hanging in waves down her back.

"Wait..." Rhys' tone turns serious. Suspicious. "What are you doing here?"

I slam the water off, spinning to see Lucy staring at me with rosy cheeks as Rhys' bright blue eyes dart between us.

"Working." It's out of my mouth before he can put two and two together. "I didn't realize Lucy worked for the company M.I.G. took over. Turns out she's my new assistant while I'm here."

Lucy visibly deflates, staring at me with a look that clearly says, 'this is the time to tell him! What are you doing?'

As Rhys' gaze swings her way, she flashes him a small smile. Her fingers tangle together, and she twists them in front of her.

"Why are *you* here, then?" Rhys questions her, still watching us both skeptically. If he knows her nervous trait, he doesn't show it.

"You know service is shit out this way. I asked her to come so we didn't get our wires crossed if I needed something." The lies keep pouring out, making me feel like absolute shit as Lucy bites her lip, either to keep her anger at bay or her disappointment.

After a few moments, Rhys makes a huffing sound. "Well, I guess this is just fate, then." He takes a small step toward Lucy, reaching up to rub the back of his neck. "I've been meaning to reach out. You know, I'm moving back." He beams at her as though he can't believe his good luck.

"Ye-yeah." Lucy has to clear her throat before forming a clear sentence. "I, uh, overheard River saying something about it to Rose. Are you excited to come home?"

"I am now." His eyes fill with that familiar gleam he always used to look at her with. "What are the chances? I was actually going to drop my stuff off, then go into town to grab dinner. Would you... maybe like to join me?"

My stomach roils as her eyes dart to me and then to the stove where our dinner is nearly done cooking. "Lawson cooked—"

"Don't mind me," I interrupt, noting how her eyes shut with annoyance. "Go for it. I don't mind."

Rhys is completely blind to the sadness that darkens her face, but I see it. I see it, and knowing I put it there pains me. Silently, I try to convey how sorry I am. This situation took me by surprise, and I'm not ready to blow my son's world up. This is a *hard* decision because I love them both so fucking much and don't want to be the reason for their hurt.

Lucy's voice is pure steel. "Okay. Let me grab my purse."

Thankfully, Rhys doesn't watch her go, so he doesn't see her enter the room we share to retrieve her things. Instead, he leans on the island and reaches for a green bean.

"It's crazy that she works for you now. It's fate, I'm telling you. The universe wants us back together."

"Back together?" I turn the burner off and pull the potatoes from the oven, careful not to use my burnt hand.

His intentions have my body reacting possessively,

wanting to make it clear that Lucy is off-limits. The sound of the oven slamming harder than I intended reverberates through the house.

"I mean, it's too good to be true, right? I'm moving back. She still lives here. She's working for you. It was meant to be." He sounds so hopeful, so *excited*, and I silently chastise myself.

How am I supposed to do this?

Lucy reappears, now dressed in a simple navy dress that highlights her assets. Her eyes harden when she looks at me and waves. "Don't wait up, Mr. Morgan. Have a nice night."

Rhys raises his eyebrows with a smirk. "Night, Dad."

# TWENTY-SEVEN

## *Lucy*

PURE, unfiltered rage rolls off me in waves as I pull apart a bread roll. We had the perfect chance to confront Rhys, and Lawson just handed me off like cattle.

*Here you go, Son, take my cow out for dinner. I've been milking her for the last two months, but you're welcome to take her for a ride around the pasture.*

Okay, I know I'm being ridiculous. But I can't help but feel so freaking pissed at how Lawson just told me to go. He didn't even *try*.

"You look really good, Luce," Rhys tells me affectionately from across the table.

I don't know why his compliment makes me bristle, but it's a far cry from the way Lawson's eyes fill with heat as they rove down my body before he tells me everything he wants to do to me. It isn't fair to compare them. I know that someday Rhys will be experienced enough to make some other woman feel like his father makes me feel— though right now, I don't feel loved *or* special.

I feel stupid and embarrassed.

Actions speak louder than words, and when the time came, Lawson fumbled pretty fucking badly. Yes, Rhys showing up was a surprise, but again, it was the perfect opportunity for us to tell him together as a united front.

"Thank you. You look great, too. Are you still playing football?"

I stopped looking at his Iconic profile before I finished my first year at Berkeley. I was holding on to the past hard enough by continuing to contact Lawson, and despite our breakup, Rhys seemed to settle into college just fine.

"Nah. Got a knee injury, unfortunately. It did push me toward sports medicine, though. I actually got a job at U of C. I'm thinking of getting an apartment in the city instead of commuting every day. Plus, I don't know if I can handle living with my dad again."

"Living in the city is great." I take a sip of my pinot noir. "It's worth it, in my opinion. Gas alone was awful. I didn't last two months back home before I was apartment hunting."

Rhys' face lights up, misunderstanding my words as an agreement that he should live in the city instead of at home.

*Shit.*

I hate how awkward this feels. And I honestly can't believe Rhys isn't picking up on any of it. He marches on through the forced sentences and long stretches of silence, and I'm relieved when our dinner arrives, so there's the added excuse of waiting to chew a bite before responding.

"I think my mom will be coming back soon, too. My parents have been talking a lot lately. I think they're getting back together," Rhys nonchalantly states.

A piece of steak gets lodged in my throat, and I cough,

beating my chest to displace it before sipping my ice water to soothe the ache as the meat rudely scrapes my insides.

"Are you okay?" Rhys' brilliant blue eyes fixate on me in alarm, yet he doesn't move from his seat.

"I'm fine." I wave a hand in the air with a choked laugh. Sipping my water again, I try to hide the curiosity in my voice as I ask, "Why do you think your parents are getting back together?"

Anxiety boils in my veins. Of course, Lawson and Charlotte talk. They have children. And eventually, if we're going to be together, Lawson will have to divorce Charlotte —something we just discussed mere hours ago.

Still, hearing that Rhys thinks they might be getting back together... There has to be a reason he believes that.

"Ah, it's nothing really. I just overheard Mom talking about second chances and how Dad seems like he's ready to forgive her." His words make me feel sick. The meaty lump that just settled in my stomach now threatens to reappear.

*Maybe he's just being nice because he doesn't want her to fight him too hard over the divorce.*

Yes, that has to be it.

"It got me thinking, you know." Rhys reaches for my hand over the table, the candlelight flickering across his face, setting a mood I'm in no *mood* for. I want to withdraw my fingers, but Rhys' grip tightens. "I know we left things on a bad note before college. And I know I don't deserve you in the slightest. I treated you poorly, and I am so sorry for that."

My palms start to sweat, chest heaving with anxious breaths as he heads to a place I don't want to revisit. "Rhys—"

"And I'm willing to go as slow as you want, but, Lucy, I miss you. I've missed you since the day I walked out of that playhouse. And I know it's a long shot, but—"

Abruptly, I pull my hand from his and exclaim, "I'm seeing someone!"

A few heads turn our way as Rhys' face turns as red as a tomato. I can also feel my cheeks warming and hide my face in my wine glass.

"I'm sorry. I didn't mean to shout."

"No. I'm sorry, I shouldn't have... Of course, you're seeing someone." He rubs the back of his neck. "It was stupid of me to think you'd be single. I'm sorry for making it awkward."

"It's okay."

After a few moments, he asks, "Are you happy?"

I can't help the smile that takes over my face or the heat rushing back to my cheeks—despite how upset I am with Lawson right now.

"Yeah." I nod. "I'm really happy."

His lips form a thin smile. "Good. I'm glad you're happy, Luce. Really, I am." He changes the subject, and the heavy, unpleasant cloud hovering over us dissipates as he cuts into his steak. "So, uh, how's working for my dad?"

"Really good. We work well together." I want to tell him just how well, but I have no desire to make a scene—which would undoubtedly happen—and it's a conversation Lawson needs to have with him. Whether I'm present or not, he needs to hear the news from his father.

"How crazy, right? That in all of Chicago, it's your company that his acquired. I never thought he'd come back. He loves New York."

*He loves me, too.*

I breathe a heavy sigh. "Yeah, well, you know what they say, there's no place like home."

"I KNOW you hate to fish, but I plan on going out on the lake early tomorrow. Wanna come with me? I'm sure Dad can spare you for a few hours," Rhys asks as we walk through the front door.

There's no sign of Lawson. The kitchen is spotless, and all the lights are off except for the recessed lighting underneath the cabinets. "Maybe you should ask your dad to go. I'm sure he'd like that."

He hums in agreement. "Looks like he went to bed. I'll ask him in the morning. Are you in the guest room on that side of the house?" He points to the left hallway, opposite the one that leads to his room.

"Yeah," I lie.

After we say goodnight, I wait for Rhys to close his door before walking down the dark hallway. As I pass the guest bedroom, I realize that I didn't lie to Rhys at all.

My bag is on the bed, and my clothes are hung up in the closet as if I'd been staying there all weekend. An icy cold feeling grips my heart as I peer into the guest bathroom and see all my hair and body products strewn across the vanity.

He kicked me out.

Tears line my eyes, and my throat feels thick as I try not to let them fall. There's a soft click, and I whirl around to see Lawson standing there with remorse painted across his features.

"Lucy... I... I'm sorry. I thought it was for the best."

He scratches his neck the same damn way Rhys does, and I blink away my tears at the unfairness of it all. When I don't respond, he asks, "How was dinner?"

"Fine," I sniff.

"Baby." He strides forward, reaching out like he's going to embrace me, but I step back.

"Why is Rhys under the impression that you and Charlotte are getting back together?" I wipe away my tears before wrapping my arms around my middle, leaning against the doorframe.

"What?" He genuinely looks surprised. "Lucy, no. I told her I wanted to see her. To discuss things. It was after the Fourth of July. She obviously took it the wrong way if that's what she thinks." He sounds disgusted, but I have to wonder why I didn't hear about this before.

"Why didn't you tell me?"

Lawson leans against the wall opposite me, expelling a deep sigh before scrubbing a hand over his face. "I don't know, rainbow. Because I didn't want you worrying about the hell she's going to put me through. I wanted to..." He looks down the hall at his room. "I wanted it to be a surprise. I was hoping to get it over and done with quickly, and then I wanted to surprise you with the news."

My body screams for me to go to him. I want to wrap my arms around him, to comfort and kiss him, but I remain rooted where I stand. "We could have told Rhys—"

"I know. I'm sorry, I wasn't prepared. I panicked." His voice is barely audible, laced with intense guilt.

It breaks my fucking heart, but I still push, hating how desperate I sound as I plead, "This is the perfect time to tell him."

Lawson shakes his head, refusing to meet my eyes. "I don't... I'm not... ready."

*Not ready to commit.*

*Not ready to ruin things with my son.*

The words he doesn't say are so much louder than the ones he does.

Hot, salty tears prick my eyes again, swelling my sinuses. I want to argue. Want to cry and demand, "Why?" But I know why. Lawson has a lot to lose by going public with our relationship. I'm only gaining.

I see where he's coming from. I really do. But I'm ready to jump all in, and Lawson has the chance to prove that he meant what he said when he told me he loves me. Yet, at the first opportunity he has, he doesn't.

How long will it be like this? It's so different when it's just us or when we're around people *he* trusts. But everywhere else, we have to pretend.

I'm so sick of pretending.

I know it's selfish of me to want him to come clean. It's so fucking unfair and thoughtless, and I know... I *know* it shows my age.

And I think that's what hurts most of all.

It's a glaring reminder of our vast age difference. Lawson has adult responsibilities that I can't even imagine —his job, his kids, his *wife.* How could I possibly begin to understand the depth of his choice to be with me?

"Lucy..." Lawson pushes off the wall, looking down the hall to ensure Rhys is still in his room.

My heart thumps, anguish ripping its way through my chest. I don't want to feel like this. I don't want him to see me this way.

"I'm fine." I quickly wipe away the stray tears starting to fall and step back into the guest room. "Goodnight, Lawson."

He steps forward, his cloudy gray eyes glowing with vulnerability as he begs, "Just give me some more time."

Before he can enter the room, I close the door. "Take all the time you need."

I hear him whisper, "I love you," through the door, and my hand flies to my mouth in an attempt to hold back my sobs as I crawl into the empty bed and curl into a ball. I don't know how such a perfect weekend got away from us —how we went from saying I love you for the first time to sleeping in separate beds. But how am I supposed to face them both tomorrow and pretend I didn't spend the night crying?

As the night goes on, I toss and turn in the cold sheets, becoming more uncomfortable with every passing minute. Finally, as the clock on the nightstand turns to two in the morning, I pack my things and write a quick note to Lawson.

I'm not going to suffer through a morning with both of them—pretending to be friendly with Rhys and hiding the fact that I'm in love with his father. I'm not going to sit there while Lawson treats me like I'm nothing to him—like he didn't just tell me twelve hours ago that he loved me for the first time and that we would figure this out.

I'm thankful for the quiet purr of the engine as I start the car and equally grateful Rhys didn't park behind it, so I don't have to do a crazy million-point-turn to get out of the driveway. Lawson will probably be upset that I took his vehicle, but at the moment, I can't bring myself to care.

I need space.

And Lawson needs time.

# Twenty-Eight

*Lawson*

SUNLIGHT CREEPS THROUGH THE WINDOW, rousing me from sleep. Reaching for Lucy, I frown when my hand hits the cold sheets of the empty spot beside me. Irritation dances through my organs, adding to the rotten lump that hasn't left my stomach since I watched her leave with Rhys last night.

Guilt spears my chest, lancing clear through my heart to leave a hole only Lucy can fill. I'm at an utter loss of what I should do: march down the hall and tell my son straight to his face that I'm in love with his ex-girlfriend, or remain quiet and potentially lose Lucy.

It should be a no-brainer.

However, my parental side keeps kicking in, instinctually reminding me I have an obligation to my son.

*Then, you should have never started things with Lucy in the first place.*

I get out of bed, pulling on a basic black shirt before quietly making my way down the hall. Pressing my ear to the guest room door, I listen for Lucy's breathing but only hear silence. I debate crawling into bed with her but decide against it, knowing she's unlikely to welcome me with open arms.

It hurts—this ache in my chest I put there myself. It should clearly indicate where my heart lies, but no matter how many times I try to talk myself into coming clean, something holds me back every single time.

Lucy deserves better.

Fuck, so does Rhys.

And me? I deserve to rot in hell for what I've done to both of them.

Scrubbing my hands down my face, I head to the kitchen to make coffee. The throbbing behind my ribs plummets into my stomach as I round the corner to see a singular piece of paper on the kitchen island.

With shaky hands, I pick it up, and the regret that's weighing me down becomes even heavier with each line I read.

*Lawson,*

*I took your car and went home. You can get a ride back with Rhys. Please don't be mad. I'm sorry.*

*Lucy*

"Fuck," I whisper. Swiftly, I return to my bedroom and grab my phone from the dresser.

She answers after only two rings. "Lawson?"

"Baby." I let out a relieved sigh. "Why'd you leave?"

Too many moments pass, with only her breathing on the other end of the line to signal she's still there.

Finally, with so much grief and sadness in her tone, she admits, "I couldn't stay there, Lawson. I... I think you have a lot to figure out, and... I think we need some space for you to do that." She sniffs, and I can hear how hard she's trying not to cry.

"Lucy..." The need to have her in my arms is overwhelming. Fear begins to creep in, settling in the marrow of my bones.

"I'm going to take a week of vacation," she informs me, voice cracking. "I'm sorry, I know it's last minute, but I... I can't do this. I can't *see* you right now."

"What would you have me do, baby?" It's a struggle to keep my own voice steady. I'm a grown-ass man, but here I am, standing in the middle of my room, trying desperately not to cry because I have to make a decision between my son and the love of my life.

"It doesn't matter what I want, Lawson." This time, her voice comes out broken, like our hearts. "It matters what you can live with. If you can't tell Rhys, then there is your answer." A muffled sob escapes her throat, and it shatters me. "And I won't be mad." She attempts to collect herself, clearing her throat as she speaks through the tears. "I promise I will respect your decision if you choose him. He's your son, Lawson. I get it. And I don't want you to divorce Charlotte because of me. If you wanted to, you would have done it already." Lucy's words grow squeaky and inaudible.

"Baby, it isn't like that." I silently curse my wife's name. "Please, rainbow, stop crying. I love you, and I promise this will work out. Don't take the week—"

"I *need* to, Lawson. I need some space, and you need some time to figure out what you're going to do—"

"I don't need space!" I interrupt as I begin pacing the room. "Fuck, that is the last thing I want from you right now."

"I'm going to hang up."

"Baby, why does it feel like you're breaking up with me?" When she doesn't answer, panic grips my lungs. "Lucy, don't—"

"I love you. Just take the time to figure out what you want, Lawson."

"I want *you*. I love *you*, Lucy." I try my hardest to express my feelings through the phone, knowing that deep down, she *knows* how much I care for her. But I still feel like I need to make the declaration anyway, as many times as it takes for her to hear me. "It's just a storm, baby. That's all this is—a storm. Remember what you said to me? That night in my car? What comes after a storm?"

"Rainbows." Lucy makes a sound of frustration and exhales deeply. "Give it a few days, Lawson. We'll talk soon."

She doesn't give me a chance to reply before she hangs up.

It only takes a few moments before rage filters through me again, replacing the anguish I feel. I dial Charlotte's number, stomping out to the kitchen because I desperately need coffee to fight the migraine settling in my temples.

As soon as she picks up, I don't even give her a chance to say hello. "What the fuck, Charlotte?"

Her haughty laugh echoes in my ear. "Well, good morning to you, too, *dear.*"

"Cut the bullshit. Wanna tell me why Rhys thinks we're getting back together?" Beans fly everywhere as I rip the lid off the container and dump them in the espresso machine.

On her end, there's a sound of a cork popping from a bottle, and I glance at the clock on the stove. Jesus Christ, it's not even ten her time. Is this what she does when River is there?

"Ahh, yes. Rhys called me last night and said you were at the lake house. And with *Lucy.* That was an interesting tidbit of information," she lilts sardonically.

"Why does our son think we're getting back together?" I repeat between clenched teeth.

"I thought that's what you wanted to talk to me about. Why you sounded so eager to see me," Charlotte tries to sound seductive, but it's like nails on a fucking chalkboard. "I told Rhys that we'd both be moving home soon."

"I wanted to see you because I want a divorce," I growl. Fuck waiting to talk to her in person. This part of my problem ends *now.*

Charlotte huffs a disbelieving laugh, her demeanor switching from hot to cold in an instant. "A divorce? Are you joking? You realize I'm entitled to half of your worth, right, Lawson? Not to mention alimony."

"I'm well aware of that, Charlotte. And I no longer give a fuck. You can expect papers within the week." I rip open the fridge for the milk as the strong scent of brewing coffee fills the kitchen.

She's silent. *Too* silent. Then, voice laced with thick suspicion, she asks, "Why now, Lawson? What's changed?"

I stare at the coffee dripping into the pot while I internally battle with myself.

*This is your moment. Tell her you've met someone.*

My tongue feels thick in my mouth, unable to form words.

Suddenly, Charlotte laughs. "It's *her*, isn't it? Oh, Lawson. Tell me you aren't sleeping with her. She's young enough to be your daughter. For God's sake, I had a feeling when Rhys told me. She always did strut around in front of you like a little hussy. I never thought you'd lower yourself to fucking a child, though."

"Do not talk about her like that!" I roar, slamming my fist on the counter, my eruption as good as an admission. "It's none of your fucking business who I'm sleeping with. Keep Lucy's fucking name out of your mouth and sign the damn papers when they get there."

I hang up without waiting to hear what else she has to say, throwing my phone against the wall. It shatters and crashes to the floor. "Fuck!"

A sharp huff has me spinning to see Rhys, wide-eyed, standing stock still on the other side of the kitchen island as if he's just witnessed a horrific trainwreck.

*Fuck. Fuck. Fuck.*

"Rhys—"

"Tell me you're not sleeping with Lucy."

My heart beats so fast against my ribs I fear it answers my son for me.

Rhys looks devastated, not even angry, but completely heartbroken—because of *me*, his *father*. And I know his anger will come eventually, and when it does, it will be explosive.

"Dad..." He shakes his head, eyes turning glassy. My heart feels like someone stuck me with a needle and is pumping pure adrenaline straight to the ventricle. "Tell me you're not fucking my ex-girlfriend."

"Rhys... it's... it's not like that." I sigh, running a hand through my hair as my own eyes fill with tears. I needed time, but here we are. I can't lie to him, not when he's staring me straight in the face.

"Then what is it like?" His words are cold and calm, and that terrifies me more than his anger.

*Just tell him. He'll understand... eventually. He loved her once. He'll get it. Right?*

"I love her, Rhys." My voice shakes, the words coming out barely above a whisper.

"She's half your age!" His rage bubbles just beneath the surface, and the tears in his eyes burn up with fury as his hands clench into fists.

"I know." I hold my hands up, trying to calm him down as I take a step toward him. "I know, Son. But—"

"But nothing! You think I don't *know* what you did when you were in New York?" He points out the window as if pointing to the state itself. "You think Mom doesn't know? And if that weren't bad enough, you came home and started fucking my ex-girlfriend?" He tangles his hands in his hair. "What the fuck is wrong with you?"

My brows furrow, confusion going off like a bomb in my brain. "What do you mean, you know what I did in New York? Rhys, what has your mother been telling you?"

Irritation prickles my skin. Charlotte and her goddamn meddling. She's twisted Rhys' opinion of me so much, I don't know why I hoped he'd listen to anything I say. She wouldn't know shit about what I did in New York. All of my indiscretions occurred at the club, which has air-tight security. Anything Charlotte *thinks* she knows is pure bullshit she spun up in her wine-drunk brain.

My son looks like he's about to go into hysterics. "Look, Rhys. I know you think I'm a terrible father—"

"Lucy told me last night that she was seeing someone." He gives me his back, mumbling to himself more than talking to me. "She looked me straight in the eye and told me how happy she was."

I can't help the spark of warmth that ignites in my chest, but it quickly diminishes as he whirls back around to face me. "Fuck you both."

He sounds so fucking broken. I didn't think my heart could shatter any further than it already had in the past twelve hours, but hearing him sound so utterly destroyed by my betrayal guts me.

I start to walk around the island, but he holds his hand up to stop me.

"I know you didn't want me. I know how much of a burden I was to you and Mom, but I never thought you *hated* me," he says through a fresh wave of tears.

Horrified, I reach for him, dread filling every crack and crevice in my chest. "Rhys, I don't hate you."

He pushes me off him, turning to walk back to his room. "Well, I fucking hate you!"

I try to stop him, but he whips around to face me instead. Pain blooms across the side of my face as his fist connects with my cheek.

Instinct tells me to pull him back, but I let him go, choosing to give him space. No amount of talking will help when he's so distressed.

"Rhys, where are you going?" I ask as he reappears, bag in hand.

My son doesn't answer me, slipping on his shoes and disappearing out the front door. His truck roars to life, and I curse. Not only do I not want him on the road when he's upset, but if he leaves, I'm stranded.

I reach the door just as he peels out of the driveway, tires squealing as he speeds away.

Slapping the side of the doorframe, I hurry back into the house, only to remember my phone is now in pieces. "Fuck!"

# TWENTY-NINE

*Rhys*

NEVER IN A MILLION years did I think something could hurt as bad as this.

My fingers fly over my phone screen, searching for Lucy's number while trying to pay attention to the road as I drive.

Pure rage blinds me—red-hot and searing through my every pore, exuding the disgust I feel for my father.

And for *her*.

Tears blur my vision, and I fucking hate that I'm crying right now.

They don't fucking deserve my tears.

I want to vomit.

Lucy's phone goes to voicemail. "How could you? You fucking slut!" I scream into the speaker before hanging up and throwing my phone at the passenger door.

Unwillingly, I think back to last night. About how she looked... almost horrified when she saw me in the kitchen. The way her eyes drifted to Dad. She didn't want to leave him.

My fingers grip the steering wheel, knuckles turning white before I slap the dashboard repeatedly, causing me to swerve into the other lane. Horns blare, and I straighten out, propping my elbow on the window to run a hand down my face.

Lucy's panic when I reached for her hand.

The way the candlelight flickered in her eyes when she told me she was happy.

Happy with my *father*.

When did this even happen?

*How* did this happen?

Deep down—deep, deep down in my bones, I know the answer.

It had to have started when we were still in high school. Dad always used to watch Lucy. Even when he thought no one was looking, he'd steal glances at her and flash his charming smile that always made her putty in his hands.

He made her his fucking cookies.

And Dad never could do anything wrong in her eyes— she was always on me for being too harsh on him. Always beaming at him like he hung the fucking moon.

*Graduation night.*

My heart races as I think of that horrible night where I fucked everything up between us—think of how she locked herself in my dad's office. Is that when all this started?

Images of them together haunt me for the entire three hours it takes to return home.

Only, I don't go home. Muscle memory kicks in, mindlessly taking me to Lucy's childhood house, where my dad's car sits in the otherwise empty driveway.

After slamming my fingers against the ignition button,

I leap out of the truck and clear the path to the front door in less than ten strides.

"Lucy!" I pound on the wood, partially hoping her parents aren't home, while also not giving a fuck because they should know what their daughter has been up to.

*My fucking dad.*

"Lucy!" I shout again, even as I hear heavy footsteps approaching.

The door swings open, and Liam steps onto the porch, clearly angry with me. "What the fuck are you doing here?"

"I want to talk to Lucy." I point behind him, sniffling from the remnants of my pitiful meltdown.

"Well, that's too fucking bad. You probably shouldn't have left her a voicemail calling her a fucking slut then." He crosses his arms with a glare, forcing me to retreat a few steps.

"Lucy!" I try to move around Liam, but he pushes me back.

"Are you fucking serious, Rhys? Go home."

Lucy's red-rimmed eyes appear around her brother, and seeing her breaks my heart all over again. It's like she personally reaches into my chest cavity and tears the still-beating organ straight from my body.

"How could you?" My voice cracks like I just hit puberty while my fucking traitorous eyes fill with tears again.

Her brows draw together with empathy as she comes toward me. "Rhys—" Her voice is soft and pleading.

For forgiveness? Acceptance? My fucking blessing? I don't know.

"*Don't.*" I begin to pace on her lawn. "It didn't matter

that you were seeing someone, Lucy. I was happy to have you back in my life as a friend, but this?" I stop and face her again, stepping into her space. Liam tenses, ready to step between us if he needs to. "How could you do this? He's my *father*!"

"I know!" Tears line her thick lashes before they stream down her cheeks. "Rhys, I know. I'm sorry. I'm so sorry that we hurt you, but I love—"

"Don't. You. Dare. Fucking say it." My voice drops to a growl as my fists clench.

This time, Liam does move between us, as if he actually believes I'd ever lay a hand on her.

"Okay, that's enough. Rhys, go home. If Lucy wants to talk to you later when you've calmed down—"

"Don't tell me to fucking calm down!" I shout in his face, pushing him away from me. "How would you feel if you found out *your* ex, someone you still had feelings for, was fucking *your* dad?"

Liam doesn't say anything as Lucy's sobbing increases. "Rhys, I'm sorry."

"I don't want your fucking apologies!" I try to get around her brother, to get in her face and rage against her with my words until I feel like she truly understands the depths of what I'm feeling.

Liam's hand shoots out to block me, and I blindly swing at him, missing as he rears back before slamming his fist across my face, just like I did to my dad earlier.

"Liam!" Lucy shouts as I stagger back from the force of his blow.

She rushes toward me, but I hold up a hand to stop her

as the other massages my jaw. I muster up as much disgust as possible so she hears the depth of my ire.

"I'm so fucking done with you. You and my dad deserve each other."

Neither of them says anything as I get back into my truck and leave, headed toward town for the nearest bar to get as shitfaced as possible.

*Welcome the fuck home.*

STAGGERING INTO THE HOUSE, drunker than I should be considering I drove, I'm relieved to see it's dark and no one else is here.

No River for me to make a bad impression on.

And no fucking *Dad*.

I stand silently in the foyer, peering around at my childhood home and thinking of all the places he probably fucked Lucy.

No matter how hard I try to forget—it's a miracle I made it home in one piece—the image of them together won't leave my brain.

Without bothering to remove my shoes, I shuffle through the house, intent on wreaking havoc on the one place he probably had her the most. The one place no one else is allowed to enter—yet he had no problem granting her access to *organize* it for him during our last few weeks of senior year.

*Fuck,* that's *probably when it all started.*

The door is locked, but it only takes a few sharp kicks before the wood splinters and gives way. Grabbing a bottle of whiskey from the minibar, I uncap it and take a swig straight from the neck, running my hands along the numerous books and binders that line the shelves.

With a roar, I sweep them all to the floor, taking another pull from the bottle before I tip it over and pour the amber-colored liquid all over the shit now littered on the ground.

"Fuck you, motherfucker..." I bark a laugh. "Guess it's actually *girlfriend* fucker."

*You're being ridiculous. She isn't your girlfriend.*

I turn my head to my proverbial angel and tell it to shut the fuck up.

"Whoops..." Another sweep of my hand plows more books to the floor, and I knock over a lamp that shatters.

"AHHH!" I rage, raking both arms across his desk, sending papers and files and a stapler flying off the surface to join the mess. The movement bumps his desktop, and the screen lights up like a beacon.

Slumping into his chair, I kick my feet up, scrubbing my hands over my face. It doesn't seem like enough. No amount of damage I can do to this office will ever seem like enough of a price to pay.

The screen's glow calls to me—the background is a picture of me, Dad, and River fishing in Florida. A folder labeled 'X' sits directly over the fish Dad holds up. I don't know why I do it, but I lean forward and move the mouse, clicking to open the folder.

Dozens of video files appear—blurred images for

thumbnails and random combinations of letters and numbers for names. I click on one.

*What the fuck?*

Harsh groans and the sound of flesh slapping against flesh fill the air through the speakers.

The whiskey I just guzzled threatens to reappear. It's a fucking *porn* video.

A man slaps the ass of the woman he fucks from behind. "Yeah, you fucking like that, don't you? Tell Daddy how much you like that."

*WHAT THE FUCK?*

As fast as humanly possible, I click out of the video.

*It's my fucking* dad.

I push the chair back, leaning over to put my head between my knees so I don't throw up.

Mom always told me that Dad fucked around on her in New York. I know she cheated on him when I was younger, but he forgave her for it—stayed with her—yet this is how he punishes her?

By fucking around on her constantly.

By fucking my ex-girlfriend.

"Seriously, fuck you, Dad," I whisper to the air as I pull up his email.

I want him to hurt as badly as I do—as bad as Mom has these last few years.

Clicking on a new message, I CC his entire office and slide the video over to attach it. I don't even pause before I hit send.

Then I throw up all over his desk.

# THIRTY

## Lucy

OVER THE NEXT FEW HOURS, I keep trying to call Lawson, but his phone goes straight to voicemail. I consider going back to the lake house, but I'm shaking so hard I don't trust myself to drive.

"Are you okay?" Liam asks, tossing a bottle of water onto my mattress next to me.

"No." My lips tremble as I fall apart.

I'm so fucking thankful my parents aren't here. That Lorraine isn't here, and she didn't have to witness that awful display. Sitting up, I hug my orange elephant pillow to my chest.

"He didn't wan–want to tell him," I sob, my words breaking with a shaky stutter. "An–and I left in the mid–middle of the night. We spoke..." A hiccup erupts from my throat. "...spoke this morning. He thought... thought I was br–breaking up with him."

My poor brother looks uncomfortable as fuck, but he sits on the edge of my bed and pulls me in for a hug anyway. "And did you? Break up with him?"

"No!" Liam lets me go but doesn't get up. His hands are shaking, knuckles bruised from where he hit Rhys. "Are you okay?"

"I'm fine." He sighs, rolling his knuckles. "Can't even feel it."

We sit in silence before a question I've been meaning to ask him pops into my mind. "Liam?"

"Hmm?" My brother repositions himself to sit against the wall next to me.

"How did you know about Lawson and me?"

I'm unprepared for the harsh bark of laughter that erupts from his throat. "Are you kidding? You two *suck* at hiding your feelings. I've been watching you two dance around each other since you were a senior in school."

Heat blossoms across my cheeks. "But at the BBQ, you accused us of sleeping together. How the fuck did you know?"

"Well, for one, if Rhys' little display earlier didn't tip me off, all of this..." He gestures to my distressed state. "...just did. But honestly, you've been happier than shit since he came back, Luce. It wasn't hard to put together if you looked for the signs."

Liam begins picking at the elastic on his wrist—a pastel pink hair tie with little cream and silver roses. Sighing, I reach over and lay my hand on his knee. "How are you?"

"Fine." He shrugs. "Bored. Thinking of taking that internship in New York that Aunt Daphne set up for me."

A ding sounds from my phone, and we both look at where it lies between us. As soon as I see the notification from Lawson's work email, I snatch my phone up and hastily click on it.

"It's Lawson. Something must have happened to his phone."

Liam rolls to his side, scooting off the bed. "I hope it works out for you guys. Mom and Dad will throw a fit... but... when you know, you know. And all that sappy shit."

His words sound far away, muddled over the blood rushing in my ears. A throb explodes beneath my lungs, and I'm pretty sure my heart stops beating.

"Lucy?"

Lawson didn't just email me. He emailed the entirety of M.I.G.'s Chicago office.

*Holy fucking shit.*

"Lucy? What is it?" Liam's voice is louder, right next to me now.

I turn horrified eyes his way. "Call Mom and Dad." My words leave my mouth in the barest of whispers.

My brother reaches for my phone, but I snatch it away, shouting hysterically, "Call Mom and Dad!"

"Fuck! Okay! Jesus Christ, you're scaring me!" He pulls his cell from his back pocket and does what I ask. I can hear him telling our parents they need to come home and that he doesn't know what's wrong.

My gaze drops back to a blown-up video attached to the email.

A homemade video of Lawson... fucking me from behind.

# THIRTY-ONE

## EARLIER

*Lawson*

To SAY I'm pissed is an understatement.

With Lucy taking my car, Rhys leaving me stranded, and my phone in pieces, I have no choice but to walk to the neighbors and ask for a ride.

Since it's a small town—and a Sunday—nowhere is open. Not a car rental or a phone store.

I had to convince the neighbor to drive me a few towns over, where I find a random personal truck rental from a website that looks suspicious. It takes hours.

I don't see my car in the guest parking lot of Lucy's building but go inside and try knocking on her door anyway. After a few minutes of silence, I let myself in with my key, only to find it exactly the same way we left it before we went to the lake house.

"Shit," I mutter under my breath. If she isn't here, it probably means she's at her parents' place. I have no clue how I'm supposed to show up there and try to talk to her without tipping anyone off to the nature of our discussion.

It takes another hour to get home, but I'm thankful

River isn't here and won't have to witness any more arguing between Rhys and me. My cheek throbs as I walk into the house. My son clocked me good, but I guess I deserve it.

I've gone and fucked all of this up for everyone.

The late afternoon light seeps through the windows, illuminating the fact that there are no shoes next to the door, and after I check the garage, I realize Rhys isn't here. Since my phone is unusable, I power up my office computer and check for the nearest phone store that's open. Rhys can't have gone far. I can drive around and look for him, and then I'll get a new phone before going to Lucy's—give myself some time to think about how I'm going to play this all out.

The proverbial cat is out of the bag now. We might as well come clean to everyone.

BY THE TIME I search for Rhys and get a replacement phone, it's nearing dark when I return home. Kicking my shoes off, I tread through the dark house, wrinkling my nose at a foul smell as I plug my new phone in and set it on the kitchen island.

It definitely didn't smell like this when I was here earlier.

I follow the smell to my office, where a splintering of wood litters the floor in the hall. Alarmed, I push the door open to find the entire room trashed. Books and binders and bric-a-brac are strewn across the floor, surrounded by smashed ceramic and puddles of whiskey.

"What the fuck?"

The glow from my computer screen illuminates a pile of puke in the middle of my desk. The stench is so strong it makes me gag.

There's solely one explanation for the destruction of the only place in this house that was truly mine.

*Rhys.*

"Rhys?" I call out, storming down the hall to the basement. His truck wasn't in the driveway, but I didn't recheck the garage. Maybe he's passed out in his room.

But the basement is dark, and the air smells stale like no one has been down here in ages. Rhys' door is shut. I know I shouldn't encroach on his space, but I open it anyway to see his bed is exactly how he left it before he went back to Mississippi. There's no sign of him anywhere—except all over my office.

Regret and concern tighten my chest. If Rhys is drunk and driving around...

Panic settles in as I hear the new phone go off upstairs —a barrage of dings, one after the other, to indicate multiple incoming texts. I take the stairs two at a time as a call comes in. Fear races through my veins as I hope it's not someone about to tell me my son was in an accident.

A little relief dilutes the anxiety when I see it's Jules' name flashing across the caller ID.

"Hey, now isn't a good time," I greet in a rush.

"No shit, it isn't. What the fuck, Lawson?!"

I've never heard her sound so worried, and my brows draw together. "What the hell did I do?"

Another beep disrupts whatever she's about to say, and I pull the phone away to see Cameron calling. "Hold on, Cam is calling. I'm merging the calls."

Might as well tell both of them about the shit that went down this morning.

As it connects, Cam's angry voice mixes with Jules' as they talk over one another to the point where I can't understand either of them. "Will both of you shut the fuck up and tell me what you're going on about?"

"I'm going to assume you got hacked. Have you not checked your email? Upper management is pissed. They've had a flood of calls from HR for the last hour," Jules says in a calmer—though still stressed—tone.

"No, I haven't checked my email. Rhys showed up at the lake house, and I stupidly sent Lucy off to dinner with him, where he told her he thought Charlotte and I were getting back together. She's pissed at me and took off with my car." I put them on speaker and pull up my email app. "Then he overheard me yelling at Charlotte this morning and put two and two together. He knows about Lucy and me now."

"Well, I think everyone knows about you and Lucy now, Law. This is bad, man," Cameron states.

"What is bad? What are you two—?" My question dies in my throat as I see an email in my sent folder dated earlier today. It's to the entire Chicago office. The only thing in it is a familiar thumbnail of a video of me and Lucy. "Jesus fucking Christ."

"Yeah," Jules drawls. "Lawson, you'll likely lose your job for this."

"I have to go." I don't wait for them to reply before I

end the call and pull up Lucy's number. I couldn't care fucking less about my job, but this will destroy her.

My stomach twists, bile rising in my throat as I grab the charger and run to the rental truck. Lucy's cell keeps going to voicemail. I try Rhys, but his doesn't even ring, and I think about calling Charlotte to see if she's heard from him.

A text comes through from Cameron.

**CAMERON**

> They've got Tailor Tech on it. The video will be wiped clean from everyone's emails within the hour. It will be harder to track who opened it already... or worse... saved it.

"Fuck!" I hit the dashboard.

There's no doubt in my mind, after seeing the state of my office, what happened. Rhys must have trashed the place before finding the videos.

Cameron is right. This *is* bad. My thoughts don't even linger on the fact that I'm probably now jobless—my son could face jail time for distributing revenge porn.

*Only if you tell people it was him who sent it.*

I keep trying Lucy on my way to her house, mentally preparing myself for the shit storm I'm no doubt about to walk into. M.I.G. headquarters calls, but I send it to voicemail. I can't deal with them right now. I need to get to Lucy, and I need to find Rhys—wherever the fuck he is.

Will's truck is next to my car in their driveway. I throw my rental into park, ripping the keys from the ignition before jogging across the lawn to pound on the front door.

Seconds barely pass before it opens, revealing Liam with an unamused glare pasted across his face.

We stare silently at each other briefly before he rolls his eyes and steps aside. As I enter the Bradee home, I hear Bree and Will arguing with Lucy, her pained cries echoing throughout the large space. Charleigh and Kendall speak into their phones, respectively, in opposite corners of the kitchen, and I can make out words and phrases like "felony" and "pressing charges."

"I don't know!" Lucy is crying when I enter the dining room, and her hazel eyes dart to me, crinkling at the corners with a fresh batch of tears.

All eyes turn to me, but I only have eyes for her. Rushing to her side, I ignore Will's outraged protest.

"You have some fucking nerve, Lawson." In my peripheral, I can see him move toward me, but Liam grabs his arm to keep him in place.

"Baby, I'm so sorry," I sink to my knees before Lucy, grasping her face in my hands. "I'm so sorry."

She launches herself at my chest. "How did this happen?" she cries, clutching me like I'm her only lifeline.

Part of me calms now that she's in my arms, even if every other part is in utter chaos. "Rhys found out. I'm so fucking sorry, Lucy. This is everything I didn't want to happen."

"You have a lot of fucking explaining to do," Bree snaps, standing at the other end of the table with her hands on her hips.

I look at both of Lucy's parents as I smooth her hair back and continue to whisper how sorry I am until she's calmed down. "The video will be wiped from everything soon. We have people working on it."

"There shouldn't be a video in the first place! I trusted you with my daughter, Lawson! What the fuck is wrong with you?" Bree screams, causing Lucy to flinch in my arms.

"The second you let go of my little girl, I swear to God I will give you a black eye to match the other one," Will growls.

Her father's threat causes Lucy to pull away from me slightly, lifting her hands to my face. "What happened? How did Rhys find out? How did he find the videos?"

"Lucy, I think you need to go upstairs," her mother suggests.

This beautiful woman—this radiant artwork, even in her deepest despair, turns in my arms to glower at her parents. "I'm not a little girl. I *love* him."

"Over my dead fucking body," her father exclaims, trying to come toward me again.

"Dad, stop!" Liam shouts.

Will whips around and gets in his son's face. "You fucking knew about this? Why am I not surprised? You're a fucking pro at keeping shit from us."

Hurt flashes across Liam's face before a stony stare replaces it. "She's an adult. She can make her own decisions."

"This is jail time, Lawson. This is a serious fucking matter. My *child's* sex tape with a man twice her age..." A visible shiver racks Bree's body. "I'm going to ask this one time, and I swear I want the truth. Did something happen between you two—"

"No." Lucy's grip on me tightens as if she's afraid her parents really will physically tear us apart. "Nothing happened until he came back," she lies, burying her face in my neck again. "It's not their business," she whispers against my skin, shielded from the intense gazes of everyone in the kitchen.

"It was Rhys who leaked the video," I inform them, untangling myself from Lucy to stand at her side after she settles back in the chair. "He's understandably upset."

"I don't give a fuck what he is, you don't share a fucking sex tape!" Bree shrieks, near hysterics as her momma bear nature comes out in full force.

"Look, I know this situation is terrible. I had hoped to come to you under different circumstances about Lucy and me, but here we are. I love your daughter." Bree and Will both scoff, shaking their heads in unison. "I know that I'm a lot older than she is, and trust me, I have grappled with the decision to pursue a romantic relationship with her. But I genuinely love her. I'm not asking you to understand, but I am asking that you don't punish her for keeping it from you."

"She isn't the one who should be punished!" Bree jabs a finger in my direction. "You should have known better and not taken advantage of a child!" Her accusation sends ice-cold dread down my spine, affirming everything that's sat in a compartment in my mind since the conference.

Lucy seems to know exactly how her mother's comments would affect me because she reaches for my hand and threads her fingers with mine. "I'm not a child, though, Mom. I can make my own decisions. And I'm going to be with Lawson."

"You realize we're pressing charges?" Bree asks pointedly, glaring at me. "How does that make you feel, Lawson?"

When Lucy doesn't correct her, I turn my gaze to the woman I love. She meets my stare, and her hazel eyes harden as she searches my face for something I can't give her at this exact moment.

Inwardly, I begin to panic. "Lucy, I—"

"He can't get away with this." My heart drops as she pulls her hand from mine. "I can't go back to work. I'm *humiliated*. I already gave my resignation."

*Fuck.*

This is all spinning out of control faster than I can manage it.

"Can we just calm down and talk about it?" I know it's the wrong thing to say by the way her eyes widen. "Lucy—"

"He has to have some kind of consequence," she says incredulously. "I understand he's upset. But this..." Tears line her lashes again. "Lawson, this is going to ruin my life. How will I ever get another job? People at work *saw* the video. How many do you think saved it and shared it to other platforms?"

"We're working on it, Luce," Charleigh calls soothingly from the kitchen. "M.I.G. has already called in Tailor Tech before Daphne could reach out to her contacts."

I don't pause to wonder why Daphne has contacts with Tailor Industries in New York, but I look back at Lucy. "Baby, I know this is awful." I ignore Will's sound of disgust. "Please, just let me find Rhys while they tackle the video. I don't know what the answer is here, but... jail?"

I let the rest of my meaning fall silently between us. Never in my life did I think I would be here, between a rock and a hard place. It's one thing to figure out how to navigate life moving forward without Rhys cutting me out entirely, but this is now a whole other mess that he's put us in.

A heavy, tangible silence spreads throughout the room, and as it does, I can see Lucy withdrawing from me more with every passing second.

"It's just a storm, rainbow..." I whisper, reaching for her. Lucy closes her eyes, tears falling down her cheeks as she turns away from me, and it feels like my heart implodes.

"Go. Find Rhys." Her words are barely audible.

"Lucy..."

"I think you should go," Bree echoes her daughter.

At a complete loss, I brush my fingers along Lucy's. "We'll talk later, rainbow."

To my surprise, Liam walks me to the door. "Tensions are high right now. They'll calm down. Especially once the video has been removed."

"The last time we spoke, I wasn't your favorite person." I notice his scraped knuckles as he reaches up to scratch his short beard. "You seem awfully calm, considering the circumstances."

"My sister loves you," he states simply. "It's up to you how the rest of this plays out."

As I leave, I can't help but feel the weight of the world sitting on my shoulders. And for once, I feel too weak to take it on.

# THIRTY-TWO

## Lucy

I WANT to crumble when Lawson leaves.

It feels like my heart is cramping, an uncomfortable ache that has me gasping for air. Aunt Kendall places a glass of water on the table before smoothing circles up and down my back as she tells me to breathe.

Mom and Dad whisper to each other angrily, which just adds to my stress. I can't bear the thought of them being so disappointed in me, but what they might do to protect their little girl terrifies me more.

The divide was so apparent in Lawson's eyes, and right now, I'm too blinded by hurt and humiliation to care much about what happens to Rhys. I'm so fucking angry with him. How could he do this? *Why* would he do this?

Surely, he had to have known how serious it would be —had to have known that his dad would most likely lose his job and all for what? A big *fuck you* to me? Rhys deserves punishment. I wasn't prepared for Lawson to fight me on that.

I saw the panic in his eyes when charges were mentioned. And while he was just as uncovered in the video as I was, everyone knows men aren't on the receiving end of the backlash for shit like this.

I feel dirty.

Exposed.

Vulnerable.

How will I ever face my friends? My phone is already blowing up with messages from Anna, Mike, and Justin. And headquarters has, of course, left a voicemail. I had to put the device on silent and leave it in my room because the anxiety was too much.

"It's a chance you take when you do something so stupid!" Mom is spitting her frustration at Dad, who nods in agreement while he looks like he wants to tear something apart with his bare hands.

My parents aren't violent people. They are caring and kind—look at how many chances they've given Liam. But the one time I fuck up—even if it's a fuck up of epic proportions—it's like I single-handedly destroyed our family.

What could happen if the video is posted somewhere else? What if this blows back on my mother's business? She works with children. This could be bad for her as well if it gets out.

"Just to be clear, we are very, *very* angry right now, Lucy, but that does not invalidate what has happened to you. This is a personal attack, and Rhys must be held accountable for his crime." Mom blows out a breath as she looks up at the ceiling. "But ultimately, it is your call."

This has to be killing her. Finding out that her child has

been lying to her all this time, creating *sex tapes* with an older man—a man she trusted.

"I think everyone should call it a night for now," Aunt Kendall chimes in. I'm so thankful she didn't out Lawson and me to my parents on the Fourth, and I'm grateful for the little wink she sends my way now. "Tensions are high, and I think what everyone needs is some good sleep. We can reconvene in the morning." She says *we* because my pseudo aunts and uncles are as much a part of the family as the ones with the last name Bradee.

Plus, crisis control is her job—literally.

Mom pulls me into a hug, squeezing me so tight it draws another wave of salty tears from my eyes, and Dad awkwardly pats me on the back. This must be so uncomfortable for him. No one says a thing as I climb the stairs to my room, and it's only when I close my door that I hear my parents and aunts start talking about how upset they are and wondering how Lawson could do such a thing.

Multiple calls and texts litter my home screen, with new ones popping up every few seconds. To my surprise, when I swipe my finger across the screen and read through them, the majority of my coworkers are worried about me instead of throwing slurs and jabs about sleeping with our boss like I expected.

**ANNA**

> I'm sure no one watched it very long once they realized what it was. Justin is in a group text with a bunch of the guys, and they all called HR right away. Are you okay? Please call me.

### JUSTIN

> Hey. I'm sure you don't want to talk, but just know we have your back. Whoever did this will get what's coming to them.

### MIKE

> So, you didn't want to date me because I was too young. That's it, right?

> I'm sorry, that was a shit thing to say. I was trying to be funny. I'm… awkward when I'm nervous.

> What I was trying to say is that it's okay if you guys are together. No one cares. But whoever leaked the video is a sick individual and deserves whatever they get.

There's even one from Molly.

### MOLLY

> No wonder you didn't want me getting my claws into him. You'd already sunk yours in. Seriously, though, what happened is fucked. I'm sorry. :(

I don't reply to anyone, but I listen to the voicemail from HQ requesting a call with them tomorrow to discuss the situation. They sound apologetic and assure me the video has been removed from the company server.

But I know they can't guarantee no one downloaded it to their personal devices beforehand.

With that last thought, I roll over and curl into the fetal position, hugging my elephant pillow to my chest. I run my fingers over the lace on my duvet. The scratchy, worn material is comforting in this time of distress.

I wish I could go back in time and say no to Lawson filming us.

"Some fucking fantasy."

"WE COMPLETELY UNDERSTAND why you would be hesitant to return, but we want you to know we are on your side. Mr. Morgan has been terminated, and if you're not comfortable returning to the Chicago office, we are willing to pay to relocate you wherever you'd like to go."

I stare at my phone, plucking the beads on my elephant pillow as a random HR lady tells me the very thing I feared —that Lawson would lose his job over this.

"It wasn't his fault." My voice is small, unsure.

I hate it. It's not me. But it's what this gross invasion of privacy has done. I *feel* small, like the HR lady is probably just saying all of this because the company wants to cover their bases, not because they genuinely care about the life of an assistant.

"Mr. Morgan took full responsibility. He said he's been in contact with your family, but if you'd like, we can certainly step in and help handle any legal action you wish to take."

*So he didn't tell them it was Rhys.*

Why does that hurt so much?

Sighing, I flop back on my bed. "Thank you, but I do not wish to take legal action at this time. I also don't want to remain with the company. Please consider the verbal resignation I gave yesterday as my official statement. And please add to it that I would like Lawson reinstated. He doesn't deserve to lose his job."

"Miss Bradee—"

"Thank you for your call. Have a nice day," I tell her curtly before hanging up.

A soft knock sounds at my door, and I know it's my mom before she even peeks her head in. Knowing her, she was probably outside listening in on the conversation.

"Can I come in?"

I don't say anything but nod my head, rolling to my side. She sits in the space next to me, running her hands through my hair like she's done since I was a little girl. We sit in silence for a while before she releases a long breath.

"When I envisioned your future, this is not what I wanted for you, Lucy."

"He's good to me, Mom. He cares about me. Isn't *that* what you want for me? Someone who will take care of me and still encourage me to do all the things I love?"

"Yes, sweetheart. I do want those things for you. But what I'm seeing right now is a broken woman who has had a very horrific thing happen to her, and that man is nowhere to be found." I can hear the tears in her voice and, in turn, my own swell.

I've cried so much over the last two days that I figured I'd run out by now.

"You ran him off with talk of jail time, Mom. What did you expect?"

"For him to fight for you." Her statement jars me. I turn to see her staring across my room at a random spot on the wall. "I think I've always known there was something there. Call it a mother's intuition. When you were younger, I didn't want to believe it. I didn't want to assume that this nice man was a predator, and I told myself I wouldn't say or do anything until he gave me a reason to or until I noticed a significant change in you that would signify any sort of assault."

Hearing her speak about Lawson like this gives me goosebumps. Never has he ever given off those types of vibes, so I wonder what exactly it was about our interactions that made her feel that way.

"Neither of those things ever came. So I chalked it up to being overprotective." She looks down at my unbound locks and smiles. "But then I did see a change. As soon as Lawson returned, I watched you light up like the Rockefeller Christmas tree. And seeing you two on the Fourth of July... you were glowing, Lucy. And I told myself maybe it wouldn't be *so* bad if something were to happen. But I figured you would at least be honest about it, that he would have the decency to come to your father and me and talk about it. I did not, in a million years, think that something like this would happen and that when things got tough, he would leave you to take care of the mess on your own."

"That isn't what he's doing! I'm sure this is excruciating for him. Rhys and he have always had a rocky relationship, Mom." I sit up, wiping the dried tears from my cheeks. "This is probably the biggest decision he's ever had to make in his life. He loves me. I know he does. But Rhys is his *son*."

"And sometimes you have to let your kids fall on their swords for them to learn a lesson!"

"That is so unfair. How many times have you bailed Liam out? How many times have you put him in rehab— expensive rehab—and then when he fucks up again, you just tell him it will be okay, and you'll find another program?" As much as I love my brother, I need my mother to hear how ridiculous she's being.

"Lucy, you're deflecting."

"I'm not, though. Parents do things like that for their kids. They take the blame, and they clean up after their messes. I can't... I can't *ask* Lawson to stand by and watch while I press charges against his son." My voice rises in pitch the longer I talk. The fact that Lawson hasn't called me all day weighs heavily on my chest, and the more I talk about the situation, the worse my thoughts get.

What if Rhys just gets away with it? Is that really fair? Is him being hurt by what we did a justifiable enough excuse for his actions?

Why *haven't* I heard from Lawson? Did he make his choice? He lost his job, of course, he wouldn't want to lose his son, too.

"So, Rhys is going to get a slap on the wrist, and you get to what? Just deal with the fallout?"

Exhaustion slams into me like a freight train, weighing me down along with all my self-pity. "Can we not talk about this anymore, Mom? Please? I'm tired. I need a nap."

She must hear the defeat in my tone because she relaxes. "Okay. Get some rest. I'll wake you for dinner."

I don't bother telling her I'm not hungry.

She leaves, and I curl up again, pulling my blanket over my head to drown out the buttery sunshine beaming through my window.

I'd rather it be storming.

I'm more comfortable when it's cloudy.

# THIRTY-THREE

## *Lucy*

An ENTIRE WEEK passes without Lawson reaching out.

Honestly, I don't know how to feel about that.

M.I.G. has been in constant contact, most likely trying to assess whether I'm going to slap a sexual harassment lawsuit on their asses. But I do know that they haven't completely fired Lawson... yet.

Anna texts me daily to say that Lawson is already in his office by the time everyone arrives and doesn't leave until everyone else has gone home. I don't know what to do with that knowledge. He's going to work but hasn't called me to check how I'm doing.

It validates my mother's worries—that he isn't fighting for me. But I can't help but think maybe it's more than that. Perhaps he's dealing with Rhys. Maybe he's preparing himself and his son for the consequences.

I don't even know what the consequences will be yet.

M.I.G. doesn't know Rhys is the one who hacked his father's email, and I don't see how they'd find out unless

Lawson tells them, which it's looking more and more every day like he won't.

I'm beginning to feel like a fool—like maybe I imagined the level of connection Lawson and I had. Yes, we said we love each other, but this isn't love. This has been traumatic and a total invasion of privacy, and instead of being a beacon in the dark, Lawson's just left me to deal with it alone.

Well, not totally alone. I have Ben and Jerry—the two most dependable men there are.

Thinking about everything makes my skin heat with irritation. I have to stretch to scratch at the middle of my back, even though it's just going to spread the hives. The attacks are a daily thing now, triggered by random things I can't pinpoint and that aren't food.

A knock interrupts my night of self-pity, echoing throughout my small apartment like an unwelcome guest. Glancing at the clock on my nightstand, I see it's nearly eight. Lawson is the only person I can think of who would be coming by unannounced at this time.

My heart skips a beat as I slam The Tonight Dough ice cream pint on the nightstand and shuffle down the hall to answer the door.

It's not Lawson.

Cornflower blue eyes and the pearly white teeth of Cameron's charming smile greet me on the other side of the door. "Hello, little Lucy."

"Cameron? What are you doing here?" Even though he's seen me completely naked, I pull my robe tighter around my magenta silk nightdress.

We haven't spoken since the night Lawson and I had

with him. He likes my photos on Iconic but never leaves a comment. So, seeing him on the other side of my door is a surprise.

"Wanted to check on you, considering everything that's going on." He waves his hand in the air like my leaked sex tape is nothing to write home about. "Gonna invite me in?"

I narrow my eyes, scrutinizing the way his happy-go-lucky countenance takes in every surface of my place like he's calculating all the ways he can fuck me on them. His Cheshire grin widens, and his gaze darkens as he runs his eyes over my body. Then his face relaxes, and his tone softens.

"Seriously, Lucy. I just wanted to see how you're holding up."

At the tenderness in his voice, my suspicion dissipates. I back up, widening the door and sweeping my arm out. "Come on in."

He enters my apartment, tucking away a stray hair that's fallen out of my messy bun as he passes by. It doesn't make my heart go pitter-patter like when Lawson does it. Even though I find Cameron attractive, it's just not the same.

"God damn, you are beautiful," he says. I expect to melt into a puddle, but I don't.

"I'm still with Lawson," I tell him flatly, swinging the door shut and returning to my ice cream. "Or, at least, I think I am."

I shove a spoonful of the softened creamy goodness into my mouth as Cameron shrugs. "He's out with Jules tonight, which was kind of surprising. He said you two haven't spoken all week."

The cold dessert sits on my tongue as I process what he just said.

*Lawson is out with Jules?*

*He hasn't bothered to speak to me all week, but he's out with* Jules?

Cameron's brows dip together, and his bottom lip rolls inward between his teeth before he says, "Ah shit, I wasn't supposed to say anything. I'm sorry. I'm not here to cause problems, I swear."

"Trust me, it's not you causing them," I grumble.

My chest hurts, and my sinuses burn with tears. But I've cried enough over the last week. And Lawson's been out having a good time, apparently.

"You look like you could use a meal. Why don't you go get yourself all dolled up and let me take you to dinner?" Cameron asks, shoving his hands in the pockets of his deep charcoal dress slacks.

He's not wearing a suit jacket, and his white dress shirt is rolled up to his elbows, the ink on his forearm a stark contrast against the bright material.

Even with the news of Lawson being out with Jules, a sense of betrayal bites at my heart. Lawson would be livid if he found out I went to dinner with Cameron behind his back.

*Do you really owe him your loyalty? You don't know where you stand with the man—if you're even together.*

"I don't know." I pick at the frayed end of the robe's belt.

"Oh, come on, little Lucy," Cameron entices with a cool, calm, casual demeanor pasted on his handsome features. "It's just dinner. Everyone's gotta eat."

"I thought you and Lawson were best friends?" In the back of my mind, I think about how I would feel if the situation were reversed... but then I remember that Lawson is out with Jules.

"The best of." He shrugs. "But if he wants to be stupid and throw away a good thing, that's on him. You're too precious to be sitting here alone, eating ice cream, and feeling sorry for yourself. Now go to your room." He jerks his chin toward the hallway. "Put on something mouthwatering, and let me take you out for a nice meal. It'll help you get your mind off everything going on right now."

His intentions are anything but chivalrous. In fact, he's looking at me like he wants to peel off my nightdress and fuck me against the wall right now.

*I bet he could get creative with the rest of your ice cream.*

I point my spoon at him. "Just dinner. Nothing more than that."

His hands fly in the air in *surrender*. "Just dinner. Promise."

Lawson creeps back into my mind while I get dressed and take my mop of hair out of its messy bun, fluffing the wayward strands into sex-kitten waves. I think about sending him a text to ask how dinner with Jules is. I consider letting him know I'm going to dinner with Cameron.

Pettiness settles in my bones as I slip into a sexy emerald dress trimmed in black lace that is meant for a lot more than *just dinner*.

A sex tape starring me front and center—or from behind, if you want to get real technical—was leaked to an entire office of my colleagues. Revenge porn at its finest served on a silver platter by my ex, and my boyfriend wants to ignore me for a week and take another woman out to dinner?

*I'm being irrational.*

I slip on a pair of shimmery gold stilettos and walk to my vanity to apply a few coats of mascara and a red lip stain that I know drives Lawson wild.

*He isn't going to see you.*

Pushing my boobs up, I secure them before spritzing my perfume over my neck.

*You're getting all dolled up for another man. This is next-level petty and something someone his age would never do.*

I'm tempted to take a photo, maybe with Cameron's arm tattoo in the shot, and post it to Iconic.

*Seriously, knock it off, Lucy. You're better than this.*

I blow out a breath as I return to the living room, and a smidgeon of pride flows through me at the way Cameron's eyes rove my body as he lets out a low whistle. "You definitely understood the assignment. Shall we?"

Taking his offered arm, I ignore his comment and let him lead me out into the cooling night air, even allowing him to help me into his rental.

All the while, the voice in my head screams that this is a bad decision, but I ignore that, too.

Apparently, I've been making bad decisions for the last few months. What's one more?

CAMERON MAKES small talk as he drives us to a restaurant I've never heard of, not that far from my apartment. It's packed, with a line of people waiting outside the gray stone building—various couples clinging to each other beneath the maroon awning.

Cam is a perfect gentleman, opening the door for me and ushering me inside with a gentle palm against the small of my back. The faintest touch from Lawson would normally set my insides on fire. But the most Cameron elicits is a slight tingle between my legs when he draws me closer as we wait our turn to be seated.

He whispers against the sensitive spot beneath my ear, "You know, you can always come work for me in New York."

There's no time to reply as we step forward, and he gives the hostess his name. I can't really read him. All his actions say he wants a lot more than just dinner tonight, but I honestly don't think he'd do that to Lawson, and I wouldn't either—regardless of what my outfit says.

A sharp screech of a chair on the hardwood floor sounds across the restaurant. As I glance up to see whatever commotion is breaking out, Cameron steals my attention by blocking my view as he ushers me forward. "Our table is ready."

We follow the hostess through the buttery light cast from dripping crystal chandeliers, twining through black leather booths and golden chairs until we reach our table.

"I mean it," he says once we're seated. "I think you'd like the city."

"I'm not moving to New York, Cameron." I browse the menu, finally realizing just how hungry I am.

One cannot live on ice cream and tequila alone.

"Well, what are your plans? You know M.I.G. is willing to help you get a job anywhere else. They really don't want a lawsuit on their hands."

Cameron doesn't even bother to look at his menu. His eyes keep darting over my shoulder, but when I start to turn to see what's caught his attention, he reaches for my hand, drawing my focus back to him as he tangles our fingers together.

Another screech sounds across the room, and for some reason, my heart hammers in my chest as Cameron's intense blue eyes crinkle at the corners, and he lifts my hand to his lips.

"What are you doing?" He's acting so weird, and I'm suddenly highly aware that I don't really know this man. I just blindly trusted him because he's Lawson's friend.

"That took longer than I expected," he murmurs against my knuckles.

"What did?"

"Three... Two... One."

A wall of black infiltrates my peripheral as the familiar, yet angry, timbre of the man I love fills my ears. "What the fuck is going on here?"

Cameron's thumb sweeps along the top of my hand as I stare up at Lawson, who is angrier than I've ever seen him. He looks like he's about to murder his friend, not bothering to grace me with his darkened storm cloud gaze.

"Hey, Law. We're just having dinner. Same as you and Jules." The words are innocent, like us being together shouldn't be a big deal. "I'm trying to talk her into coming to work for me in New York." He flashes a smile that one would give an adversary, not a friend.

Lawson finally turns his gaze to me. "Care to explain, Lucy?"

The anger in his tone sparks my annoyance. "I mean, Cameron just did, Lawson. We're having dinner. Just like you and *Jules*. I'm not sure why you care. You haven't said a word to me all week, and then I find out you're out to dinner with someone else."

His composure softens, eyes lightening a shade as he stares down at me. "It's just Jules, Lucy."

"And it's *just* Cameron." I'm hyper-aware that numerous pairs of eyes are on us as Lawson's chest heaves. He looks torn between clocking Cameron across the face and pulling me out of the restaurant.

The latter wins.

He grabs my bicep, pulling me from my chair. "Let's go."

"Lawson! What are you doing?" I scramble to get my feet beneath me, my face growing warm with embarrassment.

Cameron does nothing to stop him—just watches as I get dragged further away from the table. "Have fun, you two!" he calls out after us.

I glare at him over my shoulder just in time to see an amused-looking Jules approaching his table.

It's pretty freaking clear that we've been set up.

"What the hell?" I demand when we get outside, and Lawson lets me go to stalk toward the parking lot. "Are you seriously upset with me right now?"

"Is that a fucking rhetorical question?" I swear steam is

coming from his ears as he unlocks his car and holds the passenger door open. "Get in."

"You don't get to be mad at me!" I wave my finger in the air toward him. "You haven't said a fucking word to me all week, and then Cameron shows up to tell me that you're out with Jules. What the fuck was I supposed to think, Lawson?"

"I was giving you the space you said you needed." His words are low and growly. "Jules was helping me with a deal. But evidently, she and Cameron set this up." He grabs my hand mid-air and manhandles me into the car, slamming the door in my face.

"When did I ever say I needed space?" I yell as he rounds the car.

"At the lake house!" he screams back as he climbs in, and the engine roars to life. "And after your mother threatened jail time, and then I didn't hear from you, what was I supposed to think?"

"No. No, we are not a poorly written miscommunication trope, Lawson! I told you I needed space when you refused to tell Rhys. You should have known better after everything else happened."

"What, so that just gives you the excuse to go out with my best friend looking like that?" He gestures to my body as he whips out of the parking lot, wheels screeching as gravel goes flying. "Wanna tell me why you allowed him to have his hands all over you?"

"Oh, Jesus. He was obviously doing it to get a rise out of you!" I cross my arms with a huff and stare out the window as we fly by the familiar buildings that lead back to my apartment.

"Did you know I would be there?"

"No."

"So, you got all dolled up for *him,* then?" When I turn my head, Lawson looks like he's about ready to murder someone, and since I'm the only one in his general proximity...

I remain silent. He doesn't say a word for the rest of the drive, and when we get back to my building, I'm surprised when he turns his car off and follows me in. We barely make it into my apartment before he slams the door and crowds me against the wall.

"Tell me, Lucy. Is all this for him?" His large palm runs over the swell of my breast and along the curve of my waist before settling on my hip. "Does it turn you on knowing that he wants you?"

"Stop it." I brace my hands on his forearms, peering up at him through my lashes. "You don't get to be angry."

"Is this your way of getting back at me?" He runs his nose along the column of my neck as his knee pushes between my legs, pressing against me to create a familiar ache I've longed for all week. His fingers dig into my sides. "Did you really think another man could satisfy you? Make you feel the way I do?"

He bunches my skirt up as I pull his suit jacket off. Giving him a saucy smirk, I whisper, "Cameron felt amazing when we were together. Maybe you shouldn't abandon your toys after you loan them out if you don't want other men playing with them."

A strangled gasp flies from my lips as he snarls and spins me until my cheek is pressed against the wall. Lawson isn't rough, but he's also not gentle as he brings his hand down against my ass. The slap reverberates in the air as I moan and push my hips toward him, begging for another spanking.

This is what I've been craving all week—what I've been missing—what we could have been doing every day if one of us had just picked up the damn phone.

"Apparently, a week apart has turned you back into a mouthy little brat." The sound of his zipper reaches my ears before he slaps my ass again. Bracing my arms on the wall, I arch my back as he rips my thong to the side and positions himself at my entrance. "Such a little slut for my cock, aren't you, rainbow?"

"Lawson!" I cry out as he slams into me, pitching my body forward until my forehead presses against the wall so hard it might leave a bruise.

"Is this what you were thinking of when you got dressed up for him?" He grips my hips tightly as he pistons into me. "Were you hoping I'd see you? Tell me, Lucy. Would you have brought him back here?"

I snake a hand between my legs, desperate to relieve the tension building in my clit. Lawson twists my arm behind my back, pinning it with his chest as he takes over and begins to rub me furiously.

I'm always wet for him, but this time it's as if my pussy is angry with him, too, gripping his cock to keep him lodged inside me. There's so much friction, and I feel so full as he punishes me, reminding me of who I belong to.

"You ignored me for an entire week. I was feeling petty." He slaps my clit in response, latching onto my neck to suck at the spot beneath my ear.

My orgasm is a flood of molten heat spilling between

my legs and around his cock. He lets out a hoarse groan as my walls milk him, and I can feel his length twitch as he comes, filling me with more liquid warmth.

We stay like that for a long while, his body hunched over me as I grasp the wall for balance. When he pulls out, I turn to see him tucking himself back in his pants, so I right my dress, too.

"I'm sorry," he whispers.

Concern floods his darkened irises as he reaches up to smooth his thumb across a sore patch on my forehead. His apology doesn't seem like it's just for the rough sex but for so much more, and I feel the telltale sign of tears pricking my eyes.

"I know."

I want to reach for him. I want him to pull me into his arms and kiss away the pain. I want to tell him I would never betray him and make sure he knows how sorry I am that I even agreed to go to dinner with Cameron. I want Lawson to tell me he's sorry for not calling all week.

But neither of us speaks... we only stare at each other as our heavy breathing calms.

"It's so unfair." Unashamed, I let my tears fall. "*Everything*. I've been thinking about it all week. I know he's your son, and he should always come first, but I don't want to be second," I sob.

Tears shine in Lawson's eyes as he surges forward to cup my neck and press a kiss against my forehead. "I'm so sorry, Lucy."

It sounds more like a goodbye than an apology, and I break.

Another sob tears from my throat, my tears blurring my

vision as he lets me go. Selfishly, I wait for him to say it will always be me. For him to tell me how sorry he is that he hasn't communicated all week.

To say we're going to weather this storm together.

But Lawson looks as though he's at a loss for words, scrubbing the back of his neck while turmoil and despair battle across his handsome features. "I should get going."

My heart breaks, and an iron wall slams down around the organ to protect it from shattering further. With a more even voice than I thought myself capable, I say, "Yeah. I guess so."

Suddenly, my back hits the wall, and his lips crash down on mine. It's a kiss full of passion and desperate longing, but it's bittersweet. We're right back where we started. His words and his actions are a contradiction to everything we've been through, splitting open a chasm between us. He's always pushed me away. I don't know why I expected this time to be any different. My tears fall between our lips, the salt seasoning the saddest farewell I've ever tasted.

Then he's gone.

And I fall apart, sliding against the wall as my broken cries fill the air.

Because even though I know it's such an unfair choice, part of me really thought he'd choose me.

# Thirty-Four

*Lawson*

I fucking hate Florida.

If there's anything I hate more than the predicament I'm in right now, it's Florida.

The heat. The sticky humidity. The entitled women sitting at home nursing their daiquiris and having affairs with their pool boys while their husbands fuck their secretaries at work—and yes, I understand the irony of that statement.

I also know the latter can be found anywhere, but it seems to be extra prevalent in the little suburban Boca neighborhood, which is probably why Charlotte feels more at home here than she ever did in Chicago.

Neighbors I've never met watch my car creep by slowly while they water their lawns—wondering who the new guy on the block is.

*Not new. I just hate it here.*

As I park in the driveway, I take in the pristine appearance of the house. The bright cream stucco and red-shingled roof look like they've been recently pressure-washed, and the hedges that line the yard are freshly trimmed.

There's a fluttering of the ivory lace curtains at the front window, and I catch a glimpse of Charlotte's blonde hair as she pulls away. She greets me at the door with a wary grimace, her eyes darting to the manila envelope under my arm.

"Lawson, this is a surprise. What are you doing here?" None of her usual sarcasm fills her voice. Instead, she almost sounds scared, like she knows *exactly* what I'm doing here and is afraid of what's about to happen.

"You gonna let me in?" I ignore her question and press forward, not waiting for her to invite me into the home I pay for. "Where is Rhys?"

"I don't know," she lies.

The stale stench of alcohol permeates the house, and the liquor cart in the dining room is stocked to the brim with various bottles and mixers, all of which are nearly empty.

"He's distraught, and can you blame him? Jesus, Lawson, what were you thinking?"

Huffing a laugh, I turn to face her. Charlotte's cheeks are gaunt, and hair hangs limp around her face even though it looks clean. There's a hollowness in her frame like she's living off drinking and the misery she inflicts upon herself.

She looks like shit, so I tell her as much.

"Fuck you," she spits, her bright cerulean eyes flickering with hatred. "What, Law? You think that because you managed to talk some young, dumb pussy into bed, you're hot shit? Newsflash, you've seen better days. Lucy's more stupid than I thought if she thinks you're a catch."

For some reason, her words hurt. Most likely because I know Lucy deserves better, but my rainbow chose me. She's been choosing me since day one, and it's about damn time she knows I choose her, too.

Slapping the envelope on the kitchen table, I pull out a seat as Charlotte pours herself a drink. "This will go as easy as you want it to." I unfasten the metal clasp and dump the stack of divorce papers on the imported walnut. "It doesn't have to be messy. You can stay here, and I will continue paying the bills for this house. I get full custody of River. He only has a few years left in school, anyway. If he wants to visit, I won't stop him, but when he's here, you'll clean your act up, or I'll put an end to any visitation rights. Do you understand me?"

Charlotte keeps her back to me, but I don't miss the shiver that racks her frame. "Clean my act up?" she scoffs. "Are you implying I have a problem, Lawson?"

I cross my legs as I lean back in the chair. "Not implying. It's clear you do. This place smells like a distillery. You look like an addict, and our son has even mentioned that all you do is drink when he's here. I'm putting my foot down like I should have a long time ago. Charlotte, you have a problem. And I take responsibility for my part in it."

She turns to lean against the cart and looks at me in surprise. I motion for her to sit, and when she does, she leaves her drink on the table.

"I let our family break a long time ago. And I know it's too late to fix it, but it isn't too late to start making things right." I slide the papers over to her. "Starting with this."

Charlotte eyes them, nostrils flaring as she shakes her head. "You think I'm just going to settle for the house? You think I don't know what you're worth? You owe me, Lawson. It's why you haven't bothered to leave me yet. You should be asking yourself if she's really worth it because I won't sit idly by and let you—"

"If you'd read the damn papers, you'll see that you're getting more than your fair share," I interrupt. "And Lucy is worth all of it and more. But a judge won't grant you a dime more than I'm offering. You'll likely get less if you try to fight it."

"You don't know that."

"I do. Because I know what the papers say. If you want a lawyer to look it over, you're welcome to do so. But I'm expecting them to be signed within the week." I think I hear the sound of a car door outside, but a huff from Charlotte covers it.

"Why now? Why not just let your little fantasy play out until Lucy figures out you're not what she wants?" She smirks, but when I don't answer her, the corners of her lips pull down. Our eyes remain locked as she realizes my intentions. "Are you serious, Lawson? Rhys will hate you forever."

"I will deal with Rhys. Starting with him taking responsibility for what he's done." Bile rises in my throat as I think about the inevitable discussion I came here for.

Serving Charlotte with the divorce papers is just a bonus, but as soon as River let it slip that Rhys had run off to hide with their mother, I knew what I had to do.

"Like hell, you will! You can take the blame for it!" Charlotte snarls, her once pretty features twisting into a grotesque mask that only I have the displeasure of viewing.

"I almost lost my job. What the hell do you think that

means? I *did* take the blame for it!" My palm slams on the table to emphasize my ire. "And Lucy quit, which means she's out of a job. Her parents are talking about pressing charges. This is a serious fucking matter! This isn't something that we can sweep under the rug. It's a severe offense that could mean jail time. And that cushy new job he just landed at U of C? He can kiss it goodbye."

"So rein in your little girlfriend and make sure she doesn't press charges!" Charlotte screams, tears filling her eyes at the possibility of her little boy getting locked up.

"I'm not going to do that. Lucy's been humiliated in the worst way possible. She's within her right to go after him for what he did." It kills me to say it, but it's true. And I will stand by them both through it all if it's what Lucy decides.

"What kind of a father are you?" Charlotte grabs her drink roughly and liquor spills over the rim.

I start to argue, but a throat clearing makes me pause. Rhys is standing in the doorway, looking guilty as fuck. "He's right, Mom."

I blink.

"You don't know what you're saying, honey," Charlotte sputters as she gets up and wraps her hands around his shoulders. "Let's not speak nonsense, alright?"

Rhys gently removes her hands, folding them between his own as he stares directly into her eyes. "What I did wasn't okay. Lucy deserves an apology."

*She deserves a hell of a lot more than that.*

But hearing my son acknowledge he's in the wrong stays my hand.

"Rhys, you don't know what you're saying," his mother whimpers. "Don't let him talk you into this."

"I'm not, Mom. It's what needs to happen. I was in the wrong." Rhys finally looks at me, his eyes flashing with thinly veiled hatred. "I am still so *unbelievably* pissed at you, Dad. But I'm ready to take responsibility for my actions."

Shock ripples through me. I wasn't expecting him to *agree*.

My son gently maneuvers his mother to the side as he cocks his head toward the backyard. "We should probably talk."

Charlotte releases a dramatic sob and flees down the hall to her bedroom. Both Rhys and I wince as she slams the door.

"Okay, I guess we'll just talk here then." He takes his mother's seat, eyes darting to the divorce papers. "You're really going through with it, huh?"

I don't know what to say, so I remain quiet.

He blows out a breath as he scratches the back of his neck. "So, what? Are you going to ask her to marry you?" His words are full of grit and malice, striking me directly in the center of my chest.

"Rhys—"

He raises a hand to stop me, shaking his head. "You know, never mind. I don't think I'm ready to hear it."

A heavy silence falls between us. The clock ticking on the wall is loud as the seconds stretch on, barely concealing Charlotte's muffled cries.

Finally, I ask, "Why'd you do it?"

Rhys sighs before scrubbing his hands over his face.

"Honestly, I didn't know it was Lucy. I was drunk and pissed off, and I wanted to hurt you as badly as you hurt me. I thought it was a random woman. Never in a million years would I have thought it would have been her."

"I know I hurt you. I will never be able to express how sorry I am for that."

"I know." His eyes flicker to the papers again. "You really care about her, don't you?"

"I do." I don't elaborate. He doesn't need to hear me wax poetic on all the ways I'm in love with his ex-girlfriend. He loved her once. He knows.

"Is she really going to press charges?" he asks, eyes glued to the table.

"I don't know. To be honest, we haven't spoken all week."

My mind drifts to last night, thinking about how angry I was when she walked into the restaurant with Cameron. It literally hurt to see her—to see her beautiful face smiling at him, lips painted in a shade she knows I love, dressed to impress another man.

I still haven't replied to his *you're welcome* text. Seriously, fuck him and Jules for staging that shit.

Even if it kicked my ass into gear.

I'm ashamed of how I handled Lucy last night—even if we both wanted it. To leave her crying in her apartment after I fucked her was a dick move. But I had to get out of there and continue moving pieces around the board like I had been all week. Otherwise, I would have gotten lost in her.

And I don't want to wait any longer.

"I could lie and say I'm sorry, but I'm not," my son mutters.

"But you are sorry for what you did, and that's what matters."

"It's going to... take time... to be okay with this. But I want to be... okay with it." Rhys' admission surprises me. "I just... I don't know how I'm ever going to get there."

"Take as much time as you need. I'm not going to push you to accept it. I am, however, going to push you to apologize and face whatever consequences are necessary." I round the table to sit in the chair next to him. "Son, I've done you a great disservice all your life. I let your mother get in your head, allowing you to believe that I thought you were a burden, even though I did everything in my power to show you that you weren't. I assumed you'd see my actions and understand that I didn't feel that way. But I realize now that I never really said it. Not enough."

Rhys raises his gaze to meet mine, tears lining his lashes.

"And that is my biggest regret. That I didn't tell you enough how much I love you. I wouldn't trade you for the world, Rhys. You're my son, and I failed you. I can never apologize enough for raising you the way we did. I let the money get to me, thinking that if I could just provide as much as possible, you'd know how much I love you. But I should have been home more. Should have paid you more attention."

"Dad, stop." He roughly wipes at his eyes. "You're a good dad. I just... I fucked up. That isn't on you. Nothing you did excuses what I did."

"Well, that's... a very mature way of looking at it." I run

my hand through his shaggy, dark hair. "When did you get so grown up?"

He huffs a laugh, shrugging my hand away. "It's funny. When your parents or someone you know is saying you fucked up, you don't want to believe it. But all it takes is a stranger listening to your sob story and still telling you you're in the wrong for you to finally get it."

My brows dip together. "What do you mean?"

Rhys leans back in his chair, and a smile stretches across his face, as though he's remembering what happened. "On the flight down here, I sat next to this guy who could tell I was going through something. When I left the house, I didn't bother packing or showering, so I stank like whiskey and puke. Honestly, I'm so fucking embarrassed now that I think of it." He shakes his head in disbelief. "The guy asked me what was wrong, and I just word-vomited everything. And you know what he said when I finished telling him my sob story?"

I shake my head.

"He told me his own story about how he once followed his wife to New York and asked her husband at the time how his dick tasted." Rhys smirks, a short laugh escaping his lips as he shakes his head. "Said he ended up getting his ass beat by her husband's cronies, and she even broke up with him for a while. He said sometimes people do stupid things that result in bad decisions, but it's important to take responsibility for those actions and make amends for the wrong you've done or the harm you caused. And I don't know why his words resonated with me, but I knew immediately that I will take whatever punishment Lucy wants to give me."

I silently thank whoever took the time to talk to Rhys on the plane instead of writing him off as a drunken disturbance. "Whatever she decides, you know I'll be there for you. I'm going to be there for you both if she'll still have me."

Rhys scrutinizes every inch of my face with a neutral stare. "If she won't, maybe those are the consequences of *your* actions. What will *you* do to make amends?"

# THIRTY-FIVE

*Lucy*

A KNOCK on my childhood bedroom door interrupts my job search. "Come in."

Dad's face appears in the crack, his warm, golden-brown eyes still unable to look directly at me. "There's someone here to see you." His tone is stern, and I can see his knuckles turning white as they grip the door.

"Someone's here to see me?" I'm not expecting anyone. Unless... I scramble up and peer out the window. My heart skips a beat when I see Lawson's car in the driveway.

It hasn't even been two days, but it feels like it's been years since he walked out of my apartment on Friday and ended our relationship.

*He never ended anything. You assumed he did.*

"I'm inclined not to let him in," Dad says. "Your mother is still gone, and out of the two of us, she'd fare better in jail than I would."

I laugh as I shove my feet into my house slippers. "You're probably right. Mom would make everyone her bitch. You'd just be someone's bitch."

Finally, my dad looks me in the eye for the first time since he found out about Lawson and me. "I'm too pretty to go to jail, Luce. Make it quick."

At least he's joking with me again.

Lawson is standing just inside the door when I get downstairs, a familiar, gleaming cellophane bundle in one hand, and a bouquet of brilliant blue roses in the other.

"Hi." His eyes are bright and hopeful but filled with caution as they glance at my dad to make sure he's not going to sucker punch him when he least expects it.

"Hi." I return his simple greeting. He's got a lot of explaining to do.

Lawson licks his lips and chuckles, knowing I won't make this easy. He holds out the flowers and cookies. "I come bearing gifts."

Grabbing the flowers, I bring them to my nose, inhaling their fragrant notes. "Blue?"

Smiling softly, Lawson nods. "I told the lady at the flower shop that I needed something that celebrated attaining an impossible dream." His voice drops lower, unguarded, raw emotion filtering through. "One I want so badly to come true."

Affection warms my insides, my cheeks heating as he hands me the cookies.

I take the package and retreat a few steps, staring at him expectantly as I open it and pop one in my mouth. The silence weighs heavily between us—and my dad, who hasn't left.

"I miss you." Lawson steps toward me.

But when Dad clears his throat, Lawson stops and takes a deep breath. "Will, I'm not going anywhere. I'm here to tell your daughter that I love her, and I'm sorry. You can either stay and witness the exchange, which will probably be extremely uncomfortable for you, because after I'm finished talking, I will pretend like you're not here. Or, you can give us a little privacy. Either way, I will speak to Lucy, and when Bree gets back, I'd like to speak to you both as well."

Thankfully, Dad retreats into the kitchen after taking my flowers, mumbling about putting them in water.

Lawson looks back at me, his storm cloud eyes full of remorse and determination. "I am so sorry, rainbow. For everything. For the films. For not coming clean when you wanted to. For waiting so long to divorce Charlotte and not parading you around like you deserve." With every sentence, he steps closer until he's standing right in front of me. "I'm especially sorry for making you feel like I didn't choose you after the leak happened and for what occurred on Friday. I should have never left, not without filling you in on everything first."

I sniff, fishing another cookie out of the package. I try to act as casually as possible, but his words intrigue me. "What do you mean?"

"Charlotte signed the divorce papers. And I left M.I.G. The reason Jules was in town was because she was helping me secure my own building."

A familiar tingle blooms behind my sinuses. "Your own building?"

He nods, cupping my face in his warm hands. "Remember what we talked about? About focusing on low-income housing? I was thinking we could start a new business together. You can run the whole thing."

My lip trembles, and the cookie in my hand smushes into a large lump. "You want to start a business together?"

"I want to start a *life* with you, Lucy. I figured the business would be a good start." The corners of his lips turn up in a smirk. "I was thinking we could call it The Rainbow Rooms."

A watery laugh escapes my lips, and I wipe at the tears lining my lashes. "That is... the worst name for a building... *ever.*"

He laughs and tilts my face up to lean his forehead against mine. "We can call it whatever you want, Lucy. I just wanted to show you that I'm in this. And I'm sorry it took me so long to make things right. I love you."

My hand presses against his chest. "And what about Rhys?"

Lawson pulls back. "Rhys is prepared to face whatever punishment you deem fit."

"And you?" I ask, searching his eyes for any minuscule sign that he'll resent me for my following words. "How do you feel about me moving forward with pressing charges?"

I'm not even one hundred percent sure it's what I want to do, but I need to know where Lawson stands. On one hand, I don't think Rhys knew it was me in the video. But on the other, it isn't fair for him to get off scot-free. I looked into it. He will likely get community service and a fine—not jail time. Not unless M.I.G. catches wind and wants to go after him themselves.

The first-time offender's penalties should be enough punishment to ensure he'll never try to pull something like this again, no matter how upset he gets.

"Rhys has a lesson to learn. He's an adult and understands that his actions have consequences. I support you, Lucy. And honestly, he supports you, too." Lawson appears genuine, but in the back of my mind, I can't help but wonder if it will stay that way throughout the process of me getting justice.

"And if I need time? To process all of this?" I step out of his hold.

Lawson's arms fall to his sides, and his throat bobs as he swallows thickly. "If you need time, I'll give you as much as you require. I'll do whatever it takes to show you how serious I am."

Before I can say anything else, a car door slams outside, signaling my mom's return. We both turn to look at the front door as her string of curses becomes audible even through the walls.

She enters the house like a hurricane, and when her wide hazel eyes land on us, she points at Lawson. "You have some nerve showing up *now*."

"I agree, Bree. It shouldn't have taken me this long to get my shit together."

Mom eyes the package I'm holding and holds her hand out, waving her fingers. Smirking at Lawson, I hand the cookie ball over, and she breaks a chunk off before shoving it in her mouth.

"You have a lot of explaining to do," she says through a mouthful of marshmallowy caramel goodness.

"I am fully aware that I need to prove myself to you and Will, not just Lucy." Lawson glances down at me with warmth in his gray eyes. "I'll tell you the same thing I told her... I'm willing to do whatever it takes to show you I love your daughter, and I will never do anything ever again to hurt her."

Mom appraises us with narrowed eyes before turning and heading toward the kitchen. "Well, let's hear it then."

Lawson releases the breath he'd been holding and flashes me one of his heart-stopping smiles. I reach down and lace my fingers through his, every fiber of my being thrumming with anticipation as we follow her. *Together.*

Ready to face whatever is left of the storm as a united pair.

# THIRTY-SIX
## A FEW WEEKS LATER

*Lawson*

"GOT EVERYTHING YOU NEED?" I ask my son as I set the last of his bags on the sidewalk of O'Hare International.

Rhys nods, slinging a black backpack over his shoulders. "Yep. Mom is picking me up at the airport, and I'm gonna spend a few days with her before I head to Sugarvale."

Settling everything between Lucy and Rhys in court went quicker and easier than expected, lasting only a few weeks. He was lucky that she ended up taking pity on him, and they settled on community service and a ten thousand dollar fine he paid from his trust.

Rhys was honest with the University of Chicago about what was happening, and they let him go before he even had the chance to start working. Now, he's headed to the small town of Sugarvale, Florida, where he landed a job as the town's resident sports therapist.

"How's she doing?" I haven't spoken to Charlotte since she signed the divorce papers. Everything has gone through our lawyers, and she hasn't fought me on a single thing.

"Good. I think treatment is going well. She really wants

to see River, and I think it was pretty eye-opening to find out he wanted to live with you full-time," Rhys explains as he links a duffle bag to his hardtop luggage. He doesn't look at me as he asks, "How is Lucy?"

"She's good." I give him a simple answer. He doesn't need to know that my little vixen has been keeping me on my toes.

I've spent weeks groveling, and still, she refuses to put a label on us—which I find ironic, considering she wanted us to go public in the first place. Now, it's stolen kisses after meetings with investors and hours at her apartment between her thighs, convincing her that I'm serious about us and I'm willing to follow her lead.

I think she likes feeling like the dominant one, though I keep telling her that one of these days, my patience will snap, and she'll be in for the spanking of her life.

Rhys nods, standing to gather his things. "Well. I guess I'll see you at Christmas?"

"Come here." I pull my son into me regardless of how awkward the hug is. "If you need anything, you know I'll be there."

"I know. Thanks, Dad," he says quietly against the crook of my neck.

"I love you," I tell him, just like I've been telling him every single day since we arrived back in Chicago together.

He nods as he steps back. "You, too."

No other words need to be said as he turns and heads into the airport. I stand there, watching the crowd swallow him, and my eyes mist over the same way they did when he left for college.

My phone buzzes in my pocket.

**LUCY**

How did everything go?

**LAWSON**

Good. He just left.

**LUCY**

I'm glad to hear it.

That things went well. Not that he left. I know it must be hard on you.

Want to meet at Lauren's Fault for a drink?

It's the first time she's asked me to meet her somewhere public. I respond quickly as my pulse races, telling her I'm on my way before I even get into my car.

LAUREN'S FAULT is slow when I arrive.

The lighting is dimmer than usual, and only a few stray people are scattered throughout the space. I don't see Lucy, so I sit at the bar and order myself a whiskey neat and a shot of Patrón for her.

Barely a few minutes go by before I hear her sweet voice behind me. "Come here often?"

I turn to see her dressed in the same rainbow-patterned dress she wore the first time I saw her here, her hair is also styled exactly the same, and there's a devious glint in her hazel eyes that goes straight to my cock.

"Hi, Mr. Morgan."

"Miss Bradee. What are you doing out all alone?" I tease, playing along with her little game.

She steps in close to me, lifting the shot glass to her lips. "I was thinking we could relive this night. Make sure we get things right this time."

Lucy waves at the bartender for another shot, her other hand slipping between my legs to run her palm over my growing erection. "I waited that whole night for you to take what you wanted." Her front presses against my side as she rubs me through my pants. "Maybe you just needed more of a push. So many things would have turned out differently."

Wrapping my fingers around her wrist, I pull her hand away, twisting our fingers together instead. "What did I tell you about trying to take control, rainbow?"

Lucy shrugs innocently. "That came later. I remember having a lot of control that night. Enough to get you riled up in the back hall, at least."

"That's funny." My voice lowers to a husky purr as I whisper in her ear, pulling her flush against me as I stand. "I also remember having enough self-control to let you walk away."

The lusty haze clears from her eyes as she stares up at

me, and the golden rings around her hazel irises shine with vulnerability. "Don't let me walk away this time."

She presses up on her toes to kiss me, hands curling into my shirt as she pulls me toward the back. No one pays us any attention as we slip into the pink-lit corridor. Halfway down the hall, I push her against the wall, crowding her space just like the last time we were here.

"You're just begging for a punishment, aren't you?"

Lucy presses her chest into mine, running her palm along the front of my pants to squeeze my cock. "What can I say? I didn't feel like being a good girl tonight." She smiles at me before spinning around and flipping her skirt up.

*Fuck me.*

A quick glance tells me we're still alone, and my palm meets her exposed cheeks.

*One spanking coming right up.*

"This is what I should have done to you that night." I press my chest into her back as I spank her again. "You wanted me to claim you where anyone could have walked in on us, didn't you?"

"Maybe I wanted everyone to see who owns me," she moans, rubbing her ass along my hardened cock. "Because it's always been you."

A husky groan leaves my lips as I scrape my teeth down her neck. "Should I take you out there now and fuck you in front of everyone?"

As much as the thought turns me on, I grace her cheek with one more slap before smoothing her skirt back into place and pulling her to the bathroom.

"Lawson, I need you," she whimpers, fingers undoing my belt as I tangle my hands in her hair and tilt her head up.

"You have me, baby. You've always had me," I murmur against her lips before claiming them with my own.

Lucy pumps my length a few times before hooking a leg around my waist to line the head of my cock at her entrance. I drop my hands to her thighs, hoisting her against the wall as I sheath myself deep, bottoming out with a groan as I stretch her.

"And you have me." Her hands grip the back of my shirt as I thrust into her quickly. "I don't need any more time, Lawson. I just want to be with you."

A heavy, hot feeling bursts in my chest as we lock eyes, followed by a tingling sensation that flows down my spine and into my balls as they tense up.

"I love you," I tell her before my release rips through me.

"I love you, too," she cries out as she comes at the same time.

I hold her against the wall as we come down from our post-orgasm high, and we lazily kiss until I grow soft and slip out. She giggles as I set her back on her feet and retreat into a stall.

"We just fucked in a dirty bathroom at a bar," I mutter with mirth as I hand her a wad of toilet paper.

"Could have made a movie about it. That's some prime-time porn material there," she jests. At my grimace, she laughs. "Too soon?"

"I already tossed the camera equipment." I crowd her against the wall again. "But just wait until I get you in the club in New York."

Lucy wraps her arms around my neck, pressing her lips

against mine. "I can't wait for all the things you have yet to show me, Lawson."

"I promise you, rainbow, we have a lifetime of experiences ahead of us."

# EPILOGUE
## TWO YEARS LATER

"WOULD YOU LIKE ANOTHER DRINK?" Lawson asks softly against my ear.

I can't tell if my cheeks burn from the heat of the fire we're standing in front of or the way his arms tighten around me, pulling my back into his chest. It's been two years, and I'm not sure I'll ever get used to our public displays of affection in front of my family.

Looking around the snow-covered yard, I see that not one single person is paying attention to us. My mom and aunts are huddled on the far side of the fire, sipping their cocktails and talking about Aunt Kendall and Uncle Mark's most recent trip to Greece. Dad and my uncles are standing next to them, talking about football.

Liam is currently glaring at Rose and River, who are cuddled up on a bench beneath a large blanket, sipping from the same cup of hot chocolate.

No one cares about our age difference or the leaked sex tape anymore. Everyone cohabitates peacefully, fully accepting that Lawson and I are together and in it for the long haul.

"Sure. Thanks, babe." I give him a quick peck and hand over my champagne glass.

As he disappears inside my parents' house, I join Liam on his bench. "Stare any harder, and you'll set River on fire."

My brother huffs a laugh, and a smirk replaces his scowl. "I don't know what you're talking about."

"Sure you don't."

I look across the fire to see Rose playing with the necklace Liam gave her for her sixteenth birthday. She never takes it off. Her pretty blue eyes glance in our direction, her cheeks flushing a rosy hue before she turns her attention back to River.

"How is work?" Liam plucks the same pink and cream hair tie he's worn on his wrist for the last two years. It's wearing out, fraying at the edges, and I file the information away since I plan to finish my Christmas shopping this week.

"It's going really well, actually," I say excitedly. "We're about to open a third building, and we think it's really making a difference, you know? Other businesses have started to join in, and some are interested in collaborating. Morgan Enterprises is genuinely making a dent in the unhoused population."

"That is so like you," Liam utters. "Cleaning up the city one hobo at a time."

"Liam!" I smack his chest. "Not nice, dude." He laughs as I settle back against the bench. "How is New York? Meet anyone special yet?"

His cheeks turn pink, a shade I've never seen on his face before, and it piques my curiosity. "There *is* someone!"

"No, there isn't!" he exclaims, eyes darting to Rose again. "I mean, there's *someone*, but not... if that makes sense."

Knowing how private my brother is, I zip and lock my lips and pretend to throw away the key. "I'm here if you ever want to talk. You know that, right?"

"I know." He stands, and I turn to see Lawson approaching us.

My champagne glass appears in front of my face, only a quarter of the way full and looking like pure orange juice instead of a mimosa. "Is this your way of telling me I'm done drinking for the night? I thought it was strange you asked." I tip my glass back before I notice something sparkling at the bottom.

Everything grows quiet as I freeze, orange juice flowing into my mouth. With each gulp, a shiny diamond ring is revealed. There's a thumping behind my rib cage as tears line my eyes, and I turn to look at Lawson, only to see him kneeling in the snow behind me.

*Now*, everyone's eyes are on us.

"Lucy Bradee, I knew from the moment I met you that you were special." His eyes dart to my parents, who share an amused look. "And while our beginning might have been a massive mess, I promise you our life together won't be. I will remain as devoted to you as I always have been."

Lawson stands, taking my glass from me to tip the ring into his palm. He sticks it between his lips, sucking the sticky juice from it before grabbing my hand. "I promise to fulfill every fantasy, dream, and wish you ever have, and all I ask in return is that you take my last name and that we get started on making those babies you want so much because I'm already old and gray and don't want to be stuck in a wheelchair when our kids graduate."

"Yes!" I cry, jumping into his arms. "Yes! Yes! A thousand times, yes!"

Cheers and cries of congratulations fill the air as Lawson slips the rose gold ring on my finger, and the pear-shaped diamond in the center glitters brightly as it catches the light from the fire.

He kisses me before sliding his lips to my ear. "There's an inscription on the inside."

I pull it back off my finger. Squinting, I tilt it toward the light, and my breath catches in my throat as my chest swells with love.

*Through every storm.*

"I love you," Lawson vows against my lips as I slip the ring back on and throw my arms around his neck. "Through every single storm, I promise to love you."

"I love you, too. And I promise to be your rainbow. Always."

"Careful, little lamb. This is for one night only, but if you talk like that, I might just have to find a way to keep you."

Sign up for D.L. Darby's newsletter for a short story about Cameron and a red-hot Halloween night with a mystery girl at Désirer.

# AFTERWORD

Where to begin?

This idea came to me in early 2024, just before I released Burn With Me. I thought, how fun would it be to start a second-generation series with the kids from the Darbyverse?

Well, you give my brain an inch and it takes a few hundred miles.

The ideas came quickly, the pairings were instant, and I had written an outline for nearly the entire series by the time I could finally sit down and write.

Then Lauren, my sweet baby angel, popped into my DMs demanding a story with a main male like Lawson.

Lucy, at the time, didn't have a story yet. I wasn't sure what I wanted to do with her, but as soon as Lauren asked, inspiration struck, and within twenty-four hours, not only did Lucy have a story, but they were bumped to the top of the series to kick the whole thing off.

Lucy and Lawson were so fun to write. I loved exploring an age gap where the guy is older, since I've already written two reverse age gap stories. Something about the dynamic of an age gap resonates with me, and you will see the tried-and-true trope sprinkled throughout this series.

What I was not expecting, however, was to have to sit on them for nearly a year. Last summer, Devious Temptation was pitched traditionally, and I had no clue what that actually entailed.

I didn't realize that it meant I couldn't still self-publish it, or that I shouldn't talk about it. I spent months agonizing over a story I essentially couldn't do anything with.

So, naturally, I panicked. I pulled Starry Night Kisses out of my butt, and honestly, I'm so glad that I did because it plays into this series so beautifully for Nova's book. And then I got started on the Serial Killer Book Club, which has a completely opposite vibe from this series.

Now, I'm juggling both, but I truly believe that everything happens for a reason, and it was meant to be this way. I put DT through another round of edits since my writing style has grown, and completely threw my severe Type A personality out the window and let my cover designer take the reins... after a lot of tears and manic episodes on my part.

And what came out of it all is a beautiful love story that I'm so proud of.

I love it. I hope you loved it. And I can't wait to bring you the rest of the Devious stories over the next two years.

# Acknowledgments

Lauren, without you, this book wouldn't exist. Thank you for sticking with me, for believing in me, and for sassily demanding Lawson. #laurensfault

The rest of my team, Alex, Jessica, Cady, Ashley, Heather, and April, thank you so much for hanging in there while I complained about everything under the sun regarding this book. It was a wild ride, but I'm glad we made it to the other side of the rainbow.

Thank you to my editors, Sam and Heather, who took the time to go through this (at the time) 102k monster at the drop of a dime when I decided to do another round of edits.

My designer, Charley Jade, from now on, I'm just going to give you vibes and let you take it from there. You somehow know just exactly what's in my brain, even when I'm saying it's not what I want. You work literal magic, and I'm so thankful for you.

Victoria, with Cruel Ink. Thank you for taking the time to clean up the blurb. You're also a magic maker, and I appreciate you so much!

Mr. Darby, my husband, I adore you. You're the rainbow to my storm cloud, especially over this last year. Thank you for always being my rock.

And lastly, thank you to the readers. My darlings. The

og ones and the new. Thank you for sticking with me through sub-genres and loving all my characters, no matter their level of light or dark. This little indie author couldn't do it without you.

Xo

# About the Author

D.L. Darby lives in Anchorage, Alaska, with her husband and two fur babies.

By day, she's a hairstylist, and by night, she's continuously drafting new ideas on her "murder board" at home. While she writes across multiple romance sub-genres, you can always expect to find spicy alpha males and strong-willed women with a flair for dramatics in her stories.

www.ingramcontent.com/pod-product-compliance
Lightning Source LLC
Chambersburg PA
CBHW030338120726
47901CB00007B/1835